The Beginning Of The End

Michael T. Snyder

Chapter 1

Everything seemed so perfect.

Sam always enjoyed walking along the shore on sunny days such as this one. Today the sun had brilliantly lit up the clouds that were hanging over the water, and he loved the way that the warm grass felt under his feet. He was only ten years old, and he was still blissfully ignorant of the turmoil which had enveloped much of the planet. He was a kid that was very well cared for and that was always full of life, and he had no idea that there were millions of children around the globe that would have gladly traded places with him without any hesitation.

But Sam wasn't so carefree at the moment. He was on an errand that he did not always find pleasant.

He had been sent to tell the old man that it was time for dinner.

Sam could see him off in the distance standing on the edge of a hillside that looked out over the water. From where he was standing, the old man could watch children playing with their parents in the sand down on the beach. Sometimes the old man would spend hours at that spot, especially when the weather was good. Today was a particularly beautiful late summer day, and the old man's long, flowing white garments rippled as the breeze hit them.

Sam couldn't understand why the old man would not adopt a more modern style of dress. In fact, there were a lot of things about the old man that Sam didn't understand. It wasn't as if the old man was mean or angry. That wasn't the case at all. It was just that Sam found him to be very unusual.

His parents dearly loved and deeply respected the old man and so did the rest of the community, but Sam didn't understand why. The old man had always treated Sam very well, but there was something about talking to him that was very uncomfortable.

As Sam cautiously approached the old man, he turned and smiled at Sam. The old man had a long, white beard and a face that was very weathered. But when you looked into his eyes he suddenly seemed much, much older.

"Hello Sam," the old man said, "have they sent you to call me for dinner?"

"Yes".

"What are we having tonight?"

"Baked potatoes and broccoli."

The old man cringed inwardly. He was not much of a fan of broccoli.

"They are really doing their best to feed me right, Sam. But sometimes I must admit that I really do have a craving for some fried chicken and French fries."

Sam smiled at that. He liked that the old man was not being so serious for once.

"Sam," the old man said warmly, "you have a great future ahead of you. I really wish that I could stay and watch you grow up some more."

Sam was very puzzled by this statement. Was the old man saying that he was leaving?

The old man pointed out over the water. "Do you see those dark clouds starting to form in the distance Sam?"

Sam nodded his head.

"A great storm is coming Sam. We must get prepared. Run along and warn your parents. I will be down there for dinner shortly."

The old man looked back out over the ocean. Oh, how he was going to miss this place.

It was home to him.

No matter where his travels had taken him, this was always home.

But now he knew that he had to leave again, for indeed a great storm was coming.

The old man closed his eyes and breathed in the crisp sea air. Time seemed to slip away from him faster and faster the older that he got. There was always so much to do, and there was always so little time. It seemed like it was only yesterday that he had returned to this land. Now he had to leave once again.

At his age he figured that he would have earned some rest by now, but he also knew that he wasn't going to be getting any. Events were rapidly coming together, and now he would be needed more than he had in a very long time.

The old man opened his eyes again and noticed that the storm clouds on the horizon had gotten a little bit darker.

Time was running short. The old man turned and started walking in the direction that Sam had gone.

He knew where his next journey was going to take him, but it was not a place that he looked forward to visiting.

It was a place where people had turned their backs on the values handed down to them by their forefathers.

It was a place filled with corruption, greed and darkness.

It was a place that was not very welcoming to people such as him.

But he knew that he must go.

Tonight, he would tell his friends that he was going to America.

Chapter 2

The two men strode along the impeccably decorated hallway in absolute silence.

One of the men was a servant of the owner of the household.

The other man was a guest that had just arrived, and one could sense that he was a paradox just by looking at him.

The shorter of the two men was named Frederick. He was just barely over five feet tall, and somehow Frederick knew that the visitor would easily kill him without even thinking about it under the right circumstances. Fortunately, Frederick was a servant of the man that this shrouded visitor had come to see, so that afforded him a certain degree of protection.

But that didn't mean that this visitor did not make Frederick nervous. In fact, Frederick figured that this mysterious visitor would make just about anyone nervous.

Frederick had been ordered not to speak to this visitor and to show him in to see his master without delay, and Frederick was not about to start disobeying orders now.

Others in Frederick's position would have been tempted to start looking for a new line of work long ago. But to Frederick, such a possibility was unthinkable.

His grandfather had been a servant.

His father had been a servant in this very household.

And Frederick knew that he would be a servant of his master until the day that he died.

He just hoped that day wouldn't arrive any time soon.

The mysterious visitor that Frederick was escorting down the hall was named Killian. He was well over seven feet tall and was extremely well built, and yet he moved with a graceful athleticism that seemed almost impossible for a man his size.

A black shrouded cloak covered Killian's head and draped around his very imposing frame. This had the effect of intimidating most of the people that Killian encountered, and that was by design.

The collection of French provincial antiques that Killian and Frederick were walking past was very impressive, but it was the artwork on the wall that caught Killian's eye.

All of the paintings were full of deep occult imagery. Killian knew that this was not by accident.

Killian stopped for a moment in front of one painting entitled "The Resurrection of Apollo" and studied it carefully.

The meaning behind the dark images in the painting would have been a total mystery to most people, but Killian understood what the painting represented and he didn't like it very much.

But a job was a job, and a contract was a contract. The Order had always been very good to him and to other assassins from The Red Hand.

Killian resumed walking down the hall and Frederick fell in alongside him.

At the end of the hall was a massive oak door. Behind that door was the man that Killian had come to see.

That man was named Constantine and he was the master of the household. Constantine was about 6'4, and his very broad shoulders made him appear more bulky than he actually was. But Constantine was no brute. His dark hair and large bushy eyebrows framed a face that exuded European charm. He was a man of the world, and the world had definitely been very good to him.

He had been able to watch every move that his visitor had made since arriving at his home thanks to the surveillance cameras that monitored every inch of the 20,000 square foot estate. Constantine was paranoid by nature, but having this visitor on his property made him even more tense than usual.

Constantine normally did not like exposing himself to such dangerous men, but today it was necessary.

Constantine watched as Frederick pushed the buzzer on the security panel next to the huge oak door. He pressed a button under his desk which allowed his servant and the visitor to enter the room. Frederick opened the huge oak door and entered, and the visitor followed.

It had been a long time since the visitor had been here.

The office was absolutely enormous. It was roughly 30 feet by 30 feet, with large windows interspersed between the floor to ceiling bookshelves that ran along the exterior walls. It was tastefully decorated, but there was a feeling of darkness about the room that was almost palpable.

At the far end of the room was an enormous desk which Constantine sat behind. He was flanked by two large men in expensive Italian suits holding machine guns. Four more security thugs sat in various overstuffed chairs that were scattered about the office.

Constantine was not a man that liked to take chances.

He was even wearing body armor underneath the incredibly expensive tailored suit that he was wearing, but the visitor didn't need to know that. He trusted the visitor, but in the world in which they operated there was no such thing as absolute trust.

The shrouded visitor stood silently in the center of the room facing Constantine with Frederick at his side. Nobody said anything at first and that created a nervous tension in the room.

Constantine finally broke the ice.

"It is a pleasure to see you Killian. The Red Hand apparently meant it when they said that they would send their best. Welcome to Klausjagen."

Killian nodded in return.

"I'll get right down to business. The Order has a job for you to do. It has been decided that a reordering of the financial system in the United States is called for. Other assets will be carrying out this reordering. What we need you to do is to eliminate anyone that threatens this project. Specific targets will be assigned based on intel gathered by our agents. You are to operate in the shadows and get your work done without drawing any attention to yourself. You will receive your typical rate plus a 20 percent bonus once this project is over. Do you accept these terms?"

Killian pulled back the black shroud that was covering his head and revealed his features. Two fiercely red eyes peered out from a face that looked as if it had been chiseled out of stone. Other than his two eyebrows, he did not appear to have any visible hair whatsoever. Two very deep scars ran parallel down the left side of his forehead, over his left eye, and down his left cheek. Obviously he had sustained a horrific injury at some point, but his left eye appeared to be functioning normally.

His appearance startled a couple of the security guards and they started to reach for their guns, but Constantine held up his hands to calm them.

"Do not be alarmed. I have been told that Killian insists on looking someone directly in the eyes and shaking hands before sealing a contract. And I have been told that Killian never breaks a contract once it has been made."

Killian nodded slightly as if to confirm what Constantine had just said.

Constantine smiled broadly. Killian was even more impressive than he had remembered. Constantine much preferred to have him as a friend rather than as an enemy.

Constantine reached out to shake Killian's hand.

"So do we have a contract Killian?"

Killian shook his hand and gazed into his eyes with an ice cold stare.

"You are just as quiet as they say. Do you ever speak?"

Killian did not respond and showed no sign of emotion. At this point even Constantine was starting to get nervous.

"It is no matter. The Order needs you to depart right away. A car is waiting outside that will take you to a private plane. Needless to say, this flight has been cleared at the highest levels and you will be able to totally bypass airport security. One of our safe houses in New York City has been told to be expecting you."

Killian nodded slightly and turned to go.

He always enjoyed going to America.

There was always so much to see and always so many people to kill.

Chapter 3

One of the things that Tom McDowell truly loved was a good night of sleep, and so when his phone started ringing at 11:45 PM one Sunday night in September it immediately put him in a very foul mood.

Without opening his eyes Tom started reaching for the phone and was able to find it after a few moments. He put the phone to his ear as he tried to clear his head.

"Hello?"

The voice on the other end was female. "Tom, this is your sister Hannah. I need to talk to you about something."

It was his "crazy" sister Hannah. They had not been close growing up, and they had drifted apart even farther as adults. In fact, Tom had not heard from her in more than two years. Why was she calling him now?

"Hannah, do you have any idea what time it is?"

"Oh, I am so sorry about that Tom. I forgot that it is much later on the east coast. These time zones always confuse me. I just felt an urgent need to talk to you."

Tom cringed inwardly. He was absolutely exhausted and he really wished that Hannah would just feel an "urgent need" to leave him alone.

"What did you want to talk about Hannah?"

Hannah paused for a moment.

"Tom, have you been following the economic news lately?"

Tom was getting really frustrated now. He definitely did not want to talk about economics when he was supposed to be sleeping. "No, I haven't. Is there a reason why I should be following it?"

Hannah hesitated again, but she kept going.

"Tom, our economy is about to collapse, and there are some very powerful people out there that are determined to make that collapse as bad as possible. I am talking about an economic crisis much worse than we saw back in 2008 and 2009. In fact, it is already starting in Europe. Very soon, there will be a derivatives panic. Fear is going to sweep through the financial markets like we have never seen before. There are going to be major bank failures all over the United States and Europe, there is going to be an unprecedented stock market crash, credit is going to freeze up and huge numbers of businesses are going to be shut down. Economic activity is essentially going to grind to a standstill. We aren't just heading into a recession. We are heading into a depression. The unemployment rate is going to more than double and millions of families are going to lose their homes. What we are facing is going to be even worse than the Great Depression of the 1930s, and like I said, there are some very powerful people out there that intend to make all of this happen."

Tom was not in the mood to listen to another one of Hannah's bizarre conspiracy theories. "Hannah, isn't this something that we can talk about later?"

Hannah became even more insistent. "Look Tom, I wouldn't be calling you if this wasn't serious. Very powerful forces are going to try to crash the global economic system on purpose. We have been living in the greatest debt bubble in the history of the world and it is about to collapse. Millions upon millions of Americans are going to lose their jobs, their homes and their retirement savings. The American people deserve to be warned about what is coming."

Tom could hardly believe how delusional his sister had become. As they were growing up, she had always been regarded as the one with the brains. But now she definitely appeared to be several fries short of a Happy Meal. He was almost tempted to feel sorry for her. "So exactly how do you know all of this Hannah?"

Hannah paused for a moment as she searched for the right thing to say.

"It's...complicated. I would like you to come out here to Idaho. There are some things that I want to show you, and there are some people that you should meet. You aren't going to believe most of what I have to say if I just try to explain it over the telephone."

This statement made Tom even more angry. Tom worked for the CIA. He was accustomed to keeping secrets from other people. He was not accustomed to other people keeping secrets from him.

"You aren't winning me over Hannah."

"Tom, just take a look at what has been going on all over the financial world lately. Hundreds of top banking executives have suddenly resigned. Corporate insiders are selling off stock as if there was no tomorrow. Central banks are buying gold at an unprecedented rate. This week it was revealed that the Federal Reserve has been helping the five biggest banks in the country develop emergency plans for how to cope with the next major financial crisis. Even the

U.S. government has been very busy stockpiling food, supplies and ammunition. Everyone seems to be preparing for the end of the world but nobody is telling the American people anything."

Tom was aware that various government agencies had been submitting unusually large purchase orders lately, but he had dismissed this as "general preparedness".

"Hannah, how do you know what the U.S. government has been up to?"

Hannah smiled. "You would be amazed at what you can find out on the Internet. In any event, I was really hoping that you would want to look into this Tom. You remember what happened during the financial crisis of 2008, right? It was horrible. We still have not recovered from that. Please take a couple of days off and come out here to Idaho. There are some things that you need to see, and we could really use someone like you."

Hannah paused once again for just a moment. "And Tom, I probably should not be telling you this, but I also want to explain to you what we know about the secret government intelligence agency that you are about to be recruited into."

Tom knew that Hannah had officially gone off the deep end now.

"Hannah, who in the world is this 'we' that you keep talking about? On second thought, don't tell me. I don't want to know. And I don't know where you are getting your information from, but I am quite happy in my current position and nobody is currently recruiting me for anything."

As his frustration increased, Tom could feel his voice rising. "And I definitely am not going to fly all the way out to Idaho to listen to your latest conspiracy theories about our financial system. Despite what you may believe, the people that run our financial system are very highly trained professionals who know exactly what they are doing. They are going to do their very best to stop another major financial crisis from happening. This is not something that you or I really need to be losing sleep over. Goodnight."

With that, Tom slammed his phone down and pulled the cord out of the wall.

Despite what his "crazy" sister had just told him, Tom was still determined to get a good night of sleep.

Chapter 4

As Caroline Mancini surveyed the trading floor, she already knew that this would definitely not be a normal trading day. But she never cared much for "normal" anyway. It was way too boring. Caroline craved excitement, and she absolutely lived for days such as this one.

"Can I have your attention please?" It was more of a demand than a request. Caroline had developed a very commanding presence over the years. She had learned long ago that people tended not to respect you if you took a sweet and gentle approach to things on Wall Street.

The trading floor at Drexel & De Forest quickly fell quiet and all attention was now focused on Caroline. She had just emerged from a meeting with upper management and she was standing at the front of the room flanked by two of her most trusted aides. What she was about to say was going to really shake these traders up.

"Today, Bull Capital is going to collapse, and we are going to be there to step on their throats. Upper management has given me authorization to short as much Bull Capital stock as necessary. There have been rumors going around about the trouble over at Bull Capital for quite a while, and those rumors were true. Bull Capital has actually been on the verge of collapsing for weeks, and today is the day that it is going to happen. We are going to push them into the grave and we are going to make an extraordinary amount of money doing it."

Across the room a male voice spoke up. "This is crazy. The Federal Reserve will never allow Bull Capital to fail. Bull Capital has been around for over a hundred years. When the Fed steps in to bail out Bull Capital and their stock rebounds, won't we end up losing a lot of money and looking like fools?"

Caroline knew very well that the Federal Reserve and the U.S. government were both going to stand aside and do nothing as Bull Capital collapsed. Her sources had assured her of that.

Her long, dark hair whirled as she turned to get a good look at the trader that had just objected to her. Caroline had to squint just a bit to see him clearly. She probably should have been wearing her glasses, but Caroline absolutely hated wearing them. She was a vain woman working in an industry that greatly prized physical beauty. And without a doubt, Caroline Mancini was an extremely beautiful woman. She had a smile that could absolutely light up a room. She just didn't use it very often.

The trader that had objected to her was young.

Really young.

In fact, if you saw him on the street you might assume that he had only been shaving for a few years. Caroline did not recognize this particular trader, but she was absolutely disgusted by how unprofessionally he was dressed.

Caroline Mancini simply did not put up with this kind of nonsense.

"What is your name?"

"Ian Kelly."

"And how long have you been with us Ian Kelly?"

"For about six months."

"And where did you go to school Ian Kelly?"

"I got my MBA from Arizona State University."

Caroline was getting really angry now. She was ten minutes away from starting one of the most important trading days of her career and some wet behind the ears kid from Arizona State actually had the gall to try to tell her how to do her job.

"Well, Ian Kelly from Arizona State, let me tell you a few things about how the financial world works. I was making millions of dollars for this firm long before you ever hit puberty. I graduated at the top of my class from the McIntire School of Commerce at the University of Virginia, and I have an MBA and a law degree from Harvard. In my early years at this firm I sometimes put in one hundred hour weeks. There were many nights that I actually slept in my office. I paid my dues and I proved my worth. I never would have dreamed of openly challenging a top executive with 15 years seniority. Are you just naturally stupid or did they teach you to be that way at Arizona State?"

Ian Kelly just sat there in silence.

"This is why I never like it when we decide to hire kids from lower tier public universities. They simply do not understand how the real world works. I did not become head of trading at Drexel & De Forest by making stupid decisions. I did not wake up today and suddenly decide to go after Bull Capital while I was brushing my teeth. The wheels have been in motion for a long time. On Wall Street you either eat or you get eaten. If you can't stand swimming with the sharks then you better go back to the kiddie pool. This is a game for the big boys, and I suggest that all of you put on your big boy pants today."

Caroline paused and then pointed a finger directly at Ian Kelly.

"As for you, Ian Kelly from Arizona State, Drexel & De Forest does not put up with imbeciles. Pack up your things and go. You are fired."

Ian Kelly just sat there for a moment with his mouth wide open.

Caroline was absolutely livid now. "Do you not understand English? Gather your belongings and get to stepping. You don't belong on Wall Street, and I will personally see to it that you will not ever get another job in the financial world. Perhaps if you are lucky you can crawl back to Arizona and get a job selling life insurance down in Tucson."

Two security guards were standing next to Ian Kelly now and he was rapidly gathering his things. The entire trading floor was staring at him and he was clearly extremely embarrassed.

"Now," Caroline continued, "are there any other stupid questions?"

There was not a peep from the trading floor.

"Good. A packet with more specifics about our attack plan will be distributed to you shortly. This is one of the most important days of your careers. If everything goes according to plan and we make the amount of money that we expect to make, you will all be rewarded handsomely. Remember, we are showing absolutely no mercy today. We are going for their throats and we aren't making any apologies for it."

Chapter 5

Tom McDowell was lost in his thoughts.

Thanks to big Hollywood movies, most Americans tended to believe that working for the CIA was quite glamorous, but Tom did not feel very glamorous today.

His office at CIA headquarters in Langley, Virginia was quite cramped and his office furniture had definitely seen better days. The desk that he was sitting behind had been bumped and scraped countless times, and the chair that he was sitting in made a creaking sound almost every time he moved. The fluorescent lights in the ceiling above him constantly flickered and they emitted a faint buzzing sound that absolutely drove Tom nuts. As he took another sip of his coffee, he once again began to wonder what had happened to his life.

Things had seemed so promising when he was younger. During his time at the U.S. Air Force Academy, he had been full of anticipation about where life would take him. And during his ten years as a pilot in the U.S. Air Force he had experienced things that most people never even dream of.

But after leaving the U.S. Air Force things had taken a turn. He and his best friend had both been recruited to join the CIA, and they had both jumped at the chance. Both of them figured that they were starting to get a little bit older, and being the "next James Bond" sounded really appealing to them.

Well, it turned out that working for the CIA was nothing like what you see in the spy movies. During his first couple of years with the agency he was out in the field quite a bit, but these days Tom spent most of his time behind a desk.

There was nothing wrong with that, but it also depressed Tom to think that his life had become so incredibly "normal" and boring.

Tom took another sip of his coffee. He was feeling quite tired today. In fact, he just never seemed to have enough energy these days.

Perhaps it was time to settle down. Tom kind of regretted the fact that he had never been married. During his twenties he figured that it was just too soon to get attached to just one woman and in his thirties he was so involved with his career that marriage just wasn't a priority.

It wasn't as if women didn't like Tom. He was over six feet tall with dark hair, boyish good looks and an athletic build. In social settings, single women tended to absolutely flock to Tom.

But at this point Tom also knew that most of the "good ones" had already been taken, and whenever he reminded himself of that fact his mood became even more melancholy.

Tom understood that most men would kill for his life, but to Tom his life had become way too similar to the lives of millions of other men that spend their lives in dull, dreary offices doing the same mundane tasks day after day.

So what was on Tom's agenda today?

More meaningless reports.

More pointless meetings.

More silly small talk with self-important bureaucrats.

Tom was not sure how much more of this he could take.

Tom took yet another sip of his coffee. He could not even recall when he had begun drinking the stuff. It certainly did not taste that great. When he first joined the CIA everyone else was drinking it, so eventually he started drinking it too.

Now he needed it just to get through the morning.

The more that Tom reflected on his life the more disgusted he became.

Tom sat back and stared out his office door. The reports that he needed to get done could wait. Tom really did not feel like working on them at the moment.

Tom noticed one of his coworkers walk past his office, and Tom decided that he would be a good distraction for a while.

"Kozlowski, get in here!"

Jon Kozlowski was Tom's best friend. They had served in the Air Force together and they had been recruited into the CIA together. They used to do almost everything together, but they had kind of drifted apart since Jon had gotten married four years ago. Jon had become much more of a family man since then. But without a doubt there was still a very strong bond between them.

Jon poked his head around the door. "What's up McDowell?"

Jon always lifted Tom's spirits. "I was just wondering who keeps letting your ugly mug back into the building."

"Very funny Tom – I guess you haven't heard what is happening this morning yet."

Jon was being uncharacteristically serious. Usually he would have responded with a sarcastic quip of some kind.

"No, I have just been sitting here drinking my coffee. What's going on?"

"The financial markets are melting down Tom. The Dow is already down more than 500 points. The media says that Bull Capital has gone bankrupt and that no buyer has stepped forward and no rescue plan is in place. Millions of brokerage accounts have been frozen and it looks like there is a ton of customer money that is missing. People are freaking out because they don't know if they are going to be able to get their money back."

Tom didn't keep up with the financial markets much, and he had always just assumed that the federal government and the Federal Reserve had fixed the problems that had plagued the system back in 2008.

"Why isn't the Federal Reserve stepping in? Why aren't they bailing out Bull Capital like they bailed out all of those other banks?"

"I don't know Tom. The director is about to call a meeting. He wants us on our toes, because when the financial markets melt down just about anything can happen."

Tom wasn't sure what to make of any of this. "This is not how I expected my Monday to get started. I want to go grab another cup of coffee before this meeting. Walk with me for a bit?"

Tom headed out into the hallway and Jon walked beside him toward the kitchen.

"Is there something on your mind Tom?"

"Yeah, I just wanted to make sure that you are still coming over to watch the game with me tonight."

"I am not sure if I can Tom. Susanne gets a bit antsy when I leave her at home with the kids at night these days. She is already on my case about how much time I spend at work."

It didn't take them long to reach the kitchen where the coffee pot was located.

"Are you totally whipped Koz? Come on man. You know how much I love watching football with you. And this young quarterback that Washington has is absolutely incredible. Am I supposed to watch the game by myself?"

"I'll see what I can do Tom."

At that moment Director Del Conte walked in.

"Hey guys, is that coffee still warm?"

George Del Conte looked very much like what you would expect an overweight, balding political appointee in his mid-fifties to look like. He was certainly not a global intelligence expert, and on many days it was very clear that he was much more interested in counting down the days until his pension kicked in than he was about protecting and defending the United States.

But he was still the director of the CIA, and Tom definitely wanted to stay on his good side.

"It's warm, but it tastes absolutely horrible. But those cinnamon rolls are really good. I had one earlier."

"Thanks Tom," Director Del Conte responded, "I guess you guys have already heard about the meeting?"

Both Tom and Koz nodded.

"Good. I want everyone gathered in the conference room in about 15 minutes. And while I am thinking about it, there is something that I need to talk with both of you about today. Could you guys stick around after the meeting?"

Both Tom and Koz nodded again.

"Excellent – I'll see you guys in about 15 minutes." With that, Director Del Conte stuffed a cinnamon roll into his mouth and headed out the door.

Tom had no idea why Director Del Conte would want to talk with them. He turned to Koz with a confused expression on his face. "So what do you think he wants to talk with us about?"

Koz seemed puzzled as well. "Your guess is as good as mine bro. I just hope that we aren't in trouble again."

Chapter 6

"You're live in 30 seconds Melissa."

As Melissa Remling stood on the floor of the New York Stock Exchange, all hell was breaking loose around her. But Melissa was as cool and calm as ever. She had overcome a lot of adversity in her life, and she wasn't about to let something like another stock market crash rattle her.

In moments of great crisis, Melissa tried to remember her parents. But these days it was becoming increasingly difficult to remember their faces. The memories of her parents had become like shadows in the corners of her mind. She felt like they were constantly slipping away, but they always haunted her. She had lost her parents when she was seven years old, and she had been raised in a series of orphanages and foster homes after that. It had been an incredibly painful childhood, and Melissa had brought most of that pain into her adult life.

But instead of allowing those trials to crush her spirit, Melissa tried to use them as motivation. She had a drive to succeed that seemed to be insatiable at times, and she constantly felt a need to prove the world wrong. Sometimes she fell just short of her goals, but that just made her even more determined to excel. She had desperately wanted to be valedictorian of her high school class, but she had fallen one spot short. That just gave her the motivation that she needed to go on to the School of Journalism at the University of Texas where she graduated at the top of her class. She had desperately wanted to be Miss South Dakota, but she had to settle for runner-up. That just gave her the motivation that she needed to beat out 500 other applicants for an internship with American News Network.

That internship had eventually turned into a permanent job, and today Melissa was regarded as one of the top reporters in the industry.

Now she was standing on the floor of the New York Stock Exchange getting ready to deliver a live report on the stock market crash which would be seen by millions of people on the most watched news network in the United States.

She was not a financial expert by any means, but she always worked harder than everyone else around her and she always did her homework. There were those that attempted to disparage her by referring to her as "just another blonde infobabe", but the truth was that she had paid her dues and she could run circles around most of the reporters that had been doing this for twice as long.

Melissa was snapped out of her daydreaming by a voice in her earpiece.

"10 seconds Melissa."

Melissa could hear that the network was coming back from commercial. The anchor, Arnold Porter, would be throwing it to her very quickly. She checked herself one more time to make sure that she was ready.

"...and now we go to Melissa Remling on the floor of the New York Stock Exchange. Melissa, it looks like total chaos is breaking out around you down there. What is going on?"

"Arnold, the scene here at the New York Stock Exchange is unlike anything I have ever seen before. Traders are in a state of total panic. After falling more than 400 points on Friday, the Dow is down more than 1400 points so far today. Trading was automatically stopped for an hour earlier, but that has done nothing to stop the market from plunging. Financial stocks are being hit particularly hard. Reports that Bull Capital is insolvent have sent that stock crashing. Bull Capital started the day at about eight dollars a share and it has fallen to less than a dollar a share. There has been talk for days that Bull Capital may need a bailout, but leaders in Congress are ruling out any legislative action and the Federal Reserve says that Bull Capital is in such bad shape financially that any emergency loans would just be throwing money down a black hole.

"So it looks like Bull Capital is going to be allowed to fail. This is an absolutely stunning development and it has taken investors totally by surprise. Anyone that shorted Bull Capital today is making a tremendous amount of money.

"But the Federal Reserve is taking other action in an attempt to bolster the market. About an hour ago the Federal Reserve announced another round of quantitative easing on top of what it is already doing. The Fed says that it will conduct an 'emergency liquidity injection' of 200 billion dollars this week and will pump an extra 150 billion dollars into the financial system every month until order has been restored to the financial markets.

"Unfortunately, that announcement has done essentially nothing to calm the markets. Investors say that they have heard this story too many times before over the past couple of years.

"And the international response to this move by the Fed has been scathing. China has announced that it will no longer be buying any more U.S. debt and that it will be selling off what it has already accumulated. Saudi Arabia just announced that it may consider selling oil in currencies other than the U.S. dollar. Those two announcements have sent the value of the U.S. dollar tumbling. In fact, the U.S. dollar index has already experienced the biggest single day decline that we have ever seen and the day is far from over.

"Arnold, it would be hard to overstate how much of a disaster this is for the financial markets."

Back in the studio, Arnold Porter looked a little bit shaken, and that was quite unusual for him.

"Melissa, what are they saying about tomorrow? Will the markets be shut down?"

"At this point, nobody knows what is going to happen next Arnold. There have been reports that the president is even considering declaring a bank holiday. But some people that I have talked to down here on the floor seem to believe that such a move would just make the panic even worse.

"An even bigger concern right now seems to be about what this stock market crash is going to do to the derivatives market. Wild swings such as we have seen today tend to greatly upset the delicate balance that the derivatives marketplace depends upon. Needless to say, a whole lot of bets have gone horribly wrong today. Some firms have lost an enormous amount of money, but we won't know exactly who the losers are for a while. This is going to cause a lot of fear in the credit markets, because nobody really knows which financial institutions are essentially bankrupt at this point and which ones are still doing okay.

"I am being told that the credit freeze that we saw back in 2008 is likely to be absolutely dwarfed by what we may see over the next few weeks. The overriding emotion in the financial world right now is fear, and that is not likely to change any time soon."

Back in the studio, Arnold Porter still looked a bit shaken. "Thank you Melissa. That was Melissa Remling reporting from the floor of the New York Stock Exchange..."

Suddenly Melissa could hear another voice in her earpiece. It was her producer.

"And we're clear. Great job Melissa. Stick around though, because we're going to want a live update from you in about an hour."

Melissa knew that this was going to be a long day. Normally she would be able to relax a bit now, but on a day like this there would be no time to rest. In many ways, the events of this day reminded her of what had happened back in 2008. In fact, Melissa had already concluded that this was going to be much worse than 2008. This was unlike anything that anyone had ever seen before, and she could see the panic on the faces of the people all around her.

Was the country headed for another recession? After all, the financial crisis of 2008 had resulted in the deepest recession since the Great Depression of the 1930s. Would the U.S. economy now experience something even worse?

Melissa was determined to find out.

Chapter 7

As the meeting regarding the emerging financial crisis was wrapping up, Tom McDowell found himself wondering if it had been the absolutely most mind-numbing meeting that he had ever attended since joining the CIA. Director Del Conte had encouraged everyone to "stay alert" and had reminded everyone that a financial crisis has a way of pushing some people "over the edge", but the truth is that there wasn't anything substantive that he had been told at the meeting that he couldn't have gotten from a cable news channel.

Tom figured that he was going to have to push a little more paper around than usual this week but that was about it. The financial world may be coming apart at the seams, but Tom anticipated that it would be pretty much business as usual for him.

When the meeting was over and everyone else had left the conference room, Tom and Koz approached Director Del Conte.

Koz was the first to speak. "Are we in trouble again boss?"

"No," Director Del Conte said in a more serious tone than normal, "apparently you guys have done something right for a change. You both have gotten the call."

Tom and Koz had no idea what he was talking about.

Director Del Conte could tell they were puzzled. "You two are being called up to the big leagues. Every year, Congress allocates tens of billions of dollars for 'black budget' programs that nobody is really supposed to know anything about. Well, you two are about to experience what being part of that world is like. That is, if you choose to accept this assignment."

Tom was very intrigued. This sounded like something right up his alley.

"What would this mean? Would we be leaving the CIA? If so, who would we be working for?"

Director Del Conte lifted his right hand as if to signal Tom to slow down.

"Yes, you two would be leaving your current jobs at the CIA. No, I cannot tell you who you would be working for because that is classified. If you two are interested, a car will swing by here first thing tomorrow morning to take you to a briefing. If you choose to go to that briefing you will be required to sign a bunch of non-disclosure forms and you will be sworn to absolute secrecy. This is a 'black budget' agency that does the kinds of things that the CIA used to do back in the old days. Today, the CIA is hardly the covert agency that it once was. It has become highly politicized and it is closely watched. If we so much as squeak, the entire world ends up hearing about it. But the organization that is recruiting you operates in a bubble of total secrecy. That way they can actually get some real spy work done. After all, you can't really blame someone for doing something wrong if you don't even know that they exist."

"It seems odd that they would pick us," Koz blurted out.

"What the organization that is recruiting you values more than anything are loyalty and the ability to keep secrets." Director Del Conte paused, and he looked like he was searching for the right words to say without revealing too much. "It functions like a secret society in many ways. These kinds of organizations greatly reward those that are loyal and that serve them well. But anyone that betrays them is dealt with brutally. They operate outside of the rules that constrain normal government agencies. It would be a much different environment than you are accustomed to here at the CIA. There is not too much more that I can tell you guys beyond that."

Tom was even more intrigued now. "Can we have a couple of hours to think about this?"

Director Del Conte nodded his head. "Yes, but I will need your answer by the end of the day. Give me a call when you have made your decision."

With that, Director Del Conte made his way out of the room.

Tom and Koz just looked at each other for a moment.

Koz was the first one to speak. "What do you think we should do Tom?"

Tom already knew what he wanted to do. "I think we should go for this Koz. I definitely plan to be at that mystery briefing tomorrow. I am sick and tired of pushing papers around for a living. I have been ready for a change for a long time. I don't want to just sit behind a desk for the next twenty years while I get old, fat, bald and tired."

Koz did not seem as enthusiastic as Tom was. "I definitely hear what you are saying Tom, but things are a little different for me. I have a family now. Adventure is not as appealing to me as it once was. I am not sure that I am ready to have bullets whizzing by my head again. I don't know if I can do that to my wife. Plus, we have no idea what this other organization is all about at this point. They could be involved in some things that we would rather not be involved with."

Tom was saddened at the thought of moving on and potentially leaving his best friend behind. "Look Koz, just think about it. What is the harm in checking out this opportunity? It could be what we have always been looking for. What is it that we always used to tell each other? Life is like a coin – you only get to spend it once. Do we really want to look back someday and wonder what could have been? Doors like this don't open up very often."

Koz looked down at the floor. "Tom, we have been through so much together – first in the Air Force and then at the CIA. Part of me really wants to do this thing with you, but the family man in me really likes the safety and security of a desk job. I honestly do not know what I am going to do."

Tom could empathize with the conflicting emotions that Koz was wrestling with. "Look, I am going to be out there waiting for that car in the morning. If you show up, great. If not, I will completely understand. Either way, you will always be my best friend."

Chapter 8

"Ladies and gentlemen we did it," Caroline Mancini declared proudly as she raised a fist in triumph. A couple of subordinates uncorked champagne bottles behind her, and the trading floor erupted in spontaneous applause.

"This is likely to turn out to be the most profitable single day in the history of Drexel & De Forest and we have completely destroyed a competitor in the process. This is the first time that I have ever brought champagne to the trading floor and it might be the last, but you all definitely deserve it. Great job everyone. Bull Capital has been absolutely obliterated, and even though the rest of Wall Street is struggling to survive at this moment, we are absolutely swimming in cash. In the coming days you will hear of layoffs at major financial institutions all over the city, but our bonus checks are going to be bigger than ever at the end of the year. I want all of you to savor this moment. When you swim with the sharks sometimes you are going to get mauled. Bull Capital learned that lesson today."

A voice from the other side of the floor started chanting "Caroline, Caroline" and soon everyone joined in.

Caroline lifted her hands to calm the chanting. "So what's next? Well, tomorrow we get back to work. But for tonight we celebrate! We are going to hit some of the hottest spots in the city this evening and the firm is going to pay for everything. Vehicles are waiting in the parking garage to take us to our first stop. So don't just sit there – let's party!"

That was all the encouragement most of the traders needed. Most of them started whooping and hollering as they headed for the door. In the back of the room, one of the senior partners caught Caroline's eye and motioned for her to come over and talk to him.

Sam Van Duyn very much looked the part of a senior partner. He was in his late fifties with broad shoulders and just enough white in his hair to convey a sense of authority. His deep voice, piercing eyes and serious demeanor were tools that he used to command respect wherever he went. Very few people ever chose to mess with Sam Van Duyn.

As Caroline approached Sam, she was the first to speak. "Did you want to talk with me Sam?"

"Yes Caroline, I wanted to let you know that all of the senior partners think that you did a fantastic job today. You will receive the payment that we discussed – plus a little extra."

"Thank you Sam. I greatly appreciate the faith that you all have in me."

"You have been invaluable to us Caroline. But there is something else that we need you to do for us now. Don't ask me how I know this, but a key position at the Federal Reserve is about to open up. We plan on pulling a few strings and calling in a few favors to get you appointed to that position. In that position you would have a tremendous amount of influence over which banks the Fed gives emergency loans to and where bailout money from Congress goes. Needless to say, having a friend in such a position would be greatly advantageous for us. Of course when this crisis is finally over we will welcome you back to your current position at the firm with open arms. Plus, your resume will have been greatly enhanced by working for the Fed."

Caroline was intrigued. "So will I have to go down to D.C. for this position?"

"I am afraid so Caroline. I know how much you love New York City, but I think that you will find D.C. to be quite entertaining as well. We are really hoping that you will be willing to do this for us."

Caroline smiled. "Of course I will Sam. You know that I am always willing to do whatever the firm needs me to do. You can count me in."

Sam and Caroline continued to engage in small talk for a little while after that and then Caroline headed home. She wasn't really in a party mood tonight. Her mind was now totally focused on what was coming next for her in Washington. Yes, she was intrigued with the possibility of working at the Fed, but there was also a personal matter that she needed to attend to down in D.C. that was of even greater interest to her.

Caroline's apartment was located in one of the most exclusive buildings in New York City. It directly bordered Central Park, and the view from her apartment was literally worth a million bucks. Caroline made an extraordinary amount of money, but she also tended to spend almost as much money as she brought in. She had always dreamed of being able to look down on Central Park from her living room window, and about a year ago that dream had finally become a reality. Her 2800 square foot luxury apartment was much more than she actually needed, but to Caroline it actually felt a little bit small. She was a woman that was never satisfied with the status quo. She was always pushing for more.

When she entered her apartment on the 33rd floor, a voice spoke to her out of the darkness before she even had a chance to turn on the lights. "I told you that I could arrange to have you sent to Washington."

The voice was very familiar to Caroline, but it still made her jump a bit. "I really hate it when you do this. Can't you just knock on my door like a normal person would?"

"What kind of fun would that be? Besides, you should know by now that there is nothing 'normal' in the way that we operate."

"Yes, I know that very well," Caroline said. "So how in the world did you convince Sam and the other senior partners that I should go down to Washington? I make a lot of money for them."

"There are some things that you don't need to know Caroline. All you need to know is that we have helped you achieve a level of success far beyond anything that you ever dreamed possible. And of course we will more than make up for the reduction in salary that you will experience by taking this position at the Fed. We understand how much money it takes to maintain the lifestyle to which you have become accustomed."

"Thank you. Can I turn my lights on now?"

"Not yet. We also know that you have some personal reasons for wanting to go down to Washington, and that is fine. But don't forget - you work for us."

And with that, the voice was gone.

Caroline finally flipped on the light switch and carefully looked around her apartment. As she walked over to her open balcony door, she reflected back on the events of the past few years.

Her "friends" had been very good to her, but she wasn't sure if she really liked the idea of getting even more closely involved with them.

But at this point she was in so deep that she wasn't sure what else to do.

There appeared to be no way out, and Caroline was not sure that she wanted a way out even if one happened to be available.

Chapter 9

The next morning Tom McDowell found himself waiting alone for a car to pick him up in front of CIA headquarters in Langley, Virginia. It was an unusually chilly morning for this time of the year, and there was no sign of Koz. Tom doubted that he would show up considering how their conversation had gone the previous afternoon. Koz was very much a family man now and nothing was going to change that. Koz was very comfortable with his desk job and that was okay. Koz knew what he wanted.

But what did Tom want? That was a question that he knew that he did not have a good answer for.

A black SUV with tinted windows pulled up directly in front of Tom and the front window on the passenger side slowly opened. The driver was a very serious looking Asian-American man that Tom guessed to be about 40 years old.

The driver spoke before Tom did. "Hello Mr. McDowell. My name is Sam Park. I will be taking you to the briefing. Please get into the back seat."

Tom mumbled back a half-hearted greeting and did as requested. Sam did not appear to be interested in having a conversation, so Tom just sat in the back of the vehicle quietly. He still did not know where they were going. Tom wondered what this day would hold for him.

Tom never liked to be in a situation where he was not in control. Yet here he was on the way to a briefing for a job that he didn't know anything about for an organization that he did not even know the name of. He didn't even know where the briefing would be held. Would he have been this trusting when he was younger? Was he slipping now that he was getting older?

As Tom continued to get lost in his thoughts he noticed that the SUV had pulled on to the George Washington Parkway and that they were heading toward Washington. At least it would be a beautiful drive.

Tom actually did truly enjoy the D.C. area. If one could put up with the endless traffic and the pretentious people, it really wasn't such a bad place to be. If this new adventure with this mystery agency didn't work out, perhaps he could finally find a wife and settle down. It seemed to be working for Koz.

Tom wondered why he couldn't be more like other men. Why did he always feel the need to run after some new adventure? Was he running toward something or had he been running away from something all this time?

Tom thought back to one of the times when he almost didn't make it back from an assignment. During his early days with the CIA, Tom, Koz and four other agents had been sent into the Gaza Strip for what was supposed to be a really easy snatch and grab job. They had been told that an al-Qaeda big shot was there visiting some top Hamas leaders and that security was minimal. It was supposed to be a walk in the park.

But when they got to the house where the al-Qaeda big shot was supposed to be staying, he was long gone. Instead, a full-blown ambush was waiting for them. They got caught in a vicious crossfire and everyone on the team got hit multiple times.

Tom had been able to duck behind a concrete barricade, and even though he had been hit a couple of times he was still mobile. From where he was hiding, he could see that everyone else on his team was down. None of them was moving except for Koz.

Tom couldn't bear the thought of leaving Koz behind. He bolted out from behind cover and dragged him out of the middle of that street.

Over the next couple of hours, Tom engaged in a running gun battle with Hamas militia as he half-carried, half-dragged Koz to the extraction point.

It took Koz months to recover from his injuries, but he did eventually make a full recovery. Tom knew that Koz was incredibly grateful for what Tom had done, but the two men never spoke of it much. There was just sort of a silent understanding between them. When men bleed together in battle, it forms a bond that is not easily broken. Tom knew that if he ever needed anything, Koz would be there for him.

That is why Tom was so disappointed that Koz had decided not to come with him this morning.

It just wouldn't be the same without him.

Up ahead, Tom could see that traffic was coming to a stop. He was not very fond of traffic jams. In fact, they tended to drive him absolutely nuts. Tom decided that this would be a good time to rest his eyes for a bit.

Tom closed his eyes, but he couldn't shake the stress that was eating away at him like cancer. No matter where he was or what he was doing, he never could seem to find peace. Tom wondered if that was why he was always chasing after another adventure. Perhaps he couldn't handle being alone with his own thoughts.

Perhaps what he was most afraid of was facing the seemingly bottomless abyss of pain and frustration that was deep inside himself.

Tom opened his eyes back up and started looking out at the other vehicles on the highway. He was hoping that he could find something – anything – to take his mind off of his internal struggles.

Chapter 10

Tom figured that the black SUV was taking him into D.C., but he didn't know exactly where they were headed until the SUV entered a parking garage under a five story brick office building in Foggy Bottom. Sam Park maneuvered the SUV toward the back of the parking garage and then brought it to a stop. He turned around and looked at Tom expectantly.

"We are here Mr. McDowell. It is time for you to go upstairs to the briefing."

"Thank you for the ride. Are you coming up to the briefing too?"

"No Mr. McDowell, I will not be joining you. The briefing is on the 4th floor. They are expecting you."

Tom grabbed his things and exited the vehicle. He could see signs for an elevator in the distance so he headed in that direction. This day was getting stranger all the time. Hopefully he would be getting some explanations shortly.

Tom got into the elevator and took it up to the 4th floor. When he exited, a very professional African-American woman in a pinstripe suit was waiting for him.

"Tom McDowell – we have been expecting you. Your briefing will be in Conference Room B. It is the second door on the left."

Tom thanked her and started heading in that direction. He looked around and rapidly came to the conclusion that this office space had not been well maintained. The carpeting was very worn and there was a musky smell in the hallway. Tom began wondering what he had gotten himself into.

When Tom reached Conference Room B, he was not terribly impressed. It looked more like a college classroom than a conference room. It was filled with numerous small rectangular tables, and aging office chairs that looked quite uncomfortable were positioned behind each of them. About 15 others had already arrived and had taken seats. None of them appeared to know what was going on, so Tom figured that they were other "recruits". There was a row of chairs lined up along the back of the room and Tom decided to take a seat in one of them.

Tom didn't have to wait long for the meeting to start. Two men entered through a side door toward the front of the room. One of them had sunglasses on and was wearing a dark blue suit with a black tie. He took a seat off to the side where he could face the group and get a good look at everyone.

The other man was wearing a crisp white shirt, a black suit without a tie and was impeccably groomed. He positioned himself directly behind the podium at the front of the room.

"You are probably wondering what you are doing here," he began. "You are here because you are the best of the best, and you are about to get the answers that you have been waiting for. I am here to give you a choice. After I am done speaking, you will have the opportunity to go back to your old life and continue in your old job. But my guess is that most of you will not want to do that. My guess is that most of you desperately want to do something meaningful with your lives, and I am about to hand you that opportunity on a silver platter."

The young African-American woman in the pinstripe suit appeared in the doorway that Tom had entered through earlier. "I am so sorry to interrupt but we have one more to join the briefing. Is that okay?"

The impeccably groomed man at the podium motioned that she should bring the late arrival into the room. "That is fine – we were just getting started."

Tom's jaw just about hit the floor when he saw Koz walk in. Koz instantly spotted Tom, but he took a seat on the other side of the room.

The man at the podium spoke to Koz as he was taking his seat. "Jon Kozlowski – it is a pleasure to have you join us. Please make it a point to never be late for one of my briefings ever again."

Koz nodded and took his seat.

The man at the podium resumed his speech. "As I was saying, you all are the best, and throughout American history the best have always stepped forward to protect this nation. We live at a time when the threats to our freedoms are more insidious than ever before. Much of the rest of the world hates us. We are faced with a vast array of enemies both foreign and domestic. We live at a time when weapons are becoming much more powerful and the world is becoming increasingly unstable. A single crazed extremist with a single weapon of mass destruction could potentially wipe out millions of American lives. The next 9/11 could happen at literally any moment. We are here to do everything that we can to prevent that from happening. Once upon a time, threats to our national security were primarily handled by organizations such as the CIA and the FBI. But those organizations got soft and they became way too politicized. Meanwhile, the threats to our national security became much more serious and much more complicated. It became clear that other organizations would be needed to battle these new threats. That is where we come in. We do the kinds of things that the CIA and the FBI used to do, but we have been given a significant advantage. We are an organization without a name and we operate outside of the rules. We have been given a single mandate – to defend the interests of the United States at all costs. Some Americans may be quite disturbed if they found out about some of the things that we have to do, but most of them would be darn glad that we are out here doing them. We do the dirty work so that the rest of the country can continue to enjoy the pursuit of the American Dream."

Tom cringed when he heard this. Did this guy actually believe all this stuff?

The man at the podium continued to ramble on.

"Liberty and freedom come at a price. We take out the monsters that lurk in the shadows so that millions of families out there can continue to enjoy the good things that this country has to offer. We are the wolves that protect the sheep. We deal death so that others may live. We exist outside of democracy in order to preserve democracy.

"If you join us, your life will dramatically change. I can promise you adventure, but not safety. You will make more money than you ever dreamed possible, but we require absolute loyalty. You will do great things, but you will never be able to tell anyone about it. You will truly make a difference in this world, but you will never be recognized as a hero by the public.

"We already know that all of you love this country. You wouldn't be here if you didn't. We also already know that all of you are loyal. The question is this – do you have the guts to join the elite defenders of this nation? Are you willing to lay it all on the line for the United States of America?

"If you choose not to join us, you will be free to go after signing some non-disclosure forms and you will never hear from us again.

"But if you do choose to join us, your life will go to an entirely new level.

"Are there any questions?"

Tom raised his hand.

"Yes, Tom McDowell – what would you like to ask?"

Tom cleared his throat. "What did you mean when you said that this organization does not have a name?"

The man at the podium smiled broadly. "When an organization has a name, eventually it gets blamed for all kinds of things and it gets a certain reputation. Just take a look at the CIA. Over the years a lot of mud has been thrown at the CIA and a lot of it has stuck. But if you don't have a name, nobody can ever blame you for anything. If we do something that upsets people, who are they going to blame it on? By having no name, it becomes much, much harder for us to become a target. Nobody can threaten to shut us down or take away our funding because they don't even know that we exist."

Another recruit across the room raised his hand.

"Yes, Andy Madden – what is your question?"

Andy seemed a bit intimidated by all of this. "Well, um, if nobody knows about this organization then how is it held accountable?"

The man at the podium was clearly annoyed by this question. "Andy, I believe that you are missing the point. The major weakness of both the CIA and the FBI is that they are both directly accountable to the politicians. They can't do anything without some pathetic politician whining about it. That is why it was decided that 'black budget' organizations that Congress does not even know about were necessary. In fact, the president does not even know about our activities. That way he has 'plausible deniability' if something goes terribly wrong. Does that answer your question?"

Andy seemed unconvinced. "Well, if you don't answer to the president, then who do you answer to?"

"We answer to a higher authority than the president," the man at the podium answered back. This caused the man in the sunglasses and the dark blue suit to perk up. The man at the podium noticed his raised eyebrows and became noticeably nervous. "What I mean is that we are ultimately accountable to the American people. We are the last line of defense. If we fail, there is nobody else to back us up. Either we succeed, or the terrorists win. There are those that would like to take America in a much different direction than it is heading in today. The extremists must not win, and we are here to make sure that does not happen. Future generations of Americans deserve a future filled with peace and prosperity, but the only way that we are going to get there is if we are willing to defend America from those that seek to enslave us to the failed belief systems of the past. If you are not willing to take a bullet for this country, then you should not even think about joining our ranks."

The man at the podium was back on a roll now. "So are you in or are you out? Do you want to do something great for your country, or do you just want to be another faceless nobody? Do you want to defend freedom so that your children and grandchildren have something to look forward to, or do you want to sit on your couch and gobble down potato chips as you watch the world go by?

"If you join us, you will experience more adventure and make more money than you ever have before. If you choose not to join us, you will spend the rest of your life wondering what might have been.

"Are you ready to make a decision? If you are in, I want you to stand up right now. If you are out, I want you to remain seated."

There was a lot of noise as almost everyone in the room got up from their seats including Tom. He really wasn't buying the speech, but he was more than ready for a new adventure. Tom looked around and noticed that every single person in the room was standing except for Andy Madden.

The man at the podium was pleased. "Excellent. Those of you that have decided to join us won't regret it. Let's take a short break and we'll reconvene in five minutes."

Most of the recruits in the room got up and started milling around. A few of them asked where the bathroom was.

Tom walked over and greeted Koz. "Hey buddy, I didn't think that you were coming."

Koz was definitely not in a light-hearted mood. "These guys can be very persuasive Tom."

Tom didn't know quite what to make of that.

"What do you mean Koz?"

"I mean that after I phoned Director Del Conte to tell him that I didn't want to do this, two guys showed up at my front door and said that they wanted to have a talk with me. They told me that if I would take a position with this organization that all of the college costs that my kids would ever have would be paid for. How could I say no to that?"

This rattled Tom a bit, but he didn't show it. Instead, he decided that a little humor was in order.

"It sounds like I should have held out for a better deal myself."

As Tom said this, he noticed that the mysterious man in the sunglasses and the dark blue suit was accompanying Andy Madden out of the room.

Nobody realized it at that moment, but it was the last time that anyone would ever see Andy Madden alive again.

Chapter 11

"Let me look at the dossier again."

As Jay Helms handed the document to his partner, Roland Toler, he could see that Roland was becoming increasingly frustrated.

"Look Roland, I don't like being on a stakeout in some backwater town in Montana any more than you do. But this is how we are going to move up in the Department of Homeland Security. If we do a good job on the little things, eventually they will trust us with bigger assignments."

"I know Jay, but this guy in the dossier hasn't even been accused of any crimes. The DHS just wants us to 'gather more information' on him. We don't even know his real name. All we know about his appearance is that he is probably in his mid-forties, about 6'2, about 220 pounds, has dark hair that is thinning a bit on top and that it is believed that he is still sporting a goatee. How in the world can we hope to positively identify this guy?"

"Well, the lady that runs the 'Quack & Snack' said a man fitting this description visits this post office every couple of weeks or so. This is the best lead that we have."

Roland was getting really tired of waiting for this mystery man to show up. "I don't see why it is so important to find this blogger. It isn't as though he has done anything wrong. So what if millions of Americans read his blogs every month? Can't we just leave him alone? Is it really so important for the DHS to know everything about everybody?"

Jay really wished that someone else would have been sent with him on this assignment. "Who are we to question the orders of our superiors? There are probably things about this guy that they aren't telling us. We are on a 'need to know' basis, remember? Some people certainly feel that his writings are 'anti-government', and in this day and age it makes perfect sense that we would not want some 'anti-government' nutjob running around out there that we don't know anything about."

Roland just kind of rolled his eyes. "Whatever Jay, I'm going to go across the street and get a burger. Are you coming?"

As Roland started to open up the passenger door of the black SUV, Jay reached out to grab his left arm.

"Look over there Roland. Could that be our guy?"

Across the street they could see a man that somewhat fit the description in the dossier walking down the sidewalk toward the post office. He had sunglasses and a baseball cap on so it was hard to get a good look at him, but this was the best potential match they had come across in two days.

Roland was visibly excited. "Get out the camera Jay. We need to get some pictures."

Jay looked all around for the camera but he couldn't find it. "Where did you put it Roland? It was right here earlier."

"I moved it when we had breakfast so that I could put my waffles there. Look in the back seat."

"I don't see it back there either Roland. You are really starting to piss me off."

"Forget about the camera Jay. Let's just follow him inside. Remember, we are not here to arrest him. We are only here to gather intelligence."

The two men got out of the vehicle and awkwardly made their way inside the post office. By the time they entered the front door, the mystery man was already opening a post office box along the far wall.

"Can you tell which box number that is Roland?"

"Yes, it is box number 178. I told you that this would be an easy assignment Jay."

"Okay, you discreetly follow him outside and I will find out who is renting that post office box."

The mystery man quietly slipped out a side door and a few moments later Roland followed him out that same door. Roland was trying to be stealthy, but he was failing miserably.

Jay walked over to the counter and pushed the elderly woman that the postal clerk was helping out of the way.

"Step aside granny. This is a matter of national security."

Jay flashed his badge to the alarmed postal clerk. "I am Jay Helms from the Department of Homeland Security. I need you to tell me the name and the address of the man that is renting P.O. Box 178."

The young postal clerk turned to his computer and started typing. "Okay, it should take me just a moment. Ah – here it is. His name is Bud Weiser and he lives at 123 Seymour Beer Lane."

Jay felt like he was about to hit the ceiling. "That is obviously a fake name and a fake address you dumb redneck. How could you not see that?"

"Don't blame me. I just started here two days ago sir," the stunned postal clerk sheepishly replied.

Jay bolted out the front door and sprinted over to the SUV. When he reached the vehicle, he leaned against the hood as he pulled out his phone and dialed Roland's number. In just a moment he heard Roland's phone start to ring nearby.

Roland answered his phone and he was even more annoyed than before.

"Don't be an idiot Jay."

"Where are you Roland?"

"I am sitting in the SUV. Turn around and look."

Jay turned around and felt very stupid. Through the heavily tinted windows he could see Roland sitting in the vehicle.

"Get in Jay. Our man is over there across the street talking to that police officer. Once he gets into his vehicle hopefully he will lead us right to his house."

Jay got into the vehicle and they both carefully watched the mystery man. After a few moments his conversation with the police officer ended and he got into a black pickup truck that had obviously seen better days. The black pickup truck pulled out of the parking lot and into traffic.

Roland could hardly contain himself. "There he goes Jay. Don't follow him too closely. We don't want him to suspect anything."

After a few blocks, the black pickup truck pulled off the road in front of a gas station where some high school cheerleaders were holding a car wash.

"What should we do Roland?"

"I'm not sure. Let's pull off to the side a short distance away and wait."

Roland and Jay watched as the black pickup truck approached the crowd of cheerleaders. The man in the truck rolled down his window and had a brief conversation with one of them.

Suddenly all of the cheerleaders came sprinting over toward the SUV where Roland and Jay were waiting. One of the cheerleaders knocked on the window next to Jay.

"Thank you so much sir. Your friend told us that you are willing to donate 100 dollars to our cheerleading squad, and that you want your vehicle washed as quickly as possible because you have an important meeting to get to."

Jay wasn't quite sure how to respond to that.

All around them, girls with buckets and sponges started washing the SUV.

"No, you don't understand," Jay muttered, "we don't need our vehicle washed..."

By then, none of the girls were even listening to Jay. They were all hard at work scrubbing down the SUV.

"What do we do now Roland?"

Roland seemed very enamored with the girls washing the vehicle.

"Well Jay, to be honest our SUV is quite dirty. What is the harm in letting them wash it for a bit?"

Suddenly, Roland and Jay heard a police siren come to life behind them. The police officer pulled up to just a few inches from their back bumper and stepped out of his cruiser.

It was the police officer that the mystery man in the sunglasses and the baseball cap had been talking to just a few minutes earlier.

Jay quickly glanced over at the black pickup truck that they had been following. The man with the sunglasses and the baseball cap was looking back at them and smiling.

Jay looked back at the police officer and noticed that he had now pulled out his gun. "I want your hands where I can see them," he hollered at Jay and Roland in a commanding voice.

Both Jay and Roland carefully raised their hands.

Roland thought that he had better try to talk his way out of this mess. "You don't understand officer. We are actually from the Department of Homeland Security."

"Sure you are," the officer stated bluntly, "and I am Davy Crockett. Look...we have had a complaint that you two have been exposing yourselves in public. I am going to have to take you in."

Jay glanced over at the black pickup truck again. The man in the sunglasses and the baseball cap grinned widely, waved and drove off.

Jay felt like screaming. What were his superiors back in Washington D.C. going to think of this one?

———————

As he drove away, Russ "Diesel" Jacoby couldn't help but smile. He hadn't had this much fun in a long, long time.

Russ figured that those two clowns must be feds, and probably very inexperienced ones.

Yes, he was going to have to get rid of this truck and wouldn't be able to use that P.O. Box again, but that was okay because he had lots of other trucks and lots of other P.O. Boxes that he could use.

Russ just hoped that the numbskulls in D.C. wouldn't decide to send some real pros after him someday. If they did, that might be a problem.

Chapter 12

"...the Dow was down another 511 points today. Overall, the Dow has now fallen close to 2500 points this week. The heads of several major Wall Street firms are going to gather with the Treasury Secretary and the Chairman of the Federal Reserve this weekend to discuss this crisis. Apparently, several of the firms are potentially facing tens of billions of dollars in derivatives losses. It is believed that these Wall Street executives plan to approach Congress and ask them for another round of bailouts. Only this time the bailouts will likely need to be far larger than what we saw back in 2008. The Chairman of the Federal Reserve announced today that the Fed is ready to provide as much emergency liquidity as necessary. The Fed seems absolutely determined to avoid a repeat of the mistakes of the 1930s. Meanwhile, OPEC announced today that all member nations would begin selling more oil in other major global currencies such as the euro and the Chinese yuan. OPEC is reportedly extremely concerned about the instability of the U.S. dollar at this point. Could this be the beginning of the end for the petrodollar?"

Melissa Remling pointed the remote control at the television and turned it off. She didn't really enjoy watching herself on television. Whenever she did, all she seemed to notice were the little flaws. From where she was sitting, Melissa could see a faint reflection of herself in the television screen. She stared at it for a while. Her 1600 square foot apartment high above the West Village felt very empty once again tonight. She lived alone, and she thought that she liked it that way, but there were way too many nights like tonight when her apartment felt way too lonely.

A dim lamp on a desk next to an open window provided the only illumination now that the television had been turned off. The only sound came from the relentless traffic on the streets below. When she first got to New York, the traffic noise bothered her immensely, but now she couldn't imagine life without it. Complete silence would probably just drive her crazy.

Melissa didn't really feel like getting up from the couch. She was tired, but she doubted that she would be able to sleep. In fact, there was a good chance that she would have to take some sleeping pills yet again tonight.

She brushed a few strands of long, blond hair away from her face. Why did she grow her hair so long anyway? It was so hard to manage. Perhaps shorter hair would be nicer. But would viewers respond to her the same way?

Melissa sighed. She had always believed that a successful career in journalism would make her happy. Yes, she definitely made good money and people recognized her wherever she went, but she still felt kind of empty most of the time.

Well, except for the times when she felt extremely empty like tonight.

What was she missing out on? Why was happiness so elusive for her?

After her parents passed away, she had felt very alone for most of the rest of her childhood.

She had been convinced that things would be much different once she got older, and yet the same loneliness was still eating away at her.

So what was the answer? Should she get married?

She had certainly dated lots of men. But most of them had either been overly pretentious bankers or self-obsessed narcissists from the entertainment world. She could honestly say that she didn't miss any of her old boyfriends. In fact, she was quite certain that marrying any of them would have been pure hell.

Melissa looked back into the television screen. She was only going to get older from here, and the television industry could be a very cold, cruel world.

Was this the apex of her life? Would things only go downhill for her from now on?

That thought was too depressing for Melissa to dwell on, so she got up and headed for the kitchen. She knew her bosses would prefer that she grab a salad about now, but she was definitely in the mood for some potato chips.

She grabbed a bag and settled back in the exact same place on the couch where she had been sitting previously. She gobbled down a few chips but this made her feel even more frustrated.

Why did life have to be so difficult? She had worked so incredibly hard. In fact, she had outworked everyone around her. So where was her pot of gold at the end of the rainbow?

Melissa tossed the bag of chips on to her coffee table. Getting fat certainly wasn't going to help anything.

It seemed like the more success that she was able to achieve, the more pressure she felt. Fame was definitely a double-edged sword. It was a blessing that her reports were seen by millions of Americans every day, but it was also a curse.

What Melissa tried very hard to avoid was reading what people were saying about her on the Internet. People could be incredibly cruel, and none of them had any idea about the pressures that she experienced on a daily basis. Who were they to pass judgment on her?

Melissa felt that familiar pain in the pit of her stomach again. She was definitely going to have to go see a doctor about that at some point.

Melissa knew that there were millions of women out there that would trade lives with her in a second. Sometimes Melissa fantasized about taking one of those women up on that deal. Perhaps a simpler life would be a happier one.

Then again, maybe it wouldn't.

Melissa continued to stare aimlessly at the television, alone with her thoughts. It was going to be another very long night.

Chapter 13

Killian wondered why he always seemed to get stuck with idiot drivers.

When he arrived in the United States, a particularly annoying young man named Tony Scarlatti had been assigned to drive him around. He wouldn't stop talking, and Killian was not sure how much more of this he could take.

As far as Killian was concerned, the faster they got back to New York City the better. The Order had requested that Killian attend a "planning meeting" down in Baltimore, and Killian had reluctantly agreed to go. But Killian had not really seen the point of going to that meeting, since everyone knew that he wouldn't utter a single word the entire time.

In the old days, employers just gave him an assignment and Killian did his job and that was the end of it.

But these days a lot of people wanted to meet "the silent assassin". He had become something of a pseudo-celebrity, and word had gotten around in The Order that he had come to the United States.

The Order was becoming way too political and way too bureaucratic as far as Killian was concerned, but this was how things were done now, and so Killian was willing to play along. Attending a pointless meeting from time to time wasn't going to kill him. The Order paid very well, and so Killian was willing to put up with a little nonsense once in a while.

The worst part about the meeting today was that it had meant a very long drive down from New York City and back listening to Tony go on and on about his drunken conquests and about all of the women he was chasing and about how much he liked to work out.

Tony was the son of some big shot that operated over in Brooklyn, so Killian had to put up with him for the time being. But Killian was doing his best to try to ignore him. Unfortunately, despite his best efforts to tune him out, the young punk just kept on yammering. There seemed to be no off switch with this guy.

"Hey Killian, are you there?" Tony was looking over at him. "What's up my man? Are you listening to me?"

Killian rolled his eyes and looked over at Tony.

Tony smirked. "Hey, why is it that you never talk? Is it that you can't talk or is that you don't want to talk? If you can't talk, I feel really bad for you. I couldn't imagine going through my life without talking. A guy has got to be able to talk to the ladies if he wants to be able to charm them. You know what I'm saying?"

Killian was rapidly losing patience. All of this endless chattering was driving him absolutely insane.

Tony just kept on talking. "And why don't you have any hair man? Did you lose all your hair or do you shave your head on purpose? So what's the deal with that?"

Killian wondered why Tony didn't understand that he just wanted to be left alone. Tony had been told that Killian does not speak and that he preferred quiet, but Tony had apparently not gotten the message.

Killian figured that Tony was just like so many other young people in America today – he appeared to have absolutely no respect for his elders.

Killian looked out the window for a moment and he caught a glimpse of himself in the side mirror. He wasn't sure if he liked what he saw. Should he try to grow his hair back? He had once had very long red hair, but he had shaved it all off a few years ago when he made a vow to kill someone that was rumored to be impossible to kill.

Killian eventually tracked that man down and shot him five times in the back and then proceeded to blow up his hotel room. But after fulfilling that contract Killian had never grown his hair back.

Was now the time to start growing it again? Would it look the same as before?

Killian thought back to his childhood. His red hair had always made him stand out. He didn't even know if his parents had red hair, because he had never known his parents. In fact, he didn't know anything about his family tree at all. He was a man without any roots, and whenever he thought about that for too long it made him feel kind of sick inside.

There were stories going around that Killian had been raised by wolves, but Killian didn't remember anything like that.

What Killian did remember was an extremely painful childhood. He remembered sleeping in abandoned buildings and surviving on whatever leftover food he was able to discover in garbage bins. He remembered being found by the police on the outskirts of a remote town in rural Romania when he was seven years old. He remembered being taken in by some Irish missionaries that were running an orphanage in Romania. They had named him "Killian", because he had no records and nobody knew where he had come from.

When he reached 15 years of age, Killian ran away from the orphanage and never looked back.

In time, he learned that he was very good at killing people. Later on, Killian started killing people for money. Eventually, Killian became one of the most respected assassins on the planet.

But that didn't mean that he still didn't have to put up with some nonsense every once in a while.

Killian looked back toward Tony.

He was still chattering.

"Killian my man, when you and I get back to New York City I am going to set you up. I know exactly what you need. I am going to take you out for a night on the town amigo. You look like you could use a night of chasing women. I am sure that most of the time the ladies are pretty freaked out by how you look, but you know the silent but deadly thing can be quite sexy. Tonight we will go out and we'll hit the clubs and I will introduce you as a 'mysterious foreigner'. I think that with me as your wingman that you can do quite well."

As Tony yammered on, he wasn't paying much attention to the road. They were cruising along the New Jersey Parkway well above the speed limit, and Tony suddenly decided to change lanes without checking his blind spot. Unfortunately, there was another vehicle in his blind spot.

The Buick sedan that Tony and Killian were riding in collided with a very expensive Mercedes sedan that had been creeping up alongside them.

From the crunching sound that the impact made, Killian could tell that significant damage to both vehicles had been done.

Killian pointed toward an exit sign that was coming up, and Tony turned on his signal light hoping that the driver in the Mercedes would follow them. Both vehicles proceeded down the exit ramp and Killian pointed toward an alley behind a row of buildings that was a bit of a distance from the highway.

The Mercedes followed them down into the alley, and Tony stopped the Buick precisely where Killian directed him to. The Mercedes came to a stop about 10 feet behind them, and the driver of the Mercedes emerged from his vehicle in quite a rage.

The driver of the Mercedes was a thin man in his late forties, and he was wearing a very expensive Italian suit that had obviously been tailored for his frame. Under normal circumstances he was probably very dignified, but at that moment he looked like he wanted to take someone's head off.

Tony got out of the Buick and met the other driver about midway between the two vehicles. The driver of the Mercedes spoke first.

"You just messed with the wrong guy pal. Do you have any idea who I am? I work for one of the top law firms in New York City. I don't have time for this kind of idiocy. Do you know how much I make per hour? You didn't even look before you pulled over into the other lane and sideswiped me. Do you know how much it is going to cost to repair all this?"

Tony tried to calm him down. "Hey, don't get all freaked out man. It was just an accident. We can work this out."

The enraged lawyer pulled out his phone. "I'm calling the police. We are going to get them to do a full report and then I am going to have them arrest you for reckless driving. And I hope that you have insurance because you are going to pay for this damage one way or another. By the time I am done, you are going to wish that you had never even heard of me."

As he started to dial the police, the enraged lawyer was more than a little stunned when an arrow struck his phone, knocking it completely out of his hands.

Visibly shaken, the lawyer looked up and saw that another man had just emerged from the Buick sedan that had hit him.

The man that he was now looking at had no hair, was well over 7 feet tall and definitely weighed more than 400 pounds. He was also holding a compound bow.

"You moron," the lawyer hollered at Killian. "You guys are in really big trouble now. I am pressing criminal charges. After I am done with you two, they are going to lock you both away and throw away the key. I am the last person that you ever want to mess with."

Killian armed his compound bow with another arrow and aimed it directly at the enraged lawyer's chest.

The countenance of the angry lawyer suddenly changed, and at this point he realized that Killian was not messing around.

"Look," the previously enraged lawyer stammered meekly, "I am so sorry. I don't know what I was thinking. There is certainly no need for violence. Why don't we just forget that this ever happened? We don't have to get the police involved. I'll just go my way and you can go your way."

Killian did not lower his compound bow.

Tony tried to intervene. "Hey guy, I don't know what your deal is but this guy that I have been driving around is one really bad dude. So I suggest that you start running, because he appears to be losing his patience."

By this time, the expression on the lawyer's face had definitely changed into one of fear. He turned and started sprinting toward his car. As he did so, he pulled his keys out of his pocket, but he quickly dropped them to the ground when an arrow struck his right hand.

The lawyer pulled his right hand up to his face and he could see that the shaft of the arrow had not made it all the way through his hand. He screamed in agony and he started begging for mercy. He looked up and saw that Killian was aiming another arrow at him.

Tony smiled. He seemed to be enjoying this. "I told you man, you better start running."

The lawyer's eyes got really wide and he started running away from Killian and Tony as fast as he could in the very expensive shoes that he was wearing.

He got about 50 feet before an arrow dug very deeply into his back.

The lawyer collapsed to the ground and was dead within moments.

Killian slowly walked over to the fallen lawyer and retrieved his arrows. He took a few moments to confirm that the lawyer was indeed dead, and then he motioned to Tony that he should come over.

Together, they picked up the body of the dead lawyer and dropped it into a nearby dumpster.

Tony wasn't sure what to make of all this. "I've never seen anything like that before dude! That was wild! I mean I've seen some really messed up stuff before, but I ain't never seen nothing like that. But you've got to be more careful dude. That first arrow that you shot went right by my left ear, and if I'd made a sudden move to the left it might have hit me in the head and I could have been killed."

Yes, Killian thought, that would have been quite a shame.

As they walked back to their vehicle, Killian reflected on what had just happened. Killian certainly didn't like to kill people unnecessarily, but he just couldn't have that lawyer call 911 and get the police involved. That simply was not an option, so Killian had done what needed to be done and he had done it as quietly as possible.

Killian preferred to keep collateral damage to a minimum, but sometimes obstacles came along that had to be removed.

Unfortunately, very few jobs ever seemed to go as smoothly in the United States as they did in Europe, and Killian feared that there would be other obstacles that he would need to "remove" before all of this was over.

Chapter 14

It was a chilly day in Washington D.C., and Caroline Mancini found herself wishing that she had dressed much more warmly as she sat on the steps of the Lincoln Memorial looking out over the reflecting pool. In the distance, the Washington Monument towered over the rest of the National Mall. There were lots of white puffy clouds in the sky on this particular day, and Caroline was admiring the great architectural beauty that surrounded her. Millions of tourists came to D.C. each year, and yet Caroline knew that only a very small fraction of them understood the deep meanings behind the arcane symbols that could be found on many of the national monuments and government buildings in Washington.

Caroline understood those deep meanings, and they did not trouble her one bit.

But Caroline had not come to the steps of the Lincoln Memorial today for fun. The truth was that she was there on business. She was supposed to meet someone, and she knew that he would be talking to her about her work at the Fed.

Caroline was enjoying her new position at the Federal Reserve, even if it meant doing some things that were "questionable" once in a while. Of course Caroline had done all kinds of "questionable" things during the course of her career on Wall Street, so she wasn't exactly breaking new ground. She probably should have been disturbed by some of the things that she was currently doing at the Fed, but long ago she had gotten rid of the little voice in her heart that told her when she was doing something wrong.

Caroline's self-reflection was interrupted by a man who came and sat down right next to Caroline, but Caroline didn't even look up because she knew exactly who it was.

The man had short dark hair, he was wearing sunglasses, and he was dressed in a long black overcoat. He looked very professional, and there was nothing about him that would make him stand out from all of the other bureaucrats, politicians and lawyers in Washington.

"Caroline," the man began, "it is so good to see you again. How are you enjoying your time at the Federal Reserve?"

Caroline wasn't sure how she should respond to that question. She answered without taking her eyes off of the reflecting pool. "I appreciate you helping me get this position, and it's definitely been an eye-opening experience for me so far."

The man smiled. He liked Caroline. She knew how to play the game.

"And I trust that everything is going according to plan?"

Caroline frowned slightly. "Yes, everything is going according to plan, but I'm sure that you already knew that. All of the banks that I have been instructed to help get secret loans are getting them, and all of the banks that are not supposed to get money are being blocked from getting it."

The man in the black overcoat grinned. "Very good. We know that we can always count on you Caroline."

Caroline had a question for the man in the black overcoat.

"But what about the bailouts that are being pushed through Congress? It looks like you all are going to be a couple of votes short. What do you all plan to do about that?"

The man in the black overcoat glanced at Caroline. "That is one of the reasons why I asked you to meet me here today."

He pointed over to a bench off to the side of the Lincoln Memorial probably about 100 feet away from them.

"Do you see the senator over there?"

A man and a woman were sitting on the bench that he was pointing toward. The man was a very well-known senator. Caroline did not know the woman.

"Yes, I see him," Caroline responded.

"The woman talking to that senator is one of our people. Up until today, the senator has not been sure which way to vote on the bailouts. But right now we are informing him that if he does not vote our way that we are going to expose the affair that he has been having with one of his female staff members. This particular senator definitely would not like that to happen, because he is known as a 'family values' politician and his wife knows absolutely nothing about the affair that has been going on. If this affair came out, it would ruin both his personal life and his political career. Of course it was our organization that arranged for that particular female staff member to be hired by his office, and that particular female staff member just happens to be one of our deep cover assets, but the senator doesn't need to know about any of that."

Caroline turned slightly and looked the man in the black overcoat directly in the eyes. "You always have all of your bases covered, don't you?"

The man in the black overcoat suddenly became very serious. "Caroline, we have people everywhere. Don't ever forget that. Enjoy your afternoon."

With that, the man in the black overcoat rose and walked off.

Caroline just sat there for a moment and gazed off into the distance.

What in the world had she gotten herself into?

Was she in so deep now that she would never be able to get herself out?

Chapter 15

Tom's head was spinning.

Over the past couple of weeks, the training that Tom had been through had been unlike anything that he had ever experienced before in his entire life. Boot camp had been more physical, and the initial training that he had endured while with the CIA had certainly been no piece of cake, but nothing that he had ever gone through in the past was anything like the intense training that the agency was putting him through.

The trainees had not been given a single day off so far, and they had been going at it for 12 to 14 hours a day. Most of the training appeared to be intended to challenge them mentally and emotionally. Never before had Tom had so much information downloaded into his head in such a short period of time. To Tom, it had kind of felt like cramming for final exams all day, every day for several weeks in a row without a break.

There had been lots of lectures, and in between many of the lectures there had been films which Tom might have called propaganda films if he didn't know better. Immediately following many of the lectures and films there had been tests in which the trainees were forced to stand at attention as they answered verbal questions that were hurled at them by their instructors. If a single trainee got a single question wrong, that would add 15 minutes to the test, so there was an incredible amount of pressure on all the trainees to get their answers right.

After a couple of weeks of this, many of the trainees appeared to be near their breaking points. You could see it in their eyes. Tom knew that he was not too far away from his own breaking point.

But Tom did have to admit that many of the training sessions had indeed been extremely interesting. Tom had been amazed as he and the other trainees had been taught about the vast reach of this secret government intelligence agency. It apparently had undercover operatives embedded in almost every other federal agency, and the agency had offices of their own in almost every major U.S. city. But there were times when the agency did not want to act alone, and thanks to secret legislation that had once been passed by Congress, the agency was able to call on the help of other federal agencies whenever they needed it.

Tom and the other trainees had also learned that everyone in the agency was given multiple "cover identities" that were to be used whenever they interacted with members of other federal agencies. So members of the agency could appear to be working for the CIA, the FBI, the DHS or the NSA even though they actually weren't.

Tom was amazed at what could now be done in the name of "national security" in the post-9/11 world, and this highly secretive intelligence agency that Tom had been recruited into seemed to like to use "national security" to justify just about everything that they did.

Tom and the other trainees were certainly learning a lot about the agency, but they had become extremely weary of sitting in a classroom. They were all mentally exhausted and ready for a change. All of them had been hoping that the endless classroom sessions would soon come to an end.

So they had been elated when they had learned that the next phase of their training would involve more physical activity. Unfortunately, it turned out to be far more grueling than most of them had anticipated.

The previous night, Tom and five other trainees had been driven out to what appeared to be an abandoned military camp very deep in the woods of West Virginia. Tom didn't know that this place even existed.

They had been roused from sleep at about 4 AM and the six trainees were instructed to dress in full tactical gear and they were led on a 5 mile run through the woods at an absolutely exhausting pace.

Once they returned, they were ordered to march into a waist deep trench and stay there. The trench was then filled all the way to the top with freezing cold water. As they stood there at attention in the freezing cold water, several of the instructors carried over a huge log which spanned the entire length of the trench. It was placed in front of the trainees, and they were instructed to hold the log up with their arms and to not let it touch the water under any circumstances. So far the trainees had been holding up the log for about 10 minutes, and this was proving to be an extremely physically taxing drill.

As Tom struggled to help keep the log up, he took his mind off of the pain by reflecting on the events of the past few days. At one point when he had been having a conversation with Koz, one of the trainers had reprimanded him very loudly when he overheard Tom calling him "Jon". Things were very formal in the agency. They had been instructed that they were to address each other by their last names. So Tom would be referred to as "agent McDowell" or as just "McDowell".

Tom thought that this was a bit strange.

What made it even stranger was the fact that some of their trainers were already referring to Jon as "Koz" instead of "agent Kozlowski" or just "Kozlowski". Tom figured that perhaps they just didn't like saying such a long name.

Tom was sure that he would eventually become accustomed to the culture of this new agency, but for now it sure did seem foreign to him.

Tom just hoped that the training would be over soon. The head trainer, agent Jessup, seemed to almost enjoy being cruel to the trainees for no particular reason.

As the trainees greatly struggled to keep the massive log above the freezing cold water that they were standing in, Jessup came walking up to them. He looked them over and decided that this would be a great time to lead the trainees in some group chants.

"I am an American," Jessup screamed.

"I am an American," the trainees repeated back loudly.

"I will not fail my country."

"I will not fail my country."

"I will not whine."

"I will not whine."

"I will not complain."

"I will not complain."

"I will always complete my mission."

"I will always complete my mission."

"I will never question the agency."

"I will never question the agency."

"Failure is death."

"Failure is death."

This went on for about another 20 minutes, and when the trainees were finally allowed to drop the log and leave the trench filled with freezing cold water they were almost too exhausted to speak.

As Tom lay in his bunk later that night, he wondered why he had ever signed up for this. The only thing that gave him comfort was the realization that things would almost certainly get better once this version of "boot camp" was over.

And Tom did have to admit that he was very impressed with the seriousness of this unnamed agency. It was a huge change from what he had experienced over at the CIA. These boys did not mess around. They approached their jobs with a high degree of professionalism, and from what Tom had seen during the classroom sessions they were doing some incredible things all over the globe.

At his core, Tom really did want to serve his country, and Tom believed that this organization would give him the very best chance to do that. If he had to put up with a few weeks of absolute hell in order to be on the cutting edge of the intelligence community, then he was certainly willing to do that.

But Tom was hoping that there wouldn't be too many more days like this one. He was definitely approaching his breaking point. As he closed his eyes and dosed off to sleep, Tom found himself desperately wishing that this period of training would come to an end very quickly.

Chapter 16

One of the things that Melissa truly enjoyed about her job was the chance to sit down and do one-on-one interviews with some of the most famous names in the entire financial world.

Today, Melissa was sitting down with Conrad Crowley, one of the wealthiest and most respected investors in the entire country.

The interview was being conducted at one of the anchor desks at the American News Network headquarters in New York City. Crowley spent so much time down on Wall Street that it was usually never an inconvenience for him to stop by the ANN studios. Plus, he seemed to want to be on television as often as possible and he was the kind of man that absolutely loved to hear himself talk. So interviews with Crowley were usually not that hard to get.

"Mr. Crowley," Melissa began, "the American people have been watching the financial world implode over the past couple of weeks. The Dow has dropped by more than 4000 points during that time and many people are concerned that we could be looking at an economic crisis even worse than what we saw back in 2008 and 2009. Could you take a few moments and explain to the American people exactly what has happened and what we can expect next?"

Crowley seemed even more pompous than usual today. "Melissa, what we are witnessing is a complete and total financial meltdown caused by a derivatives panic. Most Americans still don't know what derivatives are, but you don't have to fully grasp all of their complexities in order to understand what their function in our financial system is. When you purchase a derivative, most of the time you are not actually investing in anything real like you are when you buy a stock or a bond. Derivatives are essentially side bets, and in recent years people up on Wall Street have been making side bets on just about anything that you can imagine. Usually the bets involve things like future interest rate levels or the future performance of a particular financial instrument. When the bet is over, there is usually a winner and a loser. Unfortunately, what has happened now is that hundreds of billions of dollars of these bets have gone bad, and 'the house' has gone bust. Several of the 'too big to fail' banks had made trillions of dollars of very questionable bets, and now an avalanche of those bets have gone against them and that is why they need to be bailed out. Because they cannot pay off their bets, there has been a complete and total collapse of the derivatives marketplace. Nobody is buying derivatives at this point, and nobody is selling derivatives at this point. And unless there is a massive bailout, hundreds of billions of dollars of derivatives contracts are going to go unpaid, and it would be hard to overstate how much of a disaster that would be for the financial community."

Melissa smiled slightly because she was getting some good stuff out of Crowley.

"But isn't this having far-reaching effects far beyond the derivatives market Mr. Crowley?"

"Of course Melissa. At this point the credit markets are paralyzed by fear, and banks are being extremely tight with loans right now. That means that many companies are not making their payrolls. It also means that many companies don't have the money to order new inventory or to ship goods that have already been ordered. Essentially, economic activity is grinding to a halt all over the country.

Our economy is based on credit, and right now there is a tremendous credit crunch going on. If this continues, this is going to have a dramatic effect on the daily lives of average Americans."

"And we are already starting to see this in the unemployment numbers." Melissa pulled up a piece of paper that had been sitting on the anchor desk. "Just today we learned that initial claims for unemployment benefits jumped up over the 600,000 mark this week. We haven't seen anything like this since the last major economic crisis, and many analysts believe that things are going to get far worse before they get better."

Conrad Crowley had a smug look on his face. "Oh yes, unemployment is going to get far worse. We will definitely see it go up into the double digits and I wouldn't be surprised to see it hit 20 percent eventually."

"But can the American people really handle another major economic crisis so soon?" Melissa wanted to end this segment with a bang. "Already we are hearing reports of scattered protests and civil unrest around the country. The other day a group of workers that had been laid off in Baltimore went back to the warehouse where they had been working and set it on fire. If things continue to get even worse for the economy, can we expect to see a lot more of this?"

"I honestly don't know Melissa. Obviously this is a concern. But right now the top priority should be getting Wall Street and the big banks back on track. If we can get money flowing through them again, eventually it will trickle down to the workers on Main Street. What is good for the financial community is good for all of us, so that is what the Federal Reserve and Congress should be focusing on right now. Fixing the financial system and helping Wall Street and the big banks get back on their feet is job one."

"Thank you Mr. Crowley. That was Conrad Crowley, the managing director of the Crowley Fund. We will be right back after these messages."

The lights in the studio dimmed and the network went to a commercial. Melissa thought that the interview had gone very well.

"Thank you Mr. Crowley," Melissa said as she shook his hand. "That was a great interview. It was a pleasure to see you again."

Melissa started to walk away from the anchor desk, but Conrad Crowley wasn't ready for the conversation to end just yet.

"Hold on a second Melissa," Conrad said as he followed Melissa off the set. "You're doing a great job here at ANN and a lot of people in the financial community have taken notice. I was hoping that we might have dinner tonight to discuss your career even further."

Melissa inwardly cringed. She had heard all the rumors about how Conrad Crowley was with a different woman every other week and that he was never interested in a permanent relationship.

Plus, he was about thirty years older than she was, and she was definitely not interested in getting romantically involved with a man of his age.

"Sorry Mr. Crowley," Melissa responded cheerfully, "I've got plans with my boyfriend tonight."

Of course that was not true at all because Melissa did not have a boyfriend, but she figured that her lie was good enough to get her out of the situation.

"No problem at all Melissa, thank you again for the interview."

And with that, Conrad Crowley headed for the studio exit.

Her producer, Abby Berkowitz, came over and grabbed her arm.

"What was that all about Melissa?"

"Oh it was nothing. He was just thanking me for the interview."

"It looked like a little bit more than that," Abby insisted.

"I just think that he was trying to be friendly," Melissa countered. "Was there something that you wanted to talk with me about?"

"Yes, Melissa, actually there is. We need you to go down to Washington D.C. for a while - our White House correspondent is going to be out on maternity leave for the next couple of months."

Melissa felt herself getting very excited. "You want me to cover the White House?"

"No, actually Jen Lu is going to be covering the White House. We just need you to go down there and help out with whatever else needs to be covered. As our economic problems get even worse, there is going to be a lot of pressure on Congress and on the Federal Reserve to do something. We want you to be there to report on that. And there are also rumors that a number of prominent organizations are working together to plan some huge economic protests in Washington. There will definitely be plenty to keep you busy, and I think that you will really enjoy your time down there. Plus, this kind of experience can only help you with your goal of eventually getting to the anchor desk someday."

Melissa smiled. She definitely did not mind hearing her name and the phrase "anchor desk" mentioned in the same sentence.

"Sure, I'll do whatever you guys need me to do."

The truth was that Melissa was definitely ready for a change. Her life in New York City had gotten more than just a little bit stale.

But what Melissa didn't know was that her upcoming time in Washington D.C. would dramatically change the course of her life forever.

Chapter 17

It has been estimated that there are approximately 3,000,000 "preppers" in the United States, but Russ "Diesel" Jacoby considered the vast majority of them to be total amateurs when it came to really preparing for what was coming. When things truly hit the fan, Russ knew that most of them simply would not have what it takes to survive.

To survive, one must be able to adapt, and Russ had definitely adapted to life in western Montana. With his slightly graying goatee, dark sunglasses, ball cap, flannel shirt and jeans, he definitely blended into the population of the area. He'd even done his best to try to adjust his accent so that he sounded a bit more like the people of the region.

But Russ was definitely not originally from western Montana. In fact, Russ had spent much of his life out in California. He had worked for one of the largest Internet companies in the entire world and he had made a ton of money doing it. But eventually his thirst for knowledge and his endless research had led him to the conclusion that the United States was heading for utter disaster. The politicians had turned their backs on the U.S. Constitution and on common sense, but the American people kept sending most of the same clowns back to D.C. over and over again. Russ could not understand why they would do that. Most Americans also seemed oblivious to the fact that they were living in the greatest debt bubble in the history of the world, and Russ was deeply concerned about the chaos that would be unleashed when it finally burst. He was convinced that at some point the economy would collapse and that there would be great social unrest in the major cities.

Russ desperately hoped that his family would be ready for what was coming.

He wanted to do everything that he possibly could to protect his family. He just hoped that the preparations that he had been feverishly working on would be enough.

When Russ left the big Internet firm that he had been working for down in California, he and his wife packed up their family and headed out to western Montana. When they first got out to Montana, they really didn't know what they were doing, but they were eager learners and they had plenty of money to burn, and now they had set up the kind of home that most preppers could only fantasize about.

They were totally off the grid. There were absolutely no wires or communications of any kind coming in to or out of their home. After a couple of years of living up in western Montana, they had purchased a very isolated 50 acre parcel of land way up in the mountains. A thin gravel road was the only way in and the only way out. If you were not purposely looking for their home, there was very little chance that you would ever find it.

On their property, just about everything was powered by either solar panels or wind turbines. Russ also had purchased several very large gas-powered generators, but he doubted that he would ever need those. Water was provided by a gravity fed water system, and if that ever went down they could get plenty of fresh water from several creeks that ran throughout the property. There were four very large structures scattered throughout his property where huge amounts of storable food had been stashed, and Russ also had several large caches of food buried underground. He was confident that his family could survive very easily for at least five years on the food that they had stored. But if they had to produce their own food they could do that as well. They planted an absolutely enormous garden every year, and every member of his family was proficient with a rifle in case they needed to rely on hunting for meat at some point.

Russ and his family wanted to be as independent of the system as they possibly could. His wife had compiled a checklist of more than 350 things that they would need in the event of a major emergency where they were cut off from society for an extended period of time, and they had stockpiled large supplies of all 350 items. If the rest of the world went to hell in a handbasket, Russ and his family had enough power, food, water and supplies to survive on their own for a very, very long time.

And Russ was super paranoid when it came to security. His 50 acre property was absolutely riddled with motion detectors, security cameras and other surveillance equipment. If the time came to defend his home and his family, Russ had accumulated quite an arsenal of weapons, and every member of the family knew how to handle a firearm.

Russ was insistent that no strangers ever be allowed on to the property. Over the past few years he had allowed a few close friends and a few close family members on to the property from time to time, and he had regretted even doing that.

Basically, what Russ wanted was a place that was cut off from the rest of the world and that would be completely and totally independent if everything else around them totally fell apart. Russ hoped that he had achieved that.

That is one reason why Russ did not have any Internet connection at home at all. He knew that if they had any connection to the grid, and especially if they were connected to the Internet, that they could be found very easily by the authorities.

Not that Russ was doing anything wrong. He just didn't want "Big Brother" keeping tabs on them.

But that didn't mean that Russ didn't use the Internet. Whenever Russ or another family member wanted to connect to the Internet, they took a tablet or a laptop out to one of the towns and cities scattered all over western Montana. His family had mapped out literally dozens of locations where free Wi-Fi networks were available.

And of course Russ had instructed every member of his family to never expose themselves to the public while using the Internet. That meant that most of the time they ended up sitting in their vehicles while they used the Internet. At the first sign of trouble they were instructed to drive away as fast as they could.

Not that anyone could easily tell what they were doing on the Internet anyway. Russ had installed incredibly advanced encryption security software on all of the family computers.

Today, Russ was returning home from a trip to a small Montana town where he had been working on his blogs. His home may have been cut off from the Internet, but Russ was actually a very big part of it. Over the past few years, Russ had become a very accomplished blogger. He had set up dozens of blogs on various free blogging websites, and millions of people read his articles each month. Of course he never used his real name or real address on the Internet. He always used a pseudonym. On the Internet he was known as "Diesel", and "Diesel" had become so popular that the feds were starting to take notice.

A few of the blogs that Russ had started had been taken down, and that is one reason why he had so many of them. He figured that it was better to have a multitude of targets rather than to just put all of his eggs in one basket. If he had just one site, it would have been fairly easy for the authorities to shut him down. But if his articles were popping up all over the place that would make it much more difficult to silence him.

Not that Russ ever wrote about anything illegal or was doing anything wrong. In fact, he tried very hard to avoid any conflict with the law or with the authorities. But Russ also knew that they were always watching.

Russ wrote about all of the things that were wrong with America. He wrote about how the economy was falling apart, he wrote about how the freedoms and liberties of the American people were being stripped away, and he wrote about all of the corruption in the U.S. political system. Of course Russ realized that all of this would definitely touch some nerves in Washington D.C. at some point.

But Russ felt like he was doing his part by exposing what was going on and trying to offer people some solutions. He was encouraging people to get prepared because he knew that if the country remained on the path that it was currently on that things were not going to be getting any better. Russ was convinced that great economic, political and social upheaval was coming.

Some people referred to Russ as a "doom and gloomer", but Russ didn't see it that way. Russ believed that there was hope in understanding what was happening to the United States and that there was hope in getting prepared for the storms that were coming. He was convinced that those that were not prepared and that got blindsided by what was coming would be the ones that would truly give in to despair when everything fell apart.

Today, Russ had posted a story about the great financial collapse that was in the process of unfolding on his blogs. This certainly looked like it could be the great economic crisis that so many people had written about for so many years. In his article, Russ had urged people to get as prepared as they could because the years ahead were likely going to be very, very hard.

Russ hoped that he was truly helping some people out there. He knew that his blogs reached a very large audience, and he was very thankful for that. And he was very thankful that he could still make a difference in the world even though in a lot of ways he was very much cut off from it.

As Russ drove along the single lane gravel road leading up to his home, he looked off to his right and he marveled at the natural beauty that surrounded him. He never got tired of looking at the mountains. Today the sun was out and the leaves on some of the trees were starting to change color. Off in the distance, Russ could see that there was already snow on quite a few of the mountain peaks. Russ couldn't understand why everyone didn't want to live out in this kind of natural beauty.

The gravel road ahead of him continued on for about another half a mile where it eventually ended up at an abandoned mining camp. But Russ brought his SUV to a stop and pulled out a remote control and pointed it at the steep hillside along his left hand side. A small section of the hillside slid away, revealing the entrance to his property. Russ maneuvered his SUV through the entrance, and then once he was through he pressed another button which moved the small section of the hillside back into place. It was the only way in and the only way out.

Ahead of him, a single lane dirt road eventually led to an absolutely beautiful two-story Victorian-style white house that his family called home. Their property was laid out in a deep valley that was completely surrounded by mountains.

To Russ, it was absolutely perfect.

Russ hoped to live the rest of his life here. He hoped that he would never have to move, but that meant always keeping one step ahead of the authorities.

Chapter 18

"I still don't understand why we had to come all the way out to Oregon for this Tom."

Tom looked over at his best friend, Jon "Koz" Kozlowski, and smiled. "I don't know either Koz. I'm just glad that training is over."

And that was definitely the truth. Tom had never been through such intense training in his entire life, and he had been greatly relieved when agent Jessup had told the trainees that their training was finished and that they would immediately be accompanying him on an assignment out in Oregon.

So here they were, a couple of hours west of Bend, Oregon in the middle of nowhere.

And it was no exaggeration to say that they were in the middle of nowhere. They were camped out in front of the home of a rogue pastor that the agency was apparently very concerned about, but there wasn't anything else around for miles.

This pastor had probably come out here to get away from society, but now society had come looking for him.

According to the briefing that they had been given, this pastor was a big mover and shaker in the "liberty movement" and he was extremely critical of the federal government no matter which political party was in power. He was pro-Second Amendment, radically anti-abortion and a very outspoken critic of the United Nations. All of this did not sit too well with the folks back in Washington.

And apparently he had at least one gun inside his home which had just recently been made illegal by a new United Nations treaty. At least that was the official justification that they had been given for this upcoming raid.

Several dozen agents from the Bureau of Alcohol, Tobacco, Firearms and Explosives were camped out on this pastor's driveway, and the personnel that Tom's agency had sent along were officially there in just an "advisory capacity". But of course that was not true at all.

The BATFE agents had been told that agent Jessup and the other agents with him were bigwigs with the Department of Homeland Security. Jessup would be running this show, and the BATFE agents were never supposed to know who he was really working for.

If anyone asked, Jessup and all of the other agents with him had been given identification which matched the cover story.

This was Tom's first assignment with the unnamed secret government intelligence agency that he had been recruited into, and he was definitely more than a little bit perplexed about what was going on.

Why did they have to go after a pastor that was guilty of a simple firearms violation with such overwhelming force? Tom decided that this was something that he would discuss with agent Jessup once all of this was over. It was important for Tom to know the "whys" behind what they were doing. He was not someone that just followed orders blindly when they didn't make any sense.

As Tom reflected on these things, agent Jessup came walking over toward the area where he and the other trainees were waiting. Jessup seemed even more agitated than usual. "I want all of you to come over and observe me while I brief the BATFE agents on how to handle the media. This is a very important part of our job, because even if we handle the operation successfully, if we mishandle the media the entire goal of the operation can be lost."

Tom and the other trainees followed Jessup over and watched as he briefed the BATFE agents on what they were to tell the media about what was happening here. Apparently all of the big media outlets had been called and were on their way. Jessup began to become very animated when he got to some particular points that he thought were critical to communicate to the media correctly.

"I want you to emphasize that the reason that we are raiding the home of Pastor Johnson is because he has 'illegal firearms'. That is a phrase that you need to use over and over again. We want to make sure that the media catches on to that phrase and mentions it repeatedly during their newscasts. Another thing that is extremely important is to never refer to the target of the raid as Pastor Johnson's home or Pastor Johnson's house. From here on out, only refer to it as Pastor Johnson's compound. If the media talks about how BATFE agents raided a 'house' or a 'home' that sounds kind of cruel, but if they report that we raided a 'compound' then we sound like heroes. We are out here today not just to enforce the law, but to also set an example for the rest of the nation. You see, Pastor Johnson has a very large following on the Internet. He is a widely known and highly respected figure in the 'liberty movement', and so when we take him down that is going to send a message out to literally millions of people. So we have got to get this right."

As he was finishing saying these things, several media trucks came rolling up. Agent Jessup quickly went over to tell them where to set up.

———————

Inside the home, Pastor Johnson, his wife Linda and his two daughters Blake and Brenna were very frightened. They were peeking out at all of the law enforcement vehicles that were parked in their driveway and they were wondering what was going on.

Linda looked particularly worried. "Do you know why they are here Marcus?"

"I have no idea Linda," Pastor Johnson replied. "But this definitely looks like trouble. Let's just do our best to cooperate with the authorities and I'm sure that everything will be fine."

———————

As Jessup waited for the rest of the media to show up, Tom, Jon and another brand new agent named Miguel Martinez started to get restless.

"I don't like this at all," Miguel said. "This whole operation doesn't feel right."

"Look, I know that this is a whole lot different from what we are all accustomed to, but from everything that I have seen this agency gets solid results," Koz said in reply. "The agency probably knows a whole lot more about Pastor Johnson than they are telling us. He must be a real threat to national security for them to go to all of this trouble."

"Yeah, let's just wait and see what happens," Tom added. "And remember, part of the reason why we are probably here is to see how we will respond to this kind of situation. We are being watched too."

After about another half hour, enough members of the media had arrived to finally satisfy agent Jessup. He signaled the head of the BATFE unit that it was time to proceed.

From behind one of the vehicles, a BATFE agent pulled out a megaphone and started barking directions toward the house.

"Pastor Johnson, this is the Bureau of Alcohol, Tobacco, Firearms and Explosives. We have been informed that you have illegal firearms in your compound. You and everyone else in the compound are to exit unarmed through the front door with your hands clasped on top of your heads. If this is not done within two minutes we are going to storm the compound."

Within 30 seconds the front door opened and Pastor Johnson emerged with his hands clasped on top of his head. His wife quickly followed, as did his two daughters. All of them also had their hands clasped on top of their heads.

As soon as they reached the front lawn, heavily armed BATFE agents stormed out from both sides of the house and tackled them from behind.

As they were being thrown to the ground and handcuffed, agent Jessup got on his radio.

"The two girls are resisting. I want both of them tasered."

One of the agents that was handcuffing the older girl objected to this. "Is that really necessary? We already have both of them in custody. There is no need for a taser."

Jessup was getting very angry at this point. "Those girls are resisting! I want both of them tasered now! That is a direct order!"

This time nobody objected. Instead, the agents that had just tackled the two girls got out their tasers and deployed them.

The screams of the two young girls echoed very loudly throughout the surrounding valley. Suddenly that was the only thing that anyone could hear, and the media captured all of it on video.

Lying face down on the ground in handcuffs, Pastor Johnson was absolutely furious.

"You didn't have to do that!"

Suddenly agent Jessup's voice came over the radio again. "Pastor Johnson is resisting. Use a taser on him until he shuts up."

The agent that had handcuffed Pastor Johnson deployed his taser, and this caused Pastor Johnson to start convulsing violently.

Jessup looked over at the media to make sure that they were getting good shots of all of this.

The youngest daughter, Brenna, started crying and screaming even more when she saw what was happening to her father.

Jessup couldn't resist. "Tase her again," he hollered into his radio.

One of the agents tased the little girl again and her body convulsed violently and then stopped moving altogether.

Jessup was afraid that he may have just ruined the entire operation. "What happened?"

A shocked voice responded over the radio. "She's dead. We need some medical assistance over here."

After that, all sorts of chaos broke loose. A medical team rushed over to the young girl, but it was too late.

Jessup ran over and instructed the media to turn off their cameras. He told them that they could report on the raid and show what had happened to Pastor Johnson, but that what had just happened to the two little girls was considered to be off limits for "national security" reasons.

Tom, Koz and Miguel were all completely stunned. None of them had expected anything like this.

Miguel turned to Tom and asked the question that all of them were thinking.

"What in the world just happened?"

Chapter 19

On the plane ride home from Oregon, Tom, Koz and Miguel all learned that they had been permanently assigned to an agency office right in the heart of Washington D.C. under the direct supervision of agent Jessup. When they reported for work the following day, they discovered that the office was located on the sixth floor of a very average looking Washington D.C. office building. On the floor below them was a lobbying firm, and on the floor above them was a law firm.

And of course nobody in the outside world really knew what was actually going on up on the sixth floor of that office building. As far as the management of the building was concerned, a consulting firm named Osiris Consulting had purchased that space, and all of the "workers" coming and going from the sixth floor always seemed extremely professional.

And in many ways, the sixth floor still resembled typical office space. Every agent had an office and there were big conference rooms where large meetings would be held from time to time.

But what the owners of the building did not know was that a tremendous amount of construction work had taken place up on the sixth floor. On nights and weekends, workers had transformed the sixth floor into a mini-fortress. If anyone asked, they were told that "minor renovations" were being done. But the truth was that the sixth floor had been fortified so that it could withstand just about any kind of attack.

And incredibly advanced surveillance equipment had been installed that constantly watched and monitored every inch of the sixth floor 24 hours a day. If anyone even sneezed wrong, someone was watching.

Of course if trouble did come knocking, there was an arsenal up on the sixth floor that was large enough to fight off a small army.

Tom had learned about all of this during training, so when he got up to the sixth floor none of those things was really a surprise to him.

But what did surprise him was a symbol that seemed to be everywhere on the sixth floor. It was a symbol of an all-seeing eye floating above an unfinished pyramid. Tom knew that it was the same symbol that was used on the back of the dollar bill, but Tom didn't understand why it had to be used so extensively by the agency.

The symbol was even used on the dress uniforms that were issued by the agency. The symbol of an all-seeing eye floating above an unfinished pyramid was the only insignia found on those dress uniforms. It was always placed on the left side of the chest about where the heart would be. There was a strict ban on ever wearing those dress uniforms out in public, but agents were encouraged to wear them at the office and at internal agency functions.

All the way back from Oregon, Tom struggled to come to a decision about what he should do. He figured that he should have a talk with agent Jessup about what went down out in Oregon, because he definitely did not want to be working for an organization that would abuse people like that. But Tom was a bit hesitant to say anything, because it had become exceedingly apparent to Tom during training that this was an organization that was not fond of being questioned. So Tom was trying to figure out how to approach this matter diplomatically. Tom had worked with some challenging personalities in the past, and he was sure that he could find a way to handle agent Jessup.

Tom had intended to go talk to Jessup that morning, but when he had gotten in to the office he had discovered that he was absolutely swamped with work. Finally, just before lunch, he had gotten enough done that he felt okay about going over and having a talk with agent Jessup about what had happened out in Oregon.

As Tom approached Jessup's office, he could hear that another new agent, Miguel Martinez, was already in there. The door to the office was slightly open, and he stopped in the hallway to listen to the conversation.

"I just didn't see the need to tase two young girls that weren't even resisting," Miguel was saying. "To me, that simply crossed the line."

"But they were resisting," Jessup insisted. "Are you questioning my judgment?"

"I suppose that I am sir. To me it almost seemed like you planned for all of that to happen and for the media to be there to capture it all on film."

By now the expression on Jessup's face had turned very serious. "Martinez, there are a lot of things that you simply don't understand. Sometimes there is a need to send a very public message. Sometimes there is a need to intimidate your enemies. Sometimes fear is a very powerful weapon. The threats to national security that we deal with on a daily basis in this agency are very formidable. Are you going to have the stomach to follow orders and to do what needs to be done when the time comes?"

"I just want to do what is right sir, and what happened out there at that house in Oregon didn't seem right at all."

Jessup thought about that for a moment, and then he seemed to come to a decision. "I understand what you are saying Martinez. I think that we need to send you over to one of our offices in Virginia and have you talk to someone higher up than me about this. Hold on for just a second."

Jessup picked up his phone and called agent Varnau who was located in an office on the other side of the sixth floor.

"Agent Varnau, are you busy? I need you to take agent Martinez over to our office in Alexandria. Along the way, why don't you stop and get him some lunch? I hear that he likes seafood."

Tom's heart suddenly got icy cold. Instincts sharpened by many years in the CIA told him that agent Martinez was never going to get that seafood lunch. Tom turned and quickly started walking back toward his own office.

As he rounded a corner, he almost ran head on into agent Varnau who was walking briskly the other direction.

"Excuse me agent Varnau," Tom muttered as he stepped out of the way.

"Excuse me agent McDowell," Varnau spat out as he gave Tom a dirty look.

Tom quickly returned to his office, shut the door and tried to breathe.

Tom's mind was racing as he attempted to figure out what to do next. He knew that he only had a few moments to make a decision.

He ran both hands through his hair as he wrestled with what to do.

"Come on Tom, think!"

Suddenly, he realized what he had to do. Tom grabbed his car keys and bolted toward the emergency stairs.

Chapter 20

Melissa had decided that her time down in Washington D.C. would be a great opportunity to start cycling again. Back up in New York City there just weren't that many places to ride, but one of the wonderful things about the D.C. area was that there were lots of great bike trails. Melissa had borrowed a bicycle that one of her coworkers wasn't using, and over the past few days she had taken in a lot of the D.C. area on that bike.

Melissa found that riding was a great way to clear her head, and she loved to go out and get some exercise in the middle of the day whenever she could. Earlier that morning, Melissa had interviewed a senator that was thinking of running for president, and that night she was supposed to be covering an event up on Capitol Hill, but she had an extended break in the early afternoon and she figured that it would be an excellent opportunity to take the bike out for a spin.

The Mount Vernon Trail was not too far from the apartment that she had rented, and she had heard that the views along the Mount Vernon Trail are absolutely spectacular, so she decided that she should give it a try.

———————

Tom hoped that by scrambling down the back stairs that he could beat agent Varnau and agent Martinez to the parking garage. Once he got down there he saw that he had been successful.

Tom had just enough time to slip a GPS tracking device under the rear bumper of agent Varnau's black SUV and slip into his own vehicle before agent Varnau and agent Martinez entered the parking garage. Agent Varnau appeared to be telling agent Martinez a joke, but Tom knew that if his suspicions were correct that agent Martinez would not be laughing for long.

Tom watched as agent Varnau maneuvered his SUV out of the parking garage, but Tom was not under any pressure to keep the vehicle in sight because Tom could just track the GPS device that he had planted on agent Varnau's SUV on his phone.

After a few moments, Tom started his own vehicle and also headed out of the parking garage. He knew that he had to keep a very safe distance away from agent Varnau's SUV. Both agent Varnau and agent Martinez were highly trained professionals, and if Tom got too close there was a good chance that one of them would figure out that they were being followed.

Initially, agent Varnau did head toward Alexandria, but then he drove on past Alexandria on the George Washington Parkway down toward Mount Vernon. At that point Tom realized that his worst fears were almost certainly true. Agent Varnau did intend to kill agent Martinez.

Tom had already decided that he was going to do his best to keep that from happening. He just couldn't stand by and allow agent Martinez to be murdered in cold blood. And Tom realized that he was going to have to leave the agency. He just hoped that they wouldn't decide to come after him as well. What kind of government agency would kill its own agents for expressing dissent? None of this made any sense to Tom. He wasn't sure exactly what he planned to do when he caught up with agent Varnau and agent Martinez, but Tom knew that he had a couple of surprises in the back of his vehicle just in case something special was needed.

Agent Varnau continued down the George Washington Parkway until he got to Fort Hunt Park. During this time of the year, Fort Hunt Park was usually pretty much deserted in the middle part of the day during the work week. Looking down at his GPS device, it appeared to Tom that agent Varnau had pulled up to the very edge of the water. Tom got a sinking feeling in his stomach because that probably was not good news for agent Martinez.

Tom had been following agent Varnau's SUV just out of sight, and now he knew that he needed to pull over and get ready to confront agent Varnau. Tom spotted a small parking area and found a place to park his vehicle. He popped open his trunk and pulled out a pair of binoculars and an old Russian Dragunov sniper rifle. It was a weapon that Tom had picked up during an assignment in the Middle East with the CIA, and Tom knew that if something happened the weapon and the ammunition could never be traced back to him.

Tom closed his trunk and ran through the woods in the direction of the water. At the edge of the tree line he dropped to his stomach and pulled out his binoculars. He could see that agent Varnau had backed his SUV right up to the edge of the water, and he could see agent Varnau dragging the apparently dead body of agent Martinez out of the passenger side of the vehicle.

Tom felt his stomach twist in horror. He was too late. Apparently agent Varnau had killed agent Martinez along the way as they were driving. Agent Martinez never got that seafood lunch, and now he was actually going to be fed to the fish. Agent Varnau dragged the body of agent Martinez to the very edge of the water and then pushed him face first into the Potomac River.

As the body of agent Martinez fell into the river, along the bike path a beautiful blonde woman rapidly approached the scene on her bicycle. To Tom, she seemed totally stunned by what she was witnessing as she rode past the spot where agent Varnau was standing. She started pedaling faster in an attempt to pick up speed. She obviously wanted to get away from what she had just seen as quickly as possible.

Unfortunately, agent Varnau had already spotted her, and he was not the type to leave any loose ends hanging. Agent Varnau pulled out his gun and fired two shots. The first shot went directly through Melissa's right thigh, and this caused her to fall very awkwardly off of her bicycle. Her body slammed into the ground along the left hand side of the bike path and her bicycle rolled off into the woods along the right hand side of the bike path.

Melissa was actually very fortunate that she had fallen off of her bike, because the second shot from agent Varnau would have gone directly into her chest. Instead, it safely whizzed by overhead.

Tom knew that if he didn't intervene immediately that the beautiful blonde woman was as good as dead. As agent Varnau began walking over toward the fallen woman, Tom aimed and fired. The bullet grazed agent Varnau's left shoulder and agent Varnau instantly dropped to the ground and belly crawled over behind a nearby maintenance shed.

Tom could not tell how badly agent Varnau had been hurt, but Tom could hear panic in his voice. Agent Varnau was not even attempting to be quiet. He was cussing like a sailor as he fumbled around to find the phone in his pocket. When he finally found his phone, he dialed the emergency contact number that all agents out in the field were given.

"This is agent Varnau. I am at Fort Hunt Park along the water and I am under fire. I am requesting immediate backup. Repeat, I am under fire and I am requesting immediate backup."

Tom assessed the situation. He knew that he didn't have long before that backup would arrive. But he also knew that agent Varnau was not likely to just sit there behind that maintenance shed waiting for an unknown enemy of unknown strength to close in on him and finish him off. Agent Varnau would probably try to make a break back to his SUV either to make a getaway or to grab a more substantial weapon.

So Tom kept a close eye on the space between the back of the building that agent Varnau was hiding behind and his SUV. If agent Varnau did make a break for his vehicle, Tom thought that he had a pretty good chance of hitting them with his Dragunov sniper rifle.

After a few moments, agent Varnau did make a break for it. He sprinted across the space between the maintenance shed and his vehicle and Tom fired his rifle. The bullet hit agent Varnau on his left hand side just below his rib cage. Agent Varnau collapsed in a heap behind the trunk of the SUV.

From this angle Tom no longer had a shot at agent Varnau, and Tom watched carefully to see if he should move in closer.

After a few moments, Tom could see the trunk of the SUV open. It appeared that agent Varnau was trying to find a more appropriate weapon to fight back with.

What Tom didn't know was that agent Varnau had a German H&K PSG1 sniper rifle back there. Agent Varnau was wounded, but now he definitely had the upper hand in weaponry.

Tom knew that he didn't have much longer before agent Varnau's backup arrived, so he decided to break cover. He started sprinting toward the SUV, but he only got a few steps before a rifle fired from one of the back windows of the SUV. The bullet hit Tom's left forearm like an angry hornet and ripped out a sizable chunk of flesh.

Tom immediately rolled behind a nearby garbage can. That had really hurt. Tom checked his left arm. Fortunately no bones had been hit, so he knew that he was probably going to be okay.

But Tom also knew that there was no way that he was going to get anywhere near that SUV before agent Varnau's backup arrived. Tom understood that he could make a break for his own vehicle and still get out of there safely, but he also realized that if he left now the woman that had been gunned off of her bicycle would never live to see another day.

From where he was hiding behind the garbage can, Tom knew that he would not be able to get a good shot at agent

Varnau inside that SUV. Tom looked out to see if there was any other decent cover between him and agent Varnau.

There wasn't any.

Tom sat there incredibly frustrated for a couple of moments and then a plan came to him in a flash. Tom peeked out just enough from behind the garbage can so that he could get a good view of the gas tank on the SUV. Tom aimed his Dragunov sniper rifle and fired five rounds. Gasoline started leaking from the gas tank and pooling underneath the SUV.

Tom waited for a few moments for a sufficient amount of gasoline to pour out, and then he pulled out his phone. The GPS tracking device that he had put on agent Varnau's SUV also doubled as a small explosive device. By itself, it wouldn't do that much damage, but with some help from some leaking gasoline it would be more than sufficient.

Tom pushed a button on his phone and a moment later the SUV erupted in a ball of fire.

With agent Varnau out of the way, Tom just needed to find the woman that had been shot and get her out of there before agent Varnau's backup arrived.

———————

From a hillside in the distance, a very old man with a long, white beard had watched the battle between Tom and agent Varnau unfold with great interest. The old man was dressed almost entirely in white and he was holding a weathered old book in his hands.

"It looks like they are going to need a lot of help", he whispered, but there did not appear to be anyone standing nearby.

Chapter 21

Tom realized that he didn't have any time to lose. He rushed down to the bike path and began frantically searching for the blonde woman that had fallen off of her bicycle when agent Varnau shot her.

Tom spotted the place where she fell, but she wasn't there. Tom scanned the surrounding woods and off in the distance he saw the blonde woman struggling as she attempted to crawl through the woods on her stomach.

Tom sprinted over to her.

"Are you okay?"

"Please don't kill me," Melissa pleaded. "I didn't see anything. You have my word that I won't tell the police about what happened here."

"Kill you? Don't you know that I just saved your life?"

Melissa seemed very confused. "Look, I don't want any trouble. I am sure that someone heard all of those gunshots and has already called 911. The authorities will be here any moment. So just let me go. I won't tell them anything."

Tom realized that he was going to have to take control of the situation very quickly. "Unfortunately, some very dangerous men are going to get here before the police ever arrive. If they find us here, they are going to kill me first and then they are going to kill you second. Is that what you want?"

Melissa was not convinced. "I'll take my chances here in the woods. Just please, leave me alone."

Tom knew that if he left this woman lying here that there was a very good chance that she was going to end up dead. So Tom picked her up, hoisted her over his right shoulder and started jogging back toward his vehicle.

Obviously, this did not please Melissa at all. She started pounding on his back and yelling at him.

"Hey! What in the world are you doing? Let me down!"

Tom knew that he couldn't do that, and he didn't have time to argue. "Look, you're just going to have to trust me. You can thank me later for saving your life."

Melissa quit pounding on Tom but she was still furious. "Saving my life? I feel like I'm being kidnapped!"

Tom was getting annoyed, but he didn't have time to stop. "We'll talk about your feelings later. Right now we have just got to concentrate on getting both of us out of here in one piece."

Within a few moments they reached Tom's vehicle. Tom plopped Melissa down in the back seat and then got in and started up the SUV as rapidly as he could.

Melissa would have tried to run away, but she couldn't put any weight on her right leg. But that didn't stop her from verbally objecting. "Where are you taking me? You should know that I am a reporter. If you kidnap me you are going to be in huge trouble!"

Tom ignored her and raced toward the entrance of the park. He was relieved when they got out of there without running into anyone. Tom hopped on to the George Washington Parkway and started heading back toward Alexandria. Within a few moments of getting back on to the George Washington Parkway, Tom spotted a convoy of black SUVs similar to the one that agent Varnau had been driving heading the other direction at very high speed.

"Do you see those SUVs? The men in those vehicles are trained killers. If I had not carried you out of that park you would have fallen into their hands, and I doubt that you would have lived through that experience. The agency that they work for does not like any loose ends."

Melissa was kind of half sitting up in the backseat now, and she was obviously in a tremendous amount of pain. "Are you talking about a government agency? Our government agencies don't go around shooting people for no reason."

Tom knew that he was going to have an extremely difficult time trying to explain all of this. "Trust me, there are a lot of things that you don't know about how our government works."

"Oh really?" Melissa was in no mood to be patronized. "Do you think that I just fell off the turnip truck? My name is Melissa Remling and I'm actually one of the top reporters at American News Network. I think that I know a little bit about how our government works."

Tom suddenly had a sinking feeling in the pit of his stomach. "Melissa, right now we've got to get you to a hospital. But I want you to promise me something. Please do not put any of this on the air. If you go on television and tell America what just happened, you will put my life in great danger, and you will put your own life in great danger."

Melissa rolled her eyes. "I just got shot in the leg and you don't want me to tell anyone about it? Are you insane? I'm just supposed to pretend that it never happened?"

Tom wasn't sure how to handle this. "Please, if you will just give me 48 hours I promise that I will explain everything. I know the name of the man that shot you, and I know the name of the dead man that he was dumping into the Potomac River. The dead man was a friend of mine."

Melissa admitted to herself that she really did want to know exactly why all of this happened, and if she did take this to her producer it certainly would help if she had some names to go along with the story.

"Okay hotshot, you have got 48 hours. After that I'm running with the story. Do we have a deal?"

"We've got a deal."

They drove on in silence for a couple of minutes. Eventually Tom pulled up in front of an emergency room entrance.

Tom looked back at Melissa. "Wait here for a moment."

Tom turned off the engine, got out of the vehicle and ran inside. After a few moments he returned pushing a wheelchair. Tom opened one of the rear doors and helped Melissa out of the car and into the wheelchair.

Melissa was being more cooperative now. She looked up at Tom with a curious look. "So what is your name?"

"My name?"

"Yeah, you never told me your name."

"My name is Tom, and like I said you will be hearing from me within the next couple of days. I promise to tell you the full story of everything that happened today."

Tom rolled Melissa to the admissions desk. "For now Melissa, I'm going to have to leave you here with these good people."

Melissa could see that Tom's left forearm was bleeding. "You have a bullet wound too. Don't you need treatment?"

"Don't worry Melissa. I have a long history of patching myself up, and I need to get back to work before people start asking too many questions."

"But you will keep your promise, right?"

"Yes, I will keep my promise. You will hear from me within 48 hours."

"48 hours Tom - the clock is ticking."

Tom winked at her. "I know - I'll see you soon."

And with that, Tom was gone.

Chapter 22

After Tom dropped Melissa off at the emergency room, he hightailed it over to his place. As quickly as he could, he dressed the flesh wound on his left arm and changed out of his bloody clothes before heading back to the office.

Tom was hoping that his absence would not be noticed and that nobody would ask him where he had been.

When Tom finally did get back to the agency, he was relieved to see that most of the sixth floor seemed to be empty.

He walked swiftly in the direction of his office, and when he was almost there, agent Wolfe called out to him from behind.

Agent Wolfe was a slightly pudgy woman in her early forties, and she always wore far too much makeup. She was known as "the ice queen", and even though she didn't get as much attention from men these days as she did when she was younger, she still had an extremely high opinion of herself.

She also would have made a great bureaucrat because she was an extreme control freak and she always seemed to love to get into other people's business.

"Hey McDowell," she called out, "where in the world have you been? Everybody has been looking for you."

Tom turned to face her. "I'm sorry about that, agent Wolfe. I got a tip about a potential Islamic terror cell out in Landover and I wanted to go check it out for myself. It turns out that it was a dead end."

Wolfe didn't seem satisfied with that answer. Her eyes narrowed as she stepped closer. "Why didn't you take anyone with you and why didn't you tell anyone where you were going? Jessup just about flipped his lid when we couldn't find you."

Tom tried to keep cool. "Why? What's going on?"

"Someone was shooting at a couple of our agents at a park down in Virginia. Apparently agent Martinez is dead and we are still trying to figure out what happened to agent Varnau. Jessup gathered just about all of the available agents on the floor and headed down to Fort Hunt Park to investigate earlier this afternoon."

Tom desperately hoped that agent Wolfe couldn't pick up anything in his eyes or in his expression. "That's terrible - do they need any additional help?"

"No, they've got agents crawling all over that park looking for clues right now. I don't think they need any more manpower at this point."

Wolfe suddenly seemed puzzled. "By the way, that is a great looking blue shirt. Were you wearing that earlier today?"

Tom suddenly felt his throat get tighter. "No, I was wearing a white shirt earlier, but while I was out in Landover I spilled something on it so I put on an extra shirt that I had in my car."

That seemed to satisfy Wolfe. "Well, the next time that you go running off it is important to follow protocol. Either you take another agent with you, or you make sure that you tell someone where you are going. We don't allow agents to go 'John Wayne' in this agency. We work as a team."

"I understand. I won't do it again," Tom said in reply.

Seemingly satisfied, Wolfe headed back up the hall toward her office.

Tom's mind was spinning. When he reached his own office, he closed the door behind him and tried to act as normal as possible.

What was he going to do? Certainly he could not continue working for an agency that killed its own agents. That went against everything that Tom believed in.

But if Tom left the agency immediately, that would be extremely suspicious. Someone might suspect that he had something to do with agent Varnau's death. He knew that he was going do have to stay at the agency at least for now.

Plus, Tom thought he might be able to do some good from inside the agency. Tom was absolutely disgusted that an ultra-secret government intelligence agency seemed to be able to do anything that it wanted with no accountability whatsoever. If Tom could discover their deepest secrets and expose them to the public, that might bring the agency down for good.

Tom started sorting some papers on his desk. He wanted to look "normal" for the cameras.

But inside, Tom was definitely not feeling "normal". He now knew that he was working among cold-blooded killers, and he was absolutely determined to bring them to justice.

Chapter 23

Melissa opened her eyes and realized that she was still in the hospital. It was now the second day since the shooting. Most of Melissa's injuries had been minor, but her right leg was still in a tremendous amount of pain. The doctors had removed the bullet from her right thigh, and they told her that no lasting damage had been done. She would be hobbling around on crutches for a while, but eventually she would make a full recovery. In fact, they were telling her that she should be able to go home tomorrow.

Melissa looked over to the left and noticed that on the side table next to her bed someone had left a beautiful bouquet of flowers with a card next to it.

Melissa opened up the card and started reading. It was from Tom...

Melissa:

I am so sorry for what happened to you. As I promised, I am going to tell you everything. We need to meet some place where there are not going to be a lot of listening ears around. There is a cozy little restaurant that I know called Jack's Bistro that is located over on E Street just a few blocks east of the White House. Could you meet me there on Saturday around noon? The doctors told me that you will be hobbling around for a while because of your leg, so it would probably be easiest if you just took a cab over there. Please do not share what happened to you with your bosses at ANN until we get a chance to talk. If the details of this incident are released to the public, I will be in great danger and so will you. Like I said, I promise that I will explain everything to you when we meet. I hope that you feel better soon – it looks like the nurses are taking great care of you.

Tom

Melissa put the card back down and closed her eyes. She wasn't quite sure what to make of this "Tom" character. She didn't even know if that was his real name.

Melissa had pretty much concluded that Tom didn't intend to kill her. If he had wanted to kill her, he could have easily done that out at Fort Hunt Park the other day when he had the chance. The fact that he had carried her out of that park and had brought her to the emergency room said a lot.

But could she really trust him? After all, he was some sort of a secret agent. Could anyone like that ever really be trusted?

Throughout her life, Melissa had learned some very hard lessons about trust. This was especially true when it came to men.

But Melissa desperately wanted to know the identity of the man who tried to kill her and the name of the organization that he was working for.

Melissa was not one to forgive and forget. Melissa couldn't take revenge on the man who shot her, because thanks to Tom he was already dead. But what Melissa could do was punish the organization that he had been working for.

Melissa didn't get to where she was today by letting people walk all over her. When she was lying on the ground in Fort Hunt Park, for the first time in her life Melissa thought that she was actually going to die. She didn't like that feeling, and she never wanted to be put back into that position ever again.

Melissa reopened her eyes, and there was a fire in them that had not been there earlier.

Melissa was determined to make someone pay, and she was a woman that normally got what she wanted.

Chapter 24

Melissa didn't like the look of this at all.

It was about 11:45 on Saturday morning and she was on her way to meet Tom. She wanted to get there before he did so that she could check out the place where they were supposed to meet. She didn't particularly trust Tom, and she didn't want to be walking into a set up. At the first sign of trouble, she planned to bolt.

But she wasn't going anywhere at the moment. She was still quite a few blocks from her destination and traffic was at a complete standstill.

Whenever Melissa took a cab she made it a point to introduce herself to the driver, and this time was no exception. His name was Wilbur and he had been extremely helpful.

Melissa's leg was heavily wrapped and she was on crutches, and so getting into the cab had not been particularly easy. Fortunately, Wilbur had been driving cabs for many years and had a lot of experience helping people with injuries get in and out of cabs.

But now they were sitting in the heart of Washington D.C. stuck in traffic. In fact, they had not moved at all in about 15 minutes. All around them, people were streaming toward the White House, and a lot of them were carrying signs.

Melissa was becoming quite frustrated. "Hey Wilbur, is there some kind of huge protest going on today that I didn't hear about?"

Wilbur glanced back at Melissa from the front of the cab. "There sure is. It is being called 'A Million Unemployed Americans March on Washington' or something like that. Actually, they are expecting far more than a million people to show up. There are a whole lot of angry people out there right now. Nobody can find work. In fact, a couple of my own friends just lost their jobs."

Melissa took a moment to read some of the signs that the protesters were carrying...

"Tax The Rich And Then Tax Them Again"

"It's Time For Some Robin Hood Economics"

"Tax The Greedy To Help The Needy"

"Don't Touch Our Entitlements!"

"Jobs For America Now"

"We Are The 99 Percent"

About a half a block away from the cab, a short, pudgy middle-aged man in glasses had gotten up on to the roof of a parked car. He was delivering a very passionate speech to a large group of protesters that had gathered around him. Melissa rolled down her window to see if she could catch what he was saying.

The short, pudgy middle-aged man was extremely angry. "It's time for this country to move forward, and the only way that this country is going to move forward is if the working class has jobs! Today, more than a million of us are going to deliver a message to the pompous politicians that have put the needs of Wall Street above the needs of the American people. We are going to tell them loud and clear that if they don't take care of us then they are going to pay! We are sick and tired of watching Wall Street and the big corporations thrive while the rest of us are suffering. We will not beg for crumbs! America is not broke, and it is time for our politicians to spread the wealth. It is time to take from the rich and give to the poor. It is time to stand up and start demanding change. It is time to take America back from the plutocrats. For far too long the average hard working American has been completely ignored by our politicians. Well, if they will not listen to us willingly, then we will make them listen to us! The middle class needs a cash infusion, and everybody knows who has the cash. It is the same people who crashed our financial system back in 2008 and who have crashed it again. Only in America can one percent of the population have 50 percent of the wealth. If the wealthy can socialize their losses, then they can also socialize their profits! They have taken almost everything from us, and we are here today to take it back! We absolutely refuse to live in a society where the wealthy have everything and we have nothing. We have a fundamental right to a decent existence, and we are not going to take no for an answer. If we cannot achieve our goals through legislation, then we will achieve our goals through revolution! Economic equality now!"

That started a chant of "economic equality now" which reverberated up and down the block. Melissa's cab was still not moving, and now the street was packed with even more protesters than it had been previously.

Melissa noticed that the mood of the protesters was starting to get uglier and uglier. Melissa turned around and she could see that about a block behind the cab someone had set an empty bus on fire.

Melissa was really starting to get worried. "Is there any other way to get out of here Wilbur?"

Wilbur was becoming very alarmed too. "You could try walking, but you won't be moving around very quickly through these crowds on those crutches."

Suddenly, some of the protesters started to rock the cab that Melissa was riding in back and forth. "I'm not against you!" Melissa yelled at them at the top of her lungs.

That didn't seem to help anything. Angry protesters on both sides of the cab continued to rock it back and forth and Melissa was afraid that they might actually tip the cab over.

Finally, the rocking stopped and Melissa was relieved for a moment. But then one of the protesters took a hammer and started smashing the front window of the cab. Another protester was able to open the front passenger door, and he got in and began physically dragging Wilbur out of the cab. Once he had been dragged out of the cab, a group of protesters descended on him and started beating him with their fists.

Melissa knew that she had to get out of there immediately. She didn't even bother with her crutches. She jumped out of the cab and started hobbling down the street as best she could.

Unfortunately, a group of very unpleasant looking thugs had already spotted her. Before she could do anything about it, eight or nine large men closed in around Melissa.

One of the men put his arm around her. "Well, aren't you a pretty little thing? I'll bet that we can have a lot of fun with you."

Melissa was getting desperate. "Look, I'm a reporter with American News Network and I don't want any trouble. I'm just down here on business."

The thug did not remove his arm. "Oh, we like reporters, don't we?"

Several of the men in the group nodded in approval.

"In fact, let us show you what we do to reporters."

Melissa suddenly found that she was being lifted up off the ground. She was half-carried, half-dragged over to a nearby alley. Melissa remembered that she had some pepper spray in her purse that she was still carrying over her shoulder, and with her right hand she started fumbling around in her purse to see if she could find it.

Unfortunately, one of the thugs saw what was happening and grabbed the purse away from Melissa.

"What are you looking for sweetie?"

He dug around in her purse until he found what he was looking for.

"This is pepper spray. Were you going to use this on us? That isn't very nice. It looks like we are going to have to teach you a lesson."

Melissa let out a half-muffled scream for help, but her plea for assistance was drowned out by the roaring of the crowd. Her heart sank as she realized that she was entirely at the mercy of her attackers.

Melissa decided that she wasn't going to give up without a fight. She started swinging her arms at her attackers, but there were just way too many of them. One of them landed a really solid punch on her right cheekbone, and she felt like she might lose consciousness.

The thugs tossed her body on the ground and they started to pull on her shirt. Melissa kept screaming, but it wasn't doing any good.

Suddenly, the attack stopped. Melissa was almost unconscious at that point, and she had been trying to shield her face with her arms, so she couldn't tell for sure what was happening, but it almost seemed as if her attackers were suddenly frozen in time.

A very elderly man with a very long white beard that was dressed almost entirely in white walked over to her. He picked up her purse from where it had fallen and slung it over his right shoulder. Then he went over and picked up Melissa with both arms and carried her out of the alley and away from the group of thugs.

"Don't worry," he whispered. "You are safe now."

Melissa was still groggy from the battering that she had just taken from the group of thugs, and she was basically in a state of shock. The elderly man carried her over to the other side of the street and let her rest for a few moments.

"You are going to be okay," the elderly man said reassuringly. "Take a few moments to gather yourself. When you are ready, I will escort you over to your meeting with Tom. It is extremely important that you attend that meeting."

Melissa slowly began to recover her senses. She looked up at the elderly man. "How were you able to rescue me from those thugs?"

The elderly man smiled. "Haven't you heard that the good guys are always more powerful than the bad guys? Come, we don't want you to be late for your meeting."

The elderly man put his arm around her shoulders and helped Melissa hobble down the street. The sidewalk was absolutely packed with protesters, but most of the protesters in their path stepped to the side when they saw that Melissa was injured.

"Listen," Melissa said as she turned to look at the old man, "I want to thank you for helping me. What is your name?"

"I'm just a friend that cares," he responded as he removed his arm from around her shoulders. "Look, we are at your destination. Tom is waiting for you inside."

Melissa looked up and saw the sign for Jack's Bistro. She was surprised that they had gotten there so quickly.

Melissa glanced back to where the elderly man had just been standing because she wanted to thank him once again, but he wasn't there. Melissa scanned the area in all directions, but there was no sign of him.

Melissa looked up at the sign for Jack's Bistro again and sighed. The elderly man had told her that this meeting with Tom was extremely important, so she figured that she might as well go inside.

She just hoped that this day would not get any worse.

Chapter 25

When Melissa entered Jack's Bistro, Tom spotted her right away. He could tell that she had been hurt and he rushed over to her.

"Are you okay Melissa? You've got a huge bruise on your right cheek - did something happen?"

Melissa sighed. She really wasn't too eager to tell anyone about what had just happened. "Yeah, some thugs were hassling me out in the street and it was about to get pretty bad until an elderly man stepped in and helped me."

Tom was puzzled. "An elderly man rescued you from a group of thugs?"

"Yeah, I'm still not exactly sure how it happened, but I'm very thankful. After he rescued me, he escorted me over here and told me that it was very important that I meet with you. Then he kind of disappeared."

Tom looked at Melissa with concern. He wasn't sure if she was all there mentally. "Well, you look really kind of beat up. I would definitely understand if you decided that you were not up for our meeting today. If you would like, I would be glad to escort you back to your home safely. No group of thugs will bother you with me around, I can promise you that."

Melissa had seen Tom in action and she knew what he was capable of. She was certain that he could get her back to her apartment safe and sound. But she had already decided that she wanted to go ahead with the meeting. What the old man had just told her was still echoing in her mind.

"Actually Tom, I would really like to stay here and talk, but could we get a table away from the street? I don't want to be anywhere near those protesters right now."

"Sure thing Melissa - just wait here." Tom went over and had a discussion with a couple of restaurant employees, and after a few moments he returned.

"They are clearing a table for us in the back and they are going to seat us right away."

Within a few moments a waitress was seating them at a quiet table all the way in the back of the restaurant. Tom was being very attentive, and he made sure that Melissa was able to get seated comfortably.

Tom could see that Melissa's right leg was still giving her a lot of trouble. "How is the leg doing?"

"It's getting better," Melissa responded. "But it still really hurts and the worst thing is having to take extra time and effort to do everything."

Tom nodded in empathy. "Well, I definitely appreciate you coming all the way out here to talk with me. I honestly had no idea that these protests were going to be so big today. I knew that a lot of people were angry that the unemployment rate was going up so rapidly, but I figured these protests would only draw a few thousand people at most. Boy, was I wrong. In fact, I heard on the radio coming over here that there may be as many as two million people flooding the National Mall this afternoon."

"It's okay Tom." Melissa was starting to think that Tom was actually concerned about her. "There is no way that you could have known what was going to happen. It seems like the whole world has been going crazy lately. I have never seen people so angry. On the way over here, I actually saw a bus that had been set on fire by some protesters. I shudder to think what we might see if the economy gets even worse."

Tom was hoping to lighten the mood a bit. "Let's just hope that the protesters don't get really angry and knock any of our national monuments over."

Melissa smiled slightly. "Well, if you can believe it, the Washington Monument is actually starting to fall over. It's a pretty big deal. They say that it's going to take millions of dollars to fix it."

This surprised Tom. "Are you serious? The Washington Monument is actually in danger of falling down?"

Melissa was feeling a little bit more relaxed now. "Yes, I'm afraid that it is. My network did a big story on it a couple weeks ago. I'm surprised that you haven't heard about it."

Tom smirked. "Well, things have been a bit crazy for me lately."

"You don't say," Melissa snapped back sarcastically. "Speaking of that, are you finally going to tell me who you work for?"

Tom's expression got more serious. "I promised you that I would tell you the truth, and that is exactly what I plan to do. I used to work for the CIA, but recently I was recruited into an ultra-hush-hush government agency that is so secretive that it doesn't even have a name."

Melissa was immediately skeptical. "What do you mean it doesn't have a name?"

Tom's expression didn't change. "I mean what I said. The agency does not have a name. The philosophy behind that is that it is a lot harder to pin blame on an organization when you can't even identify it. Are you familiar with the term 'black budget'? Well, my agency is funded out of the black budget and they take secrecy incredibly seriously. The most frightening thing is that they don't appear to be accountable to anyone. I don't think that the President even knows what's going on."

Melissa was slightly less skeptical now. "How in the world can that be possible? The President is the Commander-in-Chief. How can there be a government agency that is outside of his control?"

"I don't know Melissa, but I'm telling you that this is very real. These people are extremely powerful and they will kill in the blink of an eye to keep their secrets safe. That is why I urged you to keep your shooting off of the news for now. I don't want them coming after you."

Being around Tom made Melissa feel protected, and that was a change for her. Normally she was an extremely independent woman, but she kind of liked the idea of having someone out there watching out for her.

"Okay Tom, let's say that I buy your story so far. Was the man who tried to kill me a part of this ultra-secret government agency?"

Tom nodded. "His name was Nicholas Varnau. He was one of the agents that trained me. Agent Varnau had just killed another agent named Miguel Martinez and was dumping his body into the Potomac when you came riding along on your bicycle. I was trying to save agent Martinez, but I was too late. When agent Varnau shot you, I knew that I had to do something. I just could not allow him to murder you as well. I think you know how the rest of the story played out. I hope that you believe me Melissa. If you don't believe that this agency is real, I can show you the building where my office is located. It is on the sixth floor of a very boring office building down on K Street. The agency hides in plain sight, but they don't play by the rules."

Melissa was starting to realize that she had stumbled on to something really big. "So you really did save my life?"

"Yes, I am afraid that I did. If I had not been there, you would almost certainly be fish food right about now."

That sent chills down Melissa's spine. "So what can we do about all of this? Is there any way that we can expose them?"

Tom lowered his voice just a bit. "I believe that there is, and it relates to the reason why agent Martinez was killed. He had voiced objections about an operation that we had just completed out in Oregon. I was there as well, and I had concerns too, but agent Martinez expressed his displeasure to the head of our office before I was able to."

Melissa wanted to hear more. "So what happened out in Oregon?"

Tom had already decided that he wasn't going to hold anything back from Melissa. He had never trusted reporters, but somehow he trusted her.

"It was a setup from the very beginning. There was an African-American pastor that the agency obviously had a big problem with. A recent UN treaty had made one of his guns illegal, and so the agency used that as a pretext to raid his house.

"Of course the gun violation was a very simple matter that could have been handled by the local police, but this was an opportunity that the agency did not want to pass up. My boss, Eric Jessup, and the rest of the members of my team posed as big shots from the Department of Homeland Security. But the raid was actually conducted by the BATFE. The BATFE agents were put under the authority of agent Jessup, and he made sure that they were the ones that made the arrests because we never want our faces to be on camera.

"All of the big media outlets were called in, and it soon became apparent that the entire purpose of the operation was to create a huge media spectacle. Agent Jessup told us that the main goal was to 'send a message' to those in the liberty movement that admired Pastor Johnson.

"When the time for the raid came, Pastor Johnson and his family didn't put up any resistance. They walked out of their home with their hands clasped on top of their heads as soon as they were requested to. But that was not good enough for agent Jessup. He insisted that the two young daughters were resisting, and he ordered BATFE agents to taser both of them. When Pastor Johnson objected to this, he was tasered too. Of course this greatly upset the youngest daughter and agent Jessup ordered that she be tasered again. Sadly, the little girl could not handle it and she died."

Melissa was absolutely shocked by all of this. "I remember hearing about this raid, but I had no idea that a little girl had died. Are you telling me that your agency ran the whole thing and that the goal was to intimidate a certain sub-section of the American people?"

"That is exactly what I am telling you Melissa. And you didn't hear about the death of Pastor Johnson's daughter because the media were banned from reporting on it."

Melissa was shaking her head. "So what can we do about this?"

Tom looked Melissa directly in the eyes. "I think that this is a story that we can put on the air without anyone knowing that we were involved. Back at the office I have a list of the BATFE agents that were involved in that raid. I'll bet at least one of them would be willing to talk about what he saw."

Melissa was definitely eager to run with the story, but she was also concerned about the potential danger. "If I get this story on my network, won't that kind of be like sticking a pole in a nest of hornets?"

Tom nodded. "Yes, it would make a lot of people angry, but personally I have already made the decision that I'm going to expose this agency and take them down any way that I can. If something goes wrong, I might end up dead, but I once took an oath to defend the Constitution of the United States and the people that I'm working for now are definitely an enemy of the Constitution."

Melissa was impressed with his conviction. "Well, if you can provide me with that list of BATFE agents I'll definitely have someone from my network contact them. If at least one of them is willing to talk then I might have something that I can run with."

Tom looked deep into Melissa's blue eyes. There was a determination in them that he had not seen previously. Tom honestly believed that he could trust her, and it had been a very, very long while since he had found someone that he could trust so quickly.

"That sounds like a plan," Tom said to her. "I'll drop the list by your office on Monday. Now, let's eat. I'm hungry."

Melissa smiled. "I thought your name was Tom."

Tom smiled back. "Yes, my first name is Tom. Hungry is just my middle name."

Melissa chuckled. They exchanged playful banter for a while and pretty soon Melissa was not even thinking about the horrible assault that had happened to her earlier. On the street outside, huge crowds of protesters were still shouting demands and chanting various slogans. But Melissa was feeling perfectly safe and secure in the back of that little restaurant with Tom. They ate and they drank and they ended up spending most of the afternoon there.

It was the best time that either Tom or Melissa had experienced in ages.

Chapter 26

By the end of their lunch meeting on Saturday afternoon, Tom and Melissa had decided that they better get together again and talk strategy on Sunday. After spending almost all day Sunday together, they also got together on Monday evening and Tuesday evening and Wednesday evening. With each passing day, Tom and Melissa spent less time talking about their plans to expose the agency and more time talking about other things. Tom knew that dating a reporter was like playing with fire, but Tom found that he just couldn't get enough of Melissa, and he kept coming up with new excuses to spend time with her.

On Monday evening, Tom had dropped off the list of BATFE agents that were involved in the raid on Pastor Johnson's home, and Melissa had been working on trying to contact them for the last couple of days. Eventually, she was able to find one BATFE agent that was willing to talk about what had happened, and his testimony was absolutely startling. Unfortunately, Melissa was not in a position to decide what stories get airtime on her network.

It was now Thursday evening, and Tom was coming to meet Melissa for dinner at a trendy new restaurant in the heart of old town Alexandria. Things had not gone well for Melissa at work that day, but she was definitely excited to get the opportunity to see Tom again.

Melissa had already been seated at a table when Tom finally arrived. He was about five minutes late, and rain was absolutely pouring outside. But once he got inside the restaurant and spotted Melissa, a huge smile lit up his face.

"I apologize for being late Melissa," Tom said. "I was held up at the agency a little later than I expected."

Melissa was not bothered by his tardiness. "It is no problem at all Tom. It is really good to see you again. Sadly, I'm afraid that I have some bad news."

Their conversation was interrupted by a waitress. She came over and handed them some menus and took their drink orders and then walked off again.

Tom wanted to know what the bad news was. "What's going on? Is everything okay?"

"I'm fine," Melissa responded, "but I am afraid that our story about the agency is dead."

"What do you mean?"

Melissa looked slightly defeated. "This morning I took everything that I found to my producer. I told her all about the agency and I showed her the incredible video testimony that I got from the BATFE agent. And you know what? She wasn't interested in the story at all. She laughed at the notion that there was some sort of secret government agency that nobody had ever heard of, and she said that the whole thing sounded like some sort of conspiracy theory. She told me that I should know better than to come to her with such stuff."

Tom gave her an understanding look. "To be honest, all of this is a little hard to believe. I probably wouldn't believe it if I wasn't actually living through this stuff."

Melissa nodded. "Well, I figured that perhaps another network would be willing to run with the story. So I sent a copy of everything that I had discovered to two reporters that I trust at two other major networks. Unfortunately, their bosses told them almost exactly the same thing that my producer told me. So it looks like we are going to have an incredibly difficult time getting this story on the air."

Tom was not pleased by this news at all. "So what do we do?"

Melissa thought about that for a moment. "Well, I do have one other option we could try. We could attempt to get this story out to the public through the alternative media."

Tom was confused. "What do you mean? Are you saying that we should get some bloggers to write about this?"

"I guess that is exactly what I am saying. In particular, there is one very prominent blogger that I leak stuff to sometimes. I don't even know his real name. Online, he is just known as 'Diesel'. But he has a tremendous following on the Internet. Millions of people end up seeing his articles, and this is exactly the kind of stuff that he loves to write about."

Tom was skeptical. "But nobody is going to take a blogger named 'Diesel' as seriously as they would a big mainstream news network. We won't have the kind of impact that we were hoping to have."

"Perhaps, but don't underestimate the power of the alternative media. There are some alternative news websites that actually regularly get more traffic than some of the big mainstream news websites. Unless something changes and we are able to get a mainstream network to run with this story, I think this is our best shot."

"Okay." Tom was ready to concede. "Let's give it a try. It's important to get this story out there however we can."

The waitress returned to their table. "Are y'all ready to order?"

"I think that I am," Tom responded. "Are you ready Melissa?"

Melissa nodded her head. "I'll have the roasted duck breast and a Caesar salad."

That sounded good to Tom, but he decided to go in a different direction. "I'll have the seared beef tenderloin and a garden salad."

The waitress gathered their menus. "That sounds great guys. I'll be back in a while with your dinners."

Tom turned back to Melissa and smiled. "I'm glad that you aren't a vegetarian. That makes picking a place to eat so much easier."

Melissa smiled back. "I may not be a vegetarian but I definitely love animals. When I was growing up I had a cat named Kitty that I greatly cherished. Her friendship got me through a lot of hard times."

Tom was amused. "So do you have any pets now?"

"No, as a reporter I am away from home way too much to be able to take care of a pet. Someday when I don't have to travel as much I definitely want to get another cat."

Tom couldn't believe how cute Melissa was tonight. "What kind of cat do you want to get?"

"That is a good question. I don't know much about the various breeds. I figure that I'll just get a regular cat that you can get down at the cat store."

Tom howled in laughter.

Melissa wasn't sure what was so funny. "Why are you laughing?"

"There is no such thing as a cat store," Tom said as he continued laughing. "I think you meant pet store."

Melissa scowled at Tom. "Well, what kind of pet would you like to get?"

Tom got a mischievous look in his eye. "I've always wanted to get a penguin."

"A penguin?"

"Yeah, can you imagine inviting some people over to your place and then a penguin comes walking out? I think that would be hilarious..."

Tom and Melissa continued to talk quietly, oblivious to the fact that on the other side of the restaurant a very beautiful woman in a black turtleneck and sunglasses was carefully watching their every move. Her observation of the couple was so subtle that not even Tom picked up on it. An hour and a half later when Tom and Melissa finally left the restaurant, the woman in the black turtleneck waited five minutes, made a few last notes in the black notebook that she was carrying, and then slipped out the back.

Chapter 27

As Melissa was sending off an email to "Diesel" on her work computer with everything that she had found out about the raid on Pastor Johnson's home out in Oregon, she felt a hand grab her shoulder from behind.

Melissa spun around in her chair and discovered that it was Donna Taylor, one of the reporters down in D.C. that she had quickly become friends with.

Donna had an alarmed look on her face. "What are you doing Melissa?"

Melissa felt a surge of panic shoot through her. "What do you mean?"

"The teleconference is about to start Melissa," Donna said urgently. "Why are you still working? Didn't you read the memo? Everyone is expected to participate. It's a good thing that I came to get you."

"Yes," Melissa said as she breathed a sigh of relief. "Thank you for grabbing me. I almost forgot about the teleconference."

And Melissa was very much telling the truth. She had definitely forgotten about the teleconference.

Melissa followed Donna over to the conference room and took a seat toward the back. The conference room was packed with ANN personnel, and there was an unusual amount of tension in the air. Melissa wondered what was happening.

After a few moments, the large screen at the front of the conference room flickered to life. Apparently this was going to be a four way teleconference.

In the upper left hand corner of the screen, Melissa could see U.S. Treasury Secretary Paul Katzmann. Prior to becoming Treasury Secretary, he had been CEO of a major Wall Street bank.

In the upper right hand corner of the screen, Melissa could see Federal Reserve Chairman Evan Schultz. He was flanked by several subordinates in the background. One of them, a very beautiful woman with dark hair, seemed vaguely familiar to Melissa.

In the lower left hand corner of the screen was a shot of the ANN conference room in New York. The head of the news division, George Herzog, was there and Melissa thought that was very unusual.

In the lower right hand corner of the screen was a shot of the ANN conference room in Washington. Melissa noticed that some of the more ambitious reporters in the office had taken very prominent seats toward the front of the room where they would be sure to be seen on camera.

After a few moments, George Herzog started the teleconference.

"Thank you all for gathering on such short notice. Many of you are already aware that there have been some extraordinary developments in the financial world today, and that is the reason for this meeting. The government is going to be taking some very unusual steps to head off a panic, and it is very important that everyone is on the same page. I'll let Paul fill you all in on the specifics..."

U.S. Treasury Secretary Paul Katzmann was a very powerful looking man. During his Wall Street days, he was not someone that you wanted to mess with. He was known for being absolutely ruthless with his competitors.

"Thank you George. By now I am sure that a lot of you have heard what has happened. The largest bank in the country, The Bank of the Atlantic, is insolvent. It turns out that the bank was very highly leveraged, and thanks to a series of very ill-advised derivatives trades, they have experienced hundreds of billions of dollars in losses. I cannot overstate how serious this all is. Basically, they are out of cash and they are absolutely drowning in debt. They shut down operations earlier today, and they are telling the public that it is just a temporary problem caused by technical difficulties. Fortunately, today is a Friday so it isn't causing too much of a stir. Obviously we are working on a plan to save The Bank of the Atlantic, but it is going to take a few days. So for now, we need the cooperation of the media so that we can keep the public calm."

A senior reporter sitting toward the front of the D.C. conference room named Max Craig spoke up. "So exactly what do you expect us to tell the American people for the next few days? Do you expect us to lie to them?"

This visibly annoyed Katzmann. "I expect you to help us avoid a full-blown financial panic. How do you think people would react if they were told that there was no money in the bank? This is a time when cooperation between the government and the media is even more important than usual. In a few minutes you will be receiving a letter from the President ordering you to follow our instructions for the sake of national security.

Sometimes telling the truth is not the best thing for the American people."

Back up in New York, George Herzog had a question. "So exactly what is the plan to save The Bank of the Atlantic?"

"I'll field that one," Federal Reserve Chairman Evan Schultz stated coldly. "The Bank of the Atlantic is way too important to our financial system to be allowed to fail. So we will be taking extraordinary measures to save the bank. The President plans to declare a 'bank holiday' on Monday. This will apply to all U.S. banks, because we do not want to draw attention to The Bank of the Atlantic. The public will be told that Chinese hackers have exposed some very serious security vulnerabilities and that U.S. banks will be implementing some very important security upgrades on that day. But the truth is that we will be busy pumping hundreds of billions of dollars into The Bank of the Atlantic and several other major banks that we have identified that are also on the verge of collapse."

"And exactly where will you get all this money?" Max Craig did not look very happy. "Are you just going to print it out of thin air? If so, won't that cause quite a bit of inflation?"

Evan Schultz didn't like the direction that these questions were going. "We are not here today to debate how the Federal Reserve system works. Look, if it was not for the Fed, the U.S. banking system would have totally collapsed back in 2008, and we are the only thing standing in the way of a total collapse this time. I am sure that a lot of you have accounts at The Bank of the Atlantic. Do you want to be able to continue to use those accounts? If we don't step in, there will be mass panic and chaos in the streets. Instead of criticizing us, you might want to show a little gratitude."

There was a pause for a moment as nobody said anything.

Finally, George Herzog broke the silence. "Evan, you know that you can count on us. We don't want to see a financial panic any more than you do."

Schultz seemed satisfied with that response. "I know that George. We just want to make sure that everyone is on the same page. This is a moment when cooperation between the government and the media is even more important than usual. There are just a few very powerful media companies that control the news. The average American watches dozens of hours of television each week, and when you all tell them that something is true they believe it. If we are going to navigate this crisis successfully, we are going to need your help."

Chapter 28

Russ stared at the email again. His anonymous contact at American News Network had leaked him some tremendous stories before, but nothing quite like this. He was wondering if it was too good to be true.

Russ certainly did not trust the mainstream media, and it had taken him quite a while to trust this contact. He did not even know her real name. She always just identified herself as "Candy Cane", and he had always just identified himself as "Diesel". Russ believed that he was dealing with a reporter, and he believed that the reporter that he was dealing with was female, but he had no way of telling for sure.

Russ was always skeptical when he heard from this anonymous contact, but the information that she had provided had always checked out to be true, so he had learned to trust her. He just hoped that he wasn't being set up for something really big in the future.

The package of information that "Candy Cane" had sent to Russ contained a video clip of a BATFE agent discussing what had really happened during the raid on Pastor Johnson's home out in Oregon. Russ was very familiar with the mainstream news reports about what had happened that day, but he had no idea that it was all a set up from the very start and that the purpose of the entire operation was to create a huge media spectacle.

Russ started the video clip again. He was absolutely amazed by what the BATFE agent was saying.

"It was crazy," the BATFE agent in the video muttered as he shook his head. "Normally when we go on a raid, a senior BATFE agent is running the show, but this time we were told that that a hotshot from the Department of Homeland Security was going to be running things. But when those guys from D.C. arrived they sure didn't seem like DHS agents to me. If you ask me, those guys were spooks. They could've been from the CIA - I don't really know. The guy in charge was a real mean son of a gun. He wouldn't let us go in and raid the place until everyone from the media was there. He obviously wanted to create a big deal out of the whole thing on television. Finally, when everything was ready, the family was ordered to come out of the house with their hands on top of their heads and they came out right away. We got them onto the ground and handcuffed them without any problems whatsoever, but then that head spook got on the radio and started insisting that they were resisting. He ordered our agents to use their tasers on those two little girls. There was no call for that. Then Pastor Johnson said something, and the head spook ordered us to tase him too. It was insane. Then one of the little girls yelled out for her daddy and started crying, and our agent was ordered to use his taser on her again. Of course there is only so much that a little girl like that can take. Her heart gave out and she died. But of course the media was directed to cut that out of their broadcasts. Talk about twisted. They were told that it was a matter of 'national security'. So the American people never got to hear about the death of that little girl, but they got to see lots of footage of us carrying 'illegal guns' out of Pastor Johnson's home. The whole operation made me sick to my stomach. This is not what I signed up for. What in the world is happening to this country?"

Russ knew that this had the potential to be an absolutely gigantic story, and he could also see why the mainstream news networks had not wanted to touch it. This was the kind of thing that was almost too hot to handle. In fact, it could end up getting somebody killed.

But Russ felt very strongly that somebody had to get this story out to the public. Russ knew all too well that all that it takes for evil to prevail is for good men to do nothing.

But was the story actually true? Was Candy Cane actually setting him up this time? Could the BATFE agent in the video actually be an actor and faking the whole thing?

In moments like these, Russ had learned to trust his gut. And his gut was telling him that this story was legit and that he should run with it.

Russ opened up a new blog post on his website and began to write. He knew that if the story was true that it was likely to open up a huge can of worms, but he also knew that he would not be able to live with himself if he didn't tell the American people the truth about the raid on Pastor Johnson's home and about how that little girl had died.

Chapter 29

"How in the world could anyone be so stupid?"

Jessup had gathered all of the agents in the Washington D.C. office into one of the conference rooms, and he was absolutely seething with anger. Tom had never seen him so furious.

"There is absolutely no way that this idiot blogger could have gotten all of this information on his own. He obviously had a tremendous amount of help. Our internal security team believes that at least some of that help came from someone inside our own agency.

"Needless to say, this type of a leak has the potential to do a tremendous amount of damage to this agency. Fortunately, only the wacko conspiracy theorists are going to take this guy seriously. But if a report like this got on the news it could mean major problems for all of us.

"So we are going into full lockdown mode. A very thorough investigation of this matter will be conducted by our internal security team, and every agent in all of our offices will be expected to cooperate with this investigation.

"Personally, I would love to get my hands on whoever leaked information to this blogger. Whoever it is has threatened my career, this agency, and the security of the United States. If there is a traitor in this organization, that person had better hope to never get locked in a room with me. I would carve that person's kidneys out with a spoon and that would just be for starters.

"And that blogger? We're going to find him. Some of our top agents out west are hunting him down as we speak. We are going to interrogate the living daylights out of that bozo and find out exactly what he knows and who he has been talking to."

Fortunately for Tom, he had a tremendous amount of experience masking his feelings. So his demeanor was calm, but inside his stomach was churning and his mind was racing. Would they eventually find out that Melissa was involved in all of this?

———

Edmund Puckhaber had been driving a cab in downtown Portland for nearly two decades now. It didn't pay much, but it sure beat sitting in an office all day. As Edmund drove through downtown Portland that evening, he reflected on what Portland used to look like. He had to admit to himself that it sure had gotten a lot weirder over the years.

Fortunately, there was usually a lot less violent crime in Portland than in many of the other major U.S. cities. Yeah, a gun had been pulled on him a few times over the years, but if you're going to drive a cab you had to expect that type of thing from time to time.

Edmund decided that it was time for a smoke break, so he pulled over next to a five story apartment building and shut off the cab. He leaned his head back and allowed himself to think about how much he missed his ex-wife. He never could figure out why they had gotten divorced.

Suddenly, a huge object wrapped in plastic fell from above and smashed the front of his cab. It hit with such violence that it set off several nearby car alarms. Edmund bolted out of his cab to see what it was. He was horrified to discover that it was a very bloody dead body wrapped in a shower curtain.

Killian looked down from the fifth story window through which he had just thrown the dead body of BATFE agent Steve Shepherd. This had been a particularly messy assignment, but he was satisfied with his work. He had been instructed to 'send a message' to other potential whistleblowers, and Killian thought that he had done a pretty good job. Killian went back over to the kitchen sink, finished cleaning his knife, and then slipped quietly out of the apartment.

There had been panic in Melissa's voice when she had called Tom a few minutes ago. Tom rushed over to her apartment, and when she opened the door he could see the distress in her eyes.

"What's going on Melissa? Are you okay?"

"They killed him!" Melissa tried to settle herself down. "That BATFE agent - Steve Shepard - they killed him. They stabbed him 33 times, cut out his tongue, wrapped him in a shower curtain and threw him out a fifth story window.

The story just came over the wire a little while ago. The police are calling it a burglary, but you and I both know that's a load of nonsense. They killed him because he talked. I had no idea that this was going to happen. I feel so bad for contacting him and getting him to talk."

Tom became very serious. "I should have known better. The people that I am working with now do not mess around. I should have figured that they would want to make that BATFE agent pay for blowing the whistle."

"So what should we do?" There was more than a trace of fear in Melissa's voice.

"Personally, this makes me more determined than ever to take this agency down. I don't want to live in fear for the rest of my life, and I can't bear the thought that a secret government agency can run around doing these kinds of things and constantly get away with it."

Tom's resolve settled Melissa down a bit. "I can definitely respect that Tom. But I don't know if I'm ready to risk my life to go after these people. I think that I may need to lay low for a while. Is that okay?"

Tom nodded his head. "I will leave you out of my vendetta against the agency. The last thing that I would ever want is for you to get hurt. But I would definitely like to continue seeing you. I have really enjoyed spending time with you."

"Of course," Melissa said in response as she embraced Tom. "I have really enjoyed spending time with you as well. Pretty soon my bosses are going to send me back to New York, but until that happens I would definitely like to see a lot more of you while I still can."

Out in the parking lot, a slender woman in a very expensive BMW sedan stared up at the windows of Melissa's apartment. The thought of Tom running around with that airhead reporter made her sick to her stomach. Pretty soon, she decided, she would have to do something about that.

Chapter 30

As a father, Russ Jacoby knew that he wasn't supposed to have any favorites among his children, but there was no doubt that he felt a special bond with his only son Hunter. Hunter was now 17 years old, and he was the kind of son that every father dreams of. Russ recognized a lot of his best qualities in Hunter, but he also saw that Hunter had the potential to be far more of a man than Russ had ever been.

Russ and Hunter had spent countless hours together. Russ and his wife had made the decision to homeschool their children from the very start, and Russ had been Hunter's primary educator over the years. From a very early age, Hunter had exhibited a tremendous thirst for knowledge and Russ truly enjoyed teaching him. But now their student/teacher relationship had evolved into something else. Russ was learning about as much from Hunter these days as Hunter was learning from him. Russ was so incredibly proud of Hunter and wanted him to have a much better life than he had experienced. Unfortunately, the world around them was becoming increasingly unstable and Russ was not sure if that was going to be possible.

Today, Russ and Hunter had gone over to the little town of Springfield, Montana to do some work on the Internet and pick up the mail. Russ had a P.O. Box in virtually every post office in western Montana, and it had been a while since he had picked up his mail from Springfield. As they drove through downtown Springfield toward the post office, Hunter was commenting on how deserted and barren everything looked.

Hunter got particularly animated when he pointed out a large storefront that had recently been boarded up. "Look over there Dad - it looks like Joe Ferguson's hardware store has gone out of business. And next door there is a 'Going Out Of Business' sign on Grandma Jean's Variety Store."

Russ was in quite a melancholy mood. He had been writing about the coming economic collapse for several years, but even he could hardly believe how quickly things were falling apart. Unfortunately, he also knew that this was just the beginning. "It's going to get a lot worse than this Hunter."

During his travels around western Montana, Russ had witnessed scenes like this in small town after small town. Because of the recent financial crash, banks and financial institutions were hardly lending money to anyone right now. Many businesses were suddenly not able to pay their employees, and many others had been forced to shut down entirely. As economic activity slowed down dramatically, even many of the businesses that were completely out of debt had been forced to close their doors because of a lack of customers. It seemed like hardly anyone had extra money to spend right now.

The fact that things were going downhill so rapidly made Russ very sad. He had known Joe Ferguson. He had shopped in his hardware store many times. Joe and his sons had taken great pride in their little store and had always been extremely helpful to Russ. They were the kind of people that were the backbone of America. But now their store was gone. Russ wondered if he would ever see them again.

Russ pulled up in front of the post office and parked along the street. "I'm probably going to have a few packages to pick up, so it's probably going to take me a few minutes to get out of the post office. While I am in there, could you go across the street to the grocery store and pick up the things that your mother asked us to get?"

"No problem Dad", Hunter responded.

Russ got out of the bright red Chevy truck and headed into the post office, and Hunter hopped out of the passenger side and headed toward the grocery store. Inside the post office, Russ opened up his P.O. Box and discovered that he had several yellow notices indicating that he had packages waiting for him. Unfortunately, there was a very long line at the window, but Russ didn't want to come back another time for these packages so he got in line and started to wait.

After he had been waiting in line for a couple of minutes, two men wearing expensive suits and sunglasses stormed into the post office and approached the counter. One lady that was waiting in line loudly objected, but the two men totally ignored her.

One of the men spoke directly to the postal worker behind the counter that was helping customers.

"We are with the Department of Homeland Security. We need to know if you can identify the man in this photograph. We have received a tip that he might be in Springfield today."

The postal worker examined the photo for a moment. "Yeah, I know him. In fact, he is standing in line right over there..."

He pointed to the place where Russ had been standing just a moment ago, but Russ was already gone. He had bolted out the door, gotten into his truck and had already fired up the engine.

When the agents realized what had happened, they bolted out of the post office as well and sprinted toward their own vehicle which was also parked right along the street.

Russ immediately went into crisis mode. A jolt of adrenaline went through him as his truck shot up the street and into the grocery store parking lot. Russ knew that what he was trying to do was risky, but there was no way that he was going to leave Hunter behind. He slammed on his brakes as he pulled up directly in front of the grocery store entrance and he punched his horn three times very loudly.

When Hunter heard the truck horn go off three times in a row, he immediately recognized that it was their pre-arranged emergency signal. Hunter left the grocery cart that he had been using in the middle of the aisle where he had been standing, and he sprinted for the grocery store exit. His father already had the passenger door open, and Hunter bounded up into the truck and slammed the door. A moment later the truck shot out of the grocery store parking lot like a bat out of hell.

"What are we dealing with?" Hunter could tell that his father was very alarmed.

"It's the feds."

Hunter responded to that by letting a few choice profanities fly.

"What did I tell you about using those words? I don't want you to have a foul mouth like I did at your age. I really need you to focus right now. Get out the GPS and take a look at where we are. We might have to come up with a creative way home."

As Russ was saying this, the black SUV belonging to the two well-dressed agents appeared in his rear view mirror. A siren on the roof of the SUV was wailing and it was obvious that the two men inside wanted Russ to pull over.

But Russ didn't have any intention of pulling over. His red truck skidded a bit as it pulled on to the main road through town, and once the skid ended Russ pushed the accelerator to the floor.

Fortunately, there was not much traffic on the road today. The poor economy and the high price of gasoline tended to keep a lot of people at home.

But there were still red lights to deal with, and Russ was rapidly approaching one of them.

"Hunter, I'm going to go through this red light. Are both directions clear?"

"No Dad, there are actually vehicles coming from both directions."

"Well I'm not going to stop. Hold on."

The red Chevy truck shot out into the intersection. It passed easily in front of a black sedan traveling from the east, but a green minivan traveling in the opposite direction had to slam on its brakes to avoid hitting Russ.

Hunter's eyes were as wide as saucers. "Dad, we are going to have to get out of town in order to outrun these guys."

"I know, I know - once we get south of town we will be alright."

The previous red light had slowed down the SUV that had been following them slightly, but once again it closed to within just a few car lengths of Russ and Hunter.

As they rounded the next bend toward the south end of town, Russ suddenly got a sinking feeling in his stomach. Up ahead there were two more black SUVs parked across both lanes of the road. The way into town was blocked, and the way out of town was blocked.

Russ let out a string of profanities that would have made a sailor blush. Hunter would have said something about that, but at that moment he was far too scared to make a sarcastic remark.

"What are we going to do Dad?"

"Hold on Hunter."

Russ slammed the wheel to the left and his bright red Chevy truck made a skidding U-turn into the other lane. Once the truck recovered from the skid, Russ gunned the accelerator and they headed back through town in the direction from which they had just come.

It took the SUV that had been chasing them a few extra moments to get turned around, and the two additional SUVs at the south end of town roared to life and joined the chase.

As Russ and Hunter sped north through town, Russ knew that the cushion between them and the vehicles that were chasing them was not going to last for long.

"Hunter, how far is it before we can get on to Old Highway 40?"

"Old Highway 40?" Hunter was not sure what his father had in mind. "Nobody uses Old Highway 40 anymore. Before it was closed down it was considered to be the most dangerous road in western Montana."

Russ knew exactly how dangerous Old Highway 40 was. It was a very treacherous road that ran along the side of a mountain, and in many places there was no guardrail at all to protect drivers against sudden drops that were in excess of 100 feet.

But Russ knew that his Chevy truck didn't have the firepower to outrun the SUVs that were chasing them on the main road. He just hoped that his driving skills would be enough to enable Russ and Hunter to escape once they got on to Old Highway 40.

As they approached the entrance to Old Highway 40, the three SUVs trailing them had closed the gap to almost nothing. From one of the SUVs, someone was using a megaphone to tell them to pull over, but of course Russ and Hunter had no intention of doing such a thing.

Russ decided that he wasn't going to give any indication that he was going to pull on to Old Highway 40 until the last possible moment. As he got right up to the entrance to the highway, he didn't slow down at all. At the last possible moment Russ made a very sharp right hand turn on to Old Highway 40, and this caused the truck to swerve so badly that for a moment Russ feared that it might actually tip over.

The three SUVs that had been trailing Russ shot past the entrance, but Russ knew that they would be back on his tail in short order.

To say that Old Highway 40 was windy would actually be a huge understatement. It had been constructed back at a time when highway safety was not the highest priority. Russ navigated his truck up Old Highway 40 as fast as he could, but he also knew that if he made one false move that he and Hunter could end up on the floor of the valley below.

Unfortunately for Russ and Hunter, those driving the SUVs that were chasing them were extremely skilled drivers as well. Hunter looked back and saw that they had closed to within about 50 feet.

One of the agents in the lead SUV fired a warning shot over their heads.

Hunter looked over at his father. "Should I get out the shotgun and start firing back?"

"No!" Russ was yelling now. "This isn't a movie Hunter - if we start firing on federal agents and then we get caught they are going to put us in prison and throw away the key. There is no way that I'm going to do that to your mother. We're going to try to outrun them, but there will be no shooting. Do you understand?"

Hunter nodded his head. "I understand."

The vehicles that were chasing them had closed the gap even further now. They were within about 30 feet and Russ was getting nervous.

Hunter checked the GPS unit. "Dad, this GPS unit says that the road ends in about a quarter of a mile."

"I know that it does Hunter. In fact, I am counting on it."

Russ knew that up ahead there was a short wooden bridge that had been washed out by a flood several years ago. It had never been rebuilt because nobody was actually supposed to be using Old Highway 40 anymore. Some crazy teens had built ramps on both ends and had been jumping motorcycles over the very narrow river that ran underneath the bridge. Russ was hoping that those ramps would be able to handle his truck.

As they approached the washed out bridge, Hunter glanced over at his father.

"Are you actually thinking of doing what I think you're thinking of doing?"

"Hold on Hunter. If something goes wrong be ready for the airbags to deploy."

Russ pushed the accelerator all the way to the floor and raced toward the ramp that was in front of them. The truck launched into the air and landed with a thud on the other side. The back tires of the truck just barely cleared the chasm and touched down on the ramp on the other side.

Hunter looked back and was amazed to see that the SUVs that were chasing them were also attempting to make the short jump over the narrow river. The first two SUVs made it, but the third SUV came up short. It disappeared out of sight as it tumbled toward the narrow river below.

"Two of them are still on our tail Dad."

Russ let out another long string of expletives.

The truck raced along in silence for a moment and then Russ had an idea.

"Hunter, pull up Camp Five Road on the GPS unit. I've got one more surprise up my sleeve."

Chapter 31

The two remaining black SUVs were still in hot pursuit of Russ and Hunter as they raced toward Camp Five Road.

Hunter was less than thrilled about the plan that his father had come up with.

"Do you remember what happened the last time you went down Camp Five Road Dad? You were lucky to get out of there alive."

"Yes, I remember," Russ replied.

Russ most definitely did remember what had happened the last time. He had been driving this exact same vehicle, and he ended up with six bullet holes in the truck and two flat tires.

The people that lived up on Camp Five Road tended to be really hardcore militia types. Their philosophy was to shoot first and ask questions later. There weren't too many roads in America that had snipers watching them 24 hours a day. And because of the recent crash of the financial markets and the rising civil unrest all over the nation, there were rumors all over the Internet that the federal government was about to impose martial law. So the good old boys living along Camp Five Road were likely to be even more trigger-happy than normal.

In fact, Russ was hoping that they would be.

The last time he came up Camp Five Road, they did shoot up his truck, but once he got out of his truck and raised his hands and explained that he was "Diesel" from the Internet, the locals welcomed him with open arms. It turned out that they were among the millions of people that read his articles on a regular basis.

Russ was hoping that they would remember him and his truck and would shoot at the vehicles chasing him instead.

The two remaining SUVs had closed the gap to less than ten feet as Russ pulled onto Camp Five Road, and the road was in absolutely awful condition. It was a gravel road that had obviously not been maintained very well at all. There were big jagged rocks sticking up out of the road everywhere, and the road was absolutely riddled with potholes. It was definitely not a road intended to be driven on at high speed.

But Russ and Hunter were out of options, and they were desperate to get away from the SUVs that were trailing them. Russ did his best to avoid the largest potholes and the largest rocks, but their truck was still buffeted by one jarring impact after another.

Fortunately, the condition of the road was also slowing down the SUVs that were chasing them. The one in the rear hit a particularly deep pothole that almost caused it to topple over, but unfortunately for Russ and Hunter it just kept coming.

Russ glanced down at his gas gauge. It was getting very low. One way or another, this chase would end fairly soon.

As they raced up the road, Russ noticed that there were literally dozens of no trespassing signs, and some of them sounded quite ominous...

"Never Mind The Dog – Beware Of The Owner"

"If You Can Read This Sign You Are In Range"

"No Trespassing – Due To Increasing Ammunition Costs We Will No Longer Fire A Warning Shot"

"Prayer Is One Way To Meet The Lord – Trespassing Is Faster"

"No Trespassing – Violators Will Be Shot – Survivors Will Be Shot Again"

Hunter looked back to check on the SUVs that were chasing them, and he noticed that the agent riding in the passenger side of the lead vehicle had pulled out a handgun and was aiming it at them.

"Dad, they're going to shoot at us!"

"Hunter get down," Russ barked at him.

The agent fired twice and this time the bullets came much closer to their vehicle. Russ figured that they were probably still warning shots but he wasn't sure.

And Russ also figured that those shots would wake up the locals if they weren't watching them already.

The vehicles continued to race along, and they soon entered a portion of the road where there was a large clearing on each side. If Russ remembered correctly, this was the area where he had first been fired upon the last time he had come up Camp Five Road.

Suddenly, a couple of very loud gunshots rang out. Russ checked his rearview mirror and saw that the right front tire of the lead SUV had exploded. The SUV careened off the road and flipped over several times.

Russ heard several more gunshots. All four tires of the remaining SUV that was pursuing them got hit. The SUV swerved off the road and smashed head-on into a large tree.

Russ slowed his truck down and howled in triumph.

"Did you see that Hunter? That was some serious shooting! Thank goodness for the militia! I want you to wave to the snipers son. We don't want to give them any excuses to shoot at us."

Russ and Hunter both waived to the unseen snipers in the distance as they headed for home.

Chapter 32

One of the things that Tom really looked forward to each day was a turkey sub for lunch.

Most people preferred variety at lunchtime, but not Tom. He figured that once you found something great, why change? Every day as lunchtime rolled around his mouth started watering just at the thought of running out of the office and getting a juicy turkey sub.

One of the first things that Tom did when he took this new position at the agency was to scout out the local neighborhood for sub shops. He had found one that made turkey subs just the way that he liked them, and now he visited that sub shop for lunch as often as he could.

His coworkers actually joked with him about the fact that he went to that exact same sub shop and got the exact same sandwich every single day, but Tom didn't care. There were very few things in life that he enjoyed more than a great sandwich.

Of course his predictability potentially made him vulnerable. If someone wanted to get at him, they would know precisely when and where to strike.

As Tom stood in line for his turkey sub on this day, he noticed that the line was shorter than usual. The economy in Washington D.C. was not as bad as the rest of the nation, but still businesses and restaurants were really struggling. Tom wondered how much worse things were going to get.

Suddenly, Tom heard a female voice call out to him from behind.

"Tom? - Tom McDowell?? - Is that you??"

Tom spun around in the direction of the voice. A very beautiful woman with long dark hair about his age was waving to him. It took him a few moments to recognize her.

"Caroline?" A flood of bittersweet memories overwhelmed Tom in an instant.

"Yeah Tom, it's me." She was smiling broadly. "I haven't seen you in ages. How have you been?"

"I'm doing great. Are you working in D.C. now? The last that I heard you were up in New York working for some firm over on Wall Street."

"I was, but I recently took a position over at the Federal Reserve. It's been a huge adjustment, and honestly I do miss New York, but there is a certain charm to D.C. as well. I have to say Tom, you look really great. The years have really treated you well."

Tom could see that the years had treated Caroline very kindly as well. They had dated for a couple of years when they were in high school, but he could hardly remember his high school days back in Monterey, California at this point. What Tom did remember was that they had made plans for the future together, but all of that had ended when Tom went off to the Air Force Academy. Eventually they lost touch, but just seeing Caroline again brought back some very strong emotions that Tom thought that he had buried long ago.

"Thank you Caroline," Tom responded. He noticed that she wasn't wearing a wedding band. "Are you still single after all these years?"

Caroline grinned. "Yeah, I was married for a couple of years but it didn't work out. I probably was just way too dedicated to my career. What about you - are you still single?"

Tom couldn't take his eyes off of Caroline. She was absolutely stunning. "Yeah, I'm single too. I never could find the right one either."

Caroline's eyes widened. "Look, I have to get back to my office in just a few minutes. I was just passing by here on the street and I thought that I recognized you standing in line. We should definitely get together some time for dinner and catch up."

That was something that Tom was absolutely interested in. "That sounds great. How can I reach you?"

Caroline handed him a card. "You can reach me at that cell phone number any time. Let's get together soon."

"Absolutely," Tom responded. Tom found it mesmerizing just to be around her again.

"I've got to run sweetie. I'll see you soon."

As she turned to go, Caroline flashed Tom a killer smile that penetrated right to the core of his heart. He wasn't able to take his eyes off of her until she had finally rounded the corner and was out of sight.

Finally, he was jolted back to reality by the man behind the counter.

"Hey buddy, what do you want on your sandwich?"

Chapter 33

"You were being chased by the feds??"

Russ didn't quite know what to say. His wife, Dottie, was absolutely furious.

"Well, to be honest, we weren't entirely sure that they were feds."

"Who else could they have been?? The pizza delivery guys??"

"Calm down Dottie. Everything turned out okay. We got home safely."

Dottie would not be calmed down so easily. "What if everything had not turned out okay? What if you and Hunter had ended up dead or in prison? This isn't a Hollywood movie where the good guys are invulnerable. If I lost you and Hunter, it would just be me, Kinley and Brynn. Do you have any idea how hard that would be?"

Russ was nodding his head. "I know, Dottie. I had no idea this was going to happen. They have never come after us like that before."

"It's your blogging Russ - that is what is upsetting them. You need to stop writing. Let someone else expose government conspiracies for a while. Right now our number one priority has got to be protecting our family."

Hearing this saddened Russ, but he knew that Dottie was right. "I will quit writing Dottie. At least for a while until the heat dies down. I made a promise to you that I would protect our family and keep us safe, and I am going to keep that promise. You and the kids mean the world to me.

Unfortunately, even if I stop blogging that doesn't mean that the feds are going to quit coming after me. Now that I'm on their radar it is going to be very hard to get off of it."

Dottie let the implications of that sink in. "So what do we do? Should we move? Should we set up a new home in some other part of the country?"

Russ had thought about that himself. Unfortunately, it was not a practical option for them at this point. "It took us years of incredibly hard work to set up what we have here. There is no way that we could ever sell this place without exposing ourselves, and it would be virtually impossible to buy another piece of land in another part of the country and get it set up properly without someone in D.C. catching on. Our best bet is to stay here. They will never find us up in these mountains. I have just got to lay low for a while. For the time being, we will have to rely on you and the girls to do most of the shopping and run most of the errands."

Dottie felt a panic attack coming on. "Perhaps the time has come for us to leave the United States altogether. Russ, why don't we just leave and start a new life in another part of the world?"

Russ cringed. It wasn't that Dottie's idea was a bad idea. It was just that Russ knew that it wouldn't be easy to get out of the country.

"Perhaps at some point we will need to try to leave, and let's start thinking about that. But to be honest, setting up a new life in a foreign country can be extremely difficult, and even getting out of the United States is going to present quite a challenge for us."

Dottie was puzzled. "What do you mean?"

"I mean that I am almost certainly on the federal no-fly list. So flying is out. We could try leaving the country by car or by ship with fake passports, but they have photos of me and the feds are putting in facial recognition software all over the nation. Perhaps at some point trying to leave the country will be our best option, but for now I think that we should stay here."

This entire conversation was really stressing Dottie out. "If this is going to work, you have to promise me two things. Number one, I need you to promise to quit writing. Number two, I need you to promise to sit at home and stay out of public view. Perhaps if you play dead long enough, the feds will forget about you. Can you promise me those two things?"

Russ reached out and gave Dottie a hug.

"I promise. From now on, you and the kids are my top priority."

Chapter 34

It was a cloudy evening and there was a bit of a chill in the air. As Tom and Melissa strolled arm in arm through Georgetown, Melissa could tell that Tom was distracted.

"Is something on your mind tonight?"

"Yeah, I guess there is," Tom responded. "During lunch today I ran into an old friend that I went to high school with. We were really close back then, but we haven't kept in contact in recent years. It was just really strange seeing her again after all these years."

Melissa didn't appear to be alarmed. "Did it seem like she was doing well?"

"I think so. She recently moved down from New York City and she said that she was working over at the Federal Reserve now."

Melissa cringed. "Working at the Fed is not exactly something to be proud of."

Tom was puzzled. "What do you mean?"

Melissa glanced over at Tom. "You've seen the tremendous economic chaos the Fed has caused. They created the conditions for the financial crisis of 2008 and they created the conditions for the economic collapse that we are experiencing right now. The Fed was initially established to bring 'stability' to our economic system, but the truth is that they have brought us a tremendous amount of instability instead. Since the Federal Reserve was created back in 1913, the value of the U.S. dollar has declined by well over 95 percent and the U.S. national debt has gotten more than 5,000 times larger. The bankers that designed the Federal Reserve system actually intended to trap the U.S. government in an endless debt spiral from which it could never possibly be able to escape. Every year our money supply gets even larger and so does our national debt. The Federal Reserve is a perpetual debt machine that is systematically destroying our currency and the bright economic future that future generations of Americans should have had. It is a system of debt slavery that is insidious and cruel. Those are just some of the reasons why I am not too fond of the Fed."

Tom couldn't argue with that. But he didn't really want to talk about economics tonight. He had been spending almost every evening with Melissa over the past few weeks, and he wanted to make the most out of every evening that they still had left before she went back to New York. He was really starting to develop strong feelings for her.

"You never cease to surprise me Melissa. I had no idea that you knew so much about this stuff."

"Well, it is my job to know the financial world. And unlike most reporters, I actually try to dig into the history behind the stories that I cover."

Melissa hesitated for a moment. She wasn't sure if Tom was going to be pleased with what she was going to tell him next.

"Tom, it looks like the network is going to be sending me back to New York quite soon."

That statement shook Tom up a bit. He always knew that Melissa was down in D.C. on a temporary assignment, but he didn't think that things would be changing so quickly.

"How soon do you think that will be?"

"I am not sure. I will probably know more in a couple of days."

They walked about half a block in silence. Even though the economy was an absolute wreck in most of the country, there still seemed to be quite a few shoppers in the stores this evening.

It was Tom that finally said something. "I really hope that we can continue this relationship once you go back to New York. I am a bit hesitant to admit this, but I have really started to fall for you."

Melissa stopped walking and faced Tom. Her blue eyes seemed even more vibrant and alive than usual.

"I feel the exact same way Tom. Getting to know you has been a joy, and I definitely want to continue what we have started. Long distance relationships are always challenging even under the best of circumstances, but you are definitely worth it."

There was something about Melissa that made Tom feel really good inside. She was very strong, independent and successful, but she also had a way of making him feel like a man. He really liked that feeling.

Melissa took his arm again and they resumed walking along the sidewalk. Tom wished that every evening could be like this.

"There is a great Italian place a couple of blocks from here," Tom said cheerfully. "Are you ready for some dinner?"

"Of course – and you can fill me in on your next move to expose the agency."

Being with Melissa had almost made Tom forget about his vendetta against the agency. Part of him wanted to whisk Melissa away to another part of the country where nobody would ever find them. But he also realized that real life was not that simple.

"I am going to have to get something on the agency that is much bigger than last time. I need something that will take the entire organization down. Unfortunately, I am mostly on a 'need to know basis', and they don't tell me a whole lot."

"So what are you going to do?"

"I think that the head of my office, agent Jessup, is very connected to the upper echelons of the agency. If I could just get inside his head, I think that I could get a hold of some really damaging stuff."

"So how are you going to do that?"

"I am not sure yet, but I am working on a few things."

Before too long they reached the restaurant. Tom decided that he was going to forget about everything else for the rest of the evening and just focus on Melissa. The more that he got to know her, the more he began to realize that he had a real treasure on his hands. He just hoped that he was not going to mess it up somehow.

Chapter 35

Tom got back to his apartment really late after his date with Melissa, but it had been worth it. Dinner had been amazing and they had talked for hours. Tom felt like he had not just found someone that he was attracted to - he also felt like he had found someone that could be his best friend.

He just hoped that their romance would not lose too much once Melissa returned to New York.

As he stepped into his apartment, he could hear the phone ringing. Tom rushed over and picked up the phone without checking who was calling because he thought that it was probably Melissa phoning to wish him a good night.

"Hello, this is Tom."

"Hello Tom, this is your sister Hannah."

Tom cursed himself for not checking the caller ID.

"What do you want Hannah?"

"I want to talk to you. Our last conversation didn't go that great from what I recall."

Tom cringed. "Yeah, you caught me at a bad moment that night. What's up?"

"I wanted to see what you thought about what we talked about the last time, and there is some new information that I wanted to give you."

Tom tried to remember what they had talked about during their last phone call. "If I remember correctly, the last time we talked you were trying to convince me about another one of your bizarre conspiracy theories."

Hannah sighed. "Look Tom, it is very important that you start listening to me. I would have thought that our last conversation would have earned me quite a bit of credibility with you."

"Oh yeah, and why is that?"

"Well, first of all I warned you about the economic crisis that was coming. Did that not happen?"

Tom had to admit to himself that she was right about that, but he still was not impressed. "There are hundreds of half-crazed bloggers and doomsday pundits that have been predicting an economic crisis for years. It was bound to happen at some point. So what?"

Hannah was getting frustrated. "Do you not also remember that I told you that you were about to be recruited into a secret government intelligence agency? I happen to know that you are working for them right now."

Tom couldn't come up with a quick retort to that statement. He just sat there stunned for a moment.

Hannah sensed an opening. "Cat got your tongue Tom?"

"How do you know about the agency Hannah? I worked for the CIA for years and I had never even heard of this agency."

"If you will come out to Idaho, I will explain everything to you."

Why did she want him to come out to Idaho so badly? Tom never could seem to understand his older sister.

"Look Hannah, I am not going to go all the way out to Idaho just to talk to you. If you have something to tell me, you should do it over the phone."

"Okay," Hannah said in reply, "but this is very sensitive stuff. Are you sure that your phone is secure?"

"Quit with the dramatics Hannah," Tom shot back, "of course my phone is secure."

Hannah paused for a moment. "Tom, I don't know if you understand this yet, but your agency is working for the wrong side. Unfortunately, for the sake of 'national security' they have been allowed to operate in a bubble of complete secrecy and not even the President knows what they are up to. Right now, your agency is planning a major attack which will destroy the bank account records of the ten largest banks in the United States. Even the backups for those bank account records will be destroyed. Tens of millions of Americans will wake up the next day and their bank accounts will be gone. Can you imagine that? Of course all of the records for mortgages, auto loans, student loans and credit cards will not be touched. Those records are kept in separate facilities. So tens of millions of Americans will suddenly have their bank accounts vanish, but they will still owe all of their debts. If people do not have paper records that prove that they actually had money in their bank accounts, they will be told that they are out of luck. Trillions of dollars could potentially be transferred from the American people to the big banks. The banks will be recapitalized and much of the middle class will be wiped out. It will be the greatest single theft in U.S. history, and it will cause the economy to descend into complete and utter chaos."

Tom could hardly believe what he was hearing.

"Okay Hannah, let's say that I believe you. What do you want me to do about it?"

Hannah was a patient woman, but her patience was rapidly running out. "The Tom that I used to know would have been horrified to learn that the people that he was working for were terrorists. The Tom that I used to know would have done anything to expose evil such as this. The Tom that I used to know had a passion to protect the American people. Does that Tom still exist?"

Tom didn't say anything for a moment. What Hannah was saying was starting to get through to him. "Yeah, he still exists. He's just really tired. And for the record Hannah, I have already figured out that the agency I am working for is evil. I just haven't figured out what to do about it yet."

"So you will look into this plot to destroy the banking records?"

"Yes, I promise that I will look into it."

"That's what I wanted to hear. I love you little brother."

Tom hated when she called him that. "I love you too. Goodnight."

Tom hung up the phone and put his head into his hands.

Was Hannah actually telling him the truth?

If so, then Tom was mixed up in something far more insidious than he had previously imagined.

So what would his next move be?

If his agency was actually behind such a terror plot, he needed to get some proof.

Tom thought long and hard about telling his best friend Koz about everything that he had found out about the agency, but he decided against that.

Koz was a family man now, and Tom definitely did not want to endanger his wife or his children. Tom wanted to keep him out of this for as long as possible. Once the agency had been exposed and brought down, then Tom would tell Koz everything. But for now Tom wanted to be the one taking all of the risks.

Being single, Tom didn't have a family to protect. In many ways, that made things easier. If he was killed, there would be no grieving widow and no grieving children left behind.

But could Tom actually take down this agency all by himself?

Tom realized that gathering information was not going to be easy. The sixth floor of the office building where his office was located had basically been converted into a high-tech fortress. Anyone that ventured up to the sixth floor would encounter a very bored receptionist sitting behind a desk that had the logo of Osiris Consulting Group emblazoned across it. On both the right and the left of the receptionist there was an office door that led inside to the interior of the sixth floor. Nobody could tell just by looking at them, but those steel-reinforced doors were bulletproof and had been designed to be able to hold off a major frontal assault for an extended period of time.

Inside, every inch of the sixth floor was monitored by cutting edge surveillance cameras. Everything that everybody did all day long was constantly watched. The people running the agency were some of the most paranoid people on the planet. The entire sixth floor was constantly being swept for bugs, listening devices and other types of surveillance equipment. And each room on the entire floor had been completely and totally soundproofed. Once you closed your office door, nobody on the outside would be able to hear a thing.

So Tom knew that snooping on his fellow agents would not be easy.

But he had to come up with something.

By the time Tom got to his office the next morning, he had come up with a plan. Now he just needed an opportunity to implement it.

As he sat behind his desk drinking his first cup of coffee that morning, there was a knock on his office door. When Tom went over and opened the door, he discovered that it was agent Jessup that had come to see him.

"Hey there Tom, how are you doing this morning?" Agent Jessup's raspy voice sounded a bit friendlier than usual.

"I'm doing great," Tom responded. "I was just getting ready to analyze those reports about drug-running in the Midwest that you gave me yesterday."

"Excellent. Look Tom, I was wondering if you would like to have dinner with my wife and I tonight. This is something that I typically do for new agents after they have had a while to settle in. I think it's important to get to know the people under my command on a more personal level."

Tom tried not to look too excited. "That sounds terrific. What did you have in mind?"

"Do you know Antognoni's? It's just a couple of blocks from here. They make terrific steaks down there."

"That would be perfect. What time do you want to meet?"

"How about seven? And bring a date along if you would like."

"Well, I am not sure if I can rustle up a date at the last moment, but in any event I will be there. I look forward to meeting your wife and getting to know you better."

Jessup seemed satisfied. "Good stuff - I'll see you then Tom."

Agent Jessup headed back down the hall toward his office, and Tom's mind was racing as he closed the door to his own office and tried to figure out what to do next.

He knew that he definitely did not want to expose Melissa to agent Jessup and his wife. So Tom would definitely not be bringing Melissa to this dinner. In fact, he would have to cancel a date with her that he already had planned for that evening.

Tom really wanted to see Melissa, but he couldn't pass a chance like this up. A golden opportunity had just fallen into his lap, and he definitely planned on taking advantage of it.

Chapter 36

Antognoni's was not the most elegant steakhouse in D.C., but it certainly did make great steaks. Tom, agent Jessup and agent Jessup's wife had been seated at a little square table near the center of the restaurant. Tom was sitting to one side of agent Jessup and his wife Samantha was sitting on the other side. The fourth chair was empty. Tonight, Tom and agent Jessup would be addressing each other by their first names since this was a more informal setting. They were all getting along great, and they had all downed a couple glasses of wine before their steaks had arrived, and that was exactly what Tom wanted. He wanted agent Jessup and his wife to both be a little tipsy before he made his move.

In particular, agent Jessup's wife, Samantha, seemed to really be enjoying her wine.

"Tom, I'm surprised that a handsome man like you never got married." Samantha had obviously had way too much to drink. "Why do you think that you haven't found the right one yet?"

"Well, I am afraid that my relationships are just like my lawn furniture. They are both very fragile and I find that I tend to break both of them easily."

Everyone at the table laughed at that one – especially Samantha.

Agent Jessup decided that this would be a good moment to head on over to the restroom.

"If you will excuse me, it is time for me to go drain the lizard," agent Jessup said as he stood up.

Samantha looked up at him disdainfully. "Do you have to be so crude? And while you are in there, you really should do something about your breath Eric. It smells like you swallowed a dead mouse."

Samantha howled in laughter and took another sip of her wine. Agent Jessup grimaced as he walked off in the direction of the restroom. Agent Jessup had left his blazer hanging across the back of his chair. Tom realized that this was his chance.

But first he needed to distract Samantha. He pointed toward the front door of the restaurant which was directly behind her. "Hey Samantha, is that Bill Clinton?"

Samantha whirled around to look. After a few moments she turned back toward Tom. "I think you need to get your eyes checked. That is just some old guy with gray hair. He doesn't look anything like Bill Clinton."

When Samantha had turned around, Tom had smoothly reached over and had lifted agent Jessup's cell phone out of the inside pocket of his blazer. He was holding it under the table with his right hand and he was already flipping through the menus as he had practiced.

But it was not easy, because he could not afford to take his eyes off of Samantha. If she realized what he was doing, she could blow the whole thing. Tom knew that he had to keep his attention on Samantha and keep the conversation going while using his peripheral vision to watch what he was doing with agent Jessup's phone under the table.

And Tom needed to get his work done with the phone very rapidly, because he knew that he probably only had a minute or two before agent Jessup returned from the restroom.

Fortunately, Tom had learned how to charm women over the years, and Samantha was already well on the way to getting drunk. One rule that Tom had always followed was that beautiful women didn't like being constantly reminded about how beautiful they were, but unattractive women loved to hear anything positive about their appearance.

And Samantha was definitely not an attractive woman. As Tom fumbled with the phone, he figured that a little flattery would keep Samantha occupied.

"Are those new earrings Samantha? They really bring out the brown in your eyes."

Samantha smiled broadly. "Well, thank you. Eric gave them to me last Christmas. I should wear them more often."

"And I have to say that you really have a unique sense of style. You don't see too many women with a beehive hairdo anymore, but I think that it really accentuates the horn-rimmed glasses that you are wearing. You have a look that is very retro."

Tom could see that the program was downloading on agent Jessup's cell phone more slowly than he had anticipated. This was going to be close.

Fortunately, Samantha was still oblivious to what was going on. "Tom, you are one of the only people that really understands what I am shooting for. If I could live during any time in American history, it would be the late 1960s. I think that is when life was most perfect in the United States."

Tom looked past Samantha and could see that agent Jessup was emerging from the restroom. Tom realized that he was out of time.

Tom slipped agent Jessup's phone into the right front pocket of his pants and he stood up. "Samantha, I am afraid that I must use the restroom as well. Will you excuse me?"

"Of course," Samantha responded.

Tom started to leave the table, but as he turned to go he fell very awkwardly over the chair that agent Jessup had been sitting in. Tom, the chair and agent Jessup's blazer all tumbled to the floor.

From where he had fallen, Tom looked up and saw that agent Jessup was now standing directly over him.

Tom smiled. "I'm sorry Eric – I think that I have had too much to drink. Normally I am not that clumsy. I was just heading over to the restroom."

Agent Jessup took his hand and helped lift Tom to his feet. "It's no problem Tom. I think we all have had too much to drink tonight." As agent Jessup said that last part he looked over at his wife.

Tom brushed himself off and headed over to the restroom. The cell phone spyware had been fully downloaded on to agent Jessup's cell phone and the cell phone was back in the pocket of agent Jessup's blazer.

Tom breathed a sigh of relief. That had been a really close call, but he had accomplished his mission. Now he just hoped that he would be able to get some information that he could actually use.

Chapter 37

As Tom sat in his apartment listening to his phone messages, he realized that that there were a lot of people that he needed to get back to...

Beep "Tom, this is Koz. Hey, I haven't seen you much at work lately. Is everything okay? Talk to me buddy. We can get together for the football game on Sunday if you would like."

Beep "Hi Tom, this is Caroline. I apologize for the delay in returning your call. I am heading out to a Fed conference in Boston on Friday, but I would love to get together for dinner tomorrow night if you are available. Give me a call."

Beep "I really missed you tonight Tom. I know that you had to have dinner with your boss and his wife, and I hope that turned out well. Can we get together tomorrow night? I want to make the most of my time with you before I go back to New York."

That last call was from Melissa. Tom definitely wanted to spend as much time with her as he could before she went back to New York, but Tom figured that was probably still several weeks away. Plus, he felt really bad that he had not met up with Caroline yet. She had meant so much to him during his high school years, and he wanted to catch up with her before she went away to that conference on Friday.

He picked up his phone and stared at it for a few moments as he decided what to do. Finally, he started dialing Caroline's number.

Melissa had been really disappointed when Tom had called her and explained that he wouldn't be able to see her because he needed to have dinner with an old friend. Tom was obviously in an extremely dangerous line of work, but she was really starting to fall hard for him. She realized that her time in D.C. was rapidly coming to an end, and she wanted to make as strong of an impression on him as she could while she still had time. She knew that long distance relationships were never easy. If their relationship was going to work out in the long-term, both of them would have to be fully committed to putting extra effort into it.

Since she couldn't see Tom tonight, she had decided to treat herself to a great meal. There was an incredible seafood place down at Washington Harbour that Tom had taken her to a couple of times, and she had decided to go back over there by herself tonight. She started thinking about what was on the menu as she made the turn toward Georgetown.

Caroline was a half hour late getting to the restaurant, but when she walked in Tom immediately spotted her. In fact, about half of the men in the entire restaurant immediately spotted her. The elegant red dress that she was wearing perfectly framed her statuesque physique. The dress was very revealing, but Caroline wore it with poise and confidence. She had spent a lot of money on her matching red heels, but it was her stunning emerald green eyes that captured Tom's attention right away. Her long dark hair had been freshly curled and it flowed down her back like a waterfall. As Tom stood up from the table where he had been seated, he found that his jaw had involuntarily dropped.

When Caroline arrived at the table, she had the look of a woman who was completely and totally in control. "How are you doing Tom? I am so sorry for being late," she said as she leaned in and kissed him on the cheek.

When Caroline leaned in, Tom got a whiff of her perfume and found it absolutely intoxicating. Caroline was about as old as Tom was, but she had never looked like this in high school. She was someone that had obviously worked incredibly hard to maintain her appearance.

"I am doing great. Please have a seat," Tom stammered as he pulled out a seat for Caroline.

Tom suddenly found that he felt very nervous. She had looked great when they had bumped into each other in the sub shop the other day, but tonight she had literally taken his breath away.

They exchanged small talk at first, and then the conversation turned to catching up on how the last few years had gone for each of them. Tom had forgotten how much he truly enjoyed talking to Caroline. There had been times in high school when they had stayed on the phone for hours. Talking with her just seemed so incredibly natural.

Tom was curious about how she felt about the past. "Do you have any regrets in life Caroline?"

Caroline hesitated for just a moment before answering. "Not really. Sure there are many things that I would have done differently, but all the experiences that I have been through have helped make me the person that I am. If I went back and changed the things that brought me to this point, I may never have gotten to where I am today."

Tom wished that he could express such sentiments so confidently. "Sometimes I wonder what life would be like if I threw it all away and started an entirely new life in another part of the country. A few years ago, my sister bought a little log cabin up in Washington state that my uncle had owned. It is near a little town called Greenwater on the edge of the Snoqualmie National Forest. My sister told me that I can use the cabin whenever I would like, and sometimes I fantasize about dropping everything, moving out there and living a much quieter life. I think that it would suit me."

Caroline crinkled her nose. "I think you would enjoy it for about a week and then you would get incredibly bored. I know you Tom – I know how much you crave excitement."

Tom smiled. "That was the old Tom. The new Tom wouldn't mind some peace and quiet for a while. Sometimes I wonder what life would be like with a wife, a couple of kids and a couple of dogs. Am I missing out on what really matters in life?"

Caroline's eyes sparkled as the lights in the restaurant reflected off of them. She reached across the table and took his hands in her hands. "Tom it is never too late to go after what you really want in life. It isn't how our stories begin that matters. What matters is how our stories end. You still have plenty of time to write a great ending to your life."

As Caroline said this, another woman walked right up to their table and slammed her purse down on it.

It was Melissa.

"What in the world is this Tom?" Melissa was livid. "You told me that you were having dinner with an old friend tonight. Well, this tramp definitely does not look old and she definitely looks like more than a friend."

Tom was horrified. He never meant to put Melissa in this kind of a position. He stared up at her like a deer caught in the headlights.

Caroline decided that she had better intervene. "We most definitely are old friends my dear," Caroline smugly explained. "We knew each other back in high school. We are just 'catching up' if you catch my drift."

This did not settle Melissa down at all. "Oh yeah, I just bet that Tom would love to 'catch up' with you. I can't believe this! I was really starting to develop very serious feelings for you Tom. Were you just lying to me the entire time? Did you ever take our relationship seriously?"

Tom stammered as he rose from his seat. "It's – it's not what it looks like."

Melissa let out a cry of disgust. "I am so out of here. Goodbye Tom." With that, she marched out of the restaurant.

Tom turned to Caroline. "Excuse me for a moment Caroline – I need to go talk to her."

Caroline nodded her head and Tom raced out the door after Melissa. When he caught up with her, Melissa spun around to face him.

"Just leave me alone Tom." By now tears were running down Melissa's face.

"Melissa, I am not lying to you. This is the old friend that I ran into at the sub shop the other day who is working over at the Federal Reserve. I told her that I would get together with her for dinner at some point to catch up on old times. I had no idea that she was going to dress like that tonight."

This calmed Melissa down a bit. "So you never intended for this to be a date with her?"

"Of course not," Tom responded, although he wasn't entirely sure if that was the truth. He had been really looking forward to seeing Caroline, and he did still have feelings for her, but he was never going to admit that to Melissa.

Melissa started to realize that she had overreacted. "I am so sorry Tom. I should not have blown up like that. I was just coming over for a nice dinner and running into you two like that was a total surprise. I just don't want to lose you. It has been a long time since I have had these kinds of feelings."

Tom reached out and embraced her. "Me too Melissa. You mean the world to me, and I would never do anything to hurt you. Why don't you come back into the restaurant and join us for the rest of dinner?"

Melissa shook her head. "No, I would be too embarrassed. I think that I'll just head home and grab something to eat.

Go on back in there and have a good time with your friend."

Tom wasn't sure that was the best course of action, but he was willing to go with it. "Okay Melissa. But can we get together for dinner tomorrow night? I want to try very hard to repair whatever damage that I've done here tonight."

That sounded good to Melissa. They exchanged another hug and then Melissa went on her way. Tom went back into the restaurant and explained to Caroline what had happened. Caroline was very sympathetic, and she suggested that they order some more wine. Within a few minutes, their conversation was flowing very smoothly once again. They laughed, they talked and they drank wine for another two hours before finally leaving the restaurant.

As Tom walked Caroline to her car, Caroline spotted a woman that seemed to be looking right at them. She was in a car in another parking lot across the street. She was about 50 yards away from where Tom and Caroline were, and she didn't look happy. It was a dark night, but to Caroline it looked like the woman that was staring right at them was Melissa.

Caroline decided that this would be a good time to make a move. She stopped walking and turned to face Tom.

"Tom, it was so great having dinner with you tonight. It has been so wonderful to see you again after all of these years. You have really cheered me up. How can I thank you?"

Tom was clearly drunk at this point. He always did have a problem handling alcohol.

"You don't have to thank me Caroline. In fact, I should be the one thanking you."

Caroline smiled. She knew that she had him on the hook. "Well, if you really want to thank me, you can give me one little kiss. I want something to remember you by."

Tom felt a bit awkward, but inside he had to admit that he really did want to kiss Caroline.

"Okay, just one little kiss."

Caroline drifted toward Tom and he took her in his arms. A long, passionate kiss followed, and Melissa fumed as she watched the entire thing from her car.

After the kiss was over, Tom and Caroline resumed walking toward her car. As they did so, Caroline looked back over her shoulder directly toward the spot where Melissa was watching them.

There wasn't much light, but as Caroline continued to look in her direction, Melissa got the distinct impression that she was smiling at her.

Chapter 38

The spyware that Tom had installed on agent Jessup's cell phone was not your ordinary spyware. Yes, it allowed Tom to intercept all of agent Jessup's calls, record them and read all of his text messages, but it also did so much more. Tom could also continually track the GPS location of the cell phone and he could even listen to what was going on around agent Jessup even when the cell phone was turned off. As long as the battery was in the cell phone, it acted like a microphone and everything was constantly being fed to recording equipment that Tom had hidden in his SUV.

Most of the stuff that Tom had recorded so far had been incredibly boring, but then Tom came across a conversation between agent Jessup and a mysterious female visitor to his office. It was a voice that Tom did not recognize, and the conversation was about something called "Operation Ordo Ab Chao"...

"Greetings Commandant – I had no idea that you would be visiting us today."

"This isn't a social call Jessup. I am here to inform you that a decision has been made to move forward with Operation Ordo Ab Chao."

"Is that really such a good idea? There is just so much risk involved. If something goes wrong, the entire agency could be exposed."

"I didn't come here to ask you for your opinion Jessup. It is your job to follow my orders, just like it is my job to follow the orders that I get from those above me."

"I understand that. It is just that destroying the bank account records of the ten largest banks in the United

States is absolutely unprecedented and it is going to cause utter chaos all over the country. When people realize that even the backup records have been destroyed and that their bank accounts are permanently gone they are going to go absolutely nuts. If the media finds out that we are behind it, the consequences would be catastrophic."

"If you wanted to play patty-cake, you should have been a kindergarten teacher Jessup. You know very well why operations such as this are necessary. In order to make an omelette, you have to break a few eggs. A new global financial system will never be able to arise until we tear down the old one. If you cannot handle being part of this operation, just say the word and we will get someone in here who can."

"You – you know that I have always been faithful to the organization. For more than a decade I have put myself on the line for this agency. Of course I will always do whatever is asked of me."

"That is a good thing agent Jessup, because you know what happens to those that fail us."

"How could I ever forget?"

"So who is going to assist you in planting the bombs at the location that you have been assigned?"

"I have selected agent Wolfe and agent Kalon to assist me. What am I supposed to tell the rest of the agents in my office?"

"As always, they are on a need to know basis. And they don't need to know anything about any of this until after the bombs go off. When that happens, we will give them the same cover story that the media will be given. This will be blamed on certain organizations affiliated with the 'liberty movement' that have been extremely critical of the government. They will be labeled as 'domestic terrorists', and the President and Congress will devote massive amounts of resources to crushing those organizations."

"I trust the judgment of the organization my Commandant. If we are able to pull this off, it would almost be too perfect. First we wipe out the bank accounts of tens of millions of American families, thus accelerating the collapse of the economy. Government dependence soars to unprecedented heights and people start demanding change. Of course the only 'change' they will be offered is the 'change' that our bosses have in mind for them. Meanwhile, all of the blame for the crisis will be pointed at organizations that have been a thorn in our side for many years. Do you really think that the American people will believe that the 'liberty movement' is the enemy?"

"Of course they will agent Jessup. You should know by now that the American people believe whatever the media tells them to believe. As long as our bosses control the media, they are able to control what people think."

"Well, you can count on me and my team to do our jobs."

"I am glad to hear that agent Jessup. Oh, and one more thing. Operation Ordo Ab Chao has been amended. The operation has been moved up to 11:30 PM eastern time on New Year's Eve. In addition to destroying bank account records all over the nation, several dirty bombs will also go off in Times Square in New York City at the same time. Our bosses decided that just bombing financial institutions would not create enough of a media spectacle. But the sight of thousands of dead and dying people in Times Square on New Year's Eve will be something that the media will talk about for decades. It will change America forever, and it will make it much easier for our bosses to implement the much more 'structured society' that they are envisioning for the United States. Do you have any problems with this agent Jessup?"

"Of – of course not. My – my loyalty to the agency is absolute."

"I knew that we could count on you. I'll be seeing you again in a couple of days Jessup."

———————

That was the end of the conversation, and Tom played it back several times just to make certain that he had heard things correctly.

After listening to the recording several times, Tom got up and started pacing nervously around his apartment. Tom realized that his sister Hannah had been right after all, but she had not even known all of the details about this plot. His agency was planning the biggest terror attack in U.S. history.

Tom felt a surge of panic race through him.

He walked into his bathroom and stared at himself in the mirror. "What in the world am I supposed to do with this?"

Tom knew that whoever exposed this information to the public would put themselves in a great deal of danger. But he also knew that he had to do something. He had spent his entire life defending his country, and there was no way that he was going to allow those bombs to go off without trying to stop it from happening.

He sat there for a few moments just staring blankly into space. Finally he pulled out his phone and dialed a number.

"Melissa, there is something that I've got to show you."

Chapter 39

Melissa had considered confronting Tom about the kiss that she had witnessed the other night, but when Tom arrived at her place she didn't even have a chance to bring it up. Tom was freaking out about a recording that he had just made of his boss discussing some sort of a terror plot, and Tom was very insistent that she needed to listen to it.

Once Melissa finished listening to the recording that Tom had made, she was visibly stunned.

"This is serious Tom. These guys are plotting the worst terror attack in the history of the United States. If they pull this off, tens of thousands of people will be killed and our banking system will totally collapse. Our intelligence agencies need to hear this. So does the President. What are we going to do?"

That was something that Tom had been thinking about ever since he first listened to the recording. He had been mulling over the options again and again, but he still wasn't 100 percent sure about what to do.

"I have been wracking my brain trying to figure out how to handle this. If I come out publicly, I will never be able to go back to the agency and they will almost certainly try to have me killed. I think that I can do more damage to the agency by remaining hidden and working to take them down from the inside, and I am not too eager to be hunted down by assassins."

Melissa cringed at the thought of her boyfriend being murdered. "I would be horrified if anything happened to you Tom. What other options do we have?"

"I could try to anonymously get this recording to as many people in our intelligence agencies as I can. The problem is that an anonymous conversation between two people submitted by an anonymous source will probably not be taken very seriously. In addition, the agency has people embedded just about everywhere – the CIA, the NSA, the FBI, the Department of Homeland Security – and those embedded agents will do everything that they can to keep this recording from getting out. But at least I can try."

"What about me Tom? I could try to take this to my producer. I haven't been in D.C. for that long, but I trust her. This could be the biggest news story of the year if my producer is willing to run it."

Tom didn't really like that idea. It entailed a tremendous amount of risk. If anyone in the agency found out that Melissa tried to get the recording on the air it could put her in a lot of danger.

"Getting this recording aired on American News Network would be huge. But if anyone in my agency discovered that you were the reporter that handed this recording over to the network that would make you a huge target. How well do you trust this producer?"

"She is a real sweetheart Tom. Her name is Jessica and she has three young children. She looks like someone that you would run into at the PTA, and I have only gotten good vibes from her. I believe that she would keep anything that I share with her confidential."

"Well, I still don't really like this idea Melissa, but if you promise to only share this with her we could at least test the waters. If your producer was able to get this recording on the air, it could potentially blow the agency wide open and create a huge national scandal. The potential gain from such a move is great, but I still don't like the potential risk. In the end, it is you that needs to make this decision. Putting you in danger is never what I wanted to do."

Melissa smiled. She had fallen hard for Tom over the past several weeks. Even though he had kissed Caroline the other night, she still hoped that their relationship would be able to move forward. Melissa knew that Tom had probably been drunk when he had kissed her, and she was sure that he wouldn't be seeing her again. And the truth was that Melissa had started to become very emotionally invested in Tom. She had never met anyone like him before, and she only wished that she had met him sooner. In fact, after all of this craziness was over, Melissa was really hoping that they could get a lot more serious and start talking about a real future together.

"Let's both be very careful Tom. I don't want anything to happen to you either. Sometimes I think that it would be better for us just to run off to another country and leave everything behind, but I know that neither one of us could live with ourselves if we didn't try to do something to stop this plot. How could we look ourselves in the mirror if we knew that tens of thousands of people were going to be killed and we didn't do anything about it?"

Tom knew that she was right. "Once the agency is brought down, life will return to normal. I promise. Once the American people learn about this terror plot, the outrage will be off the charts. My agency and every other secret agency out there will be brought into the light, and that will be a wonderful thing. If we are able to pull this off, I will consider this my last great gift to the American people and

I will retire from the intelligence game for good. It is time for me to do something else with my life."

That sounded really good to Melissa. She embraced Tom and closed her eyes as she held him close. If they could just get through the next few weeks, maybe there was a chance that she could have the fairytale that she had always dreamed of after all.

Chapter 40

The next day, Tom decided that this might be a good time to see where Koz's head was at. Tom hadn't really talked with him much lately, and part of him was dying to share with Koz what he had found out about the agency. But part of him was also very hesitant to do that, and Tom couldn't figure out why.

Tom almost always went and grabbed a turkey sub at his favorite sub shop for lunch, but today he decided to invite Koz to join him for lunch at one of the fancy, overpriced cafes that littered the area around K Street. As they walked together toward the cafe, there were way too many awkward pauses between them. Tom decided that instead of more small talk, he would try to test the waters and see what Koz was thinking.

"Are you enjoying working for the agency Koz?"

Koz arched his eyebrows as he looked over at Tom. "What do you mean? Yeah, it's not quite what I expected, but I can't complain."

"Have you noticed anything unusual? Is there anything about the agency that concerns you?"

Koz stopped walking for a moment and turned toward Tom. "What are you referring to Tom? Yeah, that operation out in Oregon was kind of messed up, but sometimes that happens in our line of work. If I was in charge, I would run things differently, but I'm definitely not going to make waves. I am making more money than I ever dreamed that I would make, and the agency has been incredibly good to my family. And even though I may not always agree with their methods, I very much believe in what this agency is trying to do. Why would you ask these kinds of questions anyway? Is there something about the agency that is bothering you Tom? If so, you might want to keep it to yourself. It is my impression that they don't exactly have much tolerance for negative attitudes."

Tom decided that he better not test the waters any further. "It's no big deal Koz. I just wanted to see how things were going for you at the agency so far. We have been friends for a lot of years, and we have always watched out for each other. You pulled my butt out of the fire more than once. When the chips are down, you can always count on me."

Tom and Koz resumed walking toward the cafe. Koz started to tell Tom something and then he stopped himself. Tom could tell that something was bothering him, but he didn't want to push.

After a few moments, Koz turned toward Tom with a very serious look on his face.

"Tom, I hope that you know that you can always count on me too. I'll never forget what you did for me on that one mission in the Gaza Strip during our early days at the CIA. If it wasn't for you, I never would have gotten out of there alive. I will be forever grateful, and so will my family. I owe you one my friend."

———————

Melissa's producer in D.C., Jessica Evans, was not smiling. Melissa had just shared a copy of the recording that Tom had made with her, and Melissa was hoping that Jessica would want to run with the story. Instead, Jessica was visibly upset.

"What in the world has gotten into you Melissa? We don't indulge in conspiracy theories on this network. Do you actually think that we can do a story about an anonymous conversation about a plot to blow up Times Square between two 'secret agents' at a government agency that doesn't have a name and that nobody has ever heard of? Those voices on that recording could belong to anyone. This could all just be a giant hoax. Without some serious corroboration there is no way that we could ever put something like this on the air. Who gave you this recording? Is that person willing to come forward publicly?"

Melissa was afraid that this might happen. "No, my source cannot come forward because that would put my source in a tremendous amount of danger. But I can personally vouch for my source. This is solid information."

Jessica was steaming now. "I don't care if your source is the Pope himself – unless he or she comes forward this story is going nowhere. Do you even realize how upset authorities in New York would be if we ruined New Year's Eve in Times Square over some baseless rumor? Do you understand how much credibility we could lose if we put this out to the nation and it turned out that the recording was made by a couple of prankster teens? You need to start taking a much more professional approach to your job. I am ordering you to put a lid on this story and to not discuss it with anyone else at the network. If I find out that you are still pursuing this story I will personally see to it that you are fired. Am I making myself clear?"

Melissa was really wishing that she had never brought this up to Jessica. "You have made yourself crystal clear. I am so sorry for this. I won't make the same mistake again."

"You better not!" Jessica was yelling at this point. "Now get out of my office before I have you thrown out!"

Melissa hastily left Jessica's office, and she closed the door on her way out. Once Jessica was satisfied that Melissa was gone, she pulled out her cell phone and dialed a number. After a few moments, someone answered.

"This is Jessica. Look, I think we have a big problem. One of my reporters just came into my office and you will never guess what she told me. I need someone to get a message to the High Council."

Chapter 41

Tom had spent most of the day anonymously sending out copies of the recording that he had made to contacts that he trusted within the intelligence community, but he knew it was a longshot that it would do any good. A conversation between two anonymous individuals submitted by an anonymous source would simply not be considered to be very credible. But Tom had to try, even if the odds were against him. Unfortunately, Tom also knew that the agency he was working for was part of a larger network that had undercover agents embedded just about everywhere. Those embedded agents would do all that they could to protect the agency and discredit the recording. If Tom had been willing to blow his cover and go public with what he had learned, the recording would probably be taken much more seriously. But he was not willing to do that just yet. He believed that there was still much more he could uncover at the agency, and so his identity needed to remain a secret for now.

But he was torn because he definitely wanted to do everything that he could to stop the bombing plot that the agency had planned for New Year's Eve. Tom realized that at some point he would need to take more direct action.

On this particular evening, Tom had decided that he just wanted to be by himself, and he was slowly downing a bottle of beer as he sat on his sofa staring at his living room wall.

Tom was just feeling overwhelmed at that moment. He felt like the fate of thousands of lives and of the entire U.S. banking system was riding on decisions that he was making. That was a lot of pressure, and it just added to the intense stress that was constantly eating away at Tom.

At times like this, Tom didn't really want to be around anyone else. He just wanted to drink himself into a daze so that he could hopefully forget about his troubles for a while.

A loud knock at the front door of his apartment startled Tom. When he went over and opened the door, he found Caroline standing there. It was unseasonably cold outside, so she was wearing a winter coat, but on top of her head she was sporting a big red cowboy hat with a Stanford logo on it. In her right hand she was carrying a six pack of beer.

"Hey there Tom! Do you remember when the gang would all get together and watch the Stanford games when we were in high school? Well, I figured that I would swing by and see if you had the game on. Can I come in?"

Tom and Caroline had exchanged a number of phone calls since their dinner the other night, but he had not expected her to drop by this evening. Not that Tom was displeased. In fact, part of him was definitely excited to see her. Without a doubt, he was very attracted to Caroline and he liked spending time with her. And tonight Tom was definitely in the mood for a distraction.

"Of course. Come on in. I'm afraid that I don't have much to eat. I haven't done much shopping lately."

Caroline marched right over to the television and turned it on. "I can't believe that you don't have the game on. You used to be such a huge sports nut. Have the years really changed you that much?"

Tom wasn't sure what to say. "No, I've just had a lot on my mind lately."

"Well, I think that you just need to loosen up." Caroline took off her winter coat, and underneath she was wearing a very tight pair of jeans and a Stanford jersey that was several sizes too small and that did not completely cover her midsection. Not many women her age had a completely flat stomach, but Caroline had worked incredibly hard on her body and it showed. "Is it okay if we watch the game for a while?"

Tom found that he could not take his eyes off of her. Caroline had never looked this good when they were dating back in high school. "Yeah, I could use a break. I think that I have some leftover pizza in the refrigerator. Let me warm it up in the microwave. It'll be nice not to think about work for a few hours."

Tom had never told Caroline what he actually did for a living. He had told her that he was just another boring consultant in a city that was brimming with them. But even though Caroline made more money that he did and was outwardly more successful in her career, she still seemed to really respect Tom and enjoy his company.

Caroline settled down on the sofa as Tom headed over to the refrigerator to try to find the leftover pizza that he hoped was still there.

Suddenly, there was another knock at his door.

Tom opened the door to his apartment and Melissa was standing there.

"It went very badly at work today Tom. My producer flatly rejected the story. In fact, she pretty much threatened to fire me if I ever brought this up to her again. We need to talk about what we should do next."

Tom realized that he had a potential disaster on his hands if Melissa discovered Caroline in his apartment. "Now is not a really good time for me Melissa. Why don't we meet up in a couple of hours to talk about this?"

Melissa could tell that there was some activity going on inside. "Don't be silly Tom," she said as she brushed by him and into the apartment. "I just need a couple of minutes to talk to you..."

After taking a couple of steps into the apartment, Melissa froze when she spotted scantily-clad Caroline sitting on the sofa.

"I didn't realize that you had company Tom. What is she doing here?"

Caroline smiled confidently as she turned and waved at Melissa. "Hey there sweetie. We were just watching the Stanford game. Would you like to join us?"

Melissa was not amused. "What is going on here Tom? Are you guys dating? Have you been seeing someone else behind my back? Why is it that every time I turn around lately you are with this trollop?"

"He can be friends with whomever he wants sweetie. You don't own him. It's a free country the last time I checked." To Melissa, it seemed as if Caroline was really enjoying this confrontation.

Tom knew that he was in a huge amount of trouble now. He turned to Melissa and tried to explain himself. "She just dropped by to watch the game. There is nothing nefarious going on here. You know how much I care about you..."

Melissa was getting even angrier. "Let me see if I have got this straight. I come over to your apartment and I find you chugging down beers with an ex-girlfriend that is dressed up like some sort of sexed-up sports goddess and I am not supposed to be upset about it?"

"That is not what is happening," Tom said weakly, but even he was not really convinced by that statement.

By that time Caroline had gotten up from the sofa and had come over to join the conversation. "Melinda dear, if you ever want to hold on to a man you have got to tone down this jealousy. This is the second time that I have seen you explode like this. I'm tempted to think that you might be a little mentally unbalanced."

"My name is Melissa, and I'll unbalance your face if you push me any farther you little witch." Melissa angrily pointed her finger right in Caroline's face. "I know what you are trying to do, and I don't like it one bit. Be warned - most people that choose to cross me end up regretting it deeply."

In response, Caroline just grinned. She did not seem alarmed by Melissa's threats in the slightest.

Melissa turned her attention to Tom, and she was still visibly angry. "Tom, from the moment you came into my life it has been a mess. I have been shot at, I have been hospitalized, I was assaulted by a gang of thugs on the street, I have had to constantly look over my shoulder to see if 'secret agents' are following me, and today I almost lost a job that I truly love. I have risked my life and my career for you, and now I see that I cannot really trust you at all. Well, you know what Tom? We are through. Finished. Please forget that you ever knew me."

With that, Melissa turned and bolted down the hallway toward the elevators.

Caroline still had a smug little smile on her face. "What was that all about? Why would she think that 'secret agents' are chasing her around?"

Tom didn't want to reveal too much to Caroline. "I am not sure. I think that she is just upset. Wait right here while I go talk to her."

Tom bolted down the hallway toward the spot where Melissa was waiting for the elevator to arrive. Melissa saw Tom coming and was the first to speak.

"Don't worry Tom – your secrets are safe with me. I won't reveal them to anyone."

Tom wasn't concerned as much about that as he was about losing Melissa.

"She is just a friend Melissa. You have got to believe that."

"I'll believe that when you start believing that Tom. I can see how she looks at you, and more importantly I can see how you look at her. I have been through this kind of thing before, and I am not going to go through it again. I truly believed that we had a shot at something real, but now I can see that I really don't know you at all."

Tom was not that good at this sort of thing, and he found himself at a loss for words as Melissa stepped on to the elevator.

"Melissa – don't go..."

"Goodbye Tom," Melissa said sternly as the elevator doors closed.

Caroline had been trying to listen in on their conversation from just inside the open door of Tom's apartment. She had only been able to hear a little bit of it, but from what she had gathered things were moving in the direction that she had hoped. When Tom got back to the apartment, she did her best to try to comfort him.

"Is she okay? I hope that she isn't too upset with me..."

"Don't worry about it Caroline," Tom said dejectedly. "You just came over to watch the game. If she is going to get this jealous over all of my friendships, then maybe it is a good thing that we just broke up."

Caroline smiled broadly. "Well, I know just the thing to cheer you up. Let's grab a few more beers and watch the rest of this game. In the old days there were only a few things that could make you smile more than a Stanford victory."

After grabbing a few more beers from the refrigerator, they settled back down on the couch and resumed watching the game. This time, however, Caroline had cuddled up right next to him. Having her so close awakened some feelings in Tom that he had kept repressed for a very long time.

Caroline knew that after a few more beers Tom would not be able to put up any resistance whatsoever. Over the years, Caroline had learned that men that had just broken up with their girlfriends were particularly vulnerable. While Tom and Melissa had been chatting out in the hall, Caroline had pulled out her phone and had set it to record video. She had placed it up on a cabinet facing the couch at a perfect angle to catch any action that would be happening.

After a couple of more beers, Caroline pounced.

Tom didn't have a chance.

Chapter 42

After her confrontation with Tom, Melissa raced back to her apartment and eventually cried herself to sleep. When she awoke the next morning, she was feeling a bit better and she found herself wondering if she had overreacted. Perhaps Tom was just being friendly with Caroline, and perhaps they had just been innocently watching the game. Had she just ruined her best relationship in years over nothing? Were her instincts totally wrong? If she was wrong, would Tom ever be able to forgive her?

Melissa continued to mentally torture herself as she showered, dressed and had breakfast. Her head was full of doubts and she was not sure what to do next. In her heart she knew that she still definitely wanted to be with Tom, and she still very much wanted to help him stop the terror attack that his agency was planning for New Year's Eve. But there was also a part of her that was feeling extremely hurt. Would she ever be able to fully trust Tom if sexy ex-girlfriends kept coming back into the picture?

Melissa put on her coat and prepared to leave her apartment, and as she opened the door she noticed that a large manila envelope was lying on her welcome mat. On the outside of the envelope someone had written the words "For Melissa" on it. She opened up the envelope, and inside was a DVD with a post-it note on it. Someone had written the words "Watch This" on the post-it note.

Melissa was quite eager to get to the studio so that she could get some work done, but her curiosity got the better of her. She brought the DVD back inside and put it into her DVD player.

What Melissa saw next absolutely horrified her. On her television screen she could see Tom and Caroline passionately kissing on the sofa in his apartment. At one point, Caroline turned her head toward the camera and flashed an evil grin before turning back to Tom. Obviously the video had been taken by Caroline, and she apparently wanted to send a very clear message to Melissa. After a few more moments, Melissa turned off the television in disgust. She couldn't bear to watch any more. As she walked away from the television, the sting of betrayal caused her heart to flood with anger. In a fit of rage she hurled the mug of coffee that she had been holding across the room.

"I hate you!" Melissa screamed that statement several times as tears flooded into her eyes. Throughout her tumultuous childhood Melissa had felt the pain of rejection over and over again, and now it felt like all of those old wounds were being freshly reopened.

She felt like killing both of them. Melissa was normally not a violent person, but if Tom had been standing in front of her right then she would have been very tempted to take his life.

Melissa felt like a fool for trusting Tom. He had seemed so sincere.

Melissa angrily paced around her apartment for a few more minutes and then in a moment of extreme anger she grabbed the baseball bat that she kept by her front door for protection and she smashed her television with it.

Realizing what she had just done, Melissa sank to the floor and curled up into a ball and started crying like a baby. Her head was full of bitter questions. Why did life always have to turn out like this? Why did men always have to be pigs? Why did every relationship have to fail? Why couldn't she ever seem to be able to find love? Was something wrong with her?

Melissa remained on the floor for most of the next hour. Stretches of anguish and despair were interspersed with fits of frustration and rage. All of the pain that Melissa had experienced since childhood came flooding back, and Melissa knew that she never wanted to experience anything like this ever again.

Finally, Melissa decided that the only thing that would keep her from going insane would be to get everything related to Tom out of her life forever. She got up and deleted Tom's information from her cell phone and she threw all of the gifts that he had ever given to her into the trash.

She sat down at her computer and started deleting all of the emails that Tom had ever sent her. Eventually she came to the recording that Tom had made that discussed the bombings that the agency was planning for New Year's Eve. She wanted nothing to do with Tom any longer, but something in her heart told her that she should at least do something to try to keep all of those innocent people from being murdered.

She already knew that taking the story to her network again was futile and would probably get her fired. But she did know one outlet that would likely be willing to get this information out to the public.

Melissa rapidly composed an email to "Diesel" and included everything that Tom had given to her about the New Year's Eve plot. She hoped that "Diesel" would decide to get this information out to his millions of readers. Melissa hit the send button and shut down her computer.

As far as Melissa was concerned, that would be the last time that she would ever have anything to do with Tom or the crazy world that he was involved in. She was going to ask her bosses to let her go back to New York City as soon as possible, and she was going to do her best to permanently forget Tom and everything else that had happened during her time in Washington.

Chapter 43

Russ had been trying to keep the promises that he had made to his wife.

He really had been.

But lately he had been sneaking out from time to time to check his email and catch up on the news from around the world. And today, his jaw was hanging open as he read the email and listened to the recording that "Candy Cane" had just sent to him. He honestly had a really hard time believing that any of it was actually true.

Yes, "Candy Cane" had never given him bad information before, but she had never sent him anything remotely as explosive as this bombshell.

If the recording that he had just listened to was accurate, a secret government intelligence agency was planning to orchestrate a terror attack that would absolutely dwarf what had happened on 9/11. Thousands would be killed by dirty bombs in Times Square, and the bank account records of tens of millions of Americans would be wiped out. The entire nation would be plunged into utter chaos. Considering how badly the recent financial crash had already damaged the nation's economy, a blow of this magnitude would be absolutely devastating.

But then again, there was the possibility that this could be the giant hoax that "Candy Cane" had been setting him up for this entire time. If Russ put this out to his millions of readers and then nothing happened, it could destroy his credibility permanently. That is something that Russ did not want to see happen.

And if he did publish this recording and all of the other information about the terror plot that "Candy Cane" had just sent him on his blogs, Russ knew that there was a really good chance that his family could be placed in a tremendous amount of danger. Russ had promised his wife that things would be different now. Russ had promised her that he was going to make the safety and security of his family his top priority.

Russ really wished that a big network like ANN had run with this story, but he also understood why they would never do such a thing. ANN would never roll a huge national security story like this out without government approval, and if a black budget government agency was truly behind this plot then they would never get that approval.

Plus, Russ knew that there were probably deep cover agents embedded at ANN that would move heaven and earth to kill a story like this. So Russ understood why "Candy Cane" had sent this information to him after she had exhausted all of her other options.

Russ stared at his computer screen and exhaled. His wife would not approve of what he was about to do one bit.

Russ took another sip of his coffee and started typing. If he truly was going to retire from blogging, he might as well go out with a bang.

Chapter 44

Melissa had gone to sleep that night relieved that she would never have to deal with Tom or any of the craziness in his world ever again.

But when she awoke about 2 AM in the morning, she instantly knew that something was wrong and that she wasn't alone.

She reached over and turned on a lamp, and she screamed when she saw that two men were standing at the end of her bed.

One of them looked like a common street thug. His straight black hair was greased back and his leather jacket looked like something a gangster from the 1970s might wear.

The other man, on the other hand, looked like something out of a horror movie. Two devilish red eyes peered out at her from underneath a black shrouded cloak. He was much taller and significantly more muscular than the street thug standing next to him.

"What do you want? I don't want any trouble," Melissa stammered as she sat up in her bed.

The gangster in the leather jacket smiled. "We want you. I am afraid that you are going to have to come with us."

Melissa screamed in terror as she bolted toward the door to her bathroom. Once inside the bathroom, she slammed the door behind her and braced her back against it in an attempt to keep her intruders out.

"Take whatever you want. I won't call the police. Just take what you want and go."

Without warning, the bathroom door that Melissa was bracing herself against shuddered greatly and there was a loud cracking sound. Melissa looked over and saw that a huge fist had punched a hole through the bathroom door just a few inches away from her right shoulder.

The greasy little gangster peered through the hole that had just been created. "Do you see what my friend can do? Do you really think that a flimsy bathroom door is going to keep you safe?"

Melissa screamed again and frantically started searching the bathroom for a weapon.

There was another loud cracking sound and the bathroom door flew off of its hinges and into the bathroom. Melissa had pressed herself up against the far wall and she started throwing things at the intruders as they entered.

"Stay away from me! I will kill you!" Melissa pulled out a pair of scissors and pointed it threateningly at them.

The intruders did not seem concerned at all. The man in the black shrouded cloak grabbed her right arm and twisted it until Melissa released the scissors. Then he pulled out a syringe and violently injected it into her right shoulder.

As Melissa lost consciousness, she was certain that she was about to die. She felt panic consume her as she thought about everything that she had missed out on in life. She tried to summon the strength to lash out at the intruders one last time, but suddenly she felt extremely weak.

Then everything went black.

Chapter 45

Jessup cringed as he answered his cell phone. He knew who was calling and he also knew that it was not going to be pleasant. Nobody in the agency really ever looked forward to hearing from Lilith, because when she called that probably meant that you were in big trouble.

Jessup tried to remain calm as he spoke into the phone. "What can I do for you Commandant?"

"You can tell me what the hell is going on over there Jessup. Can I assume that you have listened to the recording by now?"

Of course Jessup had listened to it. Thanks to an anonymous blogger named "Diesel", the recording had gone mega-viral on the Internet and millions of people had listened to it by this point.

"Yes, I have listened to the recording Commandant."

"Can you explain to me how in the world a private conversation that we had in your own office was recorded and subsequently broadcast all over the Internet?"

Jessup felt his legs begin to tremble in fear. He had heard stories about what Lilith did to other members of the agency that had failed her.

"Honestly, I have no idea how it happened. Nobody is more paranoid about security than I am. We sweep for listening devices twice a day and I follow our security procedures to the letter. It is just unthinkable that something like this has happened."

Lilith's voice sounded very cold. "And yet it did happen. I have to answer to some very powerful people, and this has threatened to derail some very important plans that have taken years to develop. Do you have any idea how much of a mess you have made?"

Jessup felt himself swallow involuntarily. "I can assure you that nothing like this will ever happen again. You know that I have served the agency faithfully for many years. I will do whatever I can to prove my worth to the organization."

"Yes, you have served us well for many years Jessup, and so you will be given one chance to redeem yourself. One of your specialties is interrogation, and tonight a subject will be delivered to your office that you will personally be in charge of interrogating. She is a reporter for American News Network that was trying to get that recording broadcast on the air. Thankfully, The Order was tipped off about it and they sent in a 'specialist' to grab her. This 'specialist' will drop her off at your office tonight after midnight. He does not speak and you are not to speak to him. But don't worry – you can't miss him. He is over seven feet tall and he wears a black shrouded cloak. Once she has been delivered into your custody, you are to use every possible method that you can to find out who made this recording and how she got her hands on it. Am I making myself clear?"

When Lilith mentioned The Order, Jessup's anxiety instantly doubled. Without a doubt, Lilith had a well-deserved reputation for being brutal, but what Jessup had heard about The Order was truly terrifying. Jessup knew that if he messed up this assignment that he might as well consider his life to be over.

"Yes Commandant. I shall do my very best."

"Good. We are also going to make an all-out push to capture this blogger who identifies himself as 'Diesel'. Dozens of agents from our western offices are descending on western Montana as we speak. They will be blanketing the cities and towns of western Montana with passive listening devices, facial recognition cameras, automated license plate readers and mobile backscatter scanners. We are even going to have a couple of unmanned surveillance drones watching things from the air. If this guy even so much as sneezes in public we will know about it."

"I will do my best to get to the bottom of this Commandant. I will not fail you again."

"You better not fail Jessup, because if you do I shall have your head on a stick." With that, the call abruptly ended and Jessup suddenly realized that his entire body was trembling.

Jessup's hands were shaking so badly from fear that he dropped his cell phone as he attempted to put it away. He loved the agency and truly believed in what they were doing, but he also knew that failure was not tolerated and he had just failed very badly.

A burst of anger flooded through Jessup as he thought about what he had almost lost because of one stupid reporter and one idiot blogger. This was one interrogation that he was going to relish. Once he got his hands on this reporter, not only was he going to get the information out of her that he needed, he was also going to make her pay dearly. He just hoped that he would be able to get his hands on that idiot blogger at some point as well.

Chapter 46

After Melissa broke up with Tom, there was no longer anything holding him back from pursuing a relationship with Caroline, and the two of them had spent nearly every waking moment that they could with each other over the past few days. Tom had felt a really strong bond with Caroline when they were in high school, but that was nothing compared to what he was feeling now. There was almost something supernatural about how alluring Caroline could be. Just being around her was totally intoxicating, and Tom did not want to wake up from that feeling.

But Tom honestly did feel very badly about how things had ended with Melissa. He had tried to call her several times over the past few days, but he had not been able to reach her either at home or at work. Of course he fully understood that he had destroyed their personal relationship, but he did want to apologize for how he had acted and he also wanted to tell her to forget about going after the agency. He didn't want Melissa to be exposed to any more danger, and he truly wanted her to be able to go on with her life in peace.

Tom had decided that he didn't want to endanger anyone else that he cared about in his vendetta against the agency. That was especially true as far as Caroline was concerned. In fact, the more that he was around Caroline, the more he was tempted to just drop the whole thing and focus on developing his new relationship with her. He had no plans of ever telling her what he really did for a living, and he was hoping that once he left the agency that he would never even have to tell her about that part of his life.

Tom and Caroline were driving south on Interstate 495 as they headed home from a shopping trip at Tysons Corner Center. Tom had spent far more money than he could afford to on Caroline tonight, but Tom figured that since the agency had been paying him so much money that he should at least have some fun with it.

Traffic on 495 had slowed to a crawl this evening, but even that couldn't put Tom in a bad mood. "Those earrings look great on you Caroline," Tom said as he turned toward where she was sitting in the passenger seat. "I think that we made a great choice."

"I think that it was you that made a great choice, sweetie." Caroline smiled as the words came out. "You never had this kind of impeccable taste when we were in high school."

"A lot of things have changed since we were in high school. I was a pretty big idiot back then. Hopefully I have learned a lot as I have matured."

"I think that we all have."

An idea suddenly struck Tom. "One of these weekends we should really go down to Colonial Williamsburg. Have you ever been down there? It is one of those things that everyone should do at least once in their lives. It is the largest living history museum in the United States. I think that you would love it."

"That sounds wonderful Tom, but I actually had a surprise planned for this upcoming weekend. I have rented a yacht for us out at Annapolis. I thought that it would be the perfect stress reliever. We could go out Friday evening, spend the entire weekend on the boat, and then come back on Sunday more relaxed than we have been in ages. How does that sound?"

To Tom that sounded like heaven. "That sounds absolutely fantastic. But I don't know anything about sailing."

Caroline smiled, showing off her absolutely perfect teeth. "You just leave all of that to me. Like you, I have picked up quite a few tricks over the years. I think that you will be very impressed by my sailing abilities. Plus, I have a few other surprises planned for you as well."

Tom sure liked the sound of that. Right now he wanted to spend as much time with her as he possibly could. "Well, you can count me in. I can't believe how fortunate I am to be able to have found you again after all of these years. You seem almost too good to be true."

"Don't worry babe, I assure you that I am very, very real. I am the same girl that you broke up with when you went off to the U.S. Air Force Academy. Only I am much stronger and much more determined than I was back then. I've been to hell and back and I have learned a lot of hard lessons. For a long time I wondered if I would ever be able to get this opportunity. Now that I have it, I am going to make sure that you get everything that you deserve."

Those last few comments kind of puzzled Tom, but he quickly dismissed them. He was a man that was being absolutely consumed by infatuation, and men in that condition tend to overlook things. "I'm just glad for the road that eventually led me to you. I feel like I have gotten a second chance to do things right, and I don't plan on blowing it. From now on, my plan is to make your life as wonderful as I possibly can."

Tom looked over, and for a moment he thought that Caroline might be rolling her eyes at him. "Was that too sappy for you Caroline?"

"Not at all sweetie," Caroline responded. "Everything is just perfect. In fact, I can't wait to get you on the yacht this weekend. I think that when you see all of the things that I have planned for you that you will just explode."

Chapter 47

There was a little country church that Dottie and the kids liked to attend on Sunday mornings, but Russ didn't really care for church. And considering his recent troubles, he was trying to stay away from large gatherings of people as much as he could these days. So after he dropped off Dottie and the kids at church, Russ had decided to slip over to New Bern for a quiet breakfast. There was a little place right in the heart of New Bern called "Mrs. Patmire's Kitchen" that Russ just loved. Russ didn't know why it was called "Mrs. Patmire's Kitchen" since it was owned by a couple named Charlie and Kimberly Anderson. He had known Mr. and Mrs. Anderson for many, many years and they were truly gifted when it came to making breakfast.

"Mrs. Patmire's kitchen" sat up on a little hill that overlooked the rest of New Bern. During the summer, tourists would come by the restaurant for the view, but the locals kept coming back for the great food. This morning, however, the restaurant was almost entirely empty because most of the locals were still in church. Russ had already finished a huge platter of pancakes, but it wasn't time to go pick up his family yet, so he had pulled out a good novel that he had not had time to finish yet. Russ loved to read, but he never could find quite enough time for it.

After a few minutes of reading, Mrs. Anderson suddenly called out to get his attention. "Hey Russ – is that a military helicopter? What in the world is it doing right over New Bern?"

Russ looked out the window in the direction that Mrs. Anderson was pointing, and he was startled to see that a black helicopter was hovering directly over the center of town.

Russ instantly knew that this might mean trouble. Russ bolted from his table over to the south side of the restaurant. From there, he could see that the main road heading south out of town had been barricaded by black SUVs and he could see armed men dressed in black body armor all over the place.

Russ ran over to the north side of the restaurant and he could see that the main road heading north out of town had been barricaded in a similar manner, and there seemed to be even more armed men on that side. Russ could tell that they were forming a perimeter and were getting ready to move in toward the center of town.

Russ became very frantic. "Mrs. Anderson, can I use your basement for a couple of minutes?"

Mrs. Anderson had known Russ for a very long time, so this request did not trouble her. "Of course Russ. Is there anything that I can get for you?"

"No, I just need a few minutes on my computer." Russ grabbed his laptop and rapidly moved down into the basement. He was thankful that the Andersons had put in a Wi-Fi network a few years ago. Russ knew that he would only have a few minutes. He booted up his laptop and began writing...

Family, Friends and Readers:

I am at Mrs. Patmire's Kitchen in New Bern, Montana and I am about to be taken into custody by federal agents. I am going to do my best to elude them, but they appear to have the entire town surrounded. I have committed no crimes and there is no reason for them to be hunting me down except for the information that I have posted on my blogs. I have done my best to tell the American people the truth, and for that I am considered to be an enemy. If my disappearance will not convince people that the U.S. Constitution is dead, then I don't know what will.

If they are able to capture me, I am sure that they will take me far away from Montana. Hopefully they will allow me access to an attorney, but if not I hope that I will have some way of letting my family know where I have been taken. If you all don't hear anything from me in the days ahead, I hope that you will make every effort to try to find out what has happened to me. There have been stories of other patriots that have simply disappeared without a trace. I don't really believe in God, but please pray that will not happen to me. I cannot bear the thought of never seeing my wife and children ever again.

I love you Hunter. I am trusting you to take care of the family now.

I love you Kinley. Never be afraid to follow your dreams.

I love you Brynn. Be strong my sweet little one.

I love you Dottie. You have always been my best friend.

My love will always be with you all,

Diesel

Russ wrapped up what he was doing and closed his laptop. He stashed the laptop behind some very large containers of milk and moved to the bottom of the basement stairs.

What he heard next made his heart sink.

Russ could hear several agents questioning Mrs. Anderson upstairs, and he realized that there would be no magical escape for him this time.

Chapter 48

When Tom awoke late on Sunday morning, he discovered that his wrists and his ankles were wrapped in leather limb restraints similar to those commonly used in psychiatric facilities and that someone had used cords to tie those leather limb restraints very tightly to the posts of the queen size bed that he and Caroline had been sleeping on. Tom wasn't sure quite what to make of that. Was Caroline trying to play some kind of a game with him?

"Hey Caroline," he called out, but he received no response.

Caroline had definitely been right about the yacht. It was a 35-footer named "Retaliation" and it was absolutely stunning. The last couple of days out on the water with Caroline had been incredible, and it had made Tom rethink his life a bit. Maybe a quieter life would really suit him. He had definitely experienced more adventure than most other men would ever even dream about in an entire lifetime, and Tom was starting to think that now may be the time to get out of the game while he still could. But whatever happened, Tom was now more convinced than ever that he wanted his future to involve Caroline.

He was certain that it had cost Caroline a tremendous amount of money to rent the yacht for the weekend, but Caroline had done very well for herself up on Wall Street so Tom was not worried about that. He just wanted to get his hands and feet free so that he could get some breakfast.

Tom tried calling out to Caroline again. "Hey honey these restraints are cute and all, but could you untie me now? They are starting to get uncomfortable."

Caroline appeared in the doorway of the sleeping cabin with a cup of coffee in her hand. "I have no doubt that they are uncomfortable. It look me a while to get them that tight. It is a good thing that the sleeping drugs that I slipped into your drink last night did the trick."

Tom thought back to last night. They had shared quite a bit of wine as they sat out on the deck of the yacht watching the stars. Tom didn't remember much after that.

"Okay Caroline, you got me – but could you untie me now? I really am hungry for some breakfast."

"I don't think that you understand, my dear," Caroline began. "I am not going to be untying you. Otherwise you might find a way off of the yacht before it explodes."

Tom suddenly got a sinking feeling in his stomach. He struggled to free himself, but the restraints were extremely tight and were not budging.

"What do you mean Caroline? Are you trying to play some kind of little game with me?"

Caroline's voice suddenly got colder. "This isn't a game Tom. I have been planning this for a very, very long time. You have no idea how many scenarios I have imagined in my head over the years, but I always came back to the idea of killing you on a boat. There is something about an exploding boat that is just so darn dramatic."

Tom was starting to understand that she was dead serious. "Are you saying that you are going to blow up this yacht with me on it?"

"Now you are getting it sweetie. Today is the day that you are going to die. I am going to pay you back for all that you did to me, and nobody is ever going to find your body."

Panic started to pour over Tom. "Why would you do this Caroline? I honestly care about you. I thought that we had a really great time this weekend. Yes, I caused you pain in the past. I admit that. But can't we get past that? Killing me is not going to solve anything."

Caroline smiled as she pulled out a small knife. "Oh, but I think that it will. Well, at least it will make me feel better. You see Tom, you didn't just cause me pain when you broke up with me the day before you went off to the U.S. Air Force Academy – YOU RUINED MY LIFE!"

Caroline screamed as she hurled the small knife toward Tom. It sank into the headboard a couple of inches to the left of where his head was resting.

Caroline now had a crazed look in her eyes. "Don't worry Tom, I am not going to kill you yet. I just want to scare you a little first."

Caroline pulled out another little knife. "You know, they say on the commercial that these knives will cut through just about anything. Should we test out that theory Tom?"

Tom was frantically attempting to free himself now, but nothing was working. "Caroline, please, I never intended to hurt you. When I went off to the Air Force Academy we both agreed that our lives were heading in different directions. I thought that you were going to be fine."

"No Tom, I was not fine. We were both supposed to go to Stanford, remember? But then you got the bright idea that you were supposed to 'serve your country' instead. So you decided to go to the Air Force Academy. But I would have been fine with that. I would have been fine with a long distance relationship, and you said that you would be too. But then the day before you left, you called me over to your house and ended our relationship. I was absolutely crushed Tom. You have no idea."

Tom thought that maybe he could calm her down and talk her out of what she was about to do. "I am so sorry. I was a foolish young man back then. I didn't know how valuable our relationship was. I wish that I could go back and do things differently. But despite my mistakes, we finally found one another. After everything, we can finally have the future that we both wanted."

The expression on Caroline's face was resonating with extreme bitterness and resentment. Tom had never seen her like this before. "Tom, you are still as clueless as ever. Do you actually think that you can really undo all of the damage that you have done? Do you really think that you can make up for all of the years of pain that I suffered? When you broke up with me, I was PREGNANT. I was pregnant with twin boys, but I didn't tell you because I didn't want to ruin your dreams of going to the Air Force Academy."

That totally shocked Tom. "What happened? Do I have two sons out there that I don't know anything about?"

Caroline started screaming. "No, they are not alive! I had an abortion! I killed our sons Tom! Everyone was telling me that I wouldn't have any kind of a future as a single mother and so I aborted our boys and it was your fault Tom!"

Tom was stunned into silence. He didn't know what to say to that.

Caroline was sobbing as she continued her tirade. "And you know what Tom? They messed up the operation! They damaged me! After it was all over they told me that I could NEVER have any more children! For the rest of my life I would be barren!"

"I am so sorry Caroline," Tom said softly. "If I had only known..."

"What? You would have given up on the Air Force Academy to stay in California to be with me and our two boys? I seriously doubt that. You would have left just like all men eventually leave."

"Not all men are like that Caroline..."

"Don't presume to tell me about men! I have seen the same thing over and over during my years up in New York. All they want is sex, sex and more sex. When they finally tire of you they cast you aside as if nothing ever happened. Well, eventually I learned to use sex as a weapon. I used it to get what I want. And what I want right now is revenge."

"Isn't there another way Caroline? I swear that I want to make all of this up to you."

"How are you going to make it up to me Tom? After the botched abortion, I went absolutely crazy. My parents decided that they couldn't handle me anymore, and I spent most of the next two years in an insane asylum. Do you know what life in an insane asylum is like Tom? It was a LIVING HELL! Every night I stared up at the ceiling and I dreamed of what I would do to you if I ever got my hands on you. Now I finally have my chance."

As Tom looked into her eyes, all he could see was hate. It was almost as if the Caroline that he once knew was not in control and that he was talking to someone else entirely.

"Please Caroline. We once loved each other very much. I am asking for you to forgive me."

"Forgiveness? You think that you actually deserve forgiveness? I would never forgive you for what you did to me Tom. You will be lucky if I don't slice you up into a hundred different pieces and feed you to the fish before the boat blows up."

Caroline crawled up on to the bed and held her small knife right under Tom's nose. Tom struggled mightily against the restraints, but it didn't do any good.

Caroline smiled as she saw Tom squirm. "Don't struggle dear. Those are the kind of restraints that they use in mental hospitals. You aren't going to get loose."

Tom was sweating heavily now. He wasn't ready to die. "Caroline, I beg you not to do this. I don't want to die this way."

"You will die the way that I choose for you to die. I have been dreaming of this moment for a very long time. After I got out of the insane asylum, I told a few lies on my college applications and I got accepted into the University of Virginia. I packed up my car, drove across the country and I never looked back. I attended the undergraduate business school there, but I also took a number of Women's Studies courses. My professors in the Women's Studies department taught me to be strong and helped me reclaim my power as a woman. And today that is exactly what I choose to do. I choose to reclaim my power. I choose to make you feel pain for the pain that you caused me."

Caroline wrapped both hands around the handle of the knife and lifted it high above Tom. Tom rattled the entire bed as he desperately tried to shake himself loose. Caroline brought the blade down with all the force that she could muster and plunged it into his left shoulder.

Tom howled in pain and Caroline rolled off the bed and stood over where he was laying. "Oh, that is just for starters Tom. I have much more planned before the main event."

Tom looked over at his left shoulder. Not too much blood was coming from the wound, but that was because Caroline had left the knife in there. It hurt like hell, but there wasn't anything that Tom could do about it.

"Look at you," Caroline sneered as she walked over to the end of the bed. "Nobody loves you. I wrecked the only good relationship in your life. I think that reporter actually did love you. But now she is not going to miss you and nobody else will either. Even if you did have a funeral, I doubt that anyone would actually show up. Your life has been a selfish mess, and you won't even be leaving anyone behind to mourn for you. I wanted to totally destroy your life before I killed you, but the truth is that it was already a disaster before I even arrived on the scene. You have no family left, you barely have any money, and nobody will really remember you for long once you are gone. You are pathetic Tom McDowell."

Caroline turned and laughed as she headed out of the sleeping quarters. Despair flooded through Tom as he realized that she was exactly right. His life had been a total mess, and nobody was really going to miss him once he was gone.

Tom closed his eyes and he began to cry bitterly. He was not proud of how his life had turned out, and now it would be cut way too short. At that moment he would have given just about anything for a second chance to do things differently.

Chapter 49

In desperation, Tom started to look all around the cabin for anything that might help him escape. Tom had been an intelligence agent for many years, but he could see no way out of this. He screamed in frustration as he struggled to free himself from the tight limb restraints.

Finally, Tom closed his eyes and began to wonder if he should just accept that his death was imminent. He had never believed in God or had been religious in any way, but at that moment he was desperate enough to accept any help that he might be able to get.

"Please help," Tom whispered toward the ceiling.

That made Tom feel a little silly, but he didn't know what else to do. There was no way that he was going to be able to free his wrists and ankles from the limb restraints without some help.

Suddenly, Tom remembered his voice-activated phone. He looked over his left shoulder and saw that his phone was still on the nightstand where he had left it. In fact, it was only a few inches away from the post that his left arm was tied to.

In a flash, Tom knew what he had to do. It was a longshot, but it was certainly better than just waiting for Caroline to come back and kill him.

"Phone on."

Tom's phone came to life.

"Set self-destruct to maximum setting. Activate self-destruct in fifteen seconds."

For security reasons, all phones issued by the agency had a self-destruct feature. Tom had seen an agency phone explode during training, and they could pack quite a punch for such a little device.

Tom turned his head away from his phone as best he could, and he braced his body for what was about to happen. After a few moments a loud explosion filled the room. Tom felt sharp pain all up and down his left arm and left shoulder.

Tom turned his head to see what had happened. His left arm and left shoulder had absorbed some of the blast and had been damaged, but he was absolutely elated to see that the cord holding his left arm to the bed post had been severed.

He was almost free.

Wincing in pain, Tom grabbed the handle of the knife that Caroline had jammed into his left shoulder and he slowly pulled it out. The agony was excruciating, but Tom realized that he didn't have any moments to spare. Once the knife was out, he quickly used it to sever the other three cords that were holding him to the bed.

He switched the knife into his right hand, bolted out of the bed and pressed himself behind the cabin door. He knew that Caroline would return at any moment.

Suddenly, he heard Caroline call out to him from down the hall. "Did I hear some noise from in there? Are you still trying to free yourself dear? I told you that it was not going to be possible."

Tom could hear her footsteps as she approached the sleeping quarters. She was going to be in for quite a surprise.

"We still have a little bit of time before I must leave the yacht. I thought that we could have some fun with a knife and a bottle of bleach before I say goodbye."

Tom heard her stop right outside the door.

"Tom, where did you go?"

She took one step into the sleeping quarters and Tom made his move. At that point, instincts and years of training took over. The knife was in her back before Tom even realized what had happened. Tom staggered past her, down the hall and up the stairs on to the main deck.

Up on the main deck, Tom spotted the small motorized lifeboat that Caroline had obviously been planning to use for her escape. As Tom got into the lifeboat and lowered it into the ocean, everything was eerily quiet. It took a few attempts, but he finally got the lifeboat started and he headed toward the shore.

Tom was surprised to see how far from shore the yacht was. He hadn't realized that Caroline had taken them so far out. Tom knew that it was going to take him quite a while to reach land. During his journey toward shore, Tom kept looking back at the yacht to see if he could spot any signs of activity.

After about 20 minutes, there was an enormous explosion and the yacht was consumed by a massive fireball. Caroline had definitely not skimped on the explosives.

Tom was thrilled to be alive, but he also felt like a part of his soul had just been ripped out of him. Hours earlier he had been dreaming of a bright future with Caroline, and now she was gone for good.

Chapter 50

The last several days had been absolutely nightmarish for Melissa. The first thing that she remembered after being abducted was waking up lying in a fetal position in a cell that was so cramped that she could barely move around in it. Melissa estimated that it was probably about four feet long by four feet wide, and it was too short for her to be able to stand all the way up. Melissa was a little claustrophobic anyway, so this was driving her bananas. Her cell was in the middle of a row of cells that were facing outward toward a larger room. Melissa could not see into the other cells, but as far as she could tell they were not occupied.

Melissa was becoming incredibly frustrated due to the fact that she was not able to straighten up or walk around. Melissa had never felt so closed in before in her entire life. Of course it didn't help that her captors had been keeping the room incredibly cold. In fact, her captors had kept the room so cold that she could literally see her breath. She was constantly shivering hour after hour with no relief. Melissa had been dressed in a short-sleeved orange prison shirt and matching orange prison pants at some point when she had been out cold. The thought of any of the thugs that she had seen so far removing her clothing and dressing her in this outfit sent a cold chill up her spine. Melissa constantly felt like screaming, but she knew that it wouldn't do any good. Nobody would hear her screams.

At times Melissa would try to go to sleep, but her captors immediately responded by flooding the room with extremely loud heavy metal music. Melissa didn't want them to know how much they were wearing her down, but she had to admit that what they were doing was working.

She didn't even know if she had the words to describe how desperately she wanted to get out of there.

But she had already decided that she was never going to willingly tell them about Tom. She knew that if she mentioned his name that it would probably mean the end of his life. No matter how disastrously their relationship had ended, Melissa knew that Tom would never betray her and she desperately did not want to betray him.

When she first realized that they were going to torture her, she said a silent prayer asking God to keep her from saying Tom's name. Melissa wasn't "religious" by any stretch of the imagination, but at a time like this she figured that she could use all the help that she could get. They had injected her with all kinds of drugs that had really messed with her mind over the past couple of days, but as far as she knew she had not told them about Tom so far.

Of course the waterboarding had been the worst part. She had already lost count of how many times she had been waterboarded, and there had been several times when she had been absolutely convinced that she was about to die. Prior to this, Melissa had never known what it felt like to be drowning, but now she was intimately familiar with that sensation.

In addition to bombarding her with endless questions about where she got the recording from and who she may have given it to, her interrogators also frequently asked her about some organization called "the Remnant" that she had never even heard of. She made up some false information about "the Remnant" just to get the torture to stop, but when the torturers came back later they were even angrier than before because the information had turned out to be false.

Melissa figured that she would die in this place. She knew that they would never let her get out and go back on television after what they had done to her. Melissa understood that once they got the information that they wanted out of her that they would kill her.

As Melissa thought about that grisly reality, the door to the room suddenly swung open. A couple of well-dressed agents dragged a slightly overweight, middle-aged white male into the room. He looked like he had been beaten up very badly and there was blood caked all over his goatee. He appeared to be conscious even though he was in very rough shape. The agents rudely tossed the man into the cell next to Melissa, locked it, and walked out of the room.

For about an hour, neither of them spoke. There was a solid wall between them, so Melissa could not see the other prisoner that had just been brought in. But she could hear his unsteady breathing, and a couple of times it sounded like he was trying to cough up something. Melissa hoped that it wasn't his own blood that he was coughing up. Finally, she decided to say something.

"Are you okay?"

There was an answer from the other cell. "Did I look like I was okay when they brought me in?"

"I'm sorry. I know that you must be in pain. It is just that I haven't had anyone to talk to for days other than the thugs that have been torturing me."

"They have been torturing you?"

"Yeah. I am sure they will start with you in just a little while. The waterboarding is the worst. Look over toward the middle of the room. That is where they do it."

Russ peered out from his cell and he could see what she was talking about. Just the thought of being waterboarded was enough to send a wave of nausea washing over him. For a moment he thought that he was going to be sick, but then he recovered. This was much worse than Russ had ever imagined. He was almost afraid to ask the female prisoner in the other cell any more questions, but his curiosity got the better of him.

"Who are these people? CIA? FBI? DHS?"

Melissa decided that she wasn't ready to reveal everything that she knew about their captors to the other prisoner. Her torturers did not realize it, but the truth was that she was certain that she knew exactly who they were. They precisely fit the description of the agency that Tom said that he worked for, and the symbol of an unfinished pyramid with an all-seeing eye above it was everywhere. But Melissa did not trust this other prisoner enough to tell him all of that just yet.

"I don't know," Melissa responded. "I don't even know what city we are in."

"I think that we are in Washington D.C. - at least that is what I overheard some of them saying when the plane I was being transported on landed."

"A plane? Where did they capture you?"

"I was living in Montana. Apparently the feds didn't like what I was putting up on my blogs."

Melissa's eyes got really big. She suddenly realized who she was talking to.

"Diesel?"

There was silence from the other cell.

"Is that you Diesel?"

"How do you know that name?"

"I am Candy Cane."

"You are Candy Cane? So you are the reporter that has been sending me all that stuff?"

"I am afraid so."

"Did you tell them about me?"

"No. I never even knew what your real name was. All I had was an email address. I think they found you all on their own."

"And they are torturing you even though you are a reporter?"

"Yes."

"Haven't you been able to make a call or contact an attorney?"

"I don't think that is how it works in this world. I don't expect that either of us will ever get out of here alive."

The prisoner in the other cell fell silent again. At that moment, Melissa truly wished that she had never sent that recording to him. By doing so, she had destroyed his life.

"I am so sorry Diesel. I never should have gotten you involved in this."

"Don't be sorry. This is tyranny, and tyranny must be resisted. If earlier generations of Americans had not been willing to give everything in the fight against tyranny our nation never would have been free."

"That is true, but I still feel terrible that you are going to die with me in this horrible place."

"Perhaps there is still hope that the mainstream news will start reporting on this recording and that the people doing this will be exposed. If that happens, perhaps it is conceivable that we could be set free at some point. Did you send this recording to anyone else?"

"Other than the people at my network that I talked to, the only person that I sent it to was you. And you can forget about it getting aired on ANN. After my producer listened to it she killed the story and threatened to fire me."

———————

Standing on the other side of the one-way mirror, Jessup, Wolfe and Kalon were all smiling.

"See," Jessup declared to the others, "I told you that we could get them to talk if we put them in the same room together."

Chapter 51

Tom had not gone into the office on Monday. He called the agency and left word that he had come down with the flu, which seemed credible since the entire nation was in the midst of the worst flu outbreak in years.

Tom needed a day to recover physically and to patch up his wounds. In particular, the knife wound in his left shoulder was really bad. He could still use his left arm, but not without a tremendous amount of pain. At some point he knew that he would need to go see a doctor about that.

Tom also needed a day to recover emotionally. He had just lost a woman that he truly believed that he was falling in love with. How could he have misjudged Caroline so horribly? Was he really that bad a judge of character? Had he been blinded by infatuation? Those were questions that he did not have any easy answers to.

After he was done tending to his wounds, Tom wanted to catch up on what had been going on inside the agency lately. All of this time, the cell phone spyware that Tom had installed on Jessup's phone was still working, but Tom had not had a chance to listen to the conversations that had been recorded for quite a few days. Tom retrieved the computer where the recordings were being stored and he started listening to them.

When Tom got to the conversation between Jessup and Lilith about the female prisoner that was being brought in, his jaw just about dropped to the floor. Tom instantly knew who they were talking about, and he was absolutely horrified.

How had they found out about Melissa? If they knew about her, did they also know about him?

A surge of panic swept through Tom. The entire nature of the little game that he had been playing had just dramatically changed.

Tom tried to calm himself down. If his cover had been blown, then they almost certainly would have searched his apartment by now, and there was no sign that had happened while he was away for the weekend.

In addition, Tom realized that if the agency knew what he was doing that Jessup would not rest until Tom was dead. Nobody was trying to kill him yet, so Tom took that as a good sign.

But he also knew that they would torture Melissa night and day until they had gotten the information out of her that they wanted. And probably the number one piece of information on their list was the identity of the person that had given her that recording.

Tom was hoping that Melissa would be strong and not give up his name, but he also knew that almost everyone had a breaking point.

Tom realized that he needed to move quickly. He grabbed a few things, put on a jacket and headed for the door. He had no idea how he was going to get Melissa out of there, but he knew that he had to try.

He also understood that marching Melissa past 40 other agents and out the front door of one of the most secure facilities that Tom had ever seen in his entire life was not going to be easy.

There had to be another way, and Tom was going to head into D.C. tonight to take a closer look at that office building that he had been working in.

Chapter 52

When Tom went to work on Tuesday morning, he was carrying a large gym bag with him. There was nothing unusual about that, because Tom frequently went to the gym after work. But what Tom had never told anyone was that there was a large pouch in the gym bag that was made from material that made its contents invisible to metal detectors. Tom figured that someday that pouch would become useful, and today was that day.

As Tom headed to his office, he took the long way so that he could swing by the room that he believed that Melissa was being held in. Tom was certain that the room containing Melissa would be guarded 24 hours a day, and today there was only one room with a guard stationed outside of it – Room #66. Tom nodded to the guard as he walked past, and once he reached his office he quickly stashed his gym bag in the coat closet.

Tom spent the rest of the morning eliminating everything from his computer and from his files that the agency might find useful. Tom knew that this was the last time that he would ever return to his office. In fact, Tom was not entirely convinced that he would even be able to survive to the end of the day. The odds were definitely against him.

About noon, there was a knock on his office door. Tom went over and opened it, and Jessup was standing there.

"Hey there McDowell," Jessup began, "a bunch of us are headed out to lunch. Would you like to join us?"

Tom could see Wolfe, Kalon and several other agents standing there with Jessup. It was very rare for anyone to turn down any kind of an invitation from Jessup. In fact, his "invitations" were pretty much understood to be direct orders by everyone in the agency.

Tom could feel a trickle of sweat run down the back of his neck. "I think that I will just eat in my office if that is okay. I am still trying to get over this bout with the flu."

Jessup looked at him kind of funny. "Is everything okay Tom? You haven't seemed yourself lately."

"Yeah," Tom responded, "I think that it is just a little woman trouble. One of my ex-girlfriends has an explosive disposition."

Jessup smiled at that. "We've all been there at some point McDowell. But there are always more fish in the sea."

"That is very true."

"Well, we're off. But I still want to talk to you. Can we chat once I get back?"

"Sure thing boss." And with that, Jessup and his entourage headed down the hall.

Tom closed his office door and waited for exactly two minutes. Then he bolted over to his coat closet and pulled his gym bag out.

Tom wasn't going to get a better opportunity than this. Tom put on his overcoat, grabbed weapons with both hands and headed out into the hallway.

Chapter 53

Room #66 was a substantial walk from Tom's office, and as Tom marched briskly down the hall he desperately hoped that no other agents would suddenly pop out of their offices. Tom was trying to use his overcoat to shield his weapons, but if he ran into another agent he would surely be questioned about what he was doing. He didn't want the shooting to begin before it had to.

Fortunately, the hallways were completely silent. Tom got over to Room #66 in just a few moments, but there was still the matter of the armed guard at the door.

Tom spoke directly to him as he approached the door. "Hello there, agent Campbell. I am here to transfer the prisoner to another room."

Campbell had been with the agency for a very long time, and he was immediately skeptical. "Which prisoner are you talking about McDowell? And I am going to need to see some authorization."

Tom didn't count on there being another prisoner. "Jessup wants to see the female reporter right away. I am supposed to bring her to him right now."

Campbell was definitely not convinced by Tom's act, and his eyes had drifted to what Tom was carrying in his left arm. "I am still going to need to see some authorization. And hey – why are you carrying a shotgun around the office?"

Tom knew that this was not going to be easy. Without saying another word he pointed the tranquilizer gun that he was carrying in his right hand directly at Campbell and fired. The tranquilizer dart hit him directly in the stomach and he was unconscious within moments.

The commotion had not drawn anyone else into the hallway, and Tom was very thankful for that. He quickly lifted the key card for Room #66 off of Campbell's belt, used it to open the door, and dragged Campbell's body inside.

"Melissa, are you in here?" Tom scanned the room but he couldn't see her.

"I'm over here," Tom could hear a tired female voice declare from one of the short, narrow prison cells along the left side of the room.

"I'm getting you out of this place," Tom said as he opened her cell with the key card that he had taken from Campbell. "Can you walk?"

"Yeah, I think so." Melissa pointed over to the cell next to her. "But we've got to take Russ too. He is the blogger that I told you about. They dragged him in here because he posted that recording you made on the Internet."

Tom knew that trying to escape with another prisoner would make the odds against them even higher. "He'll slow us down Melissa."

"Well, I'm not leaving him behind." Melissa was banking on the fact that Tom did not have time to argue.

"Okay, okay, but we have got to go NOW. Any hesitation could cost all of us our lives."

Tom opened his cell and Russ followed them to the door without saying a word. Before opening the door to the hallway, Tom put his finger to his lips to indicate that Melissa and Russ should be silent. Tom peeked out into the hall, and once he saw that it was empty, he waved for them to follow.

Tom rapidly moved two doors down, used Campbell's key card to open up Room #64, and motioned for Melissa and Russ to come inside. Room #64 was an unoccupied office, and it had a very large window that looked out on to K Street.

"There is no way in the world that we are getting out of here through the front entrance. Russ, help me push this coat closet in front of the door. We are going to need to buy a little extra time."

Tom set his shotgun down, and in just a few moments Russ and Tom had pushed the coat closet in front of the door.

Tom picked his shotgun back up and motioned for Melissa and Russ to move away from the window. "Get behind me guys. You don't want to get hit by flying glass."

Tom fired his shotgun and it shattered the large window that looked out on to K Street. That caused a loud alarm to start shrieking.

Tom waved Melissa and Russ over to the window. He raised his voice so that he could be heard over the alarm. "Do you see the maintenance platform two floors below? I need you to jump down to it from this window. If we stay here we are dead."

Normally Melissa would have never dreamed of doing such a thing, but desperation took over and she didn't ask any questions. She steadied herself in the frame of the shattered window and jumped. She made it down on to the platform but her momentum almost carried her over the safety railing.

As soon as it was apparent that Melissa was okay and she had moved to the side, Russ also jumped. He landed a little awkwardly on his right ankle, but he knew that he didn't have time to complain. As soon as Russ was clear, Tom also jumped, still holding his shotgun.

Melissa looked at Tom skeptically. "So what do we do now? We don't know how to lower this thing, and once they figure out that we are out here we will be sitting ducks."

"We aren't going to lower this thing. Stand back." Tom reloaded his shotgun, pointed it at the office window in front of him and fired. The blast completely shattered the window. "We need to get to the other side of the fourth floor."

Tom kicked in a few pieces of broken glass that were still in the window frame and bolted into the office on the fourth floor that the maintenance platform was adjacent to. Fortunately, this office was also empty.

After they had all stepped into the office, Tom looked Melissa and Russ directly in the eyes. "This floor is occupied by a law firm, so nobody should be armed. There is a room on the opposite side of the building that we need to get to. Follow me."

Tom bolted into the hallway, and Melissa and Russ were right on his heels. A secretary screamed when she saw Tom reloading his shotgun, and there was quite a bit of commotion as frightened lawyers scurried to get out of their path. In just a few moments they had reached their destination.

Tom opened the office door and pointed his shotgun at the terrified lawyer in front of him.

"Get out."

The terrified lawyer hastily complied, keeping as much distance between himself and Tom as he could the entire time.

Once the lawyer was gone, Tom once again warned Melissa and Russ to get behind him. He fired his shotgun at the office window, totally shattering it. Tom waved the other two over, and all three of them went up to the window and peered down into the alley below.

"Do you see that garbage dumpster down there? That is where we are jumping."

"Are you insane?" Melissa did not like this at all. "What if I miss?"

Tom's expression did not change. "Don't miss."

Melissa was skeptical. "Even if I make it into the dumpster, there could be something sharp in there. Are you sure that it is safe?"

"Don't worry. I added some bags filled with big, fluffy blankets earlier this morning."

Yes, Tom had checked to make sure that the garbage dumpster was full earlier, but of course Tom had not added any bags filled with big, fluffy blankets to it. The reality was that Tom needed Melissa to jump immediately, so he bluffed.

Melissa edged out on to the window ledge and took a deep breath. She closed her eyes, took one step forward and began screaming as she felt herself start to fall toward the garbage dumpster four stories below.

Chapter 54

When Melissa's body slammed into the garbage dumpster, it bounced awkwardly. The awkward bounce caused her head and left shoulder to ram into the side of the dumpster, and Melissa felt dazed for a moment. But she got up and hopped out of the dumpster so that Russ could have room to jump.

Russ took a couple of extra moments to steady himself on the window ledge, and this started making Tom very nervous. But Russ did jump and it sounded like he hit something solid when he made impact with the garbage, but he seemed like he was okay once he got back to his feet.

Tom threw his shotgun down first, and after Russ had collected it from the dumpster he jumped. He bounded out of the dumpster almost immediately and retrieved his shotgun from Russ.

"I know that hurt like hell guys. But we have got to move. You may not feel like running about now, but you have got to. Follow me."

Tom started running up a side alley and the others followed. If Tom had been by himself, he would have been moving much more rapidly, but in this situation it was critical that they all stay together.

After a couple of minutes they reached one of the entrances to the Farragut West metro station. Tom dumped his shotgun into a nearby trash bin and handed Russ and Melissa prepaid metro cards that he had purchased earlier that morning. They moved swiftly, but not too conspicuously, down on to the platform. Unfortunately, there was no train in the station that they could jump on to immediately, and the platform that they were waiting on was fairly crowded even though it was the middle of the day.

Tom turned to face Russ and Melissa. "Just be patient – trains don't run as frequently in the middle of the day, but a train should be here in just a few minutes."

Suddenly, Tom could see Melissa's eyes get really wide. Tom spun around and saw that Koz was pointing a handgun directly at him.

"I figured that you would try to use public transportation to escape Tom. And I have to admit that I am very impressed by how rapidly you pulled off this little prison break."

In a flash, Tom pulled out the Glock that had been strapped to his hip and aimed it at Koz, but he did not fire. There were a couple of screams as people around them noticed that two men were pointing guns at each other. Some made a mad dash for the exits, but Russ and Melissa remained frozen in place behind Tom.

"You don't understand Koz. The agency is planning to bomb Times Square on New Year's Eve and these two were taken captive because they tried to expose that plot."

"No, you are the one that does not understand Tom. I know all about what is going to happen on New Year's Eve. I've been a part of the agency for far longer than you realize."

Koz could see that Tom was very confused, so he continued speaking.

"During the last four years that we were at the CIA, I was operating as an 'inside man' for the agency. When it was time for me to be pulled out of there, I suggested that they recruit you. I decided to pretend that I was being recruited too so that I could go through training with you and make sure that everything went smoothly as you got comfortable with the agency."

Tom was visibly stunned. "So all of that stuff about not wanting to join the agency was just an act?"

"Exactly. I thought that this was something that we could do together, but now you have blown everything. The agency doesn't always do things the way that I would do them, but overall they are trying to do the right thing. If it was up to me, I wouldn't bomb Times Square on New Year's Eve. But when you are trying to fundamentally transform the world sometimes you have to break a few eggs."

Tom was even more puzzled now. "What the heck are you talking about Koz?"

"Tom, if you would have stayed with the agency longer you would have understood. The world is a really messed up place, but it doesn't have to be. Under the right leadership, humanity can be truly united. We have just got to stop fighting with one another. That is why it is necessary to move the world toward one government, one economy and one religion. If humanity comes together in a single global system, we can finally have the great era of peace and prosperity that so many great thinkers have been dreaming about for so many centuries."

Tom was convinced that his best friend had gone absolutely nuts. "This all sounds like nonsense Koz. How could one secret government intelligence agency possibly unite the entire globe?"

"That's just it Tom - our little agency is not working alone. A vast global organization known as 'The Order' is running the show. You have no idea how powerful they are."

From behind Tom, Russ spoke up. "What do you mean by 'The Order'? Are you saying that the agency actually works for The Order of the Illuminati?"

Koz didn't answer.

Suddenly a train roared into the station, but Tom and Koz kept their guns trained on each other.

"This is our train Koz. Are you going to shoot us?"

"Of course not. I could never shoot you Tom. I owe you my life for carrying my nearly lifeless body out of the Gaza Strip all those years ago. Today I am repaying that debt."

The train pulled to a stop and the doors opened. Russ and Melissa swiftly boarded the train, but Tom hesitated.

"Come with us," Tom said as he lowered his gun.

"I can't," Koz responded as he also lowered his gun. "I have made my choice and I have to live with that."

"I'm sorry Koz. I have got to go." Tom stepped on to the train, but kept his gaze on his best friend as the windowed doors closed right in front of him.

The train roared back to life and started rolling out of the station. As it did, Tom lifted his hand and waved goodbye to his best friend. At that moment he knew that he would probably never see Koz again.

Russ and Melissa had moved to the far side of the train, and Melissa was looking out of the windows at the platform on the other side of the Farragut West station. She was stunned when she spotted a very elderly man with a long white beard that was almost dressed entirely in white.

Melissa pointed out the window at him and tried to get the attention of Tom and Russ. "That is the old man that rescued me when I was attacked by that pack of thugs in D.C.! Look – he's standing right there!"

As she was saying that, the car that they were riding in entered a tunnel. By the time Tom and Russ turned to look it was too late.

Tom walked over to where Melissa was standing. "Who did you see Melissa?"

Melissa had not said much during the entire escape, but seeing that elderly man had somehow lifted her spirits. "I don't know his name. But I am sure that it was him. Tom, do you remember that day when I met you at that little restaurant not too far from the White House and I was upset because I had just been attacked on the street? Well, things would have been far worse if an elderly man with a long white beard had not rescued me. I will never forget his face, and I am sure that I just saw him. In fact, I think that he was there to help us."

Chapter 55

Jessup was absolutely seething with anger as he stormed into the Farragut West metro station. He had about a dozen other agents with him, and when he got down to the platform where Koz was still standing he was in no mood to play games.

"Where are they Koz?"

Koz looked like a man that was resigned to his fate. "They're gone."

"What do you mean they're gone? Why didn't you stop them?"

"Tom is my best friend. If he had not carried my nearly lifeless body out of the Gaza Strip many years ago, I would not be standing here today. I simply could not shoot him."

The other agents standing around Jessup were visibly enraged when Koz said this, but Jessup was beyond enraged. Koz could see the murder in his eyes.

"Do you have any idea how much trouble I am in with headquarters already?" Jessup was waving his arms as he said this and was becoming very animated. "Do you have any idea what they are going to do to me when they find out that the prisoners have escaped?"

"I take full responsibility for what happened," Koz responded. "I owed Tom my life and I have repaid that debt. I have done the honorable thing."

"No, you have done the stupid thing." Jessup pulled out a handgun and fired it at Koz at point blank range.

Koz was dead even before his body hit the platform.

Jessup turned to face the other agents. "Does anyone else want to do something stupid?"

None of the other agents said a thing.

"Okay, we know that they departed on a train heading west from this platform. Kalon, I want you to call Metro headquarters and get them to shut down every train on the orange line. Wolfe, I want you to alert law enforcement and I want you to get boots on the ground in every station from here to Vienna. I cannot emphasize enough how important it is that we find those three. If they are able to escape, heads are going to roll, I can promise you that."

As he finished his tirade, Jessup's cell phone started buzzing.

"This is Jessup," he stated tersely as he answered the call.

On the other end it was Lilith. Somehow she had already found out that the prisoners had escaped.

"Have you suddenly become completely incompetent Jessup?"

"No I have not, my Commandant. I am confident that we will have the two prisoners and the rogue agent that freed them within the hour."

"You had better not fail this time Jessup. I am putting you in charge of bringing them in. If they end up jeopardizing our New Year's Eve operation, I am going to drag your sorry case out to Denver, and it won't be for a vacation."

Jessup had heard rumors about the kinds of things that happen out in Denver.

"I understand. I will not rest until I have found them..."

The phone went dead on the other end. Jessup knew that Lilith's patience was running out, and she was not a patient woman to begin with.

Chapter 56

As the train that Tom, Melissa and Russ were riding in rolled into the Rosslyn metro station, a voice came over the intercom: "Due to a law enforcement matter, all orange line trains will be holding their positions indefinitely. Unfortunately, that also means that we will need to keep all train doors closed and will not be able to allow any passengers to disembark. We greatly apologize for any inconvenience."

Russ let loose with a string of profanities when he heard this. When he was done, he turned and looked at Tom. "They know that we took the Metro. What are we going to do now?"

Tom knew exactly what needed to be done. "This is our stop anyway. We just need to get off of this train. Melissa and Russ, have all the other passengers gather at the other end of the car. I don't want anyone to get hurt."

After Melissa and Russ had herded the other passengers away from Tom, he pulled out his Glock and fired multiple rounds into one of the long windows facing the platform. That shattered the window, and Tom used his right leg to kick out some of the pieces of the window that were still hanging loosely.

In a flash, the three of them had crawled through the window, bolted up a nearby escalator and were approaching the exit to the station. As they neared the exit, an unarmed Metro worker was beginning to close the metal gate that keeps the facility secure at night.

Tom fired a couple of warning shots into the ceiling as he approached and looked the Metro worker directly in the eyes. "Don't even think about closing that gate."

The Metro worker stood aside and Tom, Melissa and Russ went sprinting through. Tom knew that the agency would have boots on the ground in every station along the orange line as rapidly as they could, so there was no time to lose.

Fortunately, there were no more signs of trouble as they left the station. They darted down one side street and then another. Tom was starting to feel like this escape might actually be successful.

"Follow me guys, I parked my vehicle at a hotel just a couple of blocks from here."

When they got to the hotel, Tom was relieved to see that nobody had disturbed the black Audi Q7 that he had left there.

Melissa was impressed. "When did you get an Audi Tom?"

Tom smiled a little as he unlocked the vehicle and they all got in. "Well, I knew that there was no way that I could use my old SUV for our escape. Every law enforcement officer in the entire region will be looking for it. So yesterday evening I went out and bought this Audi with an old false identity that I once used at the CIA."

Russ was concerned that someone could still find a way to trace the purchase of this vehicle to Tom. "But how did you pay for it? This kind of vehicle is not cheap."

Tom fired up the engine and started heading out of the parking lot. "The agency purchased it for us. The agency gives all of their agents an emergency stash of cash that is only to be used in 'desperate situations'. Well, I figured that this was a 'desperate situation', and after everything that they have put me through I figured that they owed me a nice parting gift. Plus, we still have plenty of cash in the trunk for traveling expenses."

In just a few moments, they were on Route 66 heading west. Tom finally breathed a sigh of relief, and over in the passenger seat Russ looked like he was starting to relax a little.

From the back seat, Melissa spoke up. "Tom, I will forever be indebted to you for rescuing me from that place, but I can't go with you wherever you are going. The memory of how our relationship ended is still very fresh in my mind, and I am still very angry with you. Honestly, I just want to go back to my old life. If you could just drop me off at some place that has a phone I would appreciate it."

"Are you insane??" Tom couldn't believe what he was hearing. Obviously Melissa did not understand how these things worked. "You aren't going to be able to go back to your old life Melissa. If you try to go back to your apartment or to your workplace the agency will just grab you again and you will be back in that exact same cell that I just rescued you from."

That was not what Melissa wanted to hear. "I can't accept that my old life is over just because you say so. I will just go to the police, and if they won't help me I will go to the FBI. Certainly there has got to be someone out there that will help me reclaim my old life."

Tom shook his head. "You just don't get it Melissa. The police and the FBI cannot do anything about the agency. In fact, the agency probably already has them out looking for you. It doesn't matter what the truth is. From now on you are going to be regarded as a highly wanted terrorist, and capturing you will be considered a very important national security priority."

Russ turned around from the passenger seat and looked sadly at Melissa. "He's right, Melissa. None of our lives are ever going to be the same again – at least not until the agency is fully exposed to the American public. And in order to do that, we are going to need to go somewhere secure and we are going to need to work together."

Melissa was starting to understand that she was going to have to stick with these guys – at least for now. "So where are we going? I don't have any of my things with me."

"That is a good question," Tom responded. "The odds of actually making that escape were so low that I hadn't really thought that far ahead. For the moment, I am just glad to be alive."

"You don't know where we are going?" Melissa was furious now. "What are we supposed to do? Go live in the forest and run with the wolves?"

"I have a suggestion," Russ interjected. "If we can get to Montana, my place is way up in the mountains and it is totally off the grid. Nobody knows where it is, and my family and I have taken great pains to ensure that the feds will never find it."

Tom was skeptical about the idea. "But didn't the agency just drag you in from Montana?"

"Yeah, but that was because I got sloppy and I went into a nearby town. If I had stayed home like I should have, they never would have found me. Besides, do either of you have any other ideas? We are now the subjects of a national manhunt, and we need some place where we can get seriously lost for a very long time."

Melissa was visibly exhausted, and the physical toll of the day was really starting to catch up with her. "Well, I don't have any other suggestions so it sounds good to me. What do you think Tom?"

Tom looked at Melissa in the rear view mirror. "Getting all the way out to Montana without getting caught is going to be a real challenge, but it sounds like the best option we have for now. Why don't you two get some rest for the moment, and later on we'll start planning the specifics."

Tom stared back at the road in front of him. He had no idea if they would be able to make it successfully out to Montana, but he was glad that at least they were out of immediate danger.

But what Tom didn't know was that a black helicopter had spotted them from about a half a mile away and was rapidly closing on their position.

Chapter 57

As happens so frequently on weekday afternoons, traffic on Route 66 started coming to a standstill. They were not too far from the city of Fairfax, and Tom was starting to lose his patience. If this escape was going to be successful, they needed to get far away from Washington D.C. as rapidly as they could.

As Tom sat there fuming, suddenly a black helicopter roared over their heads.

Tom let a string of expletives fly, and that got the attention of both Russ and Melissa.

Melissa spoke up from the back seat. "What is it Tom?"

Tom was visibly frustrated. "That helicopter belongs to the agency. If it knows that we are here, we are in all kinds of trouble. Let's see if it circles back or if it keeps on going."

They kept watching, and the helicopter did turn back and finally hovered directly over their position.

"We've got to get out of here," Melissa blurted out. "There is no way that I can face any more of that torture."

"We can't just sit on the highway," Russ said at just about the same moment. "As soon as that helicopter reports our position this road will be crawling with law enforcement."

"I know," Tom said through clenched teeth. "Hold on."

Tom pulled over on to the shoulder and he floored the accelerator. They were less than a mile from the next exit and Tom was hoping that they could make it in time. In just a few moments, they were traveling at more than 90 miles an hour and many of the commuters that they were passing in the regular lanes gave them some very dirty looks.

Tom had to swerve violently to avoid one knucklehead that decided to pull on to the shoulder right in front of them, and that meant scraping the paint on the right side of the Audi very badly, but they made it by and they rapidly got to the exit. Tom roared up the exit ramp and into traffic. Unfortunately, the helicopter was still following them very closely.

Tom weaved through traffic at high speed as he tried to figure out what to do. He took one side street and then another. A traffic backup at one red light caused him to get up on the sidewalk at one point. When the sidewalk ended at an intersection, he found himself making a sharp left turn at high speed across three lanes of traffic.

"Darn it Tom! You are going to kill us before the agency does!" A large delivery truck had missed the rear of their vehicle by just inches at that intersection, and for a moment Melissa had been absolutely certain that there were going to be hit.

Unfortunately, despite all of Tom's heroics, the black helicopter that was tailing them was keeping up with them very easily.

Despair started to pour over Tom. If they didn't lose this helicopter pretty soon, they would be captured for sure. It was only a matter of time.

As they roared across a strip mall parking lot toward another side street, a thought suddenly occurred to Tom.

"I can't believe that I didn't think of this earlier – I think that I know how they found us!" Tom was yelling in order to be heard over the roar of the engine. "They probably injected you two with RFID tracking chips! Check your left shoulders and see if there are any injection marks."

"Yeah, I've got a red mark on my left shoulder where it looks like something was injected," Melissa responded.

"Me too," Russ said after checking his own shoulder.

Tom knew that Melissa was not going to like what came next. "Okay, Melissa there is a knife in the long blue bag sitting next to you in the back seat. I need you to dig that chip out of his shoulder as quickly as you can, and then I need Russ to do the same for you."

"You want me to do what??" Melissa was not happy. "I can't cut open his shoulder! And you should know that I tend to faint at the sight of blood. I don't think that I can do this!"

Tom was still weaving in and out of traffic at high speed as he was trying to have this conversation. "Look Melissa, do you want to live or do you want to go back and be tortured and slowly killed in that hellhole that I just rescued you from? The choice is up to you."

Russ already had his left shoulder bared, and without saying another word Melissa took the knife and started exploring the injection point.

"I can't find it," Melissa exclaimed as blood started to pour from Russ's shoulder.

"Keep trying," Tom yelled back.

Just then, a second black helicopter passed over them. It circled back around and joined the chase.

"Come on Melissa – our lives depend on this," Russ said as he winced in pain.

"I think I've got it! I think I've got it!" Melissa held up a tiny little capsule that was covered in blood. "Is this the chip Tom?"

"Let me look at it," Tom said as he held his hand out to receive it. Once he had it in his hand, he took his eyes off the road for just a moment to examine it.

"Is that it?" Melissa was really hoping that she didn't have to dig around in Russ's shoulder any longer.

"Yeah that's it. Russ, now you have to get the chip out of Melissa's shoulder."

Melissa screamed in pain as Russ dug the knife into her shoulder. Fortunately, Russ was able to locate the chip in her shoulder and dig it out quite quickly.

"Russ, hand me that chip as well." Tom already knew what he was going to do.

Russ handed him the second chip and Tom turned down a road that was very heavily wooded. Both helicopters had to back off a bit in order to stay above the trees.

At the next intersection, a BMW convertible with the top down was in the left hand turn lane waiting for the light to turn green. It was an unseasonably warm day for early December, and the balding, morbidly obese older man that had squeezed himself behind the wheel was busy chatting with a female companion sitting in the passenger seat who was young enough to be his daughter. Unfortunately for his wife, she was definitely not his daughter. On the back bumper of the convertible was a bumper sticker with the following slogan: "Lobbyist By Day, Superhero By Night".

As Tom approached the intersection, he slowed down a bit and opened his window. As he passed the BMW convertible on the right, Tom tossed the bloody microchips into the back seat and kept on going directly through the red light. The passengers in the convertible were stunned that an Audi had just roared right past them and through a red light, but they had not seemed to have noticed what Tom had just tossed into the back seat behind them.

When the light turned green, the BMW convertible made a left hand turn and it was soon out of sight. One of the helicopters that had been tailing them changed course to follow the BMW.

"It worked," Russ declared as he pointed to the helicopter that was moving away from them.

But Tom knew that they were far from out of trouble. "Do you know how to handle a gun Russ?"

"I'm from Montana – of course I know how to handle a gun."

Tom was hoping that he actually did. "Melissa, there is a large gun in the long, blue bag sitting next to you in the back seat. Can you hand that to Russ?"

She handed it to Russ, and Russ looked it over.

Tom took his eyes off the road for a moment to glance over at him. "That is an M16. It is similar to an AR-15, except that it is fully automatic. It is already loaded. Do you think that you can operate it?"

"I can handle it." Russ seemed honestly offended.

"Are you sure?"

"I told you – I can handle it."

"Okay, wait for that helicopter to get really close again and then try to get as many rounds into the bottom of that helicopter as you can."

Tom spotted a side road that was not wooded and pulled on to it. He continued to weave in and out of traffic, but he slowed down a bit hoping that the helicopter would get closer.

After a few moments, Russ rolled down his window, aimed the M16 at the helicopter, and opened fire. He emptied the entire clip, and within a few moments smoke began billowing from the chopper and it was leaking fluid badly. The helicopter quickly distanced itself from their vehicle and then turned back toward Washington.

"Great shooting Russ!" Tom had been honestly surprised by the skill that Russ had shown with the M16. "It looks like that chopper won't be bothering us anymore."

"I wouldn't be counting our chickens yet boys," Melissa said breathlessly from the back seat. "With our luck, the entire Marine Corps will be around the next bend."

The roads had less traffic on them the farther away they got from Fairfax. Tom felt the Audi skid a bit as he accelerated into a very sharp turn. They were entering a stretch of road that was quite narrow and that was very heavily wooded along both shoulders.

As they came out of the sharp turn, Melissa screamed.

"What the heck is that thing?"

Melissa was pointing at a figure in the distance.

Tom and Russ could see it now too, and neither of them knew what it was either.

Chapter 58

Killian was standing on the double yellow line in the middle of the road about a thousand feet from them, and no traffic was coming in either direction. He was wearing a very heavily armored suit of black and red tactical armor that covered him from head to toe. The black and red helmet that he was wearing completely covered his face, making him look like something out of a science fiction movie. He had an AK-47 in his right arm, but his left arm was outstretched toward them as if he was signaling for them to stop.

"Is that a person?" Russ had never seen anything like this.

"If it is, it is an awfully large one." Tom brought the Audi to a stop as he considered his options. "That thing is definitely over 7 feet tall."

"So what do we do?" Melissa couldn't believe how much bad luck they were having. "The last turn we passed was about a half mile back the other way. If we turn around, there is a good chance that we would be running right into the arms of the people chasing us. I don't think they are too far behind us. In fact, I thought that I could hear some faint sirens in the distance just a few minutes ago. If we head back the other way now we might lose our only chance to escape."

Tom knew that she was right. "Melissa, I want you to get down on the floor. Russ, get the M16 ready. I am going to try to plow right through that thing. When we get about 200 feet away from it, open fire."

Tom jammed the accelerator to the floor and headed straight for the massive black and red figure standing in the middle of the road. After a few moments, Russ pulled out the M16 and started firing. In response, Killian raised his AK-47 and started firing at their tires.

The right front tire of the Audi went flat and Tom desperately tried to keep the Audi steady as it started fishtailing. The Audi was still heading directly toward Killian, and he acrobatically somersaulted over the vehicle just as it was about to hit him.

Tom steadied the Audi and brought it to a stop. He checked his rearview mirror, and he could see that the figure in the black and red armor was already back on his feet and was running toward them at very high speed. Tom jammed the accelerator to the floor, and the Audi roared to life. The front right tire was completely flat and was making all kinds of horrible noises, but Tom didn't have the luxury of being able to be concerned about that. He just hoped that the Audi would be able to move fast enough to outrun whatever it was that was chasing them.

Even though the thing in the black and red armor was running at a speed that Tom did not consider to be humanly possible, the Audi began to pull away. After a few moments they passed a Buick sedan that was parked along the side of the road, and there appeared to be a young man in the vehicle, but they weren't about to stop and ask if he was friend or foe. After passing the Buick, Tom quickly spotted a side street and he turned on to it.

"Are you okay Russ?" Tom glanced over and was hoping that Russ had not been hit in the exchange.

"Yeah, I'm okay. I think that thing was just firing at our tires."

"That must mean that we are wanted alive," Tom said as he turned down another side street.

Russ could not believe what he had just seen. "I know that I hit that thing a bunch of times, but the M16 rounds did not seem to bother it at all. And did you see it jump over our vehicle? That thing moves like a cat. I have never seen anything like that in my life."

"I think that I know who the man in that armor was," Melissa said as she got up off the floor in the back seat. "When I was abducted, there were two men that broke into my apartment. One of them was the tallest man that I had ever seen, and he was built like an ox. When I tried to escape by locking myself in my bathroom, he punched a hole in the door with his fist. I tried to fight him off, but I couldn't. Before I passed out, I looked up at him and I was horrified to see that he actually had red eyes. Could it be possible that he isn't even human?"

"I don't know," Tom responded. "I just hope that we never run into that thing again."

Chapter 59

The next 24 hours were fairly uneventful for Tom, Russ and Melissa. They replaced the right front tire with the spare, and they started heading south because they figured that their pursuers would believe that they would be heading west since that was their original direction. They were sticking strictly to the back roads because they didn't want to take a chance of being spotted on any of the main highways. They took turns sleeping and eventually ended up down in Fredericksburg where they found an out of the way tire repair shop that was willing to sell them a new tire without asking any pesky questions. From there they took the back roads over toward Charlottesville, and from there they headed across the border into West Virginia.

As they cruised along the back roads of southern West Virginia, Russ was sleeping in the back seat and Melissa was sitting next to Tom up in the passenger seat. As she gazed out the window, she was absolutely amazed at the poverty that she was witnessing. The roads were rapidly crumbling and were full of large potholes. Many of the bridges that they had driven over looked like they might fall apart at any moment. In some of the towns, it literally looked like a war had hit. There were abandoned homes with broken windows all over the place. In other instances, there were houses that had windows that had been boarded up, but it appeared that people were still living inside some of those homes. About a third of the stores and restaurants that they were passing appeared to be closed, and a sense of gloom and despair seemed to hang in the air everywhere they went. It was almost as if someone had sucked all of the life out of this part of the country.

"I had no idea that things had gotten this bad in some parts of the nation," Melissa said softly. "If I wasn't with you guys, I wouldn't even want to get out of the car."

Tom nodded in agreement. "Did you hear that news report on the radio last hour? They say that the unemployment rate in West Virginia is over 25 percent now. But the truth is that conditions are like this in most parts of the country at this point. Over the past couple of decades, Washington D.C. has done very well because of the growth of the federal government, and New York City has done very well because our politicians have pursued policies that have been very favorable for Wall Street, but the rest of the country has really suffered. And now that the credit markets have frozen up, economy activity in much of the country has come to a virtual standstill. Nobody can find work and crime is skyrocketing. It is getting really scary out there."

"But what about unemployment and food stamps and programs like that?" Melissa could hardly believe the scenes of poverty that she was driving past. "Aren't there programs to help people that are living like this?"

"The meager checks that people on government assistance receive don't go very far, and earlier today on the news they said that another round of federal budget cuts was coming. Due to the recent financial crisis, the rest of the world is very hesitant to lend any more money to us, and major international organizations such as the IMF and the World Bank are demanding that we implement harsh austerity measures before they give us any assistance. It is almost as if we are experiencing a replay of the economic horror that European nations such as Greece and Spain have already gone through – only much, much worse."

"So what are people supposed to do if they can't find work and they can't feed their families?"

Tom glanced over at Melissa. "They are going to do what they have to do in order to survive. Desperate people do desperate things, and even when I was still at the CIA we were tracking the rise of a 'Robin Hood mentality' in America. I would expect that we are going to see a lot of people from poor neighborhoods start to invade wealthy neighborhoods and engage in a bit of 'creative redistribution'. The tension between the wealthy and the poor in this country has been building for years, and this financial crisis has certainly brought it to a boiling point."

All of this talk about poverty and crime was depressing Melissa. The country that she loved was falling apart all around her. This made her very said, but she was also very grateful to still be alive. She didn't even want to think about what would have happened to her if Tom had not rescued her. "By the way Tom, I want to thank you for rescuing me. When you heard that I was captured, you could have bolted and left me there to rot. But instead, you risked your life to save me. I still don't understand why you did it. If it was not for you, I would have never gotten out of there alive."

Tom was not quite sure why he had done it either. The world of intelligence is a cold, cruel business. Tom had left colleagues to die in other situations, and he wasn't exactly certain why things were different this time. Something in him had just clicked and he had realized that he would never be able to live with himself if he had left Melissa behind to be tortured and killed.

Tom bit his lip as he responded to Melissa. "No matter how badly our relationship ended, I just could not bear the thought of your life being slowly ended in that place. It was my fault that you were dragged into all of this, and I knew that the only way that I could ever live with myself was if I got you out of there. I would have given my life if it would have meant your freedom. And I am going to do whatever I can to get you and Russ to safety. After that, I am going to see to it that the agency is destroyed once and for all. They will pay for what they have done."

They drove along in silence for a while. When their relationship had ended, Melissa thought that there was nobody in the world that she hated more than Tom McDowell. Melissa didn't know if she could ever forgive him for what he had done to her, but Tom had risked his life repeatedly to rescue her from torture and certain death, and that certainly had to count for something. Melissa didn't know if their relationship could ever be fully repaired, but at the moment Tom was acting as her rescuer, and that was good enough for now.

Chapter 60

It was a cold, foggy day and Killian was becoming increasingly frustrated with his driver as they raced south from Charleston, West Virginia. They had been in Charleston because several important highways intersect there and Killian had figured that there was a good chance that the fugitives that he was chasing would come through that area at some point. An unmanned aerial vehicle had just picked up an Audi fitting the description of the vehicle that the fugitives were driving about 30 minutes from Charleston, and Killian was hoping to get to them before anyone else did.

They had gotten away from him once, but they wouldn't be so fortunate the next time. He had been told that capturing these fugitives was of the highest importance, and he did not want to disappoint his employers.

But Killian was not sure how much more he could take of little Tony Scarlatti. His incessant yammering was driving him up a wall, and his incompetence had allowed the fugitives to escape back in Virginia.

"I wish that you could talk my monstrous friend," Tony blurted out as he looked over at Killian. "Chicks love big guys with muscles, but if you can't engage in some sweet talk that is a major turn off. Look, after all of this is over we'll hit the bars and I'll make up some story about you having throat cancer or something. We can try to play up the sympathy angle. Chicks tend to have a huge weakness for that kind of stuff."

Tony was absolutely shocked when he heard a very deep voice reply to him from the passenger seat. "Why didn't you block the road with the car like I wanted you to?"

"My man! You could talk all this time? Whoa! You are one freaky dude."

"Of course I can talk," Killian responded. "I just don't like to talk. Why didn't you block the road back there in Virginia like I asked you to?"

"Are you upset about that? Hey man, I didn't sign up to put my neck on the line. I figured that if they could get past you that I wouldn't want to be messing with them. I make my living with my face and not with a gun, you know what I mean?"

Killian scowled. "So you were a coward."

"Hey, I'm just a driver. If you want me to drive you some place, fine. But don't expect me to be putting my neck on the line. By the way, why does everyone believe that you can't talk?"

"Everyone believes that I can't talk because anyone that hears me talk never gets to live long enough to tell anyone about it."

"Oh-ho-ho – you are really scaring me now," Tony said sarcastically. "Did you steal that line from a bad action movie? I just heard you talk. Should I be worried?"

Tony was joking around, but Killian was not laughing.

"Yes, you should be."

A few moments later there was a loud scream and the Buick sedan that Killian and Tony were riding in started veering from the left lane into the right lane. A red Chevy truck had to swerve violently in order to avoid ramming into it. Eventually the Buick straightened back out, and then a couple of minutes later the door on the driver's side opened and the dead body of Tony Scarlatti fell out on to the highway.

The entire time, the Buick never slowed down. Killian was in the driver's seat now, and he had a contract to fulfill.

And he never broke a contract.

Chapter 61

Tom, Russ and Melissa were starting to get low on gas and they were definitely getting hungry for some dinner. Russ had spotted a billboard for "Mom's Burger Palace" in the town up ahead, and they were all looking forward to a little break from the road.

As they entered the town, a very large sign greeted them which said the following: "Welcome to Montauk – A Nice Little Place To Raise A Family". But the truth was that Montauk did not look very nice at all. In fact, it appeared to be even more run down than all of the other little West Virginia towns that they had been traveling through so far.

They finally found "Mom's Burger Palace" which was located between a sporting goods store that had been boarded up and a payday loan store that had bars on the windows. A small group of rough looking men was congregating off to one side of the parking lot. One of the men was talking on a cell phone, and he gave Tom, Russ, and Melissa a very long look as they got out of their vehicle.

"Perhaps this is not such a great idea," Russ suggested. In the pit of his stomach he knew that something was not quite right. "I think I'll be okay for food until we get into Kentucky. Why don't we just turn around and get back in the car?"

"Russ, you are just being silly," Melissa responded. "I think that you must watch too many movies. Nobody is out to get you. Just because these people are poor does not mean that they are not as nice as everyone else. I am sure that if you got to know them that you would find that they are just as friendly as anyone else you may encounter."

Russ could see that several of the men gathered in the little group on the other side of the parking lot were looking over at them now. "Okay, but could we make this a quick stop? I don't think that we should stop anywhere for too long."

The three of them ordered some burgers, fries and sodas and sat down to eat. After a couple of minutes, they suddenly heard a very loud police siren heading their way, and soon thereafter a police cruiser pulled into the parking lot and parked right next to the Audi.

A couple of very burly police officers got out of the police cruiser and marched purposefully into the restaurant. Once inside, they instantly spotted Tom, Russ and Melissa and came directly over to their table.

The larger of the two police officers spoke first. "Is that your Audi outside?"

"Yes it is," Tom responded. "Is there a problem?"

"You could say that there is," the second officer blurted out. "We are going to need the three of you to come outside with us."

Tom didn't like the sound of this at all, but the three of them got up from their meal and walked outside with the officers.

The first officer that had spoken looked over at Tom. "There have been reports of drugs being sold out of an Audi fitting this description. We are going to need you to open your vehicle."

Tom was relieved that the officers apparently did not know that they were fugitives, but he also realized that it would not look very good at all when they found all of the weapons that were in the Audi.

Tom knew that he had to move fast or things were going to get out of hand very quickly. He pulled out the Glock that was strapped to his hip and pointed it at the head of the larger of the two police officers.

"I am sorry, but I cannot allow you to search our vehicle. Now please tell your partner to put his hands on top of his head and nobody will get hurt."

In response, the other police officer and five of the men that had been congregating on the other side of the parking lot all drew guns and pointed them at Tom.

The officer that Tom was pointing his gun at smiled. "It looks like you are outgunned buddy. Either you put your gun on the ground or my friends start shooting. Trust me, none of you will get out of here alive if that happens."

Tom cursed under his breath. Russ and Melissa were unarmed, and the odds were very heavily stacked against them. Tom figured that he had better go along until he could swing things back in their favor.

"Okay, I am putting my gun down. Don't shoot."

Tom put his gun on the ground, and Tom, Russ and Melissa all put their hands on their heads. The larger of the two police officers picked up Tom's gun and the armed men from the other side of the parking lot moved closer.

The larger of the two police officers spoke to the group of unsavory looking men as they approached. "Watch these two while we search the vehicle. If they so much as twitch, blow them away."

"You got it boss," one of the armed men said in return.

"Okay," the smaller of the two police officers sneered at Tom, "will you hand me the keys or do I have to strip search you for them?"

Tom carefully handed over the keys and the officers began searching the vehicle. The larger of the two officers could not hide his excitement. "It looks like we have hit the jackpot boys! This vehicle appears to be brand new and we can sell these guns for a fortune."

"Is that what this was all about? You want to steal our vehicle?" Tom couldn't believe what he was hearing.

The larger of the two police officers approached Tom and held a little bag of white powder right up under his nose. "We aren't stealing nothing. We just found this little bag of cocaine in your car, and so we are legally impounding it and everything in it. Everything will be legally auctioned off, and let's just say that there is a really good chance that my buddies and I will be the only bidders."

Of course Tom knew that they had definitely not found any cocaine in the vehicle. It was all just a ruse to steal the Audi and everything inside.

"And if we challenge you in court?" Tom wanted to see what this corrupt police officer would say next.

The police officer looked Tom straight in the eyes and smiled. "There is no chance that you would win. My brother is the local judge. But you aren't going to get that chance."

The police officer tossed the keys to the Audi to one of the men that had been guarding Tom, Russ and Melissa.

"Billy, take this vehicle down to the station. We'll be over later after we take care of these three."

Billy got right into the Audi and drove off. That was something that Tom had not anticipated.

The sun had already set and it was starting to really get dark now. Tom knew that they were planning to kill the three of them, but he figured that they wanted to have a little more fun with them first. In fact, he was counting on that.

The two police officers and the remaining four armed men formed a tight semi-circle around Tom, Russ, and Melissa. "Okay, we are about to take a little walk, but first you three are going to tell us exactly who you are and why you are in our little town."

Melissa spoke first. "My name is Melissa Remling, and I am a reporter for the American News Network, and you guys are going to be in so much trouble when my bosses find out what has happened. In fact, I made a call from inside the restaurant when we first got here and so they know exactly where I am. If I don't show up safely for work tomorrow, this town is going to be crawling with people looking for me."

Of course this was a giant bluff, but Melissa figured it was worth a try.

"Oh crap," the smaller of the two police officers blurted out. "I do recognize her. She is telling the truth – she really is a reporter. My wife is a big fan of yours."

"Shut your pie hole Horace," the other officer responded. "Even if she is a big time reporter..."

The larger police officer never got a chance to finish that sentence. His eyes got really big and he toppled over on to the pavement with a large throwing knife protruding from his skull.

The rest of the group stared at the fallen officer and then started to scan the area for his attacker. After a moment, the other police officer fell to the ground with a large throwing knife protruding from his back.

The remaining four men were frantic now. One of them started firing his handgun at something that he thought he saw in the distance.

With their attention distracted, Tom made eye contact with Russ and Melissa and then made a break for it. The three of them ran behind the restaurant as rapidly as they could and started heading for a forested area in the distance. As they did so, they heard bloodcurdling screams from the men that they had just run away from.

They kept running as fast as their feet would carry them, and they had just about reached the tree line when a huge shadowy figure knocked all three of them over from behind.

It was Killian. When the three of them got back to their feet, he was standing in front of them with a bloody sword pointed at Tom's throat.

This time he was not wearing his tactical armor. Instead, he was dressed in loose-fitting black and red garments and he had a black shrouded cloak draped over the garments. From under the shroud, Melissa could see his red eyes staring out at her.

For a moment, they all just stood there looking at each other.

"You were one of the men who came into my apartment and abducted me," Melissa said to him.

Killian nodded.

"Don't hurt us please, we will not try to escape," Tom said as he began to shake. Tom clutched his chest and started inching away from Killian as he lowered himself to the ground. "I just – I just need to catch my breath first. Melissa, I am having chest pains. I think I am having a heart attack."

Melissa and Russ both rushed to his side and they both could see that Tom was starting to tremble violently. Tom was desperately gasping for air and was now several feet away from Killian. Melissa looked up at Killian with legitimate concern in her eyes. "We've got to do something. He needs to go to a hospital."

Killian didn't know how to handle this. He was an assassin after all. He was not accustomed to taking prisoners, and he certainly didn't know anything about providing medical care. He stood there puzzled for a moment.

During his years as an intelligence operative, Tom had learned that it always paid to have an ace up his sleeve. In this instance, it was a flashbang stun grenade. Tom continued to shake and clutch his heart with his right hand, but his left hand had slipped into his jacket and had pulled the pin on the grenade.

He pulled it out of his pocket and tossed it at the feet of Killian. He whispered "get down and cover your eyes" to Melissa and Russ just before he hit the dirt face down.

Fortunately, Melissa and Russ took his advice. The flashbang stun grenade went off and the impact knocked Killian off of his feet.

Tom got up and tried to yell "run", but he doubted that either Russ or Melissa could hear him because his own ears were ringing very badly. After a moment, Russ got to his feet, and then Melissa did, and all three of them started sprinting back toward Mom's Burger Palace as rapidly as they could.

Tom looked back as he was running, and it appeared that Killian was still lying flat on his back. When they reached the front of the restaurant, they came across the mangled bodies of the two police officers and the four armed men that had held them captive earlier. A crowd had gathered around the bodies, but Tom ignored them. Tom went over to the body of the larger police officer and grabbed the keys to the police cruiser.

He pointed over at the cruiser and Russ and Melissa instantly understood what he was telling them to do. They raced over to the vehicle and quickly got inside.

A few moments later, a still partially-stunned Killian dashed into the parking lot, but by then the police cruiser was already roaring down the street.

———————

On a hillside across from town, a very elderly man with a long white beard that was dressed almost entirely in white shook his head as he watched Tom, Russ and Melissa escape.

"They sure do get into a lot of trouble," he said quietly, although nobody appeared to be there to listen to him.

Chapter 62

Tom, Russ and Melissa knew that they were not going to get very far in a stolen police cruiser, so they dumped it outside of Charleston. Fortunately, the crooked cops that they had run into in Montauk had never gotten around to taking Tom's wallet, so he still had some cash on him. After a bit of searching, they found a truck driver at a rest stop that was willing to let them ride along out to St. Louis for 200 dollars. Under normal circumstances it would have been more difficult to find a driver willing to accept such an arrangement, but times were really tough now and they were rapidly getting tougher. In this type of economic environment, an extra 200 dollars was nothing to sneeze at.

When they reached St. Louis, the truck driver dropped them off along Route 64 not too far from the Richmond Heights area. The driver was actually headed on to Kansas City, but one of Melissa's best friends from college was living in a suburb of St. Louis called Ladue, and Melissa was hoping that she would be willing to help them. They were starting to run low on cash, and Tom didn't dare use his debit card or any of his credit cards because that would instantly tell the agency where they were.

Tom also realized that if any of them tried to call someone that it would very likely betray their position. Tom understood that virtually all forms of electronic communication in the United States are monitored by the NSA, and by now the agency surely had the NSA watching carefully for any sign of the three of them.

Melissa looked up the address of her old friend, Claire Donovan, in a public phone book and it turned out that she lived about five miles away from where they had been dropped off. Tom and Russ were absolutely famished, so they decided to grab a bite to eat before catching a cab over there.

As they were chowing down on some questionable pizza, the conversation turned a bit gloomy.

In particular, Melissa appeared to be quite worn down. "Do you really think that we will be able to make it all the way out to Montana? We don't have a vehicle, we are running out of money and the agency is probably moving heaven and earth to find us."

Due to a lack of sleep and constant travel, Tom was really dragging at this point as well. "I agree that things don't look good right now Melissa. Hopefully your friend will help us. We are starting to run out of options."

Of the three, Russ was the one that still seemed to have the most energy, and he didn't like the direction that this conversation was headed. "Look, I would do just about anything just to see my wife and my children one more time. I need you two to stay positive. The people that are chasing us are not super-human. They put on their pants one leg at a time just like we do. If we play it smart, we should be able to stay at least one step ahead of them."

———————

"What is it Kalon?" Jessup was becoming increasingly frustrated because McDowell and the two escaped prisoners had seemingly vanished into thin air, and Jessup knew that his fate depended on being able to hunt them down.

"We've found them sir. A facial recognition camera watching the exterior of a bank picked them up going into a pizza place in a suburb of St. Louis."

"Outstanding!" Jessup had not gotten such good news in a very long time, and he slammed his fists down on the table in front of him in triumph. "Are they still there?"

Kalon frowned. "No, when our agents arrived they had already left. But at least we have a lead on their whereabouts now. Checkpoints have already been established on all of the major highways leading out of St. Louis, and photos of the fugitives have already been distributed to local law enforcement. If they are still in the St. Louis area we should be able to track them down."

Jessup was pleased. "Alert the St. Louis office and let them know that we will be on a plane within the hour. This is something that I want to handle personally."

Chapter 63

By the time that Tom, Russ and Melissa finally reached Claire Donovan's home, it was starting to get dark already. Claire was thrilled to see Melissa, and she warmly welcomed the group into her home. Ladue was one of the wealthiest neighborhoods in the St. Louis area, and Claire's home was absolutely beautiful. Her late husband had been a very powerful pharmaceutical company executive, and they had never had any children, so now Claire lived in this huge home all by herself.

Melissa and Claire had been roommates for two years back in college, and they had gotten very close during that time. They had drifted apart since college, but Melissa had always remembered Claire very fondly. Apparently Claire felt the same way, because she was being extremely gracious to Melissa, Tom and Russ even though they had not showered in days and looked quite ragged.

Melissa filled Claire in on all that they had been through, and when she was done Claire was left shaking her head. Obviously these were not the kinds of things that she was accustomed to hearing.

"This is a lot to take in," Claire said to Melissa. "A government agency that is so secret that it doesn't even have a name? A plot to blow up Times Square and the bank account records of the ten largest banks in America on New Year's Eve? A seven foot tall killer that is chasing you all over the country? I can't even wrap my head around half the stuff that you just told me. But I know that you would not lie to me, and I will help you. Give me just a moment..."

Claire stepped upstairs while Tom, Russ and Melissa remained down in the formal living room. After a few moments, Claire reappeared and approached Melissa.

"Melissa, these are the keys to the Ford Mustang in the garage. I haven't even used it since Steve died. And here is an ATM card for a bank account that I had almost totally forgotten about. The account only has a few thousand dollars in it, but that should be enough to get you where you are going. I have written the pin number for the account on the back of the card. The only thing I ask is that if you do get captured that you tell them that you stole the car and the ATM card. Will all of you give me your word on that?"

Tom, Russ and Melissa all responded affirmatively, and Claire handed the keys and the ATM card to Melissa.

In the corner of the living room, a television that had been muted when they had come in was still playing. Suddenly, something on the television caught Tom's attention.

"Claire, could you turn the television up? I think this is important..."

"Of course," Claire responded. She found the remote control and started increasing the volume.

The news anchor had a very sober expression on his face, and the news that he was delivering sounded rather ominous.

"...authorities estimate that at least 1,000 young people were a part of the flash mob that terrorized neighborhoods over in Rock Hill last night. Hundreds of homes were burglarized and more than a dozen murders were reported. There are rumors that a larger flash mob is being planned for tonight, and that the wealthy enclave of Ladue is being targeted, but so far those rumors have not been confirmed. Officials continue to insist that they are doing everything that they possibly can to control the nightmarish crime wave that has erupted in the St. Louis area in recent months."

Claire turned toward the group. "Would you all mind spending the night here? If something like that does happen in this neighborhood, I sure wouldn't mind having a couple of men around."

It was now quite dark outside, and Tom had been hoping that she would invite them to stay. "Of course we'll stay for the night," Tom responded. "Thank you for your generosity."

Just then there was a loud knock at the front door.

Russ opened the curtains slightly and saw that there was a small group of teens gathered at the front door, and that a larger group of teens was roaming around on the lawn. They didn't look happy. Russ glanced over at Claire with a very serious look in his eyes. "There are a whole bunch of angry kids out there. Are you expecting anyone?"

"No, I am not," Claire said tersely in response. "Why don't you all hide in the dining room and I will see what they want."

Tom, Russ and Melissa slipped into the dining room where they were out of sight from the front door but could still hear everything that was going on.

Claire started to approach the front door, but she figured that it probably wouldn't be a good idea to get too close.

She stopped about ten feet away and she shuddered when there were more loud knocks at the door.

With all of the boldness that she could muster, she addressed the group of young thugs on the other side of the front door. "Hello – what is it that you want?"

A voice responded from the other side of the door. "We are from East St. Louis and we are here to take back what is rightfully ours. Now open the door!"

Claire was visibly shaken now. "Please just go away. I don't want any trouble."

For a moment there was no response, and then a brick shattered the living room window and a teen on the other side started hammering at the glass in the front door with a baseball bat.

Tom knew that it was only a matter of moments before the home would be overwhelmed by angry teens. "Claire get away from the door! Do you have any guns?"

Claire was shaking and it almost looked like she was going into shock. "No, Steve never believed in having any guns. Do you all have any?"

The small arsenal that Tom had originally brought with them had been lost when the Audi had been stolen from them back in West Virginia. "All I have is a knife. That isn't going to be enough to fight off all those thugs. We've got to get out of here. Where is the garage?"

"Follow me," Claire responded, and the entire group scrambled over to the other side of the house and through the kitchen to where the door to the garage was. Behind them, they could hear teens hollering threats as they opened the front door and started barging in.

Tom, Russ, Melissa and Claire entered the very large three car garage, and Melissa immediately sprinted toward the silver Ford Mustang convertible which was parked at the far end. The top on the convertible was down, and there definitely would not be time to put it up.

"I've got the keys for the Mustang," Melissa called out over her shoulder.

"Toss them to me," Tom shouted back at her.

"Not this time. Trust me, I once owned one of these. I've got this."

They didn't have time to argue, so Russ and Claire got into the back seat and Tom slid into the passenger seat. As Melissa fired up the Mustang, Tom found the button for the garage door and pressed it.

As the garage door lifted, several teens appeared behind them and blocked the driveway. Melissa put the Mustang in reverse and gunned the accelerator. The tires squealed as the Mustang shot out of the garage backwards. There were a couple of loud thumps as the Mustang made impact with several large objects on the way out to the street, but it was a very dark night so none of them could really tell if they were hitting garbage cans or teens.

Once the Mustang was out on the street, Melissa put the car in drive and she floored it. A couple of teens tried to chase them but they quickly faded into the distance.

"Great job Melissa! I never knew that you had it in you," Russ declared.

"Neither did I," Claire said as she shook her head.

Just then, a couple of black helicopters streaked overhead.

"Darn it," Tom spat out as he pointed up at the helicopters. "Those are agency choppers. They must know that we are in the area. We need to get out of here."

"I'm working on that," Melissa shot back as she raced up a hill toward an intersection. When she got to the top of the hill, Melissa slammed on the brakes.

To the left, to the right and in the direction that they had been traveling in, all they could see was a massive sea of humanity filling the streets. It looked like the flash mob "rumors" had been true, and when the crowds spotted the Mustang they started sprinting in their direction.

Chapter 64

Melissa would have put the Mustang in reverse, but two vehicles had pulled up directly behind her at the intersection. She started to perform a U-turn in the middle of the intersection, but by then it was too late.

Hundreds of crazed looters, most of them teens, suddenly surrounded the three vehicles. Since the convertible top was down, several young thugs actually decided to jump into the Mustang. Melissa couldn't even see to drive, because she was now shielding herself from the blows of one particularly cruel young man that had hopped into the front of the car.

The Mustang drifted off to one side of the road where it came to a halt. Melissa, Tom, Russ and Claire were all physically pulled out of the vehicle by the rioting crowd that was swarming all around them. All four of them suddenly found themselves fighting for their lives.

Thanks to his martial arts training, Tom was able to get to his feet rather quickly. He started decking one young punk after another, but he had gotten separated from the group. He scanned the area and he could see Russ wrestling with a couple of teen boys, but he saw no sign of Melissa or Claire.

Suddenly, out of the corner of his eye he saw a very elderly man with a very long white beard that was dressed almost entirely in white causing havoc in one area of the crowd. He was literally picking people up and throwing them twenty feet in the air. After a few moments, Melissa was able to get on to her feet next to him and started helping the elderly man fight off the crowd which was still pressing in all around them.

Tom's attention was drawn away from the elderly man and Melissa by a particularly large young thug that was coming at him with a knife. A spinning roundhouse kick to the head took care of him, but more attackers kept coming. Tom was not sure how long he could keep this up.

Just when Tom felt like he was about to be overwhelmed, a wave of extreme pain swept over him and his hands instinctively shot up to his ears. A high-pitched siren that was louder than anything that Tom had ever experienced in his entire life was shrieking, and two armored vehicles were coming through the crowd right at him.

The LRAD sound cannon was causing extreme pain for the crowd of rioters as well. Most of them covered their ears as they ran off in all directions. As the crowd of looters dispersed, Tom could see that Claire was lying flat on the ground apparently unconscious, Russ was holding his head as he walked toward Tom with a noticeable limp, and Melissa and the elderly man that had been helping her were both doing their best to cover their ears.

The two armored vehicles skidded to a stop a few yards away from them as the LRAD sound cannon stopped, and four heavily armed agents poured out of each vehicle.

One of them was Jessup.

"Well, just look at what the cat dragged in," Jessup smugly remarked as he pointed his gun at Tom. "I was always a big fan of yours McDowell. Too bad you decided to jump ship. Now all of you – get your hands where I can see them."

Tom put his hands on his head, but he was not in any mood to be nice. "Hey Jessup – we might not be the ones to do it, but one of these days you are going to get what is coming to you. When that day arrives, you will deeply regret the tremendous amount of pain that you have caused others."

Jessup smiled. "Is that so McDowell? The only thing I am regretting at the moment is ever allowing you into the agency. Soon you will be telling me exactly why you decided to betray the rest of us. I think that we both know that when I am done with you that you are going to wish that you had never been born."

Russ decided that he wanted to jump into this conversation. "You and your agency aren't even accountable to the U.S. government, are you? The Order of the Illuminati is the one calling all of the shots and you just do whatever they tell you to do, isn't that right?"

Jessup whirled around to face Russ. "How in the world do you know about The Order of the Illuminati? Actually, it doesn't matter. Your life won't last that much longer anyway. But before you die I am going to truly enjoy torturing you."

Russ wasn't finished. "How can you betray your country like this? Didn't you take an oath to defend the Constitution? How can you stand by and watch while your agency bombs Times Square and destroys our banking system? You are a traitor and you are betraying everything that our forefathers worked so hard to build. You are a disgrace to this nation."

What Russ had just said absolutely infuriated Jessup. "I want all of you face down on the ground now! I am not betraying anyone! Since the days of the Revolutionary War there have always been secret intelligence agencies such as this one, and we are working to finish the great work that our founding fathers began! Everything that we do is for the good of the American people. America has a secret destiny that you know absolutely nothing about, and the truth is that we are about to enter a glorious new age of global peace and prosperity. A new world is going to arise out of the ashes of the old one, and future generations are going to regard people like me as great heroes. We are on the correct side of history, and we will win in the end – I assure you of that."

Claire was still lying motionless on the ground nearby, and Tom, Russ, Melissa and the elderly gentleman dressed in white were all lying face down as Jessup had ordered them to do. Suddenly, they could all hear what sounded like a faint train whistle in the distance, and the elderly gentleman that had been aiding Melissa whispered just one line to the rest of the group...

"Cover your heads."

Chapter 65

The ground all around Tom began to rumble and then it began to shake violently. Tom looked up and he could see the ground going up and down all around them in waves. Suddenly, a huge wave swept underneath them, and the sickening sound of concrete cracking and crumbling filled the air. The ground shook so violently that Tom feared that the earth underneath them may open up and swallow all of them alive. The two armored vehicles were tossed up into the air like children's toys as the ground beneath Jessup and the other agents with him was thrust up into the air about a foot before completely collapsing and dropping about seven feet below the level where it had been previously standing.

This was no ordinary earthquake. It had literally ripped the earth open roughly along the middle of the road, and now the side that Tom and his group was on was seven to eight feet higher than the other side of the street. Tom tried to get to his feet, but more violent shaking knocked him off balance and back on to the ground. Once the shaking finally stopped, Tom picked himself up and walked over to where the street had been ripped open. Tom looked down and saw that Jessup was apparently unconscious and that his legs were pinned under a slab of concrete. The other agents that were with Jessup had been thrown around like rag dolls, and they all appeared to be either unconscious or seriously injured.

Tom knew that this would probably be their only chance to escape. There was no sign of the Mustang that they had been driving, so they would have to flee on foot.

"Get up! We've got to get out of here!" Tom sprinted over to Claire as the rest of the group got to their feet. Claire was motionless, but she still had a pulse. Tom threw her over his shoulder, and the entire group started running as fast as they could away from Jessup and his men.

Tom didn't know where they were going, but he wanted to put as much distance between them and Jessup's men as possible.

They ran up one side street and then another. A massive aftershock shook the ground all around them, but they just kept on running. They were all getting winded very rapidly, but they knew that they had to keep going.

Melissa looked back over her shoulder at the elderly man that had helped her earlier. It was the same elderly man that had helped her before. He was still with them, but he was obviously having a very difficult time keeping up with them.

"Why do you keep helping us?"

The elderly man was huffing and puffing as he struggled to keep up with the group. "The three of you are greatly loved. And the three of you also have key roles to play in the future. It is imperative that we keep you alive."

A thought occurred to Melissa. "Are you an angel? And did you have anything to do with that earthquake?"

The elderly man smiled a bit even as he continued to breathe heavily. "No, I am most definitely not an angel. If I was an angel, I would be in far better shape. And the earthquake was definitely not my idea."

As the elderly man was saying this, a van came up behind them, and Melissa decided to try to flag it down.

The van stopped and Melissa went over to talk to the driver. "We need help. That woman that my friend is carrying was hurt very badly in the earthquake. Can you take us to a hospital?"

The lettering on the side of the van said "Hand Of Help Baptist Church", and the driver seemed to sincerely want to be of assistance. "Of course, the four of you can get in the back. The side door is open."

"Wait, there are five of us..."

Melissa looked around, but the elderly gentleman with the very long white beard that had come to her aid was gone. He seemed to have a habit of disappearing on her.

"No, I am sorry, you are right – it is just the four of us..."

The group piled into the van and they started heading toward the nearest hospital. They moved very slowly as they drove along because the roads were in absolutely horrible shape because of the earthquake, and scenes of utter devastation were everywhere.

"This is crazy," Melissa blurted out as she shook her head. "I didn't think that major earthquakes like this happened in the middle of the country."

Russ looked over at Melissa. "Actually, the worst earthquakes in U.S. history happened along the New Madrid fault back in 1811 and 1812. The New Madrid fault zone has been reawakening in recent years, but very few people thought that anything like this would happen."

After a few more minutes, they arrived at the hospital. The church van dropped them off in front of the emergency room, and they were able to quickly get some medical help for Claire. She was unconscious and her left arm appeared to be broken, but she was going to make it.

Tom, Russ and Melissa decided to continue their journey without her. She would be safe in the hospital, and nobody was trying to hunt her down. She would be much better off not hanging around with the three of them.

It was quite late when they finally left the hospital, and as they walked down the sidewalk away from the hospital Russ turned to the others. "What do we do now?"

"We need a vehicle," Tom responded. "Do you guys have any ideas?"

"Yeah," Melissa said as she checked her right front pocket. "I still have the ATM card that Claire gave us. If we can find an ATM that is still working we should be okay."

At that moment a black helicopter went buzzing over their heads, but it did not appear to see them.

"Well, right now we need to get off the streets," Tom warned. "Let's find somewhere that we can get a few hours of sleep, and in the morning we'll purchase a vehicle. We definitely want to get out of St. Louis as quickly as we can."

Chapter 66

"I thought that you had captured them." Lilith did not sound pleased.

Jessup could hardly believe how bad his luck had been, and admitting failure to Lilith was getting very old. "We did. They were lying on the ground just waiting to be handcuffed. But then the earthquake hit..."

"You are blaming this on an earthquake? You and your men couldn't handle the ground shaking a little bit?"

"You don't understand. That was no ordinary earthquake..."

"No, you are the one that does not understand. You are in charge of tracking down this rogue agent and these two escaped prisoners because almost all of the rest of the senior personnel in this agency are preparing for the implementation of Operation Ordo Ab Chao. If you allow them to slip through your fingers, you will be held fully accountable. Is there any way that I could make myself any clearer than that?"

"You have made yourself crystal clear, Commandant. I will not fail."

The line abruptly went dead, and Jessup cursed under his breath. He knew exactly what Lilith was telling him. If he failed, he was a dead man. His wife would be a widow and his children would lose their father way too early.

Jessup ran his hands through his thinning hair. He was so frustrated that he could hardly see straight, and he was having a little trouble breathing. He had never experienced this kind of failure in his entire career. He had always been known as the one who would always get results and never make excuses.

Jessup surveyed the temporary work space that he had been allocated in the St. Louis office. This place sure was a dump compared to what he was accustomed to back in Washington. Jessup walked over to the coat closet and pulled out the dress uniform that he wore on formal agency occasions. There was a single emblem on the uniform, and when he was wearing the uniform it was located directly over his heart.

Jessup stared at the emblem for a few moments. It was an unfinished pyramid with an "all-seeing eye" above it. It was the exact symbol that was on the back of the Great Seal of the United States and that was on the back of every dollar bill.

Even most of the agents working around him did not know what the symbol really meant, but Jessup knew. To Jessup, it represented the hope for a better world. He dreamed of his children living in an era of peace and prosperity in a world that was truly united. That was one of the reasons why he took his work so seriously. The transition to a new age was drawing near, and Jessup was convinced that the old belief systems that had kept humanity in chains for so long had to be vanquished.

On a few occasions, Jessup had actually gotten to see the power that some of the "enlightened ones" near the top of the pyramid possessed. Jessup was envious of that power.

He couldn't understand why most of the world did not believe in the supernatural these days. Jessup had witnessed firsthand some of the awesome things that could be accomplished by those that possessed knowledge of the ancient secrets.

In recent months, Jessup had started to diligently study the history of The Order. He had only scratched the surface, but he knew that he desperately wanted to be one of them. He believed in what they were trying to do. He believed that a global economy, a global religion and a global government would truly unite humanity like never before. He wanted to help bring in the "world leader" that The Order believed would be coming soon. He wanted to serve the one known as the "Light Bearer", and he wanted to help crush those that were trying to hold humanity back from being enlightened.

More than anything else, he wanted his own eyes to be opened.

As Jessup stared at the emblem on his dress uniform, suddenly a wave of inspiration swept over him.

"Kalon, get in here."

Kalon appeared in the doorway. "What is it sir?"

"We have been taking the wrong approach. Instead of chasing these fugitives all over the country, we should be anticipating what they will do next. We need to figure out where they are going."

Chapter 67

Killian was receiving all of the same intel that everyone in the agency was getting, so he had heard that the fugitives had escaped from Jessup. In fact, Killian was rather glad that it had happened, because he wanted to be the one that brought them in. They had slipped through his fingers a couple of times now, and it was starting to get personal for him.

He had been directed to bring in the fugitives alive, but Killian was losing patience with that restriction. Killian was an assassin that belonged to an elite organization of assassins known as The Red Hand. If you really wanted someone dead, you hired Killian. But now The Order had him running all over the United States trying to round up some fugitives. It would have been so much easier if he could have just killed them all. If he would have been ordered to do that, they would all be dead already. But apparently these fugitives were wanted for interrogation, and so Killian had been put in the uncomfortable position of hunting people down but keeping them alive at the same time. It was awkward, and Killian did not like it, but he always fulfilled his contracts.

After the recent debacle in West Virginia, Killian had decided that he needed a different vehicle. He was now driving a Range Rover which had been specially modified by Killian. If he had to hunt these fugitives down, then he needed a vehicle which would be better suited for the job.

The agency was covering all of the main roads out of St. Louis, but Killian figured that the fugitives would continue to avoid the main roads like they had been doing up to that point. The earthquake had forced dozens of roads to close, and traffic in the St. Louis area was now a complete and total nightmare. Killian decided to drive around Chesterfield as he waited for intelligence updates on the location of the fugitives. He figured that it was roughly the direction that he would take out of the city, and he was hoping that he might get really lucky and spot the fugitives on his own.

As Killian passed an elementary school, a really old, really ugly two-tone Chevy Suburban caught his eye going down a side street. From this distance, it appeared that there were three adult passengers riding in the vehicle, and Killian decided to follow the vehicle in order to get a better look.

If the fugitives really were riding in that vehicle, they would be in for quite a surprise. Killian had already decided that he was going to take a much more direct approach this time.

———————

"Russ, I didn't know that you smoked," Melissa said from the front seat of the Suburban. "It really is a nasty habit."

In the back seat of the Suburban, Russ had rolled down the window next to him and had lit up a cigarette. When they had stopped for gas, Russ had purchased a lighter and a package of cigarettes. He had quit smoking many years ago, but at times of extreme stress he still felt the urge for a cigarette. He found that it helped him to relax.

And Russ didn't like people telling him what he could or could not do. It was bad enough that the federal government had turned into a control freak nanny state that was constantly telling everyone how to run their lives. "Hey, I know what you are going to say. I know that smoking is not good for my health. But none of us live forever, right? And don't worry – after this cigarette I won't smoke in the vehicle anymore."

"And couldn't we have gotten something a little less noisy? This thing sounds like it has been on its last legs for about a decade." Melissa was trying to get comfortable in the front passenger seat of the Chevy Suburban that they had just purchased, and she was obviously less than thrilled about the decision that had been made.

"Look," Tom responded from behind the wheel, "we had about two thousand dollars to work with and we couldn't exactly take our time shopping around town. We were lucky to find what we did."

"I liked that old Ford Bronco that we were looking at better," Melissa shot back. "This thing sounds like it might die at any moment. I kept wondering why that used car salesman looked so relieved when we said that we wanted to buy it. He was probably thrilled that we were taking it off of his hands."

"Did you know that the most watched car chase in U.S. history involved a Ford Bronco?" Russ was in the back seat behind Tom and he appeared to be in good spirits. He also seemed to enjoy endlessly bringing up useless facts. "I just couldn't see us trying to make our getaway in the same type of vehicle that O.J. Simpson tried to make his getaway in."

"Actually, O.J. was not the one driving," Melissa stated matter-of-factly. "It was actually Al Cowlings."

"I don't really care if it was the Stay Puft Marshmallow Man that was driving the Bronco," Tom said tersely, "I need you two to help me watch the road. Or did you forget that a highly sophisticated intelligence agency with seemingly endless resources is trying to hunt us down?"

They were rapidly approaching an intersection up ahead, but the light was green and there was very little traffic on this particular road, so Tom didn't slow down. In the passenger seat, Melissa turned toward Tom. "I'm sorry – things have just been so crazy the last few days that it is nice to have a normal conversation for once."

Tom glanced over at Melissa. "I understand – I just want us to keep our edge. One false move could mean the difference between life and death for us."

As Tom said this, they entered the intersection. Tom's eyes got really big as he caught sight of the Range Rover that was on a direct collision course with the Suburban. Unfortunately, it was too late for Tom to react and the Range Rover plowed directly into the right side of the Suburban at about 50 miles an hour.

Chapter 68

The collision caved in the back two-thirds of the right side of the Suburban and sent it spinning across the intersection. When it came to a stop, there was no motion inside the vehicle. Tom and Melissa both had their seatbelts on, and they both were lying motionless in the front seat of the Suburban covered in shattered glass. The impact had ruptured the gas tank, and gasoline was pouring out of the Suburban on to the street. The engine of the Suburban was still running, although not very smoothly.

Russ had not put his seatbelt on, and he had been thrown out of the left rear window that he had opened when he had lit up his cigarette. When his body hit the street, it had rolled quite a distance, and Russ was now lying motionless on the street about twenty feet away from where the Suburban had been hit.

Killian surveyed the damage from his vehicle. The very heavy steel grill that he had installed on the front of the Range Rover had worked perfectly. His Range Rover had taken a bit of damage, but the Suburban had been completely totaled.

And the crash had certainly been a shock to his system, but the airbags in the Range Rover had deployed successfully and he was also wearing his black and red tactical armor which provided a tremendous amount of protection. So he had gotten bounced around a bit, but that was about it.

Killian got out of the Range Rover and made his way over to the Suburban. He opened the front passenger door and unbuckled Melissa. Her body was limp, and Killian could not tell if she was alive or dead, but he was not taking any chances this time. He handcuffed her hands behind her back and then placed her in the back seat of his Range Rover.

As Killian headed back over to the Suburban, he could see that Tom was stirring a bit behind the wheel. Before Killian could reach him, Tom had unbuckled himself and had gotten out of the Suburban.

Killian was not about to let him get away this time. Killian closed the distance between the two of them in a flash and he grabbed Tom's left arm. In response, Tom took his right fist and smashed it into Killian's mid-section as hard as he could. Unfortunately for Tom, his fist was no match for Killian's armor. Tom tried to hit Killian again, but it was useless.

Killian grabbed Tom by the throat and lifted him up high into the air so that Tom's face was just inches away from Killian's helmet. Tom desperately gasped for air as he stared at Killian. To Tom, the faceplate on the helmet looked like something out of a horror show. Tom began flailing his arms around in a desperate attempt to free himself, but it was not doing any good.

Killian was getting tired of this. People had started to gather around the crash scene and Killian knew that eventually the police would come. Killian threw Tom on to the ground face first and then handcuffed his hands behind his back.

As Killian had been dealing with Tom, Russ had started to regain consciousness. From where he was lying on the street, Russ had watched Tom try to fight back against Killian, and he saw how futile that was.

Russ was not sure that he could even get up, but he knew that he had to try to do something. As Killian carried Tom over to the Range Rover, Russ tried to get up but that caused an immense wave of pain to go ripping down his back.

Was his back broken?

Russ didn't even want to consider that.

When Russ had tried to push himself up, he had discovered that the ground all around him was wet. Fearing that it might be his own blood, Russ lifted his right hand toward his face so that he could see it.

No, it wasn't blood. In fact, it smelled kind of funny to Russ.

That is when the light bulb went on for Russ. The pool of liquid that he was lying in was actually gasoline that had been leaking out of the Suburban.

Russ quickly reached down into his pocket and pulled out his lighter. If he could create a distraction – a fire, an explosion, anything – it might give him half a chance.

Russ could see that Killian had just finished securing Tom in the Range Rover and was headed back his way. His path would take him directly past the Suburban.

Russ very painfully forced himself to roll away from where the gasoline from the Suburban had been pooling and then he lit the gasoline on fire.

Almost instantly, fire started spreading toward the Suburban. Unfortunately for Russ, he had also set his own shirt ablaze in the process of starting the fire. Russ forced himself to roll along the ground in a direction that was away from the Suburban. After a few rolls, the fire on his shirt was put out.

But Killian was still heading in his direction and was getting very close to the Suburban already.

Russ could still hear the unsteady rhythm of the Suburban engine, and he just hoped that the fire that he had set would do something. From where he was lying, he decided that about the only thing he could do now was pray. Russ didn't really know any prayers, so he just started praying one that his wife had once taught him...

"Our Father which art in Heaven, hallowed be thy name. Thy kingdom come, thy will be done..."

Russ didn't get out another word. The Suburban exploded in spectacular fashion just as Killian was walking past it. Killian's huge frame caught the full impact of the explosion and he was thrown about 30 feet away from the blast.

A surge of adrenaline shot through Russ and he very painfully forced himself to get to his feet. Every step was agonizing, and his back was absolutely killing him, but he kept walking toward the Range Rover.

One woman that had rushed to the scene called out to him. "Sir, are you all right?"

Russ ignored her and just kept taking steps in the direction of the Range Rover.

When he finally reached the Range Rover, Tom started yelling at him from the back seat.

"Get in the front! He left the keys in the ignition! See if it will start!"

Russ got behind the wheel and started pushing the airbags out of the way the best that he could. He tried the ignition, and the Range Rover started right up.

Russ could hear some sirens off in the distance to the east, so he turned the Range Rover west and floored it.

After a few blocks, Russ glanced into the back seat at Tom and Melissa. They were still both handcuffed, and Melissa's body was completely limp and her eyes were shut.

"Is she alive?"

"There is some shallow breathing," Tom responded, "but she is not conscious and I have no idea how much damage has been done."

"So what should we do?"

"Just drive. We'll figure it out. Right now we've just got to get out of here. At least we're alive."

———————

Back where the Suburban had exploded, Killian slowly began to regain consciousness. It had been very foolish of him to try to walk past that Suburban. If he had not had his tactical armor on, he could have just been killed.

Killian sat up and looked around. A fire truck and an ambulance had just pulled up and their sirens were wailing. He looked around for his Range Rover, but it was gone. He figured that the fugitives had taken it.

Killian was hoping that the voice-activated computer in his helmet still worked.

"Computer on."

The computerized display inside his helmet sprang to life.

"Locate Range Rover."

Killian had installed a GPS tracking device inside the dashboard of the Range Rover. He didn't like surprises, and he always wanted to be able to locate his vehicle. In response to his command, the computer produced a map which showed exactly where the Range Rover was traveling.

Killian decided that he was going to keep this information to himself. Now he would be able to track these fugitives down any time that he wanted to, and he did not want the agency finding them before he did. This wasn't just about fulfilling a contract now – this was about revenge. Those three fools were going to pay mightily for what they had done to him.

As Killian was reflecting on his next move, a paramedic rushed to his side.

"Hello sir, can you hear me? Are you hurt? If you can hear me and you are not hurt, please remove your helmet. We are here to help. The police will be here in a few moments and I am sure they would like to ask you a few questions as well."

Killian turned and looked at the paramedic for a moment. Then in frustration he got up, grabbed the paramedic by both arms, and screamed as he threw the paramedic into the middle of the intersection.

Everyone in the immediate area turned to see where the scream had come from, but Killian was already on the move. As he disappeared into the surrounding neighborhood, he cursed himself for losing his temper. He was better than that, but there was something about this particular job that was starting to cause him to lose his mind.

Chapter 69

Tom, Russ and Melissa were able to get out of the St. Louis area in the Range Rover without any more incidents, but Tom and Russ both felt a tremendous amount of uncertainty about what to do next. Melissa had a pulse and she was breathing, but she was still unconscious and a large purple welt had become visible on her forehead. Ordinarily they would have taken Melissa to the hospital, but after much discussion they both agreed that would be a death sentence for her. Even if they checked her into a hospital anonymously, it would only be a matter of time before someone recognized her from television, and once her real identity became known it would be very easy for the agency to swing by that hospital and take her into custody. Once the agency had her again, they would torture her until her usefulness was over and then kill her. So Tom and Russ had decided that her best chance was to remain with them.

Tom and Russ had also agreed that they were going to have to ditch the Range Rover as soon as they could, but the bank account that was connected to the ATM card that Claire Donovan had given them did not have that much money left in it, so their options were limited. Russ had suggested that they head northeast up toward Chicago. He knew a guy up there that did custom trucks, and Russ was hoping that he would be willing to help them out. In addition, Russ argued that the agency would expect them to keep heading west, so heading off toward the northeast may give them a better chance to avoid detection. After much debate, Tom finally agreed and they started heading toward Chicago using only the back roads.

When they were getting close to Peoria, Melissa finally awakened. Melissa was in a tremendous amount of back pain, and her head was absolutely killing her, but Tom and Russ were both greatly relieved that she had regained consciousness.

In Peoria, they found a locksmith that was willing to take cash to remove the handcuffs from Tom and Melissa without asking any nosy questions.

After Peoria, Tom took over the driving so that Russ could try to catch a little bit of sleep. Tom filled Melissa in on what had happened after she lost consciousness, but other than that there was silence for much of the journey up to Chicago. They were all incredibly tired and their nerves were badly frayed.

When they got to Chicago, it was already dark and the streets were eerily quiet. Tom instantly realized that something was very wrong.

"Where is everyone? This road should be packed this time of the evening."

"Yeah," Melissa responded, "this is very strange. I don't see anyone walking around either. And all of these stores appear to be closed – they shouldn't be closed for another couple of hours at least."

As they rolled to a stop at a red light at the next intersection, a booming voice addressed them...

"You have ten minutes to get off the streets. Chicago is under martial law. If you are still on the streets after 8 PM you will be taken into custody. Once again, you have ten minutes to get off the streets."

They looked over, and off to the side of the road was parked an armored car, and standing in front of it was what appeared to be a soldier with a very loud megaphone. Standing on either side of him were two more soldiers that were heavily armed.

"Chicago is under martial law??" Melissa could hardly believe what she had just heard.

"I guess that is why the roads are so empty," Russ said glumly. "I used to write quite a bit about the possibility of martial law in America, but I never thought that it would happen so quickly."

"Hopefully only large cities such as Chicago are under martial law," Tom responded. "In any event, we need to find a motel and we need to do it quickly."

They were driving through a section of Chicago that was known to have a very high crime rate, but they didn't have the time to be choosy. They pulled over into the parking lot of the first motel they could find, and fortunately the desk clerk did not seem interested in asking them too many questions and he was more than willing to take cash. Their room was in the back of the building, and it was out of sight from the main road. Tom pulled the Range Rover right up in front of the room that they would be staying in, and they all quickly moved inside. At least for tonight they would all have a warm bed to sleep in, and all three of them were extremely thankful for that.

Chapter 70

Killian was able to track the movements of Tom, Russ and Melissa thanks to the GPS tracking device that he had previously installed inside the dashboard of the Range Rover, but due to the imposition of martial law, Killian had not been able to get into Chicago until a little after 6 AM.

Killian had not told the agency where the fugitives were, because Killian did not want anyone else to find them before he did. Despite his orders that the fugitives were to be captured alive, Killian now intended to kill them. Things had started to get personal for Killian, and these were three individuals that he very much wanted to see dead. The agency might complain a little bit when he delivered three dead bodies to them, but he would still get paid by his employers.

Killian caught up with the Range Rover in the parking lot of the "Sleep Easy Motel". It was a ratty old place in the middle of a neighborhood that could have been a poster child for urban decay. In fact, Killian concluded, people probably got killed in this neighborhood all the time. That would make things easier.

Killian decided that he would take a more subtle approach this time. Armed with only his compound bow and wearing his assassin's cloak, Killian camped out on the roof of an office building that overlooked the motel parking lot where the Range Rover was located and he waited. When the three fugitives finally emerged from their room, Killian would be ready and they would never even know what hit them.

About 7 AM, Killian noticed the drapes move slightly in the motel room that the Range Rover was parked directly in front of. Killian's compound bow was already armed and ready. The motel room door opened, and Killian prepared to fire.

All of a sudden, Killian noticed a white blur out of the corner of his eye. In the next moment, somebody tackled Killian and his compound bow went flying over the edge of the roof.

Killian roared in frustration as he and his assailant quickly rolled to their feet.

"I can't let you kill them Killian." The very elderly man that had just tackled Killian had a very long white beard and he was dressed almost entirely in white.

Killian instantly knew who it was.

"It can't be! I killed you!"

They slowly circled each other, but neither man made a move toward the other.

"I am afraid that I am not so easy to kill," the man in white responded.

Killian could not believe his eyes. "I shot you five times in the back and then for good measure I blew up an entire floor of a hotel in Rome."

The elderly man's face was extremely weathered, but his eyes had plenty of life in them. "I must admit that you got me good in Rome, Killian. And I still have the scars to prove it."

Killian continued to circle the old man as he tried to make some sense out of all this. "I got paid very well for killing you. Does The Order know that you are alive?"

"Yes, I believe that they do."

"So why haven't they told me?"

The old man sensed an opening. "There are a lot of things that they haven't told you Killian. You have been a valuable asset for them for a long time, but now they are convinced that you already know way too much about their ultimate goals. They worry about what could happen if they lose control of you. In fact, they plan to kill you off once this job is done."

"You lie!" Killian did not believe what the old man was telling him.

The old man frowned. "I am many things, Killian, but you know very well that a liar is not one of them. The Order has already hired two of your fellow assassins from The Red Hand to eliminate you once your usefulness has come to an end. They don't even plan to pay you for this assignment. So watch your back Killian – we need you to stay alive. Our side has big plans for you once all of this is over."

As the elderly man in white was finishing saying this, a very dense fog enveloped the rooftop that they were standing on.

To Killian, all of this sounded like crazy talk. "You have gone insane old man! Now I am going to make you pay and you will not escape from me this time."

Killian pulled a knife out of his boot, but the fog had become so thick that now he couldn't even see the elderly man.

"Where are you old man? Where did you go?"

Suddenly, Killian felt extremely dizzy. He lost consciousness and collapsed where he was standing.

Chapter 71

Tom, Russ and Melissa had no idea how close to death they had just come.

After leaving the motel, they headed across the city toward the custom truck business that they had come to Chicago to visit. They abandoned the Range Rover in a Waffle House parking lot, and they walked into "Mondo's Funky Wide World Of Custom Trucks" on foot.

Mondo was one of the most loyal readers that Russ had. They had never met in person, but Mondo had left more than a thousand comments on his articles over the years, and they had exchanged many emails. Russ felt like he knew Mondo very well even though they had never seen each other face to face.

But "Mondo's Funky Wide World Of Custom Trucks" was not quite what Russ was expecting.

It was definitely a funky business. It was basically one huge, messy garage that looked like it was still stuck in the 1970s. There was wood paneling on the walls of the garage and a small disco ball hung from the ceiling. There were several very old trucks in various states of disrepair inside the garage, and car parts were literally strewn all over the place. Off to the side there was a grizzly old mechanic with huge sideburns cleaning a carburetor, but there did not appear to be anyone else there other than him.

Tom, Russ and Melissa approached the mechanic, and Russ spoke first.

"Hello there – I'm looking for Mondo."

The grizzly old mechanic looked up for a moment and raised an eyebrow. "Who's asking?"

"We are," Russ responded. "We were hoping to get a truck."

"Do any of you have good credit?"

"Nope."

"Do you have cash?"

"Hardly any."

"Then you aren't getting a truck."

Russ was rapidly getting frustrated. "If I could just speak to Mondo I am sure that something could be worked out."

The old mechanic quit cleaning the carburetor and set it down. "Oh, you think that if Mondo was here that he would do something for you? Do you think that Mondo actually cares about you?"

Russ wasn't quite sure what to say next. "I would prefer to believe that people still care about one another in America."

"Anyone who actually believes that Americans still care about one another is either severely delusional, has overdosed on anti-depressants, or is madly in love with Diane Sawyer. Just look around. The economy has gone to hell and people are behaving like animals."

Russ had just about run out of patience. "Could you please just tell me how I can contact Mondo?"

"You still don't get it, do you? I'm Mondo."

"You're Mondo?"

"Yeah, who the hell are you?"

"I'm Diesel."

Mondo's eyes got really wide and his countenance immediately changed. "You better not be joking with me, because I will beat the living snot out of you if you are."

Russ smiled. "It's really me. I am sure that you saw my last post about being surrounded by the feds."

"Yeah," the old mechanic responded, "nobody heard anything from you after that. There are all kinds of rumors on the Internet that you are dead."

"No, thankfully I am not dead. But we are on the run. You may recognize one of my friends from American News Network, and my other friend is the former CIA agent that rescued us."

The old mechanic looked over at Tom and Melissa. "Yeah I do recognize her from television, and your buddy over there definitely looks like a spook. So who are you on the run from?"

"You probably wouldn't believe me if I told you."

"The Illuminati got you, didn't they?" The old mechanic was getting animated now. "I always knew that they would go after you eventually. I'd like to see those rat bastards fry in hell."

Russ wasn't sure how much he should tell Mondo. "Actually, I was captured by a government intelligence agency that is so paranoid about secrecy that it does not even have a name. It does basically anything that it wants, and as far as we can tell it is not even accountable to the president. It appears to operate under the umbrella of The Order of the Illuminati, but the same could probably be said for hundreds of other organizations. When I used to write about these kinds of things I had no idea that the conspiracy was this vast or this organized."

The old mechanic looked like he was about to lose it. "Man, things are really starting to hit the fan now! We gotta do something! This just ain't right. The last time I checked we still live in the United States of America. If super-secret government intelligence agencies are pulling people off the street just because they don't like what they are writing on the Internet, then we aren't any better than Nazi Germany. We have got to expose these tyrants!"

Tom decided that it was time for him to enter the discussion. "That is exactly what we plan to do. But first we need to get somewhere safe."

The old mechanic turned toward Tom. "Where are you guys headed?"

This time Melissa chimed in. "A place where there are a lot more mountains and a lot less people."

The old mechanic was calmer now. "So what can I do to help?"

Russ looked the old mechanic directly in the eyes. "Do you remember when you wrote to me and told me that if I was ever in Chicago and needed some help that I should look you up?"

"I sure do."

"Well, today is that day, and we could really use a truck."

Chapter 72

Mondo's shop may have looked like a total dump, but he was a genius when it came to working on trucks. He fixed Tom, Russ and Melissa up with an absolutely beautiful black 2010 Ford truck that had an extended cab and that contained all the bells and whistles. Mondo had even joked that he could have added a missile launcher to the truck if they had given him enough time.

At least they thought he was joking.

Russ assured Mondo that he would be sending him some money for the truck once he got back to Montana, but Mondo didn't seem too concerned about the money. He just honestly seemed glad to be able to help them. After spending a few hours with Mondo, they headed up into Wisconsin and then over into Minnesota. They took turns driving so that each of them could get some sleep.

As they rolled along, they spent most of the time listening to the radio. They were astounded to learn that martial law had been declared in major cities all over the nation. New York, Los Angeles, Oakland, Philadelphia, Miami, Detroit, Cleveland, Atlanta and Baltimore were all under martial law. There were even reports that the president was considering implementing martial law in Washington D.C. itself.

The economic collapse that had begun a few months ago was now accelerating, and there had been riots in almost every major U.S. city as people demanded solutions. The unemployment rate nationwide was now well over 20 percent and things were looking really grim. Of course the massive earthquake that had just hit the New Madrid fault had not helped things one bit. St. Louis had been declared a federal disaster area and large sections of the city had been flooded.

Tom, Russ and Melissa were dead tired and all of them were nursing various injuries. In particular, Melissa was in really bad shape. Sharp pain shot up her back whenever she moved, and her neck was absolutely killing her.

As they rolled into the small town of Litchfield, Minnesota she found herself wondering if her neck and back would ever be normal again. She was in a tremendous amount of pain, but she tried to block it out the best that she could.

From the passenger seat, Melissa stared out the window at a town that had obviously seen better days. Small businesses that were probably thriving just a few years earlier were now completely boarded up. There were "for sale" and "for rent" signs all over Litchfield, and a sense of gloom hung over the town like a dark cloud.

"Where are we?" Russ had just awakened in the back seat. "Are we still in Minnesota?"

"Yeah," Tom responded, "we are in Litchfield."

"This is Litchfield?" Russ was shaking his head. "When I came through here a decade ago things were so much nicer. This is so sad. I used to write about the nightmarish decline of Detroit and about how what was happening to that city would come to the rest of America soon enough, but it is truly horrifying to go through small town after small town and see it happening right in front of your eyes."

They hit a large bump in the road, and Melissa winced in pain. She turned toward Tom angrily. "Could you drive a bit more carefully? My back is really killing me."

"I'm doing the best that I can Melissa," Tom responded. "Just look at the roads. There are cracks and potholes all over the place. And as long as we are sticking to the back roads we are probably going to have to expect a lot more of this. Would it help if you went into the back seat and got some sleep?"

"No, I am fine for now. I am just getting really tired of constantly being on the road. Russ, how much longer will it be before we get to your place?"

"Well," Russ said from the back seat, "if we don't make any long stops and we drive all the way through the night we should get there some time tomorrow."

"I can handle one more day of driving," Melissa responded as she turned to look back out the window.

Melissa began reflecting on everything that she had lost. Just a few months ago she was working at the largest news network in the world and she was one of the most respected reporters in America. She was constantly rubbing shoulders with some of the wealthiest people on the entire planet, and she was living in a city that she loved. She was young, smart and beautiful and her bosses were constantly telling her that she had an incredibly bright future ahead of her.

But then she had met Tom McDowell, and it had just been one nightmare after another since then.

Her eyes started to tear up and she turned back toward Tom. "Sometimes I wake up and I forget where I am. I feel like my whole world has been turned upside down. Just a few months ago I had no idea that secret intelligence agencies that were not accountable to the president even existed, and I certainly had never heard of the Illuminati before. Yet I was a top reporter for the most important news network in the entire country. So how is that possible?"

Tom glanced over at Melissa. "I don't know how it is possible. I was in the CIA for years and I had never even heard of the agency before they recruited me. And I thought that 'the Illuminati' was just some sort of wild conspiracy that the tinfoil hat crowd tossed around to get people to come to their websites and listen to their radio shows. So what does that say about me?"

"Don't feel bad guys," Russ said in a more sober tone than usual. "I used to write about the Illuminati all the time, but even I had no idea that they were this organized or that their power was this vast. I think that most people kind of let the mainstream media define their reality for them. The average American watches 153 hours of television every month. I think that the media has much more power over us than any of us realize. After all, they don't call it 'programming' for nothing. It is almost as if we are all plugged into 'the matrix' and most of us are so comfortable with the false reality that we have been presented that we never question it. So if the mainstream media tells the American people that the Illuminati is just a bunch of nonsense that conspiracy theorists have made up, they just believe it."

Chapter 73

"Sir, we think that we know where they are heading."

After the debacle in St. Louis, the trail had gone ice cold and Jessup was becoming increasingly desperate to find the fugitives. He had gone back to Washington D.C. and had set up a situation room where more than three dozen agents were constantly pouring over every scrap of intel that looked promising, but so far nothing had panned out.

But now agent Wolfe had walked over to the back of the situation room where Jessup was standing with some apparently promising news.

"This had better be good Wolfe," Jessup shot back.

"I believe that it is sir, please follow me."

She led Jessup over to a workstation where a younger female agent known as "Newmar" was intently staring into her computer screen.

Agent Wolfe pointed at the screen. "Agent Newmar has been going through Diesel's old blog posts. Several years ago, there was a stretch of a few months where he frequently linked to a gardening blog. From the context of the posts, we strongly suspect that the gardening blog was run by Diesel's wife."

So far Jessup was not impressed. "So who cares if she had a gardening blog? What does that tell us?"

Agent Newmar swiveled in her chair and looked directly up at Jessup. "The key is the information that is embedded in the photos that were posted on the gardening blog. Many people don't realize that most smartphones have the capability of 'geotagging' the photographs that they take. In other words, many smartphones actually record the GPS coordinates of the precise location where a photo is taken. Well, it turns out that the photos posted on this gardening blog all had GPS information embedded in them."

Jessup was getting excited now. "And so where were all of the photos taken?"

Agent Newmar smiled. "They were all taken in a very remote area of western Montana. We believe that this is actually the location of Diesel's home which we have never been able to locate before. This is probably why the fugitives were heading west the whole time. They probably planned to go hole up at Diesel's place. In fact, if they moved very rapidly after they escaped us in St. Louis they could potentially even be there by now."

The importance of what Jessup had just been told started to sink in. "Great work agent Newmar. I want satellite surveillance on those coordinates immediately. Agent Wolfe, get me on the line with our Spokane office. We are going to need all of the personnel that they can muster. And I want to be on a plane out to Montana within the hour. We have only got one shot at this, and I want to make sure that nobody screws it up."

Chapter 74

Tom, Russ and Melissa were able to get from Minnesota over to western Montana without any further trouble. Their trip was quiet – almost too quiet. They hadn't even seen a traffic cop look at them funny.

And things were quiet inside the truck as well. Russ slept a lot and there was still a lot of underlying tension between Tom and Melissa. It was clear that Melissa was very grateful for having been rescued, but she also still harbored a lot of resentment toward Tom for how their relationship had ended.

Once they rolled into western Montana, Russ started perking up quite a bit. Since he was familiar with the area, he started pointing out important landmarks quite a bit, and he talked a lot about how eager he was to see his wife and kids again. It was very obvious to both Tom and Melissa that he loved his family immensely.

Tom and Melissa had never been up to this part of Montana, and they both could hardly believe how beautiful the scenery was. As they drove across one very high bridge over a river, Melissa looked into the valley below and found that her breath was almost taken away by how absolutely stunning everything was.

"It is gorgeous out here Russ. Why don't more people live out in this part of Montana?"

Russ smiled. "Well, it gets really, really cold in the winter and there is a lot of snow. A lot of people can't handle it."

Tom spoke up from behind the wheel. "I think that I could handle it. This almost seems like an entirely different planet compared to what I am used to back in the D.C. area."

"Hey," Russ said excitedly, "there are a couple of things that I want to point out to you guys up ahead. Do you see that big tree over on the right? Just after that big tree is a gravel road that leads to a lake. The gravel roads ends, but if you follow a dirt path around to the other side of the lake, there is a hillside that has a huge cave in it. Nobody seems to know about the cave, so my family has kind of designated it as an emergency 'bug out' location that we could rally at if something was to go wrong at our place. We have a bit of food and water and other supplies stashed in some storage containers near the back of the cave, but hopefully we will never have to use it."

Tom and Melissa both thought that it was a bit weird to store food and water in a cave, but they didn't say anything about it.

After a couple of moments of silence, Russ started tapping Tom on the shoulder as he pointed over to a spot that was coming up on the left side of the road.

"Over there is the other thing that I wanted to show you. It is the only spot on this road where one can look down into the valley where my home is located. I am sure that everything is fine, but we might as well take a peek. I would be absolutely amazed if they were able to find out where I lived, but the last thing we want to do is to walk straight into an ambush."

Tom pulled the truck off on to the right shoulder of the road and they all got out of the vehicle. Russ quickly moved toward the spot that he had pointed out to Tom and Melissa earlier. Melissa had to move a bit more slowly because of her injuries, and Tom watched to make sure that no traffic was coming as she slowly walked across the road.

Russ rushed over to the edge of the hillside and his jaw immediately dropped as he looked down into the valley below. Russ started to cuss up a storm as Tom and Melissa came up beside him. None of them could believe what they were seeing.

From their position, they could see that six black helicopters had landed on the property and about 40 heavily armed agents had formed a perimeter around the main house.

Chapter 75

"My wife and kids are down there! We have got to do something!"

Russ was officially freaking out. He had spent years making sure that something like this would never happen, and now his worst nightmare was coming true.

"Settle down Russ," Tom said sternly. "Perhaps when they realize that we aren't down there they will leave your wife and kids alone."

"Yes," Melissa interjected, "let's wait and see how this plays out. Will they be able to see us up here Russ?"

"No way," Russ responded, "we are much too far away for them to spot us. But we just can't sit up here and do nothing. This has 'Waco' and 'Ruby Ridge' written all over it. I just can't stand by and watch them storm my home."

"And exactly what do you propose that we do?" Tom was starting to lose his patience. "If you will remember, we lost all of our guns when the Audi was stolen in West Virginia. Are we going to run down there and throw rocks at them?"

"You are right," Russ conceded, "we can't fight them. But perhaps I could go down there and give myself up. If they have me, they might let my family go."

"Or they might not," Tom shot back. "You don't understand how these guys operate Russ. The normal rules don't apply to them. From everything that I have learned about them so far, once they have you in custody they will most likely want to 'sanitize' the entire area. That would include killing anyone that could ever tell the public about what happened. In the end, the only thing keeping your family alive right now is the fact that they don't have you yet. As long as the agency considers your family to be valuable as 'bait', they will probably keep them alive."

Russ knew that Tom was telling him the truth, but it still absolutely horrified him.

"I hate myself. I never should have started blogging. If I had just stayed off the Internet and never talked about any of this stuff, my family would not be in this kind of danger. We could have lived out our lives in peace and safety. But instead, my desire to 'make a difference' has ruined our lives."

"You can't blame yourself Russ," Melissa said in an attempt to calm him down. "Is running into a hole and hiding any way to live? There are already way too many cowards in America. The fact that so many people have failed to speak out against evil is the reason that secret organizations like this can exist in the first place. Unless people start standing up to these evil people, they will just keep on ruining lives."

"Melissa is right Russ," Tom said. "All it takes for evil to prosper is for good men to do nothing. You should be proud of the work that you have done over the years. And if it wasn't for you, millions of people would not have learned the truth about the New Year's Eve plot to bomb Times Square and destroy the bank account records of the ten largest banks in America. Let us just hope that someone out there is taking action to stop that plot from becoming a reality."

Russ understood what they were saying, but he was not about to calm down. "Right now, all I care about is the safety of my wife and my three kids. If anything happens to them I will never forgive myself."

"Well," Melissa responded, "let's just keep watching and hopefully once they realize that we aren't there they will go away. I don't think that we really have any other options right now."

Chapter 76

Jessup was seething with frustration as he stared up at the big white house that the agents under his command had formed a perimeter around.

"What do you mean they aren't here?"

Agent Wolfe did not like being barked at by Jessup, but it was part of the job so she put up with it.

"What I am saying, sir, is that thermal imaging shows that there is just one adult female, one young male and two young females in the home. It is believed that those are his wife and kids. There is no sign of anyone else on the property."

"Damn it! I knew that we should not have barged in like this. We should have just set up covert surveillance and waited for them to arrive." Jessup scanned the hills surrounding the property. "Now if they see us they will be scared off. In fact, they could be looking down at us right now and we would never even know it."

Agent Wolfe's expression did not change. "So what should we do sir?"

Jessup thought about that for a moment. "Well, we may have lost the element of surprise, but we still have some cards to play."

———————

Inside the house, Dottie Jacoby was about to totally lose it.

"I knew this would happen! This is why I warned your father to quit blogging. I knew that someday the feds would find our home. I've already lost him, and now I am going to lose the three of you."

Little Brynn looked up at her mother. "You aren't going to lose us Mommy. We are right here."

Hunter decided that he had better take charge of things. "Kinley, why don't you take Brynn down into the basement? Mom and I will handle things up here."

Kinley took Brynn by the hand and led her down into the basement. That left Hunter and his mother alone up on the main level.

"You know that there is no way that we can shoot our way out of this Hunter. It looks like there are several dozen armed men out there."

"I know Mom. But we've got to think of something."

Suddenly, a loud voice coming from what sounded like a megaphone interrupted their conversation.

"The house is surrounded. You are to come out the front door unarmed and with your hands raised. You have five minutes."

Dottie's eyes got really big and she turned to look at Hunter. "So what do we do?"

"We've got to go talk to them," Hunter responded. "I'll be the one to go out there first."

Chapter 77

"Sir, thermal imaging shows that one of them is approaching the front door."

Jessup nodded to Wolfe and then trained his binoculars on the front of the house. After just a few moments, a young male walked out with his hands high above his head.

Jessup considered what he was about to do. He still needed this kid for bait, but he also wanted to do something to draw the fugitives out if they happened to be watching.

Jessup looked over to his left. "Sniper team one, are you ready?"

"We are ready sir."

Jessup looked back toward the house. "I instructed the entire family to come out of the house, but only the boy has come out. This must be a trick. Sniper team one, I want you to target the legs. You may fire when ready."

Two shots rang out and Hunter collapsed to the ground.

From high above, Jessup and all of the other agents could hear a deep male voice crying out in excruciating pain.

———

"NOOOOOOOOOOOOOOOOOOO! Not my son! Not my only son! I'm the one you want! Take me and leave my family alone! Just please don't shoot my family! Please don't shoot my family!"

Tears were flowing down his face as Russ cried out into the valley below. He had stepped out from behind cover and he had raised his arms high above his head.

"I surrender! PLEASE just get some medical attention for my boy! Don't let him die! I surrender!"

Russ continued to yell out to the agents below. As he did so, Tom rushed over to Russ. Tom grabbed him by the shoulders and spun Russ around so that he was now facing Tom, but Russ hardly seemed to notice. Russ just kept sobbing and crying out to the agents in the valley below.

Tom knew that there was no time to lose. He slammed his fist across Russ's face as hard as he could, and Russ dropped to the ground like a sack of potatoes.

Chapter 78

Hours later, Russ awoke. He was lying on cold, damp ground inside a cave.

"Dottie? Hunter? Kinley? Brynn?"

"No Russ," a woman's voice responded, "it is just me."

Russ recognized that the voice belonged to Melissa.

"Where are we?"

"We are in the cave that you told us about. After you started yelling, we kind of went into panic mode. Tom knew that we had to get out of there before they got those helicopters up in the air. Tom and I dragged you into the truck and then Tom drove like a madman toward this cave. The entrance of the cave was just big enough for us to be able to pull the truck into it, and so we were able to get it out of sight of the helicopters. Right now Tom is out looking for some large rocks and tree branches so that we can cover up the mouth of this cave the best that we can."

Russ was still kind of in a daze. "What about my family?"

"We don't know what happened to your family. But that was really stupid what you did back there Russ. Do you really think that you could have saved anyone by surrendering? Yes, you and your family would have probably stayed alive long enough for them to get all of the information out of you that they wanted, but after that they would have killed all of you. At least now your family has a chance. They will probably keep them alive in case they need them for bait or leverage."

Russ realized that his face was throbbing. He reached up and touched his left cheekbone. It felt like it had been broken.

"Why did Tom hit me?"

Just then, Tom came walking back toward them from the entrance to the cave. He was not pleased.

"You don't get it, do you? You just about got me, Melissa and your entire family killed with the stunt that you pulled back there. These people don't play by the rules and they sure don't have any mercy. Do you actually believe that they would have spared a single member of your family in the end?"

"You are right Tom," Russ responded, "but until you see one of your own children shot right in front of your eyes you will have no idea what I am going through right now. I feel like I am in hell."

"I can't even imagine how much pain you are in right now," Melissa said comfortingly. "Just get some rest for a while Russ. Tom and I will look through the supplies in the back of the cave and see if we can find something for us to eat."

Tom and Melissa walked off toward the back of the cave, and Russ pulled himself up to a sitting position. He had survived, but until he found out what had happened to his family he wasn't going to be sure if his life was still worth living.

Chapter 79

Tom, Russ and Melissa stayed in the cave for the next seven days, but the weather was really starting to get cold, and even though they slept inside the truck at night they were having a very hard time staying warm.

Finally, they decided to venture out to get some gasoline for the truck. On the way, they stopped at the spot on the highway that allowed them to look down into the valley where Russ's home was located. What they saw really shook them up. The main house and every other structure on the property had been burned to the ground.

Russ couldn't control his tears. He still had no idea what had happened to his wife and family, and now everything that he had worked to build for so many years was destroyed.

Russ turned toward Tom and Melissa and they could see the anguish on his face. "I need to go down into the valley and see if the bodies of my wife and children are there."

"It's not safe," Tom responded.

"You know that I have to do this Tom."

Tom nodded his head. "I know. But it is not safe for Melissa and I to come with you. The agency could still be watching this valley."

Russ looked like all of the life had just been sucked out of him. "I can hike down there by myself. I know these hills like the back of my hand. You two take the truck and go back to the cave. If I don't make it back by tomorrow afternoon, get out of here and never look back."

Melissa seemed hesitant. "Are you sure Russ?"

Russ nodded his head. "I am sure."

Tom could see the determination in his eyes. He knew that he had to let Russ go down there. "Okay my friend. Good luck."

Tom and Melissa hugged Russ and then they took off in the truck. Russ slowly started making his way down into the valley, very afraid of what he might find.

Chapter 80

Early the next morning Tom and Melissa were just starting to pack up the truck with supplies from the cave when Russ came walking in.

Tom was the first to speak. "What did you find?"

Russ seemed a bit calmer today. "Fortunately, I didn't find any dead bodies. That doesn't mean that they are still alive, but at least it gives me hope. On the downside, the agency literally destroyed everything. They even found my underground food caches and destroyed those. They definitely did not leave a single stone unturned."

Melissa walked over and gave him a hug. "I am so sorry."

"Thank you Melissa," Russ responded.

Then he noticed that a bunch of supplies were already packed in the truck. "Have you guys discussed where we are going next?"

"Yeah," Tom said sleepily. "My sister owns a cabin in the mountains over in the state of Washington. She always told me that I could use it whenever I want, so I think that it is about time I took her up on that offer. It is very isolated, but it does have satellite television and high speed Internet service. I think that it would be perfect for us, unless someone has a better idea."

"Don't look at me," Russ said in reply, "all of the preparations that I spent years working on have just gone up in smoke."

"I think that the cabin sounds perfect," Melissa said as she picked up a box of storable food. "Tom, what town did you say that the cabin was closest to?"

"It is near the little town of Greenwater," Tom said cheerfully. "I absolutely love it there. We used to go up there when I was a kid. When my uncle died, my sister bought it. It is nice and quiet there, and nobody will bother us."

Back in Washington D.C., Jessup was going out of his mind. He felt like he had been so close to capturing McDowell and the two escaped prisoners in Montana, but now they seemed to have disappeared into thin air and there had not been a single decent lead on their whereabouts in a week. Jessup was becoming increasingly concerned that he had lost them forever, and he knew what that meant.

He was pacing back and forth in the back of the situation room that he had assembled to coordinate the search for the three fugitives when a woman that he did not recognize boldly came walking in.

Jessup was in no mood to put up with unexpected visitors. "Excuse me, who are you and what are you doing here?"

The woman was extremely beautiful, but she did not look happy.

"Perhaps I should be asking you the same thing," she shot back at Jessup.

Jessup's face started to get red. "Look, I am not in any mood for games lady. If you do not identify yourself in about five seconds I am going to have you taken into custody."

"Look chubby, I am here to do you a favor. I am probably the only one in the world that has any idea where your three precious fugitives are going next."

Jessup was completely out of patience at this point, but he was also desperate for any information that would lead him to the fugitives.

"Okay, I'll bite. Where are they going and why haven't you come forward with this information before now?"

The beautiful lady with the dark hair smiled. "They are almost certainly heading out to a cabin that Tom McDowell's sister owns near the town of Greenwater, Washington. I have not come forward with this information before now because I have been in the hospital. I was in a very bad boating accident."

She definitely had Jessup's attention now. "Okay, let's say that I believe you. How in the world did you come across this piece of information? And you still haven't told me who you are..."

The beautiful lady with the dark hair grinned widely as she pulled up a chair and sat down.

"Oh, I know that you will believe me because you haven't had another solid lead on their location in a week. The people that I work for have sent me here to make sure that

you don't royally mess things up this time. If you do screw
things up, I am going to make your life a living hell. You
see, the truth is that Tom McDowell is my ex-boyfriend.
My name is Caroline Mancini and I work for The Order of
the Illuminati."

Chapter 81

Roaming around in the woods in the middle of the night was just about the last place that Killian wanted to be, but he still had a job to finish. It had been raining for most of the last several days, and even though the rain had now stopped and there were no clouds in the night sky, everything around Killian was still extremely damp. Somehow Killian's socks had even gotten wet, and that made Killian feel even more miserable. Tonight the temperature had dipped down into the upper thirties, and a brisk wind made it feel even colder. It wasn't just cold – this was a bone chilling cold that Killian could feel down to his core.

After Chicago, he had lost track of the fugitives, but fortunately he still had access to all of the intel that the agency was being fed. He had traveled up to the Northwest after the fugitives had slipped through the agency's grasp in Montana, and once he had learned that the fugitives were likely holed up in a cabin near Greenwater, Washington he headed out that way as quickly as he could. Killian had been hoping to get out to the cabin before the agency did, so he had been a bit disappointed when he saw that they had already barricaded the only road going in toward the cabin. Killian knew that the agency had very big plans elsewhere tomorrow night, but they had still committed at least 50 agents to this particular operation. From where he was hiding, he could see agents starting to spread out and form a perimeter around the cabin.

Off toward the south, Killian could hear more rumbling coming from Mt. Rainier. The plume of ash that was rising from the volcano that had started a couple of hours earlier was getting much larger, and every few minutes Killian could feel the ground tremble under his feet. The sickening smell of sulfur was starting to become overpowering, and volcanic ash had begun to fall from the sky all around him. There had been reports on the evening news that had discussed how scientists were extremely concerned about the possibility of a major eruption. If it happened tonight, that could potentially disrupt his plans. Killian knew that he was going to have to act quickly.

"Sir, our scouts have confirmed that there are two adult males and one adult female in the cabin."

Jessup smiled broadly. "Outstanding! Kalon, let me know when the assault team is in position. And please remind them that we want these fugitives alive. If they are dead they will not be able to answer any of my questions."

Kalon walked away to coordinate things with the assault team, and Jessup turned back toward the cabin. He was absolutely thrilled that this crisis was about to come to an end. Once he had Tom McDowell and the two escaped prisoners in custody, all of the mistakes that he had made over the past several weeks would hopefully be forgotten. Perhaps Lilith would even let him keep his position as the head of the D.C. office.

Jessup was jolted out of his daydreaming by a very loud explosion that came from the direction of Mt. Rainier. Jessup looked over toward the volcano and he could see that the entire top of the mountain had exploded. A massive amount of volcanic dust and ash was being forced up into the atmosphere, and it appeared that a full-blown eruption of Mt. Rainier was now underway.

Jessup went running over toward Kalon. As he did so, he almost lost his balance as the ground beneath him shook violently. He knew that he had to get his team out of there quickly. "Hey Kalon – thanks to that volcano our plans have just changed. We are going to have to strike faster than I anticipated. We are storming that cabin in three minutes whether the assault team is ready or not."

———————

One of the things that Tom McDowell truly loved was a really good night of sleep, so when he was jolted awake at 2 AM by a ringing phone it instantly put him in a very foul mood.

The phone was on the nightstand next to his bed. He had hardly noticed it when they had first arrived at the cabin, and he couldn't think of any reason why anyone would be trying to call them. The truth was that nobody was even supposed to know that they were there.

He thought about not answering the phone, and in fact for security reasons he definitely should not have answered it, but a little voice inside his head urged him to pick it up.

So he did.

"Hello?" Tom tried to clear his head and wake up, but he was extremely groggy. "Who is calling?"

"Tom, this is your sister Hannah. Do not turn on the lights. Federal agents have formed a perimeter around the cabin and they are getting ready for an assault."

Tom's eyes popped wide open when he heard this. He bolted over to the curtains and took a quick peek outside. It was very dark, but it did appear to Tom that there were some shadowy figures moving around off in the distance.

"How do you know that we are here Hannah? And how do you know for sure that there are federal agents out there? I just looked outside and I could hardly see anything."

Hannah's voice was urgent. "There is no time to explain. There is an elderly man standing in the kitchen right now. You need to wake up the others that are with you and you need to go with him if you want to live. Hang up and walk into the kitchen NOW."

Tom hung up the phone and walked into the kitchen. An elderly man with a very long white beard that was dressed almost entirely in white was standing there. Tom recognized that it was the same man that had helped them in St. Louis.

The elderly man spoke first. "Tom, please wake up Melissa and Russ. I need all of you to put on your shoes. I am afraid that we do not have much time. We must go now."

Instead of asking any of the dozens of questions that were suddenly shooting through his mind, Tom decided that he had better listen to the old man. He quickly went back into the bedroom that he had been sleeping in and woke Russ up, and then he went over to the other bedroom and woke Melissa up.

When Melissa rushed into the kitchen, she recognized the elderly man right away.

"I know you."

"Yes," the elderly man responded, "but we do not have time to talk now. We must leave."

Tom and Russ came stumbling out of the front bedroom with their shoes on, and the elderly man already had his hand on the doorknob of the back door of the cabin which was right off of the kitchen.

The elderly man had a very serious expression on his face, but he spoke very softly.

"Follow me closely. We will be moving very rapidly and a single mistake could cost all of us our lives. We must go now."

With that, the elderly man bolted out the door, and Tom, Russ and Melissa quickly followed him.

Chapter 82

"Sir, the assault team is in position on the west side of the house and they have indicated that they are ready. Thermal imaging still indicates that all three fugitives are asleep in their beds. It looks like the eruption over at Mt. Rainier is not showing any signs of letting up, so we might want to hurry."

"Very good Kalon," Jessup responded. "Send them in."

Through his night vision goggles, Jessup could see agents dressed in black riot gear starting to silently move toward the cabin and he smiled.

Hidden up on a ridge southeast of the cabin, Killian suddenly realized that he was out of time. It was either now or never. He checked his thermal imaging equipment one more time. It told him that both adult males were still sleeping in their beds in the front bedroom and that the adult female was still sleeping in her bed in the second bedroom.

Killian understood that the agency wanted these fugitives alive, but Killian wanted them dead.

He lifted his FGM-148 Javelin missile launcher to his shoulder and fired.

The agents that had been storming toward the cabin dropped and took cover when they spotted the missile that was suddenly streaking through the sky.

It slammed into the front bedroom of the cabin, and an instant later there was a deafening explosion. A massive fireball consumed the cabin and lit up the night sky.

To say that Jessup was stunned would be a massive understatement. He just stood there with his mouth hanging open. After a few moments of complete bewilderment, he finally came to his senses.

"What the hell was that??" Jessup was screaming into his radio. "Who fired that missile??"

Kalon came running up to his side. "Sir, it wasn't one of us. Someone fired that missile from a ridge southeast of the cabin. Should I send a team up to investigate?"

Jessup thought about that for a moment. As he did, another massive explosion rocked Mt. Rainier off in the distance. Even more dust and ash shot up thousands of feet into the air and an enormous river of volcanic mud started to pour out of the side of the mountain.

Jessup knew that he had to get his team away from that erupting volcano. "There is no time!" Jessup was yelling at Kalon so that he could be heard over the roar of the volcano. "Just send some agents over to check the wreckage of the cabin. We want to make sure that there were no survivors. After that let's get the heck out of here."

———————

The missile hit the cabin just a few moments after the elderly man had led Tom, Russ and Melissa away from it. The explosion knocked all four of them off of their feet.

Tom was in the trail position, and he had gotten the worst of it. He had been knocked sideways into a large tree, and when he tried to get back up he found that he could not put any weight on his right leg.

"Are you okay Tom?" Melissa rushed to his side once she realized that he had been hurt. She could see that his leg was very badly damaged. "Can you get up?"

"No, I think that it is broken. You guys go ahead without me. I will only slow you down."

Without saying a word, the elderly man came over and picked Tom up like a sack of potatoes and threw him over his shoulder.

"I've got him," the elderly man whispered. "Follow me."

———————

By this time, Killian was already well away from the ridge where he had fired his weapon. Nobody could possibly have survived that explosion, and Killian considered his job to be done.

As he jogged away, he stopped to take one more look back at his handiwork. Using his night vision goggles, Killian could see that the cabin had been completely obliterated, but beyond the cabin out in the distance he spotted something that made his jaw drop.

The old man that he had tangled with in Chicago was standing on top of a hill and was staring directly back at him. He was carrying the body of one of the fugitives on his shoulders, and even at that great distance he seemed to know exactly where Killian was.

Killian thought about reloading his missile launcher and taking a shot at the elderly man, but as Killian was considering this the elderly man rushed out of sight down the other side of the hill.

Chapter 83

Even though he was carrying Tom on his shoulders, the elderly man was moving very rapidly through the woods. So rapidly in fact that Russ and Melissa were really struggling to keep up.

Another loud explosion caused all of them to turn and look over at Mt. Rainier. Earlier, the moon had been providing quite a bit of light, but now ash and smoke had covered much of the night sky and that was making things very dark. None of them had a flashlight, and moving through the woods on a night this dark was proving to be quite difficult.

As they rushed along, they passed one agent on the ground that was either dead or unconscious and then another one. Russ and Melissa both wanted to ask the elderly man how this had happened, but they kept their questions to themselves.

After about another ten minutes of hard walking through the woods, the elderly man stopped and put Tom on the ground. He kneeled down and looked Tom in the eyes.

"How does your leg feel?"

Tom was not doing well at all. "It feels like it has been shattered."

The elderly man had a tremendous amount of compassion in his eyes. "I would like to roll up your pants and take a look. Is that alright?"

"Yes, that would be fine," Tom responded. "Are you a doctor?"

"No, but I can help," the elderly man replied back as he examined Tom's broken right leg.

The leg was definitely in bad shape. The tibia was sticking out through the skin and the entire lower leg was turning purple.

Melissa gasped when she saw how gruesome it was.

Tom was in an extreme amount of pain but he wanted the truth. "How bad is it Melissa?"

"It looks really bad Tom. The bone has penetrated all the way through the skin."

The elderly man rolled his pant leg back down, grabbed the lower section of Tom's right leg with both of his hands and closed his eyes.

"Don't worry Tom," Russ said hopefully, "we'll get you out of here and get you some medical help somehow."

Tom was not as optimistic. "Are you kidding? I can't walk, we are in the middle of nowhere and on top of everything else Mt. Rainier is erupting. What we need is a major miracle about now."

The elderly man reopened his eyes, took his hands off of Tom's leg and stood up.

"Well," the elderly man said cheerfully, "that should about do it. You should be able to walk now Tom."

Tom felt his right leg. There was no more pain and his tibia was not protruding out of the skin any longer.

Tom turned and looked up at the elderly man.

"How did you do that?"

The elderly man shook his head. "You don't understand. I did not do it."

"Then who did?"

The elderly man looked at Tom with great love. "Y'shua is the one that has healed you. In English, you call him Jesus. You have much to learn, but now is not the time. Right now you all need to get away from this volcano as rapidly as you can. Much of Greenwater is going to be covered by a lahar and the parts that aren't are going to be absolutely buried by volcanic ash."

Melissa and Russ were both absolutely stunned by what they had just seen.

"Thank you for helping us," Melissa said to the elderly man. "What is your name?"

"You can call me Yochanan."

Tom had gotten back to his feet by this time and was in a noticeably better mood.

"Well Yochanan," Tom said as he smiled at the old man, "I also want to thank you for all that you have done for us. If it was not for you, we would all be dead right now. I don't understand why you keep popping into our lives, but obviously you are here to help us. So where do we go now?"

The elderly man handed a compass and a set of keys to Tom. "Use this compass to go directly north for another half mile. If you hit the button on the right side of the compass, it will light up so that you can see it. When you get to the road, you will find a blue SUV parked along the shoulder. Those are the keys for the vehicle. Inside the SUV you will find a GPS navigation device. There is just one address stored in the memory. Travel north to that address. It is not too far from Bellingham. You will be safe there."

Russ was a bit skeptical. "But what about the people that are chasing us? Won't they find us if we take to the road too quickly?"

The elderly man shook his head. "The secret government intelligence agency that was chasing you believes that you are dead. Even thermal imaging equipment can be fooled. There is one man that knows that you are still alive, but he will not be coming after you anymore. But it is not wise to stand around here much longer. We should get going."

"He is right," Tom said as he turned toward Russ and Melissa, "can you guys make it another half mile?"

"Yeah," Melissa replied cheerfully, "I am quite tired but I can definitely make it a half mile. What about you Russ?"

Russ grinned broadly. "After what we have been through, a half mile is nothing."

"Great," Tom said as he turned back to look for the elderly man. "Where did Yochanan go?"

They all looked around but he was gone. After a few moments they realized that he wasn't coming back and they started following the compass north.

Chapter 84

It was only a couple of hours before sunrise when Killian finally returned to the dumpy little motel where he was staying. He was eager to get out of his tactical armor, take a bath and get some sleep.

When he opened the door to his motel room, he immediately sensed that something was wrong. Someone had spilled M&M's all over both beds and that could only mean one thing.

There were two twin female assassins in The Red Hand, Mira and Mikaela, that used M&M's as their calling card. In a flash, Killian realized what was about to happen. He dove face down between the two queen size beds in his room just as dozens of armor-piercing depleted uranium rounds ripped through the front window.

Killian waited for a pause in the firing and then he sprang to his feet. He knew what was likely to come after the deleted uranium. Killian ran toward the back window of his motel room and dove through it head first. He rolled to his feet and began sprinting as the motel room behind him exploded in a massive ball of fire.

Killian had been correct – Mira and Mikaela had followed up the depleted uranium rounds with an RPG.

Killian sprinted into the woods as fast as he could and just kept going without looking back.

He knew that there was only one organization in the world that could turn members of his own assassin clan against him.

Killian cursed under his breath as he weaved his way through the woods. The old man had been right after all. The Order of the Illuminati wanted him dead, and so now there would be no place on earth that he would be truly safe.

But now there would also be no place on earth where they would be truly safe either. They had just made a very dangerous enemy, and Killian intended to make them pay dearly.

Chapter 85

When Tom, Russ and Melissa finally reached the address up in Bellingham that they had been given, they discovered a very large country house that was surrounded by about 20 acres of land. Apparently someone was expecting them, because they were greeted right away by two large men.

One of them introduced himself as "Tommy Sims" and the other introduced himself as "Rick Florian", but Tom suspected that those were not their real names. The two men explained that they ran this house along with their wives, but that after some rest Tom, Russ and Melissa were to be moved to an even more secure location.

After being given an opportunity to wash up, Tom, Russ and Melissa were ushered into a huge dining area where they were served a very large meal. The conversation was light but not very substantive. Tom, Russ and Melissa were so tired that they didn't really feel like asking too many probing questions of their hosts, and "Tommy" and "Rick" and their wives were being pretty evasive anyway.

After the meal, Tom, Russ and Melissa were told that a doctor was coming over to take a look at them since they had been through so much. They were led upstairs to a room that looked like it could have belonged in a hospital. It contained six twin size beds that were neatly made up, and they were all encouraged to lie down and wait for the doctor.

When the doctor arrived, he looked them all over and made some notes. He seemed particularly concerned about Melissa's neck and back. She was still in a tremendous amount of constant pain.

"All of you really need some time to rest and recover," the doctor said as he was finishing up examining Melissa. "I don't know that I have ever examined a group of people with so many injuries."

"We take a licking but we keep on ticking," Melissa remarked. "But the past few weeks have definitely been very hard on the three of us. Are we all going to be okay?"

"Yes," the doctor responded, "in time all of you should hopefully make a full recovery. But for now it is important to get as much rest as possible. In fact, let me give you all something that will help you sleep."

The doctor handed each of them a large red pill and a glass of water. Tom, Russ and Melissa had no reason to distrust the doctor, and they were all looking forward to a good night of sleep, so all of them quickly swallowed the red pill.

Within a few moments of swallowing the red pill, Tom realized that what he had been given was no normal sleeping pill. He was rapidly losing consciousness and he tried to sit up in his bed to fight back. He reached over to grab the doctor, but it was too late. Tom lost consciousness and he collapsed on his bed, as did Russ and Melissa.

The doctor smiled. He opened the door to the room and called down to the others.

"They are ready," the doctor declared.

Chapter 86

On New Year's Eve, Operation Ordo Ab Chao went off without a hitch.

Thanks to the efforts of Tom, Melissa and Russ, millions of Americans had heard about it beforehand, but the agency had been ordered to go ahead with the operation anyway.

The dirty bombs that went off in Times Square killed more than 10,000 innocent people and tens of thousands of others had either been seriously injured or had been exposed to very high levels of radiation. New York City went into a panic unlike anything that had ever been seen before.

The destruction of the bank account records of the ten largest banks in the United States was also successful. Those bombings were greatly overshadowed by what happened in Times Square, but the truth is that they actually did far more long-term damage to the country. All of the backup records had also been destroyed, and so all of the bank account data was permanently lost. Of course the agency had been very careful not to touch the records of the mortgages, loans and credit card accounts that those banks were holding. Those were in separate facilities that had not been bombed.

So tens of millions of Americans woke up the next morning only to discover that their bank accounts had been wiped out but their debts had not been.

In the coming weeks, their bank accounts would be restored if they had paper records that proved that they actually did have money in their accounts, but most Americans had not held on to such records.

Needless to say, there were a lot of incredibly angry people and the financial system completely collapsed.

Of course the media had a field day with all of this. It was the story of the decade, and there was wall to wall coverage 24 hours a day for weeks.

The "official story" that law enforcement and the mainstream media had been given just hours after the bombings was that a rogue CIA agent named Tom McDowell and a crazed "conspiracy theorist" named Russ Jacoby had been the "masterminds" behind the bombings. No mention was made of Melissa Remling.

According to the "official story", Tom McDowell and Russ Jacoby had attempted to pin the blame for the bombings on the U.S. government by releasing a fake recording on the Internet ahead of time. Their supposed goal was to create civil unrest and to turn the American people against the federal government.

The American people celebrated wildly a couple of days after the bombings when it was announced that the president had authorized a daring raid on the "compound" where Tom McDowell and Russ Jacoby had been hiding. Of course Tom and Russ had supposedly been "killed" in the raid, but the president assured the American people that the "domestic terror threat" was just beginning.

A new set of "terror watch guidelines" was quickly issued to law enforcement authorities all over the United States. The following groups were identified in those guidelines as "potential terrorists"...

-"conspiracy theorists"

-"Tea Party sympathizers"

-"anti-abortion activists"

-"militia groups"

-"those with extreme religious views"

-"bloggers with extremist ideologies"

-"assault weapon owners"

-"anyone that expresses negative opinions about the United Nations"

-"anyone that is suspicious of centralized federal authority"

-"anyone that has a fear of communist regimes"

-"those that talk about a 'New World Order' in a derogatory manner"

Thousands of people were rounded up and brought in for questioning in the aftermath of the attacks.

Most were eventually released, but some were never heard from again.

The president promised the American people that he would do everything that he could possibly do to prevent terror attacks like this from ever happening on American soil again. Strong new "national security" legislation was rushed through Congress and funding for the Department of Homeland Security was doubled.

Funding for "black budget" government intelligence agencies was also doubled.

Fewer voices than ever spoke out against the government. As people started to disappear and rumors started spreading, people became very afraid. Pretty soon there was very little open opposition to the government at all.

Chapter 87

When Tom awoke, he was in a completely different bed in a completely different room.

"Don't worry Tom," a female voice said to him. "You are safe now."

Tom recognized the voice. "Hannah?"

"Yes Tom, it is your sister. Don't be alarmed. Everything is okay."

Tom sat up in his bed and looked around. He was sleeping in a queen size bed in a large bedroom enclosed by stone walls. A fire was roaring in a fireplace along the far wall, and his sister was attending to the fire. Nobody else appeared to be in the room.

"Where are Russ and Melissa?"

Hannah smiled. "They are fine. They each have their own rooms."

Tom was very confused. "Where are we?"

"You are in Idaho Tom. I apologize for the cloak and dagger stuff. Tommy and Rick are quite paranoid, and they were not entirely sure that they could trust you. They figured that it would be safer for everyone if all of you were asleep for the journey."

Tom was still in the same clothes that he had been wearing in Bellingham. He got out of his bed and walked over to the fire that his sister was tending.

"Why did you bring us here?" Tom's mind was racing. "Don't you know that the entire country is looking for us?"

"The people that were searching for you think that you are dead," Hannah responded. "And we plan to keep it that way."

His sister seemed to know far more about what was going on then he did, and this was starting to really frustrate Tom. "Hannah, who is this 'we' that you keep talking about? Are you a part of some larger organization?"

Hannah turned and looked Tom directly in the eyes.

"Have you ever heard of 'the Remnant' Tom?"

Tom thought about that for a moment. During his training with the agency, "the Remnant" had been mentioned as a domestic terrorist organization numerous times, and when Russ and Melissa had been captured they had been questioned repeatedly about any affiliation with "the Remnant" while they were being tortured.

"I think so. Are you a part of a terrorist organization?"

Hannah laughed. "Of course not, although that is what some of our enemies would like people to believe that we are. The truth is that we strive to love all people and we do not wish harm on anyone. The real terrorists are the ones that use violence to spread fear and hate. They want to use fear and hate to control the world, while we want to use love and forgiveness to change it."

"So if you are not a terrorist organization, then what are you?"

Hannah handed a book to Tom. "Our enemies hate us because of what we believe. We are entering a time in human history that God refers to as the last days. It will be an incredibly tumultuous time. In fact, it will be a darker time than humanity has ever known before. But as darkness increases, so will the true light. All over the world, God is raising up His Remnant for these last days. We are those that keep the commandments of God and that share the good news about salvation through faith in Y'shua the Messiah. You can read about us in that book."

Tom looked down at the book that he had been handed.

It was a Bible.

Tom set the book down. None of this made any sense to him yet.

"You are confusing the heck out me Hannah."

Hannah felt herself become a little frustrated, but she reminded herself to be patient. "Tom, you still don't understand how important you are, do you?"

Tom gave her a puzzled look.

Hannah realized that she had some explaining to do. "Why do you think I called you and told you what we knew about the economic problems that were going to happen? Why do you think I called you and told you what we had found out about the New Year's Eve bombings that your agency was planning? We wanted you to get involved. We wanted you to turn on the agency. In the end, we wanted to get you out here so that you could be with us."

Tom could hardly believe what he was hearing. "You used me as a pawn?"

Hannah frowned. "Of course not. You are far more important than that Tom. There is a reason why such an effort was made to keep you alive. You have a very big future ahead of you, even though you don't realize it right now."

Tom sat down in a chair next to the fire. He didn't know what to think. Had his sister gone completely insane?

"How am I supposed to have any sort of a future Hannah? I am one of the most wanted men in America and the instant that I show my face in public I will be arrested as a terrorist."

"Actually," Hannah responded, "you have no idea how famous you have become. Despite your efforts, the New Year's Eve bombings that your agency was planning went ahead as scheduled. The news channels are reporting that more than 10,000 people were killed in Times Square. When you are feeling better, I will show you some of the footage. It was absolutely horrifying. New York City is basically paralyzed by fear at this point. And the bank account records of the ten largest banks in the country were totally wiped out. Even the facilities where the backup records were being held were bombed. Tens of millions of Americans have lost all of the money in their bank accounts, and those that did not keep their paper bank statements will never see any of that money again. The level of anger in this country has reached a fever pitch, and you and Russ are being blamed for planning the entire thing. They are saying that you posted a fake recording on the Internet ahead of time in order to make it look like a government agency was planning the attacks. According to the story, you two wanted to create civil unrest and start a violent rebellion against the government. Your photos are being shown on the news channels 24 hours a day. You guys will soon be even more famous than Osama bin Laden."

Tom just sat there stunned for a few moments. Could the American people actually be that gullible? Would the history books remember him as one of the greatest terrorists to ever live? "Oh great," Tom said dejectedly. "Some future, eh?"

"Well, fortunately the agency believes that you guys are dead and that is what the American people have also been told. In fact, there was great celebration when it was announced that you had been killed. But if you ever showed your faces in public again all of that would change very quickly. That is why the three of you need completely new identities. Our organization has access to some of the best doctors, plastic surgeons, computer hackers and document forgers in the world. We are going to give you new faces and new voices. We are also going to create all of the personal identity documents that you will need to start entirely brand new lives."

Tom's jaw just about dropped to the floor. "Why are you doing all of this?"

"Well, number one, you are my brother and I love you. Number two, like I said, you are extremely important to the future of our movement."

Tom started walking back toward his bed. "Hannah, I appreciate everything that you are doing for us, but I don't plan on joining any movement. Right now all I want is to get some rest."

Hannah smiled confidently as she rose and started heading for the door. "Yes, get some rest for now Tom. We will talk more later."

Chapter 88

A few days after the Operation Ordo Ab Chao bombings, Caroline Mancini decided to pay another visit to Jessup's office.

When she walked in, she could tell that Jessup was not exactly thrilled to see her, but she also knew that he had no choice in the matter.

"It's so nice to see you again Jessup," Caroline remarked as she pulled up a chair across from his desk.

"Yes," Jessup shot back, "it's a real pleasure."

"You see Jessup," Caroline said smugly, "this is your problem. You don't know how to grovel appropriately. If you did, you might not be in so much trouble."

Jessup held his tongue for a moment. He realized that he was on thin ice, and he also knew that the woman sitting across from him could make his problems a whole lot worse.

"We found the fugitives and they were eliminated. In the end, Operation Ordo Ab Chao unfolded beautifully and we were able to pin the blame on Tom McDowell and Russ Jacoby. So why would I be in trouble?"

Caroline clearly was not persuaded by Jessup's reasoning. "Oh, but were they really 'eliminated'? Your people didn't find any bodies when they searched the wreckage of the cabin."

Jessup was starting to get frustrated. "Nobody could have survived that blast. Everything that was inside that cabin was basically incinerated. The cabin did not have a basement and nobody saw them leave. There is no way that any of them could have survived."

Caroline was not buying it. Her eyes narrowed as she peered over at Jessup. "There should have been some sign of them in the wreckage. Didn't your people find anything at all?"

"We didn't have time to do a thorough search. In case you forgot, the largest eruption of Mt. Rainier ever recorded happened that night. We were fortunate to get out of there when we did."

Caroline scowled at Jessup. "Not good enough. You had the opportunity to confirm the death of the most wanted criminals in America, but you were more concerned about your own personal safety. I would go check the wreckage for myself, except that the entire area is now completely covered by several feet of volcanic mud."

Suddenly Jessup's cell phone rang. He looked at it to see who was calling.

"I've got to take this," Jessup said to Caroline, and then he walked out of the room.

Caroline already knew who had called Jessup. In fact, Caroline had talked with her just a few minutes earlier.

As Caroline waited for Jessup to come back into the room, she reflected back on the events of the past few days. When she had first been told that Tom McDowell was dead, she did not believe it. If he was dead, she should have felt some peace in her spirit. But instead the ache for revenge was now stronger than ever.

Caroline's suspicions were made even stronger when she had learned that no bodies had been found in the wreckage of the cabin.

Tom McDowell was still alive. Even though everyone else seemed to be convinced that he was dead, Caroline knew that he was still alive.

She would find him someday. Caroline was absolutely certain of that. And when she found him, she would make him pay for everything that he had done to her.

Jessup walked back into the room, but now he looked completely different. He looked like a completely defeated man.

"I never had a chance, did I?"

Caroline smirked at him. "No, I am afraid that you did not."

Jessup looked like he was about to pass out. "Did you have anything to do with this?"

"Yes I did," Caroline shot back, "and you deserve it. You are a totally worthless cretin and you have failed us for the last time."

"Please," Jessup pleaded with her, "I just want some more time with my family. Please give me some more time."

There was a knock on the door, and two armed security guards entered the room.

"You better get going Jessup. You don't want to miss your flight."

Jessup just glared at her.

"Punctuality is a virtue," Caroline said to Jessup as she smiled broadly. "There are some hungry people waiting."

Chapter 89

Jessup knew that it would be pointless to try to run.

Even if he did escape, there was no place on the face of the earth where they would not be able to find him.

Originally he had figured that it would be best to accept his fate with whatever dignity he had left, but now he was not so sure.

He had heard rumors about what happens in Denver, but now as he sat in a holding cell deep under Denver International Airport he started to understand that the reality of what he was about to experience was probably going to be far worse than any rumors that he had ever been told.

Jessup's hands and feet were chained, so he couldn't run even if he wanted to. He looked around his dark cell in a desperate attempt to find a way to escape, but it was hopeless. He knew that he would never see his family again, and that tore him up inside. He started wondering how the Illuminati were ever going to unite the whole earth if this was how they treated those that were loyal to them.

After a few minutes, 6 men dressed in black robes came and released him from his cell. Jessup could see that they were all heavily armed, and the chains on his feet would only allow him to kind of shuffle along anyway. There was no way that he was getting out of there.

The 6 armed men escorted him toward a very large underground amphitheater. Jessup could hear loud chanting coming from the amphitheater, but he did not understand what was being said. If Jessup had studied ancient languages, he would have recognized that two of the languages that were being chanted were Latin and Sumerian.

Around the perimeter of the amphitheater were hundreds of men and women in black robes. Many of them had their faces covered by masks.

As Jessup was escorted toward the center of the amphitheater, he was able to recognize several of the people around the perimeter that did not have masks on. In particular, he was quite distressed to see the head of the agency, Lilith, standing there. They locked eyes for a moment, but her ice cold expression did not change.

Jessup cursed her inwardly. There was no way that he would have been there if she had not signed off on it.

As Jessup was led to the very center of an inverted pentagram on the floor of the amphitheater, the chanting got even louder. He was unchained and stripped of all of his clothes by the armed men.

A woman that had a robe that was decorated more elaborately than anyone else in the room stepped forward on to a raised platform that was facing Jessup.

She pulled back her hood and Jessup could see her clearly. She was extremely pale, and she had red eyes and jet black hair.

Jessup could almost feel the evil coming from her.

The woman with the jet black hair held up her hand and the chanting stopped.

Jessup tried to speak, but he found that he could not. Some invisible force was holding his mouth shut.

The woman with the jet black hair began to address the assembled crowd...

"Fellow Enlightened Ones:

"We are here tonight to celebrate the circle of life. One life will end and somewhere else other lives will begin.

"This cycle of birth, death and rebirth has always been with us and it will always be with us.

"It is only through great sacrifice that the kingdom of the Light Bearer will be brought forth on this earth. We welcome it and we look forward to the return of his son Osiris. He is the one that will unite the world in peace and prosperity and restore the ancient paths.

"Order only comes out of chaos. Light only comes out of darkness. Life only comes out of death.

"When there is sacrifice, it makes the rest of us stronger. May this sacrifice hasten the day when we are all strong enough to bring the reign of the Kingdom of Lucifer to this world."

After she said that, the woman with the jet black hair took a step back and the underground amphitheater got even darker.

Suddenly, the Pentagram under Jessup's feet opened up and he fell into a very large pit below.

In the dim light, Jessup could tell that there were others with him in the pit.

A lot of others.

A few of them started staggering closer to Jessup, and for a moment Jessup was hopeful that he had just been dropped into a common holding cell.

But as they began getting even closer, Jessup started to realize that these creatures were only partially human at best.

Jessup's mouth was loosed from the invisible force that had been holding it shut and he started crying out in fear. He screamed and yelled for someone to help him, but nobody came.

Instead, the hybrid creatures that had surrounded him were now trying to grab his arms and legs.

Jessup tried to fight back, but it was useless. A couple of the hybrid creatures got a solid hold on him and then it was over. They literally ripped his limbs apart as the assembled Illuminists up in the amphitheater listened with delight.

Chapter 90

Constantine had not even considered what might happen if Mira and Mikaela failed to take out Killian. After all, they had never failed before, and Constantine had been absolutely certain that they would be able to kill him.

But they had failed, and now Constantine was deeply worried. He had tripled security at his mountain estate known as Klausjagen, but he feared that it might not be enough. Killian was one of the top assassins in the entire world, and Constantine knew that he would be coming for him at some point.

The High Council had ordered Constantine to dispose of Killian. They believed that he knew too much and that he could become a problem. They believed that he was becoming way too independent and that nobody was able to control him any longer.

They had compared Killian to a rabid animal that needed to be put down.

But rabid animals never escape assassination attempts.

As Constantine paced back and forth in his office, his phone suddenly started ringing.

It was an unfamiliar number. Constantine picked it up anyway.

"Who is this?"

A very deep male voice answered on the other end. "You were told what would happen if you ever broke a contract with me."

Constantine became very nervous. "Is that you Killian? I am afraid that there has been a tremendous misunderstanding. Mira and Mikaela went rogue and they tried to kill you. Thank goodness that you are still alive. We were all so worried."

"Cut the crap Constantine. Where is my money? I fulfilled my end of the contract and I expect to be paid."

"Of course," Constantine responded as he rushed over to his computer. "I apologize for the delay. There has been some confusion on our end. I am sending the money now."

"You better be sending it," Killian shot back.

Constantine nervously typed the required information into his computer and he was hoping that this would be enough to appease Killian.

"Okay, the money was been sent," Constantine said as he wiped sweat off of his brow.

Killian looked down at the tablet computer that he was carrying with him. The money had been successfully transferred into his account.

"Thank you Constantine. So tell me - why did you try to have me killed?"

Constantine began to shake. The money had not been enough to satisfy Killian. "I told you, Mira and Mikaela went rogue. I don't know why they tried to kill you. But I didn't have anything to do with it."

Killian was not about to be blinded by Constantine's lies. "Then why did you transfer a million euros into their account the day before they destroyed my motel room?"

Constantine knew that he was in trouble now. "I don't know where you are getting your information. I never made such a payment. We would never turn our back on you Killian. You are greatly valued by The Order and we hope to have a very profitable relationship with you for many years to come."

Killian frowned. He was getting tired of this little game.

"Constantine, from where you are standing are you able to look out a window toward the east?"

"Yes."

"I am standing on the top of a large hill off in the distance and I am waving at you. Can you see me?"

"Yes, I can."

"I have spent the last several hours wiring your entire estate with plastic explosives. In my right hand you can see that I am holding the detonator."

Constantine started trembling with panic. "Killian, don't do anything stupid. We can work this out..."

"Shut up Constantine. I'm the last thing that you are ever going to see."

Killian pressed the detonator, and Klausjagen exploded in a thousand different directions.

Killian smiled as he walked down the hill away from the explosion, but he also knew that Constantine was just middle management as far as The Order of the Illuminati was concerned.

There were much, much bigger fish to fry, and Killian was going to truly enjoy getting his revenge.

Chapter 91

It took some convincing, but Tom, Russ and Melissa all eventually agreed to undergo the surgeries necessary to radically alter their appearances. All of them came to realize that they would never be able to go out in public again if something dramatic was not done.

Fortunately, the surgeons that the Remnant had access to were extremely skilled, and even though they all now looked very different, the truth was that all of them probably looked even better than before.

All of the surgeries had been performed at the very large house in Idaho where they had been staying. Hannah had told them that it was called "the Rock House", and that this was because stone and rock had been used extensively in its construction.

The Rock House was absolutely huge. It was nearly 8,000 square feet in size, and there were several other very large buildings on the property as well. It was located on a 200 acre parcel of land way up in the mountains, and it appeared to be extremely isolated.

There were about two dozen other people living on the property in addition to Hannah, and Tom, Russ and Melissa had gotten to know all of them over the past several weeks. They appeared to truly love and care about one another, and that was very different from what Tom was accustomed to. The notion that you should "love others as you love yourself" was very foreign to him. But Tom did have to admit that it really did seem to be working for the people that lived in this small community.

After their first few days in the Rock House, Tom, Russ and Melissa had not spent much time together.

Russ was deeply mourning what had happened to his family. He still did not know if they were dead or alive, and that was eating him up on the inside. He tried to deal with his stress by spending a lot of time either in his room or walking through the woods. Everyone knew that he would eventually go after them. He just had to come up with a plan first.

Melissa was doing a different kind of mourning. She was mourning the loss of her former life. She would never again appear on camera and that realization was extremely depressing for her. Her job as a reporter at American News Network had been the culmination of everything that she had ever worked for, and now it had been taken away from her permanently. She was also dealing with mixed feelings about Tom. She was incredibly grateful that he had rescued her, but she also blamed him for the loss of her former life and for how their relationship had ended. Instead of hanging out with Tom or Russ, Melissa had been spending a lot of time with Hannah. They had gotten very close over the past few weeks. Melissa's neck and back were feeling much better now, and Melissa could even be seen smiling here and there from time to time.

Tom had spent a lot of time sitting outside and reading as he recovered from the various surgeries that he had been through. He wanted to understand the ancient conflict that he had been dropped into the middle of. At the Rock House there was an extensive library, and Tom spent hours reading about The Order of the Illuminati. He was shocked at how little he had actually known about them. He had also spent some time reading about the Remnant.

Apparently the conflict between the two groups went back a very, very long time.

Today, Tom, Melissa and Hannah had gathered up in the main dining area of the Rock House which was located up on the second floor because Russ wanted to tell them all something. The main dining area was more than 600 square feet in size, and it was often used for other sorts of gatherings when it wasn't being used for meals. A fire was roaring over in the corner, and along the wall that faced west there were some very large windowed doors that led out on to a huge deck that provided a spectacular view of some of the snow-covered mountains that surrounded the property.

When Russ walked in, the others could immediately tell that he had something serious to say. He had a couple of airline tickets in his hand.

"I have come to say goodbye," Russ said to the group. "I am going to go find my family."

Tom and Melissa didn't know quite what to say, but they always knew that this day was coming at some point.

Hannah, Tom and Melissa all rose from where they were sitting and went over and hugged Russ.

"We are going to miss you Russ," Melissa said as she embraced him.

"I'm going to miss you guys too," Russ replied back.

They all sat down and Tom turned toward Russ. "So where are you headed?"

Russ seemed happier than he had been in a long time. "Well, my first stop is the Cayman Islands. The feds found all of my U.S. bank accounts, but I still have some money stashed overseas that they have not gotten to yet. I need to move that money before they find it. It should be more than enough to keep me going as I search for my family. If they are still alive, I will find them, and when I find them I am going to move heaven and earth to rescue them."

"We certainly wish you the best as you go after them," Tom said to Russ sincerely. "Please keep in touch and let us know how the search is going."

"I will," Russ responded. "So what about you guys – do you all have any future plans yet?"

"Not me," Melissa said. "Personally I am just glad that my neck and back are doing so much better. I can't explain it, but I really feel at peace in this place. I could sit and look at those mountains forever. And I am so thankful for everything that Hannah has done for me – I feel like I have made a true friend and I am learning so much. Thank you."

"You are welcome Melissa," Hannah said in return. "I feel like I have made a true friend as well."

Russ turned toward Tom. "So what about you buddy?"

Tom thought about what he was going to say for a moment.

"I have really been enjoying all of this rest, but at some point I know that I will get the itch for another adventure. I just have to figure out what that adventure will be first. I spent many years in service to my country, but now everything that I always assumed about how the world works has been turned upside down.

"Six months ago if someone told me that I would be dropped into the middle of an ancient conflict between The Order of the Illuminati and the Remnant I never would have believed it. Even when I was first recruited into the agency, I had no idea that it was being directly controlled by The Order of the Illuminati. When Hannah first mentioned 'the Illuminati' to me, I accused her of being a conspiracy theorist.

"But now I can see what the Illuminati are trying to do. They want a one world economic system, a one world religion and a one world government. They believe in creating order out of chaos, and they are not afraid to tear down the existing structures of society so that they can build new ones to replace them. They believe that they are going to truly be able to unite all of the nations of the planet and usher in a glorious new age of peace and prosperity which will be ruled over by a Messiah figure that they believe is coming. But it is a much different Messiah figure than the Remnant believes in."

Tom glanced over at his sister. "Am I pretty much on the right track Hannah?"

Hannah nodded and smiled. "I think that you are starting to get it. But remember, our battle is not against flesh and blood. We serve Y'shua, and His Kingdom operates very differently than the kingdoms of this world do. Right now, God is bringing things full circle. The Remnant of the last days is going to look just like the original Christians did back in the days of the New Testament. The Remnant is going to keep the commandments of God, it is going to boldly proclaim the gospel of salvation through faith in Y'shua the Messiah, and God is going to perform mighty works through the Remnant just like He did through the

Christians of the first century. Things in this world are going to get much darker in the years ahead, but as they do, the true light will also become much brighter. The greatest move of God that the world has ever seen is rapidly approaching, and it is going to change the world. The Illuminati will do all that they can to persecute it and try to stop it, but in the end they will not be victorious."

Tom smiled too. "I still don't really understand a lot of the things that Hannah has been trying to explain to me yet, but I have been doing a lot of reading. For way too many years, I let other people do my thinking for me. I let my teachers tell me what to think, I let the politicians tell me what to think and I especially let the mainstream media tell me what to think. But now I am going to question everything. I am finding out that I have been lied to for a lot of years, and to be honest I am quite angry about that. I feel like a man that is just waking up for the first time in his life. There is so much that I don't know, but I am eager to learn, and a journey of a thousand miles begins with a single step, right?"

As Tom was finishing saying this, beautiful music suddenly began to pour into the house from outside.

Tom, Russ, Melissa and Hannah all jumped up and hurried out on to the deck.

At first, they couldn't tell where the beautiful music was coming from. It sounded like some sort of a victory march, but it was unlike any music that any of them had ever heard before.

They scanned the entire area, and after a few moments they all spotted him.

On a hillside about 100 yards from where they were standing was Yochanan. Tom, Russ and Melissa had not seen him since the night that he had rescued them from the cabin.

Yochanan was waving at them and smiling. There was a look of great love in his eyes.

Tom, Russ, Melissa and Hannah all smiled broadly and waved back.

For a moment, they were all hoping that he would come over and say hello to them.

And then he was gone.

Nobody said anything. They all just smiled and glanced at each other with knowing looks in their eyes.

The beautiful music was still playing, and off in the distance the sun was setting behind the mountains. As it did, it painted the sky in some of the most beautiful colors imaginable.

Tom, Russ, Melissa and Hannah gathered along the railing of the deck and admired the sunset.

In the future, there would be great challenges ahead for all of them.

But for right now, in this moment, everything was absolutely perfect.

The Most Important Thing

I hope that you truly enjoyed the novel that you just read. Although I write for a living, this was my first attempt at writing a novel, and I learned a lot going through this process.

In my novel, there are some characters that identify themselves as followers of Y'shua the Messiah. In English, he is more commonly referred to as Jesus Christ.

I feel like I would be doing a disservice if I didn't explain to you the most important thing that you could take away from this book. If I had not given my life to the Lord Jesus Christ, I would probably be dead today. He has taken the broken pieces of my life and has made them into a beautiful thing, and He can do the same thing for you.

If you would like to know how you can become a Christian, I encourage you to keep reading. A lot of the time people find Christianity to be very confusing. In the following pages, I have tried to explain the core of the Christian faith in a way that hopefully just about everyone will be able to understand.

Fortunately, the Christian gospel is very, very simple to understand, and the stakes are incredibly high.

If Christianity is true, then it is possible to have eternal life.

I am not just talking about living for millions of years or billions of years.

I am talking about living for eternity.

If you had the opportunity to live forever, would you take it?

Many people would respond by saying that they are not sure if living forever in a world like ours would be desirable, but what if you could live forever in a world where everything had been set right?

What if you could live forever in a perfect world where there is no more evil or suffering or pain?

Would you want that?

The truth is that is exactly what God wants for you. He loves you very much and He wants to spend forever with you.

If you could, would you want to spend forever with Him?

If God is real, and there really is an afterlife, who wouldn't want to spend eternity with Him?

To be honest with you, if eternal life really exists, there is not a single issue of greater importance to every man, woman and child on earth.

Who would not be willing to give up everything that they own to live forever in paradise surrounded by people that love them?

All over the world people perform all kinds of religious acts, desperately hoping that they will gain favor with God. Some religious nuts even blow themselves up during suicide attacks, hoping that their "sacrifices" will earn them favor with God. But are those really ways to get to heaven? What does the Bible have to say?

The truth is that the plan of salvation described in the Bible is very simple.

It starts with God.

The Bible tells us that God created humanity and that He loves us very much.

In fact, God loves you more than you could possibly ever imagine. The Scriptures go on and on about how great the love of God is and about how deeply He cares for each one of us individually.

But there is a huge problem.

The problem is that humanity is in deep rebellion against God.

Humanity has rejected God and is continually breaking His laws.

Most people like to think of themselves as "good" people, but the truth is that none of us are truly "good". Each one of us has broken God's laws over and over again. We are lawbreakers and criminals in the sight of God. The Scriptures call us sinners.

Perhaps you think that you are a "good person" and that God should let you into heaven based on how good you are.

If that is what you believe, ask yourself this question...

Have you ever broken God's laws?

Posted below is a summary of the Ten Commandments. Are you guilty of violating His rules?...

#1) You shall have no other gods before Me. (There is only one true God – the Creator of all things. Have you ever served a different God? Have you ever expressed approval for a false religion just because you wanted to be polite? Have you ever participated in activities or ceremonies that honor other religions?)

#2) You shall not make any idols. You shall not bow down to them or serve them. (The Scriptures tell us that we are to love God with everything that we have inside of us. Even if you have never bowed down to an idol or a statue, you may have created a "god" in your own mind that you are more comfortable with. That is sin. In fact, we are not to have any "idols" in our lives that we love more than God.)

#3) You shall not take the name of the Lord your God in vain. (Have you ever used God's holy name as a profanity or as a curse word? Have you ever failed to give His holy name the honor it deserves?)

#4) Remember the Sabbath Day, to keep it holy. (Is there anyone alive that has kept this commandment perfectly?)

#5) Honor your father and mother. (Have you ever been rebellious or disrespectful to your father or your mother even one time? If so, you have broken this commandment.)

#6) You shall not murder. (Even if you have never killed anyone, it is important to remember that Jesus considers hatred to be very similar to murder.)

#7) You shall not commit adultery. (Sexual promiscuity is absolutely rampant in society today, but you don't even have to sleep with someone to break this commandment. In Matthew 5:27-28, Jesus said that "whosoever looketh on a woman to lust after her hath committed adultery with her already in his heart".)

#8) You shall not steal. (Have you ever stolen anything from someone else? It doesn't matter if it was valuable or not. If you stole something, you are a thief.)

#9) You shall not lie. (Have you ever told a lie? If so, you are guilty of breaking this commandment.)

#10) You shall not covet. (Have you ever jealously desired something that belongs to someone else? This sin is often the first step toward other sins.)

The first four commandments are about loving God. In the Scriptures, you are commanded to love God with all of your heart, all of your soul, all of your mind and all of your strength.

The final six commandments are about loving others. In the Scriptures, you are commanded to love others as you love yourself.

Have you always loved God and loved others like you should have?

Sadly, the truth is that we are all guilty of breaking God's laws.

In fact, if we took an honest look at how guilty we truly are we would be horrified.

Take a moment and imagine the following scenario...

One of the biggest television networks has decided to do a huge two hour prime time special about your life. It is going to be heavily advertised, and tens of millions of people are going to watch it.

Doesn't that sound great?

But instead of a two hour documentary about how wonderful you are, the network has discovered all of the most evil and horrible things that you have ever thought, said or did and they are going to broadcast those things to tens of millions of people all over the world for two hours during prime time.

What would you do if that happened?

Sadly, the truth is that whoever that happened to would be utterly ashamed and would never want to be seen in public again.

Why?

Because we have all done, said and thought things that are unspeakably evil.

We are sinners in the eyes of God, just as the Scriptures tell us...

"For all have sinned, and come short of the glory of God" (Romans 3:23).

God created us to have fellowship with Him, but He also gave humanity the ability to choose. Unfortunately, humanity has chosen to be in deep rebellion against God and we have all repeatedly broken His laws. When we broke God's commandments, our fellowship with God was also broken. By breaking God's commandments, we decided that our will would be done instead of God's will. And if you look around the world today, you can see the results. Evil and suffering are everywhere. God hates all of this evil and suffering very much. In the Bible, our rebellion against God is called sin.

As a result of our sin, the Scriptures tell us that we are separated from God...

"The wages of sin is death" [spiritual separation from God] (Romans 6:23).

So what can be done about this separation from God?

Why doesn't God just forget about our sins?

Well, the truth is that God cannot just sweep our evil under the rug. If God did that, He would cease to be just.

For example, how would you feel about a judge that decided to issue a blanket pardon for Hitler and all of the other high level Nazis for the horrible things that they did?

Would that be a "good" judge? Of course not.

There is a penalty for evil, and because God is just, that penalty must be paid.

Fortunately, Jesus Christ paid the penalty for our sins by dying for us on the cross. He took the punishment that we deserved...

"But God commendeth his love toward us, in that, while we were yet sinners, Christ died for us." (Romans 5:8).

We were guilty, but the Son of God, Jesus Christ, died in our place.

Being fully man, Jesus could die for the sins of mankind.

Being fully God, Jesus could die for an infinite number of sins.

Jesus paid the penalty for your sins and my sins so that fellowship with God could be restored.

Not only that, but Jesus proved that He is the Son of God by rising from the dead...

"Christ died for our sins...He was buried...He rose again the third day according to the Scriptures" (1 Corinthians 15:3-4).

You see, if there was any other way for us to be reconciled to God, Jesus would not have had to die on the cross. He could have just told us to follow one of the other ways to get to heaven. But there was no other way. The death of Jesus on the cross is the only payment for our sins and He is the only way that we are going to get to heaven. In the Scriptures, Jesus put it this way...

"I am the way, the truth, and the life: no man cometh unto the Father, but by me." (John 14:6).

But it is not enough just for you to intellectually know that Jesus is the Son of God and that He died on the cross for our sins.

The Scriptures tell us that we must individually commit our lives to Jesus Christ as Savior and Lord. When we give our lives to Jesus, He forgives our sins and He gives us eternal life...

"But as many as received him, to them gave he power to become the sons of God, even to them that believe on his name" (John 1:12).

"For God so loved the world, that he gave his only begotten Son, that whosoever believeth in him should not perish, but have everlasting life." (John 3:16).

"That if thou shalt confess with thy mouth the Lord Jesus, and shalt believe in thine heart that God hath raised him from the dead, thou shalt be saved." (Romans 10:9).

So exactly how does someone do this?

It is actually very simple.

The Scriptures tell us that it is through faith that we enter into a relationship with Jesus Christ...

"For by grace are ye saved through faith; and that not of yourselves: it is the gift of God: Not of works, lest any man should boast." (Ephesians 2:8,9).

If you are not a Christian yet, then Jesus is standing at the door of your heart and He is knocking. He is hoping that you will let Him come in. He loves you very much and He wants to have a relationship with you...

[Jesus speaking] "Behold, I stand at the door, and knock: if any man hear my voice, and open the door, I will come in to him" (Revelation 3:20).

Jesus asks that you give Him control of your life. That means renouncing all of the sin in your life and making Him your Savior and Lord. Just to know intellectually that Jesus died on the cross and that He rose from the dead is not enough to become a Christian. Having a wonderful emotional experience is not enough to become a Christian either. You become a Christian by faith. It is an act of your will.

Are you ready to make a commitment to Jesus Christ?

If you are ready to invite Jesus Christ into your life, it is very easy.

Just tell Him.

God is not really concerned if you say the right words. What He is concerned about is the attitude of your heart.

If you are ready to become a Christian, the following is a prayer that can help you express that desire to Him...

"Lord Jesus, I want to become a Christian. I know that I am a sinner, and I thank You for dying on the cross for my sins. I believe that you are the Son of God and that you rose from the dead. I repent of my sins and I open the door of my life and ask You to be my Savior and Lord. I commit my life to You. Thank You for forgiving all of my sins and giving me eternal life. Take control of my life and make me the kind of person that You want me to be. I will live my life for You. Amen."

If you are ready to enter into a personal relationship with Jesus Christ, then I invite you to pray this prayer right now. Jesus will come into your life, just as He has promised to do.

If you do invite Jesus Christ to come into your life, you can have 100 percent certainty that you have become a Christian and that you will go to heaven when you die. In 1 John 5:11-13, the Scriptures tell us the following...

"And this is the record, that God hath given to us eternal life, and this life is in his Son. He that hath the Son hath life; and he that hath not the Son of God hath not life. These things have I written unto you that believe on the name of the Son of God; that ye may know that ye have eternal life".

Do you understand what that means?

It means that you can know that you have eternal life.

The Bible says that if you have invited Jesus Christ into your life, your sins are forgiven and you now have eternal life.

What could be better than that?

But your journey is not done.

In fact, it is just beginning.

The Christian life is not easy - especially if you try to go it alone.

There are four keys to spiritual growth for any Christian...

#1) The Bible - If you do not have a Bible you will need to get one and read it every day. It is God's instruction book for your life.

#2) Prayer – Prayer does not have to be complicated. The truth is that prayer is just talking with God. God wants to hear from you every day, and He will fundamentally transform your life as you pray to Him with humility and sincerity.

#3) Fellowship - The Scriptures tell us that we all need each other. Find a fellowship of local Christians that believe the Bible and that sincerely love one another. They will help you grow.

#4) Witnessing - Tell others about the new life that you have found in Jesus Christ. Helping even one person find eternal life is of more value than anything else that you could ever accomplish in this world.

If you have invited Jesus Christ to come into your life, I would love to hear from you. You can write to me at the following email address...

TheEconomicCollapseBlog @ Hotmail.com

As was mentioned in the novel, we are entering a period of time that the Bible refers to as the last days. It will be a period of great darkness and the world is going to become increasingly unstable. According to Jesus, there has never been a time like it before, and there will never be a time like it again. But in the middle of all of this, God is going to do great things. He is raising up a Remnant that will keep His commandments, that will boldly proclaim the gospel of salvation through faith in Jesus Christ, and that will see their message confirmed by the power of the Holy Spirit just like the very first believers in Jesus did. This is already happening all over the globe even though no organization is in charge of it. You can read about the Remnant in Revelation 12:17 and Revelation 14:12. God is starting to bring things full circle. The Remnant of the last days is going to do things the way that the Christians of the first century did things. Have you ever wondered why so many Christian churches of today do not resemble what you see in the Bible? Well, the sad truth is that over the centuries churches got away from what the Scriptures tell us to do, but now God is restoring all things. Without God we can do nothing, but with God all things are possible.

Today, we have an even greater opportunity than the first century Christians did in some ways. During the first century, there were only about 200 million people on earth. Today, there are more than 7 billion. That means that there are about 35 times as many people living on the planet today than there were back then.

The global population has experienced exponential growth over the past couple of centuries, and that means that we have the opportunity to impact more lives than anyone else ever has. I believe that the greatest move of God that the world has ever seen is coming, and I believe that millions upon millions of souls will be brought into the Kingdom. I encourage you to be a part of what is happening.

As the global economy collapses and unprecedented troubles break out around the globe, people are going to be looking for answers. Hundreds of millions of people will have their lives totally turned upside down and will be consumed with despair. Instead of giving in to fear like everyone else will be, it will be a great opportunity for the people of God to rise up and take the message of life to a lost and dying world.

Yes, there will be great persecution. The world system absolutely hates the gospel and the Bible tells us that eventually Christians will be hunted down and killed for what they believe.

But those that have read the end of the Bible know that we win in the end. God loves you very much and He wants to make your life a greater adventure than you ever imagined that it possibly could be. Yes, there will be hardships in this world, but if you are willing to pursue God with a passion and become totally sold out to Him, you can make an eternal difference in countless lives.

When you get a chance, go read the book of Acts. Do you want your own life to look like that?

It can.

In these last days, those that have a passion for God and a passion for reaching the lost are going to turn this world upside down with the gospel of Jesus Christ.

The Scriptures tell us that "there is joy in the presence of the angels of God over one sinner that repents." When a single person makes a commitment to Jesus Christ, there is great celebration in heaven.

As millions upon millions of precious souls are brought into the Kingdom in the years ahead, what do you think the atmosphere in heaven is going to look like?

Yes, darkness and evil will also prosper in the days ahead. A one world government, a one world economy and a one world religion are coming. This world system will utterly hate the Remnant and will try to crush us with everything that they have got.

It is going to take great strength and great courage to stand against the world system in the times that are coming. You have the opportunity to be a part of a greater adventure than anything that Hollywood ever dreamed up, and in the end it may cost you your life.

But in Revelation chapter 2, Jesus tells us that if we are "faithful unto death" that He will give us "a crown of life".

Do you want that crown? I do.

For those of us that have a relationship with Jesus, we know that we have the ultimate happy ending. Jesus has forgiven our sins and has given us eternal life, and nobody can ever take that away from us.

Life is like a coin – you can spend it any way that you want, but you can only spend it once.

Spend your life on something that really matters.

God is raising up a Remnant that is going to shake the world. You do not want to miss out on the great move of

God that is coming. It is going to be unlike anything that any of us have ever seen before.

If you enjoyed this book, I encourage you to also connect with me on the Internet. You can find my work at the following websites...

The Economic Collapse Blog: http://theeconomiccollapseblog.com/

The American Dream: http://endoftheamericandream.com/

The Truth: http://thetruthwins.com/

Thank you for taking the time to read my book. I would love to hear any feedback that you may have.

My wife and I are praying for all those that visit our websites and for all those that will read this book.

May the Lord bless you and keep you.

May the Lord make His face shine upon you and be gracious to you.

May the Lord lift up His countenance upon you and give you His peace.

Thank you again for reading my novel.

Michael Snyder – The author of The Beginning Of The End

CPSIA information can be obtained at www.ICGtesting.com
Printed in the USA
LVOW11s0305160615

442542LV00002B/793/P